CHOSEN OF THE VALKYRIES

CHOSEN OF THE VALKYRIES

Twilight Of The Gods II

CHRISTOPHER G. NUTTALL

Text copyright © Christopher G. Nuttall

ISBN: 1533232202
ISBN-13: 9781533232205

http://www.chrishanger.net
http://chrishanger.wordpress.com/
http://www.facebook.com/ChristopherGNuttall
Cover by Brad Fraunfelter
www.BFillustration.com

All Comments and Reviews Welcome!

AUTHOR'S NOTE

I'm not particularly fond of books, even alternate history books, that attempt to reproduce foreign accents or make excessive use of foreign terms. Unfortunately, writing a book set in Nazi Germany makes it impossible to avoid the use of *some* German words, including a number specific to Nazi Germany and the SS. I've done my best to keep this to a bare minimum and, just in case the meaning of the word cannot be deduced from context, I've placed a glossary at the rear of the book.

Please don't hesitate to let me know if there's a word I've missed during the editing.

CGN

PROLOGUE

Near Cottbus, Germany, 1960

Sturmann Jordan Haizmann allowed himself a sigh of relief as the train pulled into the station - with nary a welcoming committee in sight. He'd been granted a week's leave two days ago, but the Mayor of Cottbus had welcomed him and his fellow graduates from Wewelsburg Castle with a parade and a whole series of endless speeches. Attendance was technically voluntary, yet Jordan had been in the SS long enough to know that it was actually mandatory and their absence would be counted against them. By the time he'd finally been allowed to board the train to his hometown, he couldn't help feeling as though he'd been cheated of some of his hard-earned leave.

He rose to his feet, picked up his bag and made his way to the door, silently enjoying the way the other passengers made way for him and his uniform. The SS was as much feared as loved, he knew; their duty, to defend the *Reich* from internal as well as external enemies, made them few friends. But Jordan refused to allow himself to take it personally. The good citizens of Cottbus and the surrounding towns could sleep easily in their beds, knowing that Jordan and his comrades stood between them and the barbarians at the gates. This time, the *Reich* would endure a thousand years. Adolf Hitler had promised no less.

The two policemen on duty at the barrier glanced at his uniform and nodded him through, even as one of their comrades berated a Slavic *Untermensch* for daring to ride in a carriage, rather than one of the cattle cars attached to the rear of the train. Jordan paid no heed, even when the policemen started to beat the Slav with their truncheons. Serve the *Untermensch* right for daring to think he could sully a German train with his filthy presence! He'd be in the camps by nightfall, if the policemen didn't beat him to death. No one would care, either way. He was just an *Untermensch*.

Jordan glanced around, looking for his driver. He'd been told that...*someone*...would be there to meet him, although his uncle hadn't been very specific about *who* It was odd - Uncle Rudolf was a Town Clerk, with the breed's passion for being as specific as possible - but perhaps his uncle merely wanted to surprise him. Maybe he'd even come himself, leaving the office in early afternoon. His superiors wouldn't object too strongly if he wanted to welcome his adopted son home.

"Jordan!"

He turned as he heard the voice - and stared. A young woman was hurrying towards him, her arms outstretched. For a moment, he didn't recognise her. The ugly uniform concealed almost everything, save for her pale face and bright green eyes. And then it struck him.

"Kathie!"

Kathie blushed. "I'm glad you remember," she said, as they hugged. "Your father thought you'd like to see me again."

Jordan blushed too as she took his hand and led him towards the gates. They'd courted, on and off, over the last two years before he'd gone off to Wewelsburg Castle, then exchanged letters infrequently. Her parents had not raised any objection to their courtship, but Uncle Rudolf had insisted that Jordan complete his training before he formally approached her parents for a betrothal. It had made their relationship more awkward than it had any right to be. Kathie was eighteen. Most of her friends from school were already married, with children on the way. It was what was expected of a young girl in the *Reich*.

He found himself staring at her as they walked towards his uncle's car. Kathie had changed in the last two years. The skinny girl he recalled from childhood was gone, replaced by a stunningly attractive young woman. Her uniform concealed her curves, but it couldn't hide her face - or the sparkle of light in her eyes when she smiled. He wondered, feeling a pang of bitter pain, if anyone else had tried to court her while he was gone. They might have had an...understanding, but he found it hard to imagine the young men leaving her alone indefinitely. But he wasn't sure he wanted to know.

"My father isn't too keen on me driving," Kathie said, as she opened the passenger door for him. "But your uncle thought it would be good for me."

Jordan shrugged. "And is it?"

"It has its moments," Kathie said. "Your uncle keeps me busy."

Jordan nodded as the car rumbled to life. Uncle Rudolf was the Town Clerk - and that made him a very powerful man, easily one of the biggest fishes in a very small pond. He might not have the fame of the mayor - who'd been decorated for bravery during the war - but very few people would willingly get on his bad side. Certainly, no one had objected to Uncle Rudolf adopting Jordan after his parents had been killed. Jordan would never have known that Uncle Rudolf and Aunt Mary weren't his real parents, if they hadn't told him so. They'd been nothing but loving to him.

Kathie chatted happily as they drove through the streets, heading down to Uncle Rudolf's house. Jordan listened, torn between the desire to get home as quickly as possible and a mad impulse to suggest she drive out into the countryside. He resisted the temptation, somehow, even though he wanted to take her in his arms and kiss her. He'd completed his training, now. He could ask Uncle Rudolf to approach her parents this evening, if he wished, and be married in the office tomorrow. But he wasn't sure if she'd want a formal ceremony...

"It's been a while," Kathie said, as she parked the car. For a moment, she sounded utterly unsure of herself. "Did you...did you find someone else while you were gone?"

Jordan shook his head, hastily. Recruits weren't allowed to leave the castle until they graduated, unless they quit or were so badly injured that they were given a medical discharge and granted a pension for the rest of their lives. The old sweats had talked about sneaking out of the grounds and going to a nearby brothel, but anyone who tried had been in for a nightmare of punishment. It had been safer to stay in the castle and concentrate on preparing themselves to go to war.

"There were no women at the castle," he said. It was true. There were rumours of female soldiers, true, but most of them sounded more than a little absurd. Women were just too delicate to fight, even if they weren't required to bear children for the *Reich*. "All I had was your letters."

Kathie smiled, then turned to face him, leaning forward very slightly. Jordan leaned forward himself and kissed her, as gently as he could. They'd kissed before, when he'd taken her to dances and formal events, but this was different. His heartbeat was suddenly pounding so loudly that he wondered if she could hear it. It was all he could do to pull back from her, knowing they were in the middle of a public street. His uncle would be severely displeased if the police pulled Jordan and Kathie from the car.

"Later," Kathie promised.

Jordan blinked. "You're not coming inside?"

"I have to park the car," Kathie said. She gave him a smile that melted his heart. "Go see your aunt and uncle."

Jordan kissed her again, then opened the door and stepped out onto the street. His uncle's house loomed up in front of him, easily two or three times larger than they needed. But then, Rudolf and Mary *had* hoped for more children, even after they'd adopted Jordan. They'd just never had them.

He waved to Kathie - who started the engine and drove away - and pushed the doorbell, hearing it echoing inside the house. Perhaps he could talk his uncle into going to Kathie's family tonight…but he knew it was unlikely. Uncle Rudolf would want to talk about his training, while Aunt Mary would want to discuss how Jordan could support a wife on his salary. Kathie wouldn't be permitted to work, once she was married. Her family would never allow it, even if she was working for her father-in-law.

The door opened. "Jordan," Uncle Rudolf said. "Welcome home."

Jordan hugged the old man, then stepped backwards to take a good look at him as he led the way into the house. Uncle Rudolf was *old*, easily old enough to have fought - and been wounded - in the war. Jordan didn't know much about his military service, but the small cluster of medals his uncle wore for Victory Day parades told their own story. Maybe he wasn't *Waffen-SS* - his training officers had told him that the *Waffen-SS* was the best of the best - yet even the *Wehrmacht* didn't give out medals like candy. Uncle Rudolf had been in some of the most intensive fighting of the war.

"Kathie's just parking the car," he said, suddenly awkward. He was no longer a child, but not quite a man either. "Uncle…"

"We have to talk," Uncle Rudolf said. "Mary will take care of Kathie."

Jordan felt a sudden lump of ice forming in his chest as Uncle Rudolf led the way into his study. It was a large room, crammed with books and bookshelves; Jordan, as a young man, had been absolutely forbidden to enter the chamber. Uncle Rudolf had always made sure to keep the door locked. But now, it just felt cramped and uncomfortable as Jordan took one of the hard wooden seats and sat down. His uncle had never been one for comfort while he was working.

Uncle Rudolf closed the door and took a seat himself, his blue eyes studying Jordan narrowly. "There's something I have to tell you," he said. "Something I wasn't sure if you should be told - or not - at all."

Jordan frowned. His imagination supplied too many possibilities. "Is it about Kathie?"

Uncle Rudolf blinked. "No," he said. "It's about you - and your parents."

"My parents?" Jordan repeated. "You never told me *anything* about my parents!"

He swallowed, hard. His uncle was a calm and dignified man, rarely raising his voice…but he'd been furious when Jordan had started to ask questions about his parents. Jordan had been just over nine, yet old enough to get the impression that some questions were better not asked. He had no idea why. Hadn't they been taught, at school, to honour their ancestors?

"No, we didn't," Uncle Rudolf said. "What you didn't know, Jordan, you couldn't tell."

Jordan stared.

"You…you were six months old when your parents were uncovered," Uncle Rudolf said, curtly. "Mary and I were already starting to realise that we would never have children of our own. She knew your mother, Jordan. When it became clear that there was no hope of escape, she insisted on taking and adopting you. I altered the records to create a false record, then took you far from your natural parents."

"Uncovered?" Jordan repeated. "Uncle…"

"My elder brother was killed in the wars," Uncle Rudolf said. "Even before then…we were not close. We certainly never lived together. It was easy enough to convince people that you were *his* son."

He took a breath. "Jordan…your parents were Jews."

Jordan felt his mouth drop open in shock. Jews? It was a joke. It *had* to be a joke! He'd been told, time and time again, that Jews were subhuman monsters. The pictures he'd been shown in school were of shambling cripples, twisted parodies of the human form. But *he* was no cripple, no monster! He'd showered beside hundreds of other recruits at the castle and noticed no difference. Jews…

"There weren't many left at the time," Uncle Rudolf said, remorselessly. "The smart ones fled to Britain or America before the war. Your parents were isolated, their names changed; they thought they could hide forever. But they were wrong."

Jordan swallowed desperately to keep from throwing up. He wasn't a Jew. He *couldn't* be a Jew. And yet, his uncle wouldn't have played such a ghastly practical joke on his adopted son. Jordan still remembered just how furious his uncle had been after Jordan and a handful of friends had played a nasty prank on the nearby shopkeeper. Uncle Rudolf had no sense of humour at all.

"I can't be a Jew," he said. The doorbell rang. Kathie would be standing outside, blissfully unaware of Jordan's true nature. She wouldn't want to marry him after she learned the truth…she'd never be able to marry, once word got out that she had kissed a Jew. "Uncle…"

"I am sorry," Uncle Rudolf said. "But we told your parents that we would tell you once you were a man."

Jordan wanted to scream. His world was spinning around him. Uncle Rudolf…Kathie…his real parents…and his comrades! What would they say if they knew they had welcomed a Jew into their ranks? And what would happen if the truth came out? A *Waffen-SS* Stormtrooper might pass unnoticed, but anyone who wanted to be promoted to high rank had to have Germanic ancestry that stretched back at least four generations. Uncle Rudolf was the Town Clerk, in a perfect position to alter the records to hide someone's true origins, yet what would happen if the investigators discovered the truth? Even not being able to *prove* one's roots would bar any future promotion. And the truth…

He shuddered, helplessly. It would come out eventually, he was sure. Kathie might be fine - her family roots were solid - but *he* would be killed… and so would his children, if they had any. If Kathie could bear the thought of touching him after he told her…and he couldn't keep it from her, could he?

"Go to your room and think," Uncle Rudolf said. "We'll discuss possible options in the morning."

"Damn you," Jordan snarled. "You could have said nothing…"

"You needed to know," Uncle Rudolf said. "I did try to keep you from joining the SS."

Jordan bit off a curse as he headed for the door and walked up the stairs to his room. It was true. Uncle Rudolf *had* tried to forbid him from joining the SS, but Jordan had been determined. Everyone knew the SS was the finest fighting force in the world, always ready to protect the *Reich* against those who would tear it down. He'd wanted to be part of it, desperately. And he'd made it through training when so many others had not…

He closed the door and sat down on the bed, trying to gather his thoughts. But it was impossible. He was a Jew. Everyone *knew* Jews were inferior, yet he'd passed one of the hardest training courses in the world. And everyone knew Jews were monsters, but he was no monster. If he'd been lied to about that, what *other* lies had he been told? And Kathie…how could he marry her now? How could he *live* with the possibility of discovery hanging over his head like the Sword of Damocles? There was no way he *could* live!

Quite calmly, he drew his pistol from his belt, placed it to his temple and pulled the trigger.

CHAPTER ONE

Berlin, Germany
1 September 1985

Berlin felt...different.

Leutnant der Polizei Herman Wieland strode down the street, feeling oddly exposed for the first time in his long career. *Nothing* was the same any longer. People who had once eyed him with respect, or fear, were now meeting his gaze challengingly, while political agitators walked through the streets openly, surrounded by hordes of admiring supporters. *Anyone* could speak now, without fear of arrest. It seemed as if everyone in Berlin had something to say.

He sighed inwardly as he turned a corner and saw yet another speaker, a middle-aged man standing on a box, telling the crowd what needed to be done to save the revolution from itself. Apparently, all of the former servants of the state were to be herded into the concentration camps and exterminated, even though the *Reich* couldn't *survive* without the bureaucrats and former regime officers who ran the state. There were quite a few Herman would cheerfully have watched die - he wouldn't have crossed the road to piss on them if they were on fire - but it was hard to separate the truly dangerous ones from the bureaucrats who were necessary. And yet, the crowd was murmuring in approval.

Nothing is the same any longer, he told himself, glumly. *Too many people have too many grudges to pay off.*

He forced himself to look back, evenly, as some of the crowd eyed him in a distantly hostile manner. No one would have *dared* to look at him like that, even a year ago, but things had changed. These days, the police had strict

1

orders to use as little force as possible, even when dealing with riots. Herman was all too aware that a number of police officers had been waylaid and killed, their bodies brutally mutilated by their murderers. There were just too many possible suspects for the police to track down even one of the killers. The police had few friends on the streets of Berlin and they knew it.

The crowd scowled at him, but made no move to attack. Herman kept his relief off his face as he strolled past, forcing himself to walk normally. He had a pistol, of course, but he couldn't have hoped to kill more than a handful of rioters before they tore him apart. The old fear was gone, leaving a civilian population that was growing increasingly aware of its strength. And they *definitely* had far too many grudges to pay off.

His companion elbowed him. "So tell me," *Leutnant der Polizei* Hendrik Kuls said. "What's it like to have powerful relatives?"

Herman groaned, inwardly. Nepotism was epidemic in the *Reich* - he didn't expect *that* to change anytime soon - but *his* case was unique. His *daughter* was a *Reich* Councillor, under Chancellor Volker Schulze. His *teenage* daughter. Herman honestly wasn't sure what to make of the whole affair - Gudrun had defied him to his face, not something any self-respecting German father could tolerate - but she *had* avenged her boyfriend and forced the *Reich* to change. He was torn between pride and a sense of bitter horror. The youngsters might believe they'd won, yet Herman knew better. It wouldn't be long before the SS mounted a counterattack from Germany East.

"It has its moments," he said, finally. Gudrun hadn't done *anything* for his career, as far as he knew. Certainly, his superiors hadn't moved him to a safer post in one of the police stations, rather than allowing him to patrol the increasingly dangerous streets. "And your relatives are doing *what* for you?"

"Getting out of the city," Kuls said. "They're convinced that Berlin is going to tip into anarchy at any moment."

"They might well be right," Herman commented.

He frowned. Berlin was on a knife-edge these days, torn between hope and fear. The provisional government had doubled military and police patrols through the city, but it would take a far larger army to keep the entire city under control. Berlin was the largest city in the world; miles upon miles of sprawling government buildings, apartment blocks, factories and *Gastarbeiter* slave camps. A riot in one place might easily do some real damage before it could be crushed, now the fear was gone.

And with a quarter of the police force gone, he thought, *we don't have the manpower to keep running regular patrols through a third of the city.*

"I think so," Kuls agreed. "What happens when we run out of food?"

"We starve," Herman said, flatly.

He pushed the thought aside as they walked down the long road, striding past a row of apartment blocks. They were new, designed more for young unmarried professionals rather than men with wives and families; now, their windows were decorated with political slogans and demands for change. Herman wondered, absently, just what would happen when the young professionals realised that change wouldn't come as easily as they hoped, then shrugged. They'd just have to learn to cope, same as everyone else.

Some of them will have military experience, he thought. *They'll be able to join the defence force, if nothing else.*

He jumped as a door banged open, a middle-aged woman running out onto the street and waved desperately to them. Herman tensed, wondering if it was a trap of some kind, then walked over to her, keeping one hand on his pistol. Up close, the woman was at least a decade older than his wife, although time seemed to have been kind to her. Her hair was going grey, but otherwise she seemed to be in good health.

"I need help," she gasped. "One of my tenants is wounded. There's blood under the door!"

Herman blinked. "Blood?"

"Blood," the landlady said. "It's coming out from under the door!"

Herman exchanged a glance with Kuls, then allowed the woman to lead the way into the apartment block. Inside, it was dark and cold, the only illumination coming from a single flickering light bulb mounted on the wall. A shiver ran down his spine as he carefully unbuttoned his holster, glancing from side to side as his eyes struggled to adapt to the dim light. It grew brighter as they walked up two flights of stairs and stopped outside a single wooden door. Blood was dribbling from under the door…

"Call it in," Herman snapped.

"*Jawohl,*" Kuls said.

Herman tested the wooden door, then pulled a skeleton key from his belt and inserted it into the lock. Legally, locks *had* to be designed so a policeman could open them with his key, but it wasn't uncommon to find a door that had been designed before 1945 or one put together by a crafty locksmith. He allowed himself a moment of relief as the door opened without a fuss, then swore out loud as he pushed it open. A body - horrifically mutilated - lay on the carpeted floor. Behind him, he heard a thump as the landlady fainted.

"Take care of her," he ordered. "Did you get any reply?"

"Not as yet," Kuls said. "The dispatcher merely logged the call."

"Tell them we have a body," Herman said. He frowned as he peered at the corpse, careful not to touch the remains. "And one that doesn't look to long dead."

He felt his frown deepen as he silently listed the wounds. The murderer - or murderers - had been *savage*. They'd cut their victim's throat, stabbed him several times in the chest and castrated him, probably after force-feeding him some kind of anticoagulant. The blood should have started to clot by now, but it was still liquid. He'd been bled like a pig. Herman shuddered - he hadn't seen anything like this outside a brief tour in Germany East - and then glanced around, looking for clues. But there was nothing to be found.

"His penis is missing," he said, out loud. "They must have taken it."

Kuls looked pale as he peered through the door. "An *Untermensch*, perhaps?"

"It's possible," Herman agreed. An *Untermensch* would have nothing to lose, if he attacked a German. Why *not* mutilate the body? It wasn't as if he could be killed twice. Hell, *Untermenschen* were routinely executed for the crime of *looking* at good Germans. "But where would an *Untermensch* get the drugs?"

He sighed as he heard the landlady starting to stir. "See what you can get out of her," he said, as he rose. "Did you get anything from dispatch?"

"Still nothing," Kuls said. "They may have no one they can spare."

Herman nodded, shortly. "Get the landlady to her apartment, then see what you can pour into her," he ordered. "I'll search this place."

He closed the door, then turned and took one final look at the body. It was impossible to be sure, but it looked as though the attack had been deeply personal. The murdered man might well have *known* his killer; the murderer

4

could not have inflicted so much damage without some degree of feeling being involved. Indeed, judging by the body's position and the way the blood had splattered, it was quite possible he'd been trying to run when the fatal blow had been struck. But there was no way to know.

Nothing appeared to be missing, he decided, as he peered into the kitchen. It looked surprisingly bare, compared to the kitchen at home, but an unmarried man would probably have eaten at work, rather than cook for himself. A bottle of milk and two cartons of juice sat in the fridge; otherwise, the fridge was empty. Herman checked the drawers and found almost nothing, save for a small selection of imported - hence rare and expensive - British teas and coffees. No doubt the murder victim hadn't liked drinking the cheap coffee served all over the *Reich*.

I can hardly blame him for that, Herman thought. *I don't like drinking it either.*

He smiled to himself as he walked into the bedroom, then frowned. The bed was easily large enough for two people - it was larger than the bed he shared with his wife, at home - but there was no trace of a feminine presence. He opened the drawers, feeling his frown deepen as he noted the complete lack of female clothes and products. A homosexual? The man had been in his late forties, if Herman was any judge. It was staggeringly rare for a man of that age to be unmarried, although it *was* possible that he'd been married and then lost his wife to an accident. But homosexuality carried a death sentence in the *Reich*. Even the mere *suspicion* of homosexuality could be enough to destroy someone's life.

Herman shook his head slowly as he checked the bathroom. There was nothing, apart from a simple shampoo and a toilet that didn't look to have been cleaned regularly. No, there was no woman in the apartment: no wife, girlfriend or mistress. Indeed, if there hadn't been so many male clothes in the drawers, he would have wondered if the apartment wasn't being used as a covert rendezvous. The upper-class prostitutes - too expensive for the average soldier - often used them for their clients, once their pimps paid out bribes to all and sundry. But it was clear that *someone* had lived in the apartment...

He turned his attention to the photographs hanging from the walls and scowled, darkly, as he recognised the murder victim. He was wearing an SS uniform - a *Standartenfuehrer* - in one picture, shaking hands with a man

Herman vaguely recognised from a party propaganda broadcast. It took him a moment to recognise the Deputy *Führer*, a non-entity who had only been given the job because it provided a convenient place to dump him. But he'd clearly been younger then, maybe not even a politician. There was no date on any of the photographs.

He looked up as he heard the door opening. Kuls stepped into the apartment.

"The landlady says her tenant was a schoolmaster," he said, shortly. He eyed the body darkly, then stepped around it. "Apparently, he taught at the school just down the road."

"Oh," Herman said.

He looked back at the body. A schoolmaster? Maybe it was just his flawed memory - he hadn't been a schoolboy for nearly forty years - but the man didn't look anything *like* intimidating enough to be a schoolmaster. They were all kicked out of the SS for extreme violence - or so the schoolboys had joked, as they lined up each day, rain or shine, to enter the building and begin their lessons. He'd believed it too, back then. School might have toughened him up, but he remembered it with little fondness.

"She said he was normally out of the door at the crack of dawn," Kuls added, darkly. "He was rarely home until late at night, at least until the government fell. Since then, he merely stayed in his room and never left."

Herman snorted. "Did she happen to know when he had visitors?"

"Apparently, one of the boys would occasionally come and clean the apartment for him," Kuls said. "But he never had any other visitors."

"I see," Herman said. A landlady in Berlin could be relied upon to know *everything* about her tenants, from where they worked to how often they slept together. They were often the best sources a policeman could hope for. "Did anyone come today?"

"Not as far as she knows," Kuls said. "But that proves nothing."

"No," Herman agreed.

He contemplated the possibilities, one after the other. An SS officer - a *Standartenfuehrer* - would have been very useful, if he'd reported to the provisional government. It wasn't as if there weren't *other* SS officers helping to rebuild the *Reich*. But he'd stayed where he was, hiding. A spy? A coward? No, *that* was unlikely. He'd disliked the SS long before it had arrested his daughter, but he had to admit that SS officers were rarely cowards. They often led their men from the front. And yet, this one had become a schoolmaster. Jokes aside, schools weren't *actually* war zones...

But he would probably have impressed the brats, Herman thought, grimly. *A man who has marched into the teeth of enemy fire isn't going to be scared of a naughty teenage boy.*

Herman shook his head. The victim had known his killer, he was sure; he'd let him directly into the apartment. Or killers, if there had been more than one. And yet...

He sighed. Normally, a team of experts would tear the dead man's life apart, looking for the person who'd killed him. A murderer could not be allowed to get away with killing a *Standartenfuehrer*, even if the *Standartenfuehrer* had retired. It set a bad example. And yet, with the police force in such disarray, it was unlikely there would be a solid attempt to find the killer. Herman doubted they'd even take the time to dust for fingerprints before dumping the body into a mass grave and handing the apartment back to the landlady.

Unless we find something that leads us straight to the killer, he thought. *But what?*

"We search the apartment, thoroughly," he said. "And if we find nothing, we'll just have to make arrangements to dispose of the body."

"Of course," Kuls said.

Herman shot him a sharp look as they walked back into the kitchen and began to search with practiced efficiency. The landlady would be furious, when she discovered all her drawers dumped on the floor, but there was no help for it. Herman's instructors - when he'd joined the police - had shown him just how easy it was to conceal something, particularly something small, within a kitchen or bedroom. Taking the whole edifice apart was time-consuming, but it was the only way to be sure there was nothing hiding there.

"My wife would have a heart attack," Kuls said, when they'd finished the kitchen. "No tools at all."

"Mine too," Herman said.

He smirked at the thought as they walked into the bedroom and started dismantling the wardrobe, piece by piece. It was an older design, practically fixed to the wall. And yet, there was enough space behind the panel for something to be hidden...he grinned in sudden delight as he felt a concealed envelope. It refused to budge until he tugged the panelling back completely, then pulled. The envelope came free and fell into his hand.

"He *was* hiding something," Kuls observed.

"Looks that way," Herman agreed.

He led the way back into the living room and opened the envelope. A handful of photographs fell out and landed on the floor. He sighed, picked the first one up…and froze in horror as he saw the picture. It was…it was unthinkable.

"Shit," he breathed. He'd seen horror, from burned homesteads and raped women in Germany East, but this…this was far worse. He had to swallow hard to keep his gorge from rising. "No *wonder* someone wanted him dead!"

"He must have taken the photographs himself," Kuls observed. "Trying to buy this sort of shit…it would get him killed."

Herman looked back at the body, fighting down the urge to kick it as hard as he could. A schoolmaster with connections to the SS…even if someone had suspected something, they would never have dared take their concerns to higher authority. The boys - his victims - would have been compromised for life. They would have known they were doomed, when he tired of them…

…Until now. Until the SS's power had been broken. Until they'd found the nerve to brutally murder their tormentor. Until…

That could have been my son, he thought, numbly. Few would have dared to pick on a policeman's child, but an SS officer - even a retired one - might have had other ideas. *It could have been any of them.*

He glanced at his partner. "You know what? I don't want to find the killers."

Kuls nodded. "I don't think I want to find them either," he agreed. He kicked the body savagely. "Looks like an ironclad case of suicide to me."

CHAPTER TWO

RAF Fairford, United Kingdom
1 September 1985

"We've picked up a pair of escorts, sir," the pilot said. "Air Traffic Control is redirecting us around London."

Andrew Barton nodded as he peered out of the window. A pair of RAF Tornados were flying near the small jet, the air-to-air missiles clearly visible under their wings. There would be others too, he knew; RAF Tornados and USAF F-15 Eagles, patrolling the English Channel and the North Sea for signs of trouble from the *Reich*. It wasn't likely that the Germans would cause trouble - both sides in the brewing civil war had too many other problems - but it was quite possible that a rogue officer might consider sparking a global war in hopes of using it to reunite the *Reich*. He would have to be out of his mind, if he thought that would actually work...

"As long as we get there," he said, glancing at the radar screen. "Has there been any update from the Joint Command Network?"

"Nothing," the pilot said. "Skies are clear."

Andrew leaned back into his seat. He'd never been a comfortable flyer, even in the jet permanently assigned to the Berlin Embassy. Indeed, he would have preferred to take the train to Dunkirk and board one of the ferries to Dover, but time was pressing. He'd been summoned to Britain and knew he couldn't disobey. Besides, the sooner he was finished in Britain, the sooner he could return to Berlin. There were too many interesting things happening in Berlin for him to want to be elsewhere.

The RAF Tornados peeled off as RAF Fairford came into view. It was a smaller airfield than the fast-jet fighter bases to the east, serving the British

Government as a private airport and conference chamber - although he was fairly sure the British would have plans to turn it into a fighter base if the long-feared war between the North Atlantic Alliance and the Third *Reich* finally became a reality. The pilot spoke briefly to the ground, then steered the plane towards the runway. Andrew had a flash of a blue and white plane parked at the far end of the airfield before the aircraft shook, violently, as it touched the ground. He closed his eyes and kept them closed until the plane finally rumbled to a halt near a small cluster of buildings.

"I'll be refuelling the plane while you're gone," the pilot said. "Do you know if we're going to be heading straight back?"

Andrew shrugged. He'd had the *impression* that he wouldn't be kept for long, but Washington - and London - operated on their own timescale. He might be expected to remain overnight, if there was a need for further debriefing, or he might just be ordered back to Berlin within the hour. But there was no way to be sure.

"Get a nap, if you can," he advised. "I have no idea when we'll be leaving."

He rose to his feet and headed for the hatch. The ground crew, working with commendable speed, had already pushed a mobile staircase against the plane, allowing him to descend to the ground. He couldn't help noticing that security had been doubled or tripled; armed soldiers patrolled the fence, backed up by armoured cars, while Rapier missile launchers had been scattered around the airfield. It had been years since Britain had faced a terrorist threat, since the last remnants of the IRA had been crushed or convinced to lay down their arms, but it was evident that no one was taking chances. A strike at RAF Fairford could decapitate two governments at once.

"This way, sir," a young man said. He wore a black suit and tie, rather than a uniform, but he couldn't hide his military training. "We have to get you through security."

Andrew nodded, unsurprised, as he was led into the nearest building. The guards were polite, but firm; they searched him thoroughly, examined everything in his pocket with cynical eyes and finally waved him through. Andrew was tempted to make a crack about one of them buying him dinner afterwards, but thought better of it before he could open his mouth. The guards probably wouldn't find it very funny.

"This is your badge," his escort said, once Andrew was passed through the gate. "You are scheduled to enter the main room in thirty minutes. Do you want to take a shower and freshen up before then?"

"Yes, please," Andrew said. He felt grimy, even though the flight hadn't taken more than three hours. "And is there coffee?"

"There are *gallons* of coffee," his escort assured him. "I'll have some brought into the room for you."

Thirty minutes later, feeling much better, Andrew was escorted into a comfortable conference room. He stiffened, automatically, as President John Anderson rose to his feet, hastily snapping out a salute. Beside the President, Prime Minister Margaret Thatcher nodded politely as Andrew was shown to a chair. There was no one else in the room, but Andrew would have been surprised if the meeting wasn't being recorded. The government - both governments - would want a solid record of just what had been said, even if the recordings never saw the light of day.

"Mr. Barton," Anderson said. "Thank you for coming."

"Thank you, Mr. President," Andrew said.

He took a moment to study them both as an aide brought two cups of coffee and one of tea, placing them on the table. They made an odd pair. President Anderson looked more like a schoolteacher than a President, while Prime Minister Thatcher reminded him of one of the fearsome old biddies who'd dominated his hometown. The *Reich's* propaganda machine had turned her into a monster, even to the point of insisting she was really a man in drag. They'd had some problems coming to terms with female politicians, Andrew recalled; they'd never really seen women as anything more than mothers, daughters and wives.

And now a young girl started a movement that sundered the Reich, Andrew thought, *will they change their attitudes?*

"This is not a formal debriefing," Anderson said, once the aide had retreated. "We would merely like your impression of the current situation."

Andrew took a breath. "At last report" - he wasn't going to go into specifics, not when the recording wouldn't be kept in the US - "the provisional government has a reasonably firm grip on Germany Prime, but very limited control outside it. Germany North and Germany South seem to be waiting to see who comes out on top, while Germany Arabia has effectively declared for Germany East. That gives the rump government in Germany East the ability to pressure the Turks into allowing shipments of troops and supplies through their territory. I don't expect the Turks to refuse."

"I imagine the prospect of being devastated from one end of the country to the other will concentrate a few minds," Thatcher said, dryly.

Andrew nodded. The *Reich's* allies knew, beyond any possibility of doubt, that resistance to the *Reich* would be utterly futile. Vichy France, Spain, Portugal, Turkey, Italy, Finland…the slightest hint of resistance, of disagreement, would be enough to start the Panzers rolling in their direction. They were utterly prostrate before the *Reich*. And yet, with the *Reich* itself torn in two, who knew which way the former allies would jump?

But they'd have to be sure of themselves first, he thought. *Whoever comes out on top will certainly seek revenge, if they feel that they were betrayed.*

"It is hard to be sure just where the military balance actually stands," Andrew continued, after a moment. "The rump has a more deployable military force at its disposal, but the provisional government should be able to generate a larger force, given time. I believe they will certainly *try* to recall troops from South Africa, yet there's no way to know which way those forces will jump. It might be better to keep them in the south until after the civil war is settled, one way or the other."

President Anderson leaned forward. "What do *you* think is going to happen?"

"The rump will attack," Andrew said. "I'm sure you've seen the orbital imagery of forces being moved westwards and positioned in place for a full-scale advance. Launching an offensive and pushing it forward with maximum force has been part of German military doctrine for well over a century. There's no way they will allow a bunch of rebels - and that is how they will see the provisional government - to take and hold Berlin."

He paused. "In the long-term, it's quite likely the remainder of the *Reich's* economy will collapse," he added. "But I don't know if that will happen in time to prevent the civil war from devastating the country. The *Reich* stockpiled vast qualities of military supplies over the past forty years."

"Which leads to the obvious question," Anderson said. "What about the nukes?"

Andrew took a long breath. "Officially, the *Reich's* stockpile of nuclear weapons can only be launched with command codes held within the Berlin Bunker," he said. His source within the provisional government had told him as much, although he wasn't high enough to be absolutely sure that was true. "The missile silos in Siberia should be unable to launch without those codes, while the bombs assigned to the *Luftwaffe* cannot be detonated. In theory, the rump should be unable to deploy nuclear weapons.

"In practice, Mr. President, I believe they may well be able to detonate tactical nukes."

The President scowled. "How?"

"I'm not a nuclear weapons expert, but I discussed the matter *thoroughly* with an officer at the embassy," Andrew said, carefully. "The problem with any sort of security system is it needs to strike a balance between two competing imperatives; the need to keep the weapon from detonating at the wrong time and the need to ensure that the weapon actually detonates at the *right* time. It's quite possible that a designer could accidentally ensure that the weapons *cannot* be detonated through making the security system too good."

"Too good," the President repeated.

"Yes, Mr. President," Andrew said. "If the wrong code is inputted, the security system will fry the detonator and render the weapon useless."

He paused. "We do not know the specifics of the *Reich's* version of our Permissive Action Links," he added. "However, my expert believes that someone with a good knowledge of tactical nuclear weapons might well be able to remove the PAL and replace it with a makeshift detonator. Indeed, given that a lucky strike on Berlin might destroy the command codes, it's quite possible that the *Reich* was very careful *not* to make their PALs too good. In the absence of a working model to examine, there's no way to know for sure."

"So the rump may have access to tactical nukes," Thatcher commented.

"Yes, Prime Minister," Andrew said. "They may also be able to fire the ICBMs from Siberia, given time."

"It sounds careless of them," Thatcher observed.

"They need to strike a balance, Prime Minister," Andrew said. "I don't think they envisaged civil war when they were planning how best to secure their nuclear arsenal."

"Probably not," Anderson said. "Do you think the rump will deploy nukes?"

Andrew hesitated. "I think they would be reluctant to take the risk," he said. "The provisional government could certainly retaliate in kind. However…"

He took a breath. "Germany East has always been the most *fanatical* part of the *Reich*," he added, after a moment. "The SS isn't just tolerated there, it's actually *popular*. Neither their leadership nor their population are likely to view the provisional government as anything more than a bunch of filthy traitors. Indeed, they may even have a *point*. By overthrowing the former government, the rebels have actually weakened the *Reich*. I don't expect them to be reluctant to deploy nukes if they think they need them."

"Wonderful," Anderson said, sourly.

Thatcher nodded in agreement. "Are they likely to try to pick a fight with us?"

"I don't know, Prime Minister," Andrew said. "They would have to be insane to try, in hopes of convincing the *Reich* to reunite, but I don't believe Karl Holliston is quite sane."

He didn't blame Thatcher for worrying. *America* was protected, first by vast oceans and then by the FIELD GREEN ABM network, but Britain was bare moments from German-occupied France. There would be barely any warning before the first missile reached its target. A nuclear war would turn Britain into a radioactive slagheap and both sides knew it; hell, with thousands of German jet fighters sitting on airfields in France and Germany, even a *conventional* war would give the British a very hard time.

"That's not reassuring," Anderson said.

Andrew nodded. He'd met *Reichsführer-SS* Karl Holliston once, two years ago. The man was a fanatic, as reactionary as they came. Calculating, ruthless…and utterly dedicated to the ideas of the Third *Reich*. Andrew had no difficulty in believing that Holliston would deliberately set out to kill as many protesters as possible, then expend a dedicated Special Forces assault team in trying to kill the provisional government. A man like Holliston would do *anything* for his cause.

"There's nothing reassuring here, Mr. President," Andrew said. "I believe there was some talk of accepting a permanent split between the two sides, leaving us with two German states, but I don't think that either government would willingly accept it. Their dispute will have to be settled by war."

Anderson nodded, glancing carefully at Thatcher. "And *that* leads to a very different point," he said. "Should we be trying to intervene?"

Andrew winced, inwardly. He'd expected that question from the moment he, instead of Ambassador Turtledove, was summoned to RAF Fairford. The Ambassador was there to be diplomatic, while *Andrew* worked for OSS, trying to develop new sources and covert networks within the *Reich*. If there was a determined attempt to support the provisional government, *he* would be running it…

But he wouldn't have the final say. There would be factions in Washington - and London too, he suspected - that would be arguing for intervention, after reading a handful of carefully-slanted reports. Other factions, having read different reports, would be arguing for staying firmly out of the growing conflict. And *neither* faction would have a real *feel* for what was going on in Germany. Their leadership certainly wouldn't be stationed in the *Reich*.

Andrew took a moment to compose his thoughts. This - *this* - was a chance to influence policy on a truly *global* scale. His words would shape the thinking of the most powerful man and woman in the world, a terrifying thought. He was no stranger to danger - he knew he ran the risk of being arrested, tortured and disappeared every time he made contact with one of his sources within the *Reich* - but this was different. Lives hung on his words. His mouth was suddenly very dry.

"There are a number of factors that should be considered, Mr. President," he said, carefully. "First, perhaps most importantly, the provisional government is *strongly* nationalistic. They will not be pleased at an open suggestion of military support. Even if they were, the presence of American and British troops fighting alongside their men will hand their rivals a major propaganda coup. Entire *generations* of Germans have been raised to consider us the enemy. It may well undermine their position."

He paused. "And they will suspect us of wanting to weaken the *Reich*," he added, after a moment. "Will we demand German withdrawal from France, for example, as the price of our support?"

Anderson frowned. "I thought they wanted freedom."

Thatcher smiled. "So did George Washington and his fellows," she pointed out. "That didn't stop them keeping black slaves in bondage."

"Touché," Anderson said. He met Andrew's eyes. "But should we not use this as a chance to remove the threat permanently?"

"If we back the rump into a corner, they will use nukes," Andrew said, flatly. "And we could not *guarantee* that they wouldn't be able to fire the missiles at us."

He sighed. "Ambassador Turtledove has been trying to forge links with the provisional government, but - frankly - the government has too many other problems at the moment. If they lose the coming war…well, our opinion isn't going to matter."

Thatcher nodded, curtly. "What would *you* advise?"

"I would suggest providing limited intelligence support and nothing else," Andrew said. He understood the urge to do *something*, but they were playing with nukes! "We can let them know, quietly, that we may not be averse to providing further help. But really, getting involved in their civil war would be a major commitment."

"Particularly with the troubles in South Africa," Anderson observed. "There are demands for intervention there too."

"Another political headache," Thatcher agreed. Her lips quirked into a smile. "Although, really, one that doesn't involve nukes."

Andrew nodded. South Africa had tried but failed to produce nuclear weapons. Or so he'd been told. South Africa's nuclear program had taken a body-blow when South Africa had been expelled from the NAA, while the *Reich* wasn't in the habit of providing nuclear weapons or nuclear technology to anyone. But even if South Africa *did* have nukes, what could they *do* with them? Blow up their own cities?

"Thank you for coming, Mr. Barton," Anderson said. "I'm afraid there are quite a few others waiting to debrief you, but hopefully we should have an idea how to proceed before you return to Germany."

He paused. "Do you anticipate any problems in returning?"

"No, Mr. President," Andrew said. He rose. "The provisional government has seen fit to honour the treaties we made with their predecessors."

"Let's just hope it stays that way," Anderson said. "This could spin out of control very quickly."

"I would say that was a given, Mr. President," Andrew said. "Both sides have enough military power to ensure that the coming war is far from short."

CHAPTER THREE

Reichstag, Berlin
1 September 1985

Volker Schulze, Chancellor of the Greater German *Reich* - he'd refused to take *Führer* as a title - stood at the window and peered out over the city as the sun started to sink towards the distant horizon, feeling a gnawing concern within his gut. Berlin looked surprisingly calm, from his viewpoint, but he knew it was nothing more than an illusion. Gudrun and the Valkyries had unleashed forces he doubted they knew how to control, even if control was possible. The government's absolute control over its population was gone, once and for all…

We were held in a cage, Volker thought, grimly. *And now the bars are gone, some of us are leaving the cage.*

He cursed the former *Reich* Council under his breath, wishing with all his heart that he'd been able to get his hands on the *truly* guilty men. *Reichsführer-SS* Karl Holliston had made his escape, while several of the other former councillors had fled to Germany East, rather than face the wrath of their fellow countrymen. Volker would have given a great deal for the chance to get his hands around Holliston's neck and squeeze, even though he'd been an SS officer himself. The bastard had not only gotten Volker's son mortally wounded; he'd had the gall to lie about it to the people. Volker wouldn't have known *anything* about his son's injury - and death - if Gudrun hadn't sneaked into the hospital. It had been enough for Volker to switch sides and start a - highly-illegal - union. And now he was the head of the provisional government.

The thought made him smile, sourly, as he turned to face the table. His councillors - the *new Reich* Council - were slowly filling up the seats, looking as grim as he felt. Volker had no idea just how far any of them could be trusted, even though they were all under sentence of death if they were captured by the SS. Finance Minister Hans Krueger, at least, could be relied upon to try to mend the increasingly broken economy, but Volker had no illusions about some of the others. Two of them, at least, were ambitious enough to unseat him if they thought they could get away with it.

He surveyed the room, half-wishing that Gudrun was there. The mere presence of a woman - and a teenage girl, at that - was enough to agitate many of the older and more reactionary councillors. Volker hated to admit it, but he took a perverse pleasure in watching them being forced to take a woman seriously. Gudrun didn't hold a portfolio - there had been no way to justify giving her a ministry - yet she was the single most popular councillor in Germany. It gave her a power her older counterparts could neither deny nor subvert.

She would have made one hell of a daughter-in-law, Volker thought, as the doors were firmly closed. *And Gerde would have had real problems trying to bully her.*

He smiled at the thought as he strolled over to the table, nodding to the guards positioned against the walls. The *Reichstag* was guarded by heavily-armed soldiers these days, men drawn from the toughest regiments in the *Heer*. After the SS had dropped an assault force into the building and done their best to destroy the provisional government before it had formed, he wasn't inclined to take chances. Some of the councillors had insisted that the men posed a security risk, but they hadn't dared say it very loudly. They knew, all too well, that most of them would be dead if the Berlin Guard hadn't switched sides.

"Let us begin," he said, sitting down and resting his elbows on the table. He had no time for elaborate formalities. "Field Marshal. What is our current state of readiness?"

Field Marshal Gunter Voss leaned forward. He'd taken up the post of Head of OKW - the uniformed head of the military - after Field Marshal Justus Stoffregen had resigned, citing a refusal to fight his fellow Germans. Volker had no idea if Stoffregen genuinely felt that way - or if the SS had somehow brought pressure to bear on him - but some of his advisors insisted that losing Stoffregen wasn't a bad thing. Voss was almost certainly high on the list of individuals the SS intended to purge, if they ever recovered Berlin. He'd opposed Holliston far too often.

"Better than I'd feared, but worse than I'd hoped," Voss said, bluntly. "Much of our heavy armour was placed near the beaches, for fear of a British invasion. We're starting to ship it back to the east now, but it's going to take time before we have the divisions formed up and ready to go to war. The resignations and defections haven't helped either. Right now, we barely have two scratch divisions digging in along the border with Germany East and two more held in reserve."

He smiled, rather tightly. "We *are* recruiting as fast as we can, sir, and most of our recruits have some military experience, but it will still take weeks - if not months - before they're ready for deployment. Until then, we will be committed to a mobile defence of the eastern border, slowing the SS down until we are ready to drive them back."

Volker nodded. "And the men in South Africa?"

"Getting them back is going to be a nightmare, even if we trusted them," Voss said. "Much of our heavy-lift capability was deployed to the south, which made them easy targets for American-designed missiles. And the South Africans aren't particularly keen to see them go."

"Too bad," Volker said, tiredly.

He shook his head. His son had been wounded in South Africa. He certainly had no love for the country. But even without that, he knew there was no way the *Reich* should have supported South Africa. Fighting to preserve white civilisation was one thing, but South Africa was right on the end of a very long logistics chain. Better to ship the South Africans to Germany East and invite them to blend in with the population. It wasn't as if Germany East was short of territory.

"Most commanding officers in South Africa have secured their bases, but there's little else they can do," Voss added. "A handful of officers have refused to answer my calls. I think we have to assume they're on the other side."

"Understood," Volker said. The *Wehrmacht* was not used to civil wars. Soldiers fought for the *Reich*, not for factions *within* Germany. Now, with the country torn in two, everyone in uniform had to ask themselves where their loyalties lay. And not everyone was willing to fight for the provisional government. "Start making preparations to get the others home."

"Of course, sir," Voss said.

And hope to hell the French don't decide to play games, Volker thought, privately. Vichy France had been restless for decades, before the *Reich* Council had collapsed. Now, the French might try to take advantage of the *Reich's* troubles to reclaim their independence and recover the territory they'd lost. *If they decide to shut down the airfields between South Africa and the Reich, getting those troops home will be impossible.*

He shook his head - Gudrun had been dispatched on a diplomatic mission to France, in hopes of preventing the French from trying to take advantage of the chaos - and met Voss's eyes. "How are our chances?"

"Mixed, sir," Voss said. "The *Waffen-SS* has the armour and supporting elements they need to punch through our defence lines, even if they don't have covert supporters within our ranks. I believe we will see a major offensive within two weeks, perhaps less. They have to know that matters will become a great deal harder if they give us time to mobilise. On the other hand, we can lure them into fighting grounds where their advantages are strongly reduced - urban conflict in Berlin, in particular."

Volker winced. He was no stranger to combat. Military operations in built-up terrain - street-to-street fighting - were always nightmarish. But he knew Voss was right. The SS - and Holliston in particular - would want to recover Berlin as quickly as possible. Letting them overextend themselves, while gathering the forces necessary to cut their supply lines and crushing their advance elements...Holliston was many things, but he was no Adolf Hitler. The first and greatest *Führer* would never have made such a deadly mistake.

"Very well," he said. "Luther? How are they placed for an attack on Berlin?"

Luther Stresemann, Head of the Economic Intelligence Service, frowned. "Holliston has reshaped his...*cabinet,* sir," he said, "so many of our original sources within the SS have been reshuffled out of power. I don't believe that was intentional - they still appear to be alive - but it makes it harder for us to get a window into their deliberations. However, many of our lower-level sources are still in play."

He paused. "All their reports indicate that Holliston has called up both Category A and Category B reservists, both *Heer* and SS," he continued. "As you know, the reservists in Germany East have often been called up at the drop of a hat, so we don't anticipate it taking very long for them to brush up on their tactics and return to their units. However…they will have problems securing many of the settlements if they call away their defenders. We believe that *Untermenschen* attacks on German settlements will increase rapidly, as the *Untermenschen* realise that there are fewer defenders in place."

Volker frowned. "Is that likely to cause Holliston problems?"

"Not immediately," Stresemann said. "In the long run, the reservists are unlikely to be *pleased* at marching away from their homes, with the *Untermenschen* ready to attack, but right now Holliston has all the tools he needs to render their opinions immaterial."

"That *was* what the old council thought," Voss pointed out, dryly.

"The old council was also worried about the knock-on effects of heavy repression," Finance Minister Hans Krueger countered. "I doubt Holliston gives much of a damn about the side effects."

Volker tapped the table before Krueger and Voss could start bickering. "How long can Germany East survive, economically?"

"It depends on what you mean by *survive*, sir," Krueger said, bluntly. "My staff have run the figures but too much depends on factors that are unfortunately unpredictable. Germany East is perfectly capable of feeding itself, and of supplying its own wants in small-arms ammunition, but it doesn't have many factories capable of producing tanks, railway locomotives and heavy machinery. However, they do have massive stockpiles of everything they need for war. It may take *years* before they drain their stocks dry."

"Maybe less than that," Voss commented. "Ammunitions expenditures are always far - far - higher than predicted. I imagine that their logistics problems would turn into nightmares soon enough."

Krueger nodded. "The problem, sir," he added, looking directly at Volker, "is that we're in a mess too."

He went on before anyone could say a word. "Our industries were pushing the limits long before the…the uprising," he continued. "Machinery was becoming outdated, workers were working longer hours for less pay. We were robbing Peter to pay Paul right across the *Reich*, sir, and the real value of our currency was declining sharply. The push for unionising the workforce only made matters worse, as it added another factor to our considerations."

"I believe I am aware of that," Volker said, lightly.

"Then you have to face up to the implications," Krueger said, bluntly. "There are just too many problems, deeply rooted within our industrial base, for a quick fix to work. We need to replace vast quantities of machinery and train up hundreds of thousands of new workers very - very - quickly, which will come at a staggering cost. Frankly, sir, we may have to concede that we have lost the arms race with the Americans."

"Then the Americans will crush us," Voss snapped.

"The Americans are hardly our problem at the moment," Volker pointed out.

"Not now, no," Krueger agreed. "Our best estimate is that it will cost upwards of a hundred billion *Reichmarks* to rebuild our economic base - and we don't *have* a hundred billion *Reichmarks*. We'll have to start on a smaller scale…"

"…During a war," Voss reminded him.

"Exactly," Krueger said. "We have a colossal shortage of money."

Volker swallowed. A *hundred billion Reichmarks?* He couldn't even *begin* to imagine such a vast sum of money. There was no way he'd ever be a millionaire on his salary, let alone a *billionaire*. And getting the money was only the *start* of the problem. The unions would resist, strongly, training up more than a handful of new workers. They'd see it as an attempt to undermine their power and they'd be right. Hell, Volker *himself* would have opposed it when he'd been a Union Chief.

And how can we do all that, he asked himself, *when there is a war underway?*

"Loot it from the French," Voss suggested. "Or the Italians. They bend over to give us anything we want."

"They don't have the money or machinery we need," Krueger snapped. "Their currencies are pegged to ours, so the real value of *their* money is declining too. The best we can hope for, from either of them, is more poorly-trained workers and food supplies. And looting them would mean drawing forces away from the eastern border!"

Volker held up his hand. "Can we supply the demands of the war?"

"Perhaps," Krueger said. "But right now, even our ammunition plants are in trouble."

"And without ammunition, we can't fight," Voss said. He sounded tired and harassed. "Stop producing ladies underwear and start turning out more shells!"

"It isn't that easy and you know it," Krueger snapped. He sounded tired too. "A plant designed for producing one thing cannot easily be modified to produce something else!"

Volker took a long moment to think as the bickering began in earnest. On one hand, Krueger was right. The economy was in a mess. He had no real dislike for the Americans - both sides had supported rebels, insurgents and terrorists - but he had to worry about the long-term effects of an economic collapse. And yet, on the other hand, there *was* a war on. The economic issues were secondary to preserving the provisional government.

He tapped the table, again. "Hans," he said. "How long can you paper over the cracks?"

"I've been doing that for the last five years," Krueger said. He rubbed his eyes. "There are just too many variables, sir. I can do my best to freeze prices, but unless we manage to stop our money declining in value...well, all we'd do is shift sales into the black market. I don't think it will be easy to force farmers to sell at a loss."

"Then confiscate their stocks," Voss said.

"That would ensure we wouldn't get any harvests *next* year," Krueger said. "The Russians learned - too late - that collectivism reduced yields. We don't want to make the same mistake ourselves."

He looked at Volker. "I think we might just be able to stretch matters out for another year, but a single major disaster will almost certainly set off a chain reaction that will bring our economies down," he added. "As it is, we may have to go back to rationing food very quickly. We're just not getting any additional supplies from Germany East - or the French."

Gudrun will have to discuss that too, Volker thought. *And hope to hell the French don't demand too much in return.*

"See to it," he ordered. It wasn't going to go down well with the population - it seemed as though everyone had a political opinion these days and was willing to share it - but there wasn't any choice. "I'll announce it once you've got the groundwork in place and explain the problem. Maybe there won't be too many objections."

"Hah," Voss commented.

Volker suspected he was right. The German population knew better than to believe what someone said on the radio, particularly now. They might be *told* that things were getting better - or they had been, before the uprising - but they could *see* that costs were steadily rising higher, when products were available at all. It was ironic, he had to admit, that people conditioned to disbelieve whatever they were told by the previous government wouldn't believe him either, yet it would just have to be endured. There was nothing that could be done to make the population trust him, save for carefully building up a reputation for telling the truth. But that would take years.

"I think a basic supply of food each week would be reassuring to most people," Krueger said, bluntly. "It's going to get worse before it gets better."

"And we're moving people from the east," Voss added. "We're going to have to feed them too."

"I know," Krueger said. It was yet another headache. "And people *here* aren't going to welcome them either."

Volker sighed, inwardly. The refugees were unlikely to be welcomed, not by people who barely had enough to eat and drink themselves. But they had to be moved from their homes, if only to keep them safe. The SS was unlikely to be *pleasant* to anyone who hadn't already declared themselves for Germany East. Indeed, it was quite likely that any civilians they encountered would pay a steep price.

He sighed, again. He needed his sleep; he needed to lie beside his wife and pretend, if only for a few hours, that he was nothing more than a simple factory worker. But there were too many things they needed to discuss - and hash out - before he could seek his bed. A mistake now might come back to haunt them when the SS finally started its advance.

At least Holliston has his own problems, he thought, dryly. *But does he have so many bickering subordinates?*

CHAPTER FOUR

Germanica (Moscow), Germany East
1 September 1985

Karl Holliston had always loved Germanica.

He stood on the balcony and gazed out over the city. Moscow - old Moscow - was gone, save for a handful of buildings that had once been the beating heart of the long-dead Union of Soviet Socialist Republics. Schoolchildren were taken there every year, where they were told about how Stalin had been trying to flee Moscow when he'd been killed and just how much the *Reich* had done for the country. Russia was now the breadbasket of the *Reich*, the source of true Aryan greatness. The fact that the Russians themselves were a threatened minority in their own country was neither here nor there, as far as Holliston and his fellows were concerned. They were, after all, *Untermenschen*.

Adolf Hitler had wanted to be an architect, Karl recalled, and Albert Speer had been more than happy to make his dreams reality. Germanica was larger-than-life, dominated by towering gothic buildings and monuments to the great victories won by the Third *Reich* over its many enemies. There was something about the sheer grandeur of the buildings that made *Untermenschen* feel small and puny, Karl knew, even though *he* felt the buildings suited him and his dreams. Here, there were no limitations on the *Volk*. No accountants to quibble over the cost, no bleeding-heart westerners moaning and whining about 'human rights;' nothing to stand in their way as they built the Thousand Year *Reich*. And not a single *Untermensch* in sight!

He leaned forward, enjoying the view. Blond young men, wearing a multitude of uniforms, strolling beside blonde-haired young women who were clearly readying themselves for a happy life of *Kinder, Küche, Kirche*. They would birth and raise the next generation of Germans - *true* Germans, Germans who would not let anything stand in their way between them and true greatness. It was with them, Karl was sure, that he would take the entire world and remake it, as Hitler himself had dreamed. And now the time was at hand.

Smiling, he took one last look, then turned and strolled back into the office. It was large, a duplicate of the giant room Hitler had occupied before he'd died in 1950. Two SS flags hung from the walls, surrounding a giant map of the world. Germany East was immense, stretching from what had once been Poland to Kamchatka, but he knew better. It would be the work of generations before Germany East was tamed. Until then, it would continue to breed strong and hardy Germans willing to do whatever it took to keep themselves alive.

"*Mien Führer*," Maria said. His assistant was standing by the door, seemingly unwilling to walk over to the desk. It had been decades since the *Reich* had a true *Führer* and no one was quite sure how to react. "*Oberstgruppenfuehrer* Alfred Ruengeler is here, as you requested; he's currently waiting in the antechamber. Your...other guest is currently passing through security."

Karl smiled. He hadn't missed the hint of disapproval in her voice. Maria was, in very many ways, a strict conservative. Quite how she squared that with actually working outside the home was beyond him, but it hardly mattered. Maria couldn't hope to wield power on her own, not in the remorselessly masculine SS. She was loyal because none of Karl's rivals would trust her any further than they could throw her.

"Have her wait in the antechamber, once she arrives," he ordered. "And show the *Oberstgruppenfuehrer* in."

He sat down at the desk and smiled to himself as *Oberstgruppenfuehrer* Alfred Ruengeler entered the room. Ruengeler had been working a desk for the last four years, but he was still a tall powerfully-built man with short blond hair and a badly-scarred face. Karl knew that he took every opportunity he could to get out of the office and tour the settlements personally, despite the risk of assassination. Ruengeler had just never been very comfortable serving behind a desk. Indeed, he'd even requested a transfer to South Africa, even though it would have meant an effective demotion.

A fighter, Karl thought, as Maria brought them both coffee. The SS blend, not the weak slop served in Berlin. *And I need fighters.*

"*Mein Führer*," Ruengeler said. "I have the report you requested."

Karl leaned forward, eagerly. "Can you complete the mission?"

"I believe so, *Mein Führer*," Ruengeler said. "Our tactics were designed for a rapid advance against stiff enemy opposition. Here, we are intimately familiar with much of the terrain involved, an advantage we had no good reason to expect during training. A combined-arms thrust involving both armour and elite forces should be more than sufficient to open the route to Berlin."

He paused. "The true danger is the enemy withdrawing *into* Berlin."

Karl snorted. "They'll never be able to hold the city."

Ruengeler looked doubtful. "The Slavic *Untermenschen* held Leningrad for three years, even though they were grossly inferior to us," he said. "They were eating one another when the defences finally fell. I would expect better from the Berliners. If we fail to take Berlin quickly, we will have real problems imposing our will on the remainder of the *Reich*."

"Then we will thrust as hard as we can," Karl said, firmly. "Do we have any major problems?"

"Our air support arm is going to have problems," Ruengeler said, flatly. "Much of the forces at our disposal were designed for close-air support, not air supremacy. We have a number of jet fighters at our disposal, but the traitors have more. They also have all five aircraft carriers into the bargain."

"We are already taking steps to handle their advantages," Karl said. It was wasteful, but he would sooner lose half the *Luftwaffe* than the *Reich*. Soldiers, sailors and airmen were *meant* to be expended, if necessary. "And the *Kriegsmarine* is unlikely to take a major role in events."

"They do have marines, *Mein Führer*," Ruengeler reminded him. "And their ship-mounted cruise missiles may be a major problem."

Karl shrugged. "They will not be a problem," he said, firmly.

"As you say, *Mein Führer*," Ruengeler said.

He cleared his throat. "The offensive should be ready to launch in two weeks, perhaps less," he said. "By then, all the forces will be in place and our logistics support network will be well underway…"

"I believe it should be possible to launch the offensive earlier," Karl said. "Is that true?"

"We would be launching the offensive with what we have on hand," Ruengeler said. "I believe that waiting at least ten days would allow us to throw a much harder punch into their defences. We need reserves to handle any unanticipated little…problems."

Bloody noses, Karl translated, mentally. *Or outright defeats.*

He studied the map for a long moment. It was just over three hundred miles from the front lines to Berlin, assuming nothing slowed the assault force down as it mounted the first true *Blitzkrieg* in forty years. The forces that had stormed into Russia, back when the *Reich* had been embarking on its grand plan of conquest and transformation, had done as well, yet they'd faced *Untermenschen. His* forces faced *Germans.* Degraded Germans, perhaps, but still Germans. A delay - a setback - might prove fatal. His only consolation was that the enemy couldn't really afford to trade space for time.

They can't surrender Berlin, any more than we can refuse to try to take it, he thought, stroking his chin grimly. *Giving up the capital will doom their cause.*

He looked up at Ruengeler. "And that is your considered military opinion?"

"Yes, *Mein Führer*," Ruengeler said. He was strong, too strong to wilt easily before a *Fuhrer.* "Too much can happen when an offensive finally begins. I would prefer to have forces on hand to…deal with the problems before they get out of hand."

Karl sighed. "You do realise that you'll be giving *them* an extra two weeks too?"

"I understand the factors involved," Ruengeler insisted, calmly. "But give us two weeks and we will be ready to deal with any countermoves they make."

"I hope you're right," Karl said.

He ground his teeth in frustration. He *wanted* to order his forces to attack instantly, but he knew better. Expending an entire team of crack commandos was one thing - his forces weren't significantly weakened by their absence - but thousands of tanks and hundreds of thousands of infantry? Losing a *Waffen-SS* division would be costly, very costly. It would certainly encourage his enemies to consider overthrowing him. Karl Holliston, after all, was no Adolf Hitler.

"I'll be flying to Warsaw tomorrow morning," Ruengeler added. "I should have more than enough time to get everything organised before the offensive starts in earnest. Ideally, *Mein Fuhrer*, we should have enough time to make our gains before winter sets in."

Karl nodded, tightly. Winters in Eastern Europe weren't *quite* as nasty as winters in Germany East, but the coming winter would still impose limitations on military operations. His troops were trained and experienced in arctic warfare - the insurgents didn't let up just because it was cold enough to kill a grown man - yet they'd be needed back home. God knew the insurgents would take advantage of the chaos to launch additional attacks against German settlements.

"Very good," he said. "Make sure you send anyone on the purge list back to Germanica for trial and punishment."

"Of course, *Mein Fuhrer*," Ruengeler said, as he rose. "It will be done."

He sounded faintly displeased at the thought of having his *Waffen-SS* troopers mistaken for *Einsatzgruppen* extermination squads, but Karl had no doubt he'd do his job. The purge list included thousands of Germans who had come under suspicion for one reason or another, as well as everyone closely related to them. All traces of heresy had to be exterminated, even if it meant catching a few innocents along with the guilty. They had to die so that the *Reich* could live.

"Good luck," Karl said.

He held up his hand in salute. Ruengeler returned it, then about-faced and marched out of the giant office. Karl watched him go, wondering just how long it would be until he had to dispose of the older man. Ruengeler was extremely competent, but he asked too many questions - and, besides, he was just a little too squeamish for the task ahead. Purging the first set of names was one thing, yet that would only be the beginning. Germany had to be purified before she could rise from the ashes.

Maria stepped into the office. "Should I show your other guest into the room?"

"Yes, please," Karl said. Maria's disapproval was almost amusing. One would think he'd called a prostitute from the gutter. "And then hold all my calls."

He rose as Maria left the office, only to return a moment later with a tall woman wearing a black SS uniform. The thought of a woman wearing such a uniform had seemed absurd, he recalled, until he'd first *met Hauptsturmfuehrer* Katharine Milch. She was impressive, he had to admit; tall, blonde, her curves clearly visible through her uniform. And yet, her file made it very clear that she was one of the most ruthless people - male or female - in the *Reich*. The string of successes to her name warned him that Katharine Milch was not a woman to take lightly. Her cold blue eyes silently challenged him to do just that.

"*Mein Fuhrer*," she said. Her voice was a warm contralto, but there was a hint of sharpness in it that made his hindbrain sit up and pay attention. "I understand that you have a special task for me?"

"I do," Karl confirmed. There was something about her that flustered him, more than he cared to admit. "Please, take a seat."

He sat down facing her, studying her carefully. She was beautiful, in the ice-maiden fashion that was so popular in the *Reich*. Her face looked to have been carved out of flawless marble, her hair was tied up in long braid that fell over her shoulders and her uniform drew attention to the size of her chest. And yet, the more Karl looked at her, the more he became aware that she moved like a professional…that she *was* a professional. She didn't show him a single wasted movement.

This woman is dangerous, he thought, as he leaned back in his chair. Part of him wanted to take her to bed, but the remainder knew it would be a dangerous mistake. *She might even have a realistic shot at the top job.*

"In two weeks, perhaps less, we will be launching a military operation to recover Berlin and eliminate the rebels," he said, flatly. Katharine could be trusted - and besides, the rebels weren't fools. They'd *know* an offensive was coming. "You and your unit have been held back for a reason. I have a specific task for you."

He met her eyes, levelly. "Can you get into Berlin?"

Katharine showed no visible response to the question. "I believe it shouldn't be too difficult," she said, after a moment. But then, he knew she wouldn't have shown any traces of doubt, whatever her real feelings. She wouldn't show any weakness in front of a man. "We would not have travel papers, of course, but the system for producing and tracking paperwork seems to have collapsed. If necessary, we would pose as refugees making our way westwards until we reached Berlin. Unfortunately, they have gained control of the air defence network to the west."

Karl nodded. They'd slipped one assault team to Berlin via helicopter, but that trick wouldn't work twice. He'd be astonished if they even managed to get a helicopter over the front lines without it being intercepted and shot down.

Any assault teams would have to make their way over the border on foot, just to make sure they avoided detection. Katharine would have to do the same herself.

"Very good," he said. "Once you're in Berlin, you are to make contact with underground elements that have remained in place and plan the capture or assassination of the so-called provisional government. This is to be done when they are coping with our offensive, so they have no time to put replacements forward to take command. Ideally, I want them held in place until they can be forced to issue an order to surrender; if necessary, you are to kill them and smuggle their heads out as proof."

"They would be fools," Katharine observed tonelessly, "if they all stayed in one place."

"Capture or take out as many as you can," Karl said. He shrugged. "Taking them alive would be nice, but killing them is acceptable."

He reached into his desk drawer and produced a file. "Except for this one," he said, holding the file out to Katharine. "I want her alive."

"Gudrun Wieland," Katharine read. She skimmed through the file with ease, her brow furrowing slightly. "The one who started all this."

"So they say," Karl said. He wasn't sure it was true. Katharine might be a professional killer, but very few women could match her. Gudrun Wieland's file made it clear she was nothing more than a university student. Maybe they *claimed* she'd started the chain of events that led to the uprising, but Karl rather doubted it. There was a man hiding behind her, he was sure, someone who remained unidentified. "I want her alive."

Katharine quirked her eyebrows. "May I ask why?"

"They have turned her into a symbol of their cause," Karl said, bluntly. "A true flower of German womanhood, the lover of a wounded boy, the hero-ine who avenged him...such a symbol cannot be merely *killed*. She must be forced to recant before she is patted on the backside and told to go back to the kitchen."

He felt a sudden hot flash of anger that disturbed him. It was impossible to *believe* that Gudrun was the true leader of the uprising, the person who'd started the first pebble rolling down the hillside. Her background - father a policeman, brother a soldier, boyfriend an SS stormtrooper before he was badly wounded - told against it. And yet...if she *was* guilty, Gudrun had fooled a great many people. She'd even been *arrested*, only to be released for lack of evidence. It was far more likely that *someone* had talked her into posing as the founder, after she'd been arrested.

And if she is guilty, he thought, *she will pay for it.*

There were...*techniques*...used for breaking women, women and their male relatives. He wouldn't hesitate to order them used, just to make it absolutely clear that Gudrun Wieland would not be able to hide behind her sex. If she was guilty, she'd be tortured to death...it went against the grain to inflict such horrendous punishment on a German girl, but it had to be done. And then her entire family would be killed too...

Serves them right for letting her get out of hand, he thought, nastily. *Her father should have beaten any trace of rebelliousness out of her before she grew into a young woman.*

"I will certainly do my upmost to ensure she is brought here," Katharine said coolly, breaking into his thoughts. "But you do realise that smuggling one prisoner, let alone a dozen, out of Berlin will not be easy?"

"You may have to keep them under wraps in the city until it falls," Karl said. Berlin was vast, easily large enough for an experienced team to hide for weeks if necessary. The normal surveillance systems were completely offline. "I know it won't be easy, but it has to be done."

"I understand, *Mein Führer*," Katharine said. She rose, a movement that drew his attention to her chest. "And we will do our very best to deliver the traitors to you in chains."

CHAPTER FIVE

Near Vichy, France
2 September 1985

"Wake up," Horst said, poking her shoulder lightly. "We're almost there."

Gudrun opened her eyes, then stretched. Sunlight was pouring in through the windows, revealing that they were driving up a mountainside road towards a large French building half-hidden in the foliage. Guards could be seen everywhere, manning the gates and patrolling the grounds, wearing desert tan uniforms and flat caps that reminded her of something she'd seen back in school. The Foreign Legion, she recalled, as the driver took them through the gates and parked outside the chateau. Foreigners who'd travelled to France to fight for her - and leave their pasts behind.

Horst scowled. "They're not supposed to be here," he said, grimly. "By treaty, the Foreign Legion isn't meant to return to Mainland France."

"They're probably making a statement," Gudrun said. "Trying to tell us they won't be pushed around any longer."

She rolled her eyes in irritation. Being a councillor - even one without portfolio - had been an education in more ways than one. She'd known there was something deeply wrong about the *Reich* ever since she'd discovered just what had happened to her former boyfriend, but she'd never truly grasped the full extent of its evil. The Vichy French had been Germany's unwilling allies since 1940, trapped within the *Reich's* network of satellite states, unable to move to partnership or escape Germany's grasp. The slightest *hint* of nationalist sentiment would have been enough to get the panzers moving, back before the coup.

And the French were lucky, compared to some of the others, she thought, numbly. *At least there's still a nation that calls itself France.*

"Here we are," Horst said, as a man in a light brown suit opened the car door. "Just remember not to give away more than we *have* to give away."

Gudrun shot him a dark look as she stepped out into the warm air. France was warmer than Germany, she'd been told, particularly as the world inched remorselessly towards winter. A number of her teachers had even made fun of the French, insisting that they were weak because they'd grown up in such a pleasant climate. Gudrun wasn't sure if that was true - she'd been told thousands of lies at school - but she put the thought firmly out of her mind anyway. This was a bad time for a three-sided war.

"We cannot afford major trouble on our western borders," Volker Schulze had said, before she'd departed Berlin. "If we have to make concessions to keep the French quiet, we will make concessions."

Horst stayed behind her as she was escorted through a pair of doors and into a sitting room that was, quite evidently, a place for holding clandestine discussions. She'd half-expected to travel to Compiègne Forest, where Hitler had laid down the terms for France's surrender and submission to the *Reich*, but the French had offered the Chateau Picard instead. In some ways, it was a relief. Her predecessors might have enjoyed rubbing France's collective nose in just how helpless it was before Germany, but she had to admit it would make it harder to hold talks now. They needed the French in a reasonably cooperative mood.

"*Fraulein* Wieland," the French Premier said, in excellent German. "Welcome to Chateau Picard."

Gudrun took his hand and shook it, firmly. Premier Jean-Baptiste Jacquinot was an old man, easily in his seventies. Vichy France didn't bother to hold elections. Jacquinot had been deemed suitable by the *Reich* and any attempt to undermine him would have drawn the wrath of the *Reich* Council, as long as Jacquinot served them faithfully. His position now was somewhat ambiguous, according to Horst. Vichy might not overthrow him, for fear of what the *Reich* would do, but his real power was declining by the day.

The younger man beside him underlined it. Bruno Ouvrard was tall, with dark hair and dark eyes. It was hard to be sure - the files hadn't been clear - but

Gudrun suspected he was only five or six years older than her. Old enough to be experienced, young enough to gaze upon her with interest. His mere presence was a sign of just how badly events in Vichy were slipping out of control, she knew. It said a great deal about the situation that the official government and the growing independence movement knew perfectly well how to talk to one another - and had probably done so for some time.

They should have locked him up, she thought. *They could have locked him up.*

She sighed, inwardly. The files had made it clear that Vichy had promised to do its upmost to keep the growing movement from disrupting food supplies to the *Reich* - and failed, miserably. France had been on the verge of starvation for years now, as German demands grew harsher and harsher. It was hard to blame the French for wanting to fight - or simply downing tools and refusing to serve the Germans at the expense of their own population. But they didn't realise they might face a far worse threat in the near future.

"Thank you, Premier," she said. "Shall we get down to business?"

"Of course," Jacquinot said. He nodded towards the comfortable chairs. "Please, take a seat."

Gudrun sat, schooling her face into the impassive mask that every German schoolchild learned to master before reaching their second decade. Showing what one was *really* thinking in school could mean a beating or worse. She still shivered when she remembered one of her friends being expelled for questioning their teacher over a relatively minor point, even though her family were good Germans. Gudrun had no idea what had happened to her after that, but she doubted it had been anything pleasant. The SS hadn't tolerated any open dissent.

"I am curious," Ouvrard said. "Why have they sent you, *Fraulein?*"

He made *Fraulein* sound like an insult, Gudrun noted with some amusement. Perhaps it was, to him. *Fraulein* was hardly used to address French girls, let alone *Untermenschen* servants and slaves. The Racial Purity Laws insisted that good Germans could not marry French women, let alone have children with them. Gudrun could marry a Norwegian or a Dane, if she couldn't find a pure-blooded German, but a Frenchman would be right out. They were forever isolated from the *Reich*, trapped between the *Volk* and the *Untermenschen*.

"I started the movement that brought down the *Reich* Council," she said, simply. "Chancellor Schulze felt you would listen to me."

"We would listen to anyone, *Fraulein*," Jacquinot assured her. *He* didn't make it sound like an insult. "But doing what you want is quite another matter."

"I would expect as much," Gudrun said. She cursed under her breath. She knew how to haggle in the market - her mother had taught her - but not how to hold a sensitive diplomatic discussion with a foreign power. "May I be blunt?"

"Of course, *Fraulein*," Jacquinot said.

Gudrun leaned forward. "Right now, the SS is readying its offensive against us," she said, curtly. There was no point in trying to hide it. The BBC and Radio Free Europe had been broadcasting the truth for the last week. Normally, the *Reich* would have tried to jam the outside broadcasts, but right now the jamming stations were offline. "If they successfully retake Berlin, the most you can expect is a return to your previous status - servitude to Germany."

"Unacceptable," Ouvrard said.

"You do not have the firepower to keep them from pushing into Vichy France and putting your people to the sword," Gudrun said, bluntly. "And you have already compromised yourselves, in the eyes of the SS."

"Just by being born French," Ouvrard sneered.

Gudrun nodded. "If we win the war, however, we will be in a position to make a number of concessions," she added. "And we have no inclination to keep France permanently subjected to Germany."

"A pretty speech," Ouvrard said. "Why don't I believe you?"

He met her eyes. "Why should we not ally with the SS to regain our independence?"

Gudrun stared at him in genuine astonishment. The French ally with the SS? Were they out of their minds? It was so absurd that she refused to believe it was anything more than a negotiating gambit, yet it was *worthless*. The SS had tormented France ever since 1940, conscripting slave labourers and purging the French of anyone they deemed anti-German. No Frenchman in his right mind would ally with the SS.

"That's what the Arabs said," Horst said, into the silence. "And remind me - what happened to the Arabs after they were no longer useful."

"They were slaughtered," Jacquinot said, flatly.

"Quite," Gudrun said. She regained her balance and pushed forward. "If we have to fight you, now, it may well cost us the war. Therefore, we would prefer to avoid fighting you…"

"So would we, *Fraulein*," Jacquinot said.

"But we also need food supplies from you," Gudrun continued. "Our stockpiles are already dangerously low."

"So we have leverage," Ouvrard said.

"Not as much as you might think," Gudrun countered. "We might simply *take* what we want, devastating France in the process…or we might lose, leaving you exposed to a vengeful SS that intends to use you as the enemy to reunify the *Reich*."

"You make a convincing case, *Fraulein*," Jacquinot observed.

Ouvrard leaned back in his chair, resting his hands on his lap. "There are terms, of course."

"Of course," Gudrun echoed.

She looked from one Frenchman to the other, wondering precisely what the balance of power actually was. Jacquinot controlled the government, in theory, but Gudrun knew from bitter experience that the government was hardly a solid monolith. Who knew which way the different departments would jump, if their loyalty was tested? The French generals had to know they were badly outmatched, if push came to shove, but the French soldiers might want to fight. And, while the French were constantly mocked as military weaklings, they *did* have a hard core of tough professional soldiers, men who had served multiple terms defending French North Africa from insurgents. Overrunning France would be a distraction the *Reich* could not afford.

"First, we want political and economic independence," Ouvrard said. "Once the war is over, we want complete freedom to make whatever political alliances we like and trade with whoever we like, on even terms. You will no longer be allowed to dominate us."

Gudrun nodded. Volker Schulze and Hans Krueger had expected as much, when they'd discussed the different possibilities with her. The French economy was in a mess, at least in part, because they were forced to sell their wares to Germany at ruinously cheap prices. They wouldn't want to *remain* under the *Reich's* economic thumb. She was just surprised they hadn't demanded military independence too.

But that would worry us, she thought. She'd taken the time to study the true history of German-French relations and they hadn't proved encouraging. France and Germany had been at loggerheads from the very first day of the Second *Reich*. *A France armed with modern weapons - and perhaps even nukes - would be a lethal threat.*

"Those terms are acceptable, with one caveat," Gudrun said. "You may not join any outside military alliance or allow outside forces to station troops, aircraft, ships or anything else within your territory."

The two Frenchmen exchanged glances, but neither of them looked particularly surprised by her response. Only the Americans or the British could have moved forces into France - and they had to realise that the *Reich* would not tolerate such a move. France would become the first battleground of the final war.

"Understood," Ouvrard said. "Second, we demand the return of our stolen territories."

Gudrun reminded herself, savagely, to keep her face impassive. Alsace-Lorraine was historically *German,* she'd been taught in school, even though it had changed hands several times in the last century. Every German schoolchild was told about French atrocities against the Germanic population… atrocities that were far outmatched by the horrors the SS had committed against almost everyone, even the Germans themselves. She could not simply abandon German territory to the French…

…And if she did, she knew Volker Schulze would renounce it as soon as she returned home.

Because the SS will turn it into a propaganda ploy, she thought, numbly. *They'll tell the Volk that the government is planning to surrender German territory…and they will be right.*

It wasn't just Alsace-Lorraine either, she knew. There was a swath of French territory - the entire western coastline - that had been annexed by the *Reich*. It was now dominated by hundreds of military bases and fortifications, preparations to meet an Anglo-American invasion that had never come. Much of the native population had been moved out too, when they hadn't been quietly 'encouraged' to leave, and replaced by Germans. The French settlers in French North Africa had been uprooted from their homes and bitterly resented it, but they couldn't return. There was no way she could make *any* territorial concessions.

"Let me be blunt," she said. "Occupied France - and Alsace-Lorraine - have been thoroughly Germanized. The people living there are *Germans*. Forcing them to move will only spark off another major confrontation at the worst possible time."

She scowled, inwardly. The vast majority of the troops in Occupied France, certainly the reservists, had homes and families there. They would not be keen to force their own people to leave, nor would they sit there quietly while outsiders did the dirty work. And the SS would be *delighted* to offer support to any insurrection. A major crisis in the rear would be at least as bad - perhaps worse - as going to war with France.

And the loyalty of our own military could not be taken for granted, she thought, grimly. *Our entire government could disintegrate, allowing the SS to come back and take over.*

"Those territories are *ours*," Ouvrard insisted. "They cannot be surrendered!"

"You *did* surrender them," Horst said, amused.

Gudrun gave him a sharp look as Ouvrard purpled. Horst was no more a diplomat than *she* was. The SS had never been about diplomacy. It rarely even *bothered* trying to be polite.

"That was when we lay prostrate before you," Ouvrard said. "Now…you *need* us."

Horst leaned forward. "There's such a thing as overplaying your hand," he said. "I concede that we need your help, but we don't need it so badly that we're ready to deal with the consequences of giving you what you want. If you push this too far, you may wind up with the SS on the border *instead* of us."

Jacquinot smiled. "So you're saying we should quit while we're ahead?"

"Yes," Horst said. "You can get some concessions from us now - and we will honour them - but you can't get *everything*."

"True," Jacquinot said. "*Fraulein*, with your permission, we will write up the terms of the agreement and make them public, once they are signed. Our public needs to know that we are making progress."

Gudrun nodded. The French economy had been hit by multiple strikes, but - unlike in the *Reich* - the strikers hadn't gained any real concessions. They were growing tired of waiting for change, she'd been told. It wouldn't be long before Jacquinot and Ouvrard found themselves on opposing sides, if they failed to put the brakes on now. A civil war in France *might* keep the French from causing trouble, but it would definitely interfere with the shipment of supplies to the *Reich*.

"That would be acceptable," she said.

"There is one other condition," Ouvrard said, softly. "We want the conscripted labourers returned from the *Reich*."

Gudrun wasn't entirely sure if that was a good idea or not - for France. Hans Krueger had pointed out that hundreds of thousands of Frenchmen were in Germany, Frenchmen who would have problems finding employment when they got home. Dumping so many workers onto the French economy would probably cause all sorts of headaches for the French Government, which might be why Ouvrard wanted it. But it wasn't as if anyone in Germany wanted to *keep* the *Gastarbeiters*.

"They will be returned home," she said, bluntly. She had no idea what would be done - if anything *could* be done - about the *Gastarbeiters* from Germany East, but that wasn't her problem. "Do you have any other demands?"

Ouvrard smiled. "Not at all, *Fraulein*."

"We thank you for coming, *Fraulein*," Jacquinot said. "And we will have the terms of the provisional agreement written up now."

"Of course," Gudrun said.

She watched the two Frenchmen leave, then sat back and waited - doing her best to keep her face impassive - until Jacquinot returned with the provisional agreement. It was nothing more than a list of points, but it covered everything they'd discussed. She signed both copies, then passed one back to Jacquinot. The provisional government would have to hold a formal signing ceremony later, once the agreement was approved.

And there's no reason why they won't approve it, she thought. *It gives us what we want.*

As soon as both copies were signed, she rose and followed the escort out of the room, back to the car. Horst walked beside her, looking pensive. He hadn't liked the idea of negotiating with the French at all, Gudrun knew, even though he'd seen no alternative. But then, as far as everyone was concerned, he was nothing more than her bodyguard. His objections had been strictly private.

"Well," Horst said, as the car passed through the gates and back onto the road leading to the private airfield. "That could have gone worse, I suppose."

"Yeah," Gudrun said.

She wanted to hug him - they'd been lovers ever since the *Reich* Council had fallen - but she didn't know if she could trust the driver. He might well be keeping an eye on her for his superiors. God alone knew what having a premarital affair would do to her reputation, now everything was up in the air. Once, it would have been harmless, as long as she'd intended to get married. Now…

"They didn't offer us troops," Horst added. "Did you notice?"

"We were going to refuse, if they offered," Gudrun reminded him. "I don't know how well they'd fight, but the SS would turn them into a propaganda weapon."

"True," Horst said. "But they didn't even make the offer, when they know as well as we do that an SS victory means their destruction. I find that rather odd."

He leaned back into his seat, staring out at the French countryside. "We'll get the latest reports when we return to Berlin," he added. "And we'll see what the council has to say about it."

CHAPTER SIX

Near Warsaw, Germany Prime
2 September 1985

The town wasn't much, *Leutnant* Kurt Wieland thought, as they drove into the town square and parked the lorries under a giant statue of a soldier he didn't recognise. A few dozen homes, a handful of shops, set a couple of miles from the *autobahn*…it was the kind of place his parents had talked about going to live when they retired and their children had flown the nest. *He* suspected that he would have found it rather boring, if he'd had to live there, but he was still in his twenties. His parents might have a different attitude.

He jumped down to the ground and barked orders to the soldiers, who scrambled out of the lorries and hurried to take up position near the Town Hall. The entire town was due to be evacuated and turned into a strongpoint, hopefully one that would slow up the SS for a few hours before they continued advancing towards Berlin. Kurt had no illusions about just how weak the defence line actually was, even though his actual experience of combat was practically non-existent. Between the resignations, the deaths and a number of desertions, the forces facing the SS were badly disorganised. It would take longer than they had, he feared, to get the army into proper shape.

"The population should have left already," *Oberfeldwebel* Helmut Loeb commented. "But some of them won't have left."

Kurt nodded. The young men and military veterans would have already been called up, although it was anyone's guess just how many of them would bother to report to the training camps. They'd signed up to fight the enemies of the *Reich*, not their fellow Germans. Quite a few veterans had already been caught trying to slip across the border to the east, or merely hiding in the countryside and hoping not to be found. They found it impossible, they'd claimed when they were caught, to choose a side.

And I would find it difficult too, if I hadn't been in Berlin, Kurt thought, as the town was rapidly searched and a handful of stragglers pushed into the square. *I saw the SS mowing down innocent Germans as if they were Slavs.*

He glanced down at his hands, wondering if he should feel guilty. He'd broken his oaths when he'd opened fire on the SS, triggering off the Battle of Berlin. It wasn't something he *should* feel guilty for, he told himself, but he knew he'd feel responsible for everyone who died in the coming war. There could be no doubting it would come, either. Everyone knew the SS was moving troops up to the borderline and preparing their offensive. It was only a matter of time before the shit hit the fan.

"This is an outrage," a loud female voice declaimed. "We *paid* for our house!"

Kurt tried hard to suppress a flicker of tired - and utterly inappropriate - amusement. The speaker was an older woman, easily twenty years older than his mother if she was a day, standing next to a skinny older man who looked thoroughly henpecked. Kurt wouldn't have cared to try to impose his will on *that* woman, no matter what the law said about German womenfolk obeying their husbands. She was swinging her fists around like a navvy as she argued with the soldiers. Kurt wouldn't have been surprised to hear she'd been a boxer in her youth, even though women were technically forbidden to take part in blood sports.

Which would have merely driven them underground, he thought, as he strolled over to rescue his men. His first trip outside the wire, during basic training, had been an eye-opener in more ways than one. There were all sorts of forbidden pleasures available in the *Reich*, if one knew where to look. *And now…who knows what will happen?*

"*Gute Frau*," he said, dismissing his men with a nod. "This town is about to become a battleground."

The woman glared at him. "We have lived here for thirty years and…"

"And it is no longer safe," Kurt snapped. The nasty part of him was tempted to leave the woman for the SS, but her mouth would probably get her and her husband shot down. If the rumours from the front lines were true, the SS was purging Germany East of anyone whose political loyalties were even slightly suspect. "The SS is coming!"

"The SS?" The woman repeated. "Why would they come here?"

Kurt swallowed his first angry reaction. It had been nearly two weeks since the Battle of Berlin. The news had been on the radio…although, he had to admit, he had a habit of not believing what the radio said either. But surely she must have heard rumours of the change in government, if nothing else. He doubted she was the kind of woman who disdained rumours and gossip as beneath her.

"A civil war is about to begin," he said, instead. "You and your husband will be shipped to a refugee camp to the west, where you will be held until the war is over. At that point, you will be allowed to return home."

If your home is still there, he added, silently. *When they hit this town, they'll advance with all the force they can muster.*

He kept his face impassive. He'd seen footage of the SS pacification troops in action, burning down entire Russian towns and villages in response to a handful of shots aimed at them from a distance. There was no way to know - even - if they were getting the *right* village, but the SS didn't care. Spreading terror was more important to them than capturing or killing specific individuals. And yet, their terror tactics hadn't put an end to the South African War. It had only burned brighter than ever.

The woman's expression tightened. "And if we choose not to go?"

"Then you will also be shipped west, but not to a refugee camp," Kurt said, allowing his voice to harden. Too many people were already in the detention camps, simply because they couldn't be trusted…he had no desire to add two more. "We do not have time to debate the issue. Pack yourselves a bag and prepare for the journey."

He glanced at the woman's husband, wondering if he could be relied upon to say something to his wife. But it didn't look like it. Kurt couldn't understand how any self-respecting husband could allow themselves to be so dominated in public - he couldn't imagine his father allowing his mother such freedom - but it wasn't his problem. All that mattered was getting them out of the town so it could be turned into a strongpoint.

The woman turned and marched back towards her home, muttering angrily to herself. Her husband shot Kurt an apologetic look, then followed;

Kurt watched them go, shaking his head at their antics. But as long as they were happy, he supposed it was none of his business what they did in private. Turning to the other refugees, he was relieved to discover that none of them looked willing to question him. Most of them were older men and women, the former too old for military service, but there were a handful of younger girls and children amongst them. The town's teenage boys would already have been conscripted.

"A few of those girls are quite pretty, *Herr Leutnant,* " Loeb muttered warningly, as they wanted towards the edge of the town. "Better keep an eye on the men."

"Do so," Kurt ordered. Loeb was right. Two of the girls were pretty enough to turn heads anywhere, he had to admit, which could cause problems until they were shipped west to a foster family. The remainder might not be so pretty, but soldiers who hadn't had leave for far too long developed new standards of beauty. "We don't want any incidents."

He surveyed the edge of the town, peering into the distance towards Germany East. It was ideal panzer country; rolling fields, very little in the way of natural obstacles and a reasonably well-maintained road heading east. There were a handful of hedges and ditches, but he doubted they would cause any problems to a modern tank. A Panther would crush the hedges beneath its treads and roll over the ditches as if they weren't there. Hell, they could just charge into the town and keep going. It was unlikely any of the buildings were tough enough to stop a tank.

"We'll need to be ready to fall back," he said. A fluid defence was their only hope, according to Field Marshal Voss. He hadn't bothered to ask Kurt's opinion, naturally, but Kurt couldn't disagree with his ultimate superior. "Get off a couple of shots, then fall back before they get the range and start pounding us."

"I'll have antitank missiles placed in the nearest houses," Loeb stated. He paused. "And we'll mine the fields leading up to the town. It should give them a few nasty moments."

"One would hope so," Kurt agreed.

He had his doubts. The insurgents who menaced Germany East couldn't stand up to the SS in pitched battles, if they were foolish enough to try. Instead, they fought from the shadows; they sniped at isolated Germans, hurled the occasional mortar shell into German settlements and mined roads the Germans needed to move supplies from place to place. None of their attacks were particularly significant, individually, but collectively they represented a major drain on Germany's manpower. And God help any German soldier unlucky enough to be captured by the insurgents. Kurt had heard enough horror stories to know that *he* never wanted to go there.

And the SS knows precisely how to deal with minefields, he thought, darkly. *The only real question is just how far they're prepared to go to intimidate good Germans.*

It was a bitter thought. He'd been raised to believe that the SS existed to *protect* Germans - and indeed, many of the SS Stormtroopers he'd met had been good guys. Konrad had certainly been a *very* good guy, even though - as Gudrun's boyfriend - Kurt had been obliged to detest him on sight. He certainly hadn't deserved his fate, let alone being abandoned by his own superiors and left to rot. But his superiors? How far were they prepared to go to keep their power? They'd already slaughtered countless *Untermenschen*, he knew, but were they prepared to slaughter vast numbers of *Germans?*

Probably, he thought, as they worked their way through the town. *They think that we're traitors.*

"Just gives us reason to fight," he muttered.

Loeb glanced at him. "*Herr Leutnant?*"

"It doesn't matter," Kurt said. He heard the buses entering the town and allowed himself a moment of relief. "Let's go."

He sucked in his breath as he walked back to the square and saw the older woman - the same older woman - arguing with one of the drivers. She had four large bags beside her, the smallest easily five times as large as the knapsack Kurt had been issued when he'd reported for basic training. He found it hard to understand how she'd packed them so quickly, let alone carried them to the square. Her husband didn't look strong enough to have carried them for her...

"I need all of these clothes," the woman was saying. "I need..."

"No, you don't," Kurt snapped. *Gudrun* liked clothes, but she was much more practical than this silly cow. "You need only the bare minimum."

He allowed his temper to show as the woman rounded on him. "I don't have time to deal with this any longer," he snarled, feeling his patience snap completely. "Take one bag and leave the rest here!"

"I need them," the woman repeated. "I can't just leave them here!"

"Yes, you can," Kurt said. He made a show of unsnapping his holster and placing his hand on his pistol. Her eyes widened with shock. "Take one bag and get into the bus, now. Or I'll shut you up permanently."

The woman glared at him for a long moment, but there was a flicker of uncertainty in her gaze. She'd been told, of course, that the entire region was under martial law. Kurt could shoot her down in front of a dozen witnesses and it was unlikely he'd get in any real trouble for it. Those witnesses would argue that she had impeded the evacuation and defence preparations, if nothing else. He braced himself, unsure what she'd do, then breathed a sigh of relief as she picked up one of her bags and marched onto the bus. Either the bag was lighter than it seemed or she was stronger, he noted. She didn't seem to need much effort to carry it.

"What an idiot," someone muttered from behind him.

Kurt ignored the comment and watched as the remaining evacuees were hustled onto the buses. He couldn't help noticing that some of the girls waved cheerfully at the soldiers, blowing kisses as the bus roared to life. No doubt there had been some flirting going on, even though the soldiers were *meant* to be helping convert the town into a strongpoint. Who knew? It might even lead to marriage. Soldiers were encouraged to marry young, just to sire the next generation of Germans before they were killed in one of the *Reich's* wars.

Or it might lead to nothing, he thought, as he made his way towards the makeshift command post. The radio antenna had been positioned some distance from the CP, just to ensure the SS didn't take out the CP as well as the radio when they tracked it down. *The flirters may never see one another again.*

"Message from HQ," the radio operator said. "*Generalmajor* Gath is on his way to inspect the defence lines."

Kurt swore, inwardly. They'd barely started…had the main offensive begun already? He peered through the window, looking eastwards for some signs of trouble, but all seemed safe and tranquil. Maybe *Generalmajor* Gunter Gath - the CO of the Eastern Defence Line - merely wanted to get a feel for the terrain before the shooting actually began. Or maybe he thought that Kurt - who was handling responsibilities well above his pay grade - should be supervised.

Or maybe he wants to kiss my ass, he thought, darkly. He'd never met Gath in person. *I have a sister on the Reich Council, after all.*

"Acknowledge the message," he said. *Generalmajor* Gath was already on his way. There was no point in trying to deter him, not now. "And then request additional landmines and AT weapons from stores."

He sucked in his breath as he walked back outside. His men were already hard at work, digging trenches, fortifying a number of houses and emplacing antitank weapons in the most advantageous positions. Kurt had no idea *precisely* how the SS intended to advance, but the town was right in the middle of the shortest route to Berlin, controlling one road and far too close to the *autobahn*. They practically *had* to secure the town to keep their flanks unmolested. But he had no illusions about how long his men could stand off a determined offensive.

"We should have time to run through two of the drills before nightfall," Loeb said, as he joined Kurt outside the CP. "Once we know what we're doing, it should be easier to fall back to the next set of defences."

He leaned forward. "Morale is high, *Herr Leutnant,*" he added. "But there's plenty of concern about the SS."

Kurt nodded. The men had *reason* to be concerned. Apart from the old hands, like Loeb, they had very little actual *experience.* Sure, their training had been savage - it wasn't uncommon for a handful of recruits to die in training accidents - but no amount of training could compensate for actual experience. The Berlin Guard had been earmarked for deployment to South Africa, yet the uprising had taken place before they'd been redeployed...

...But the SS had no shortage of experience.

It was a sobering thought. The men in black, the men on the far side of the border, were combat veterans. They would have been in almost continuous combat against insurgents in Germany East, when they hadn't been deployed to South Africa. They'd know tricks his men had never had a chance to master; they'd know what worked and what *didn't* work. And they would feel it in their bones. *They* wouldn't be dependent on textbooks to tell them what to do.

"They have to be stopped," he said. "We *did* beat off an attack on the *Reichstag.*"

"True," Loeb agreed. "But that was pretty much a gamble on their part. Victory would have brought them everything; defeat...didn't really harm them, one way or the other. Here…they will be bringing to bear everything they can against us."

"I know," Kurt said. "And we will defeat them."

He frowned as he heard the helicopters clattering through the sky, a single transport escorted by a trio of armed attack helicopters. *Generalmajor* Gath wasn't taking any chances, Kurt saw; the SS wouldn't hesitate to try to assassinate him if it could. There were too many holes in the command network for *Generalmajor* Gath to be replaced quickly, if something happened to him. No doubt Gath was right on top of the list of officers to be killed…

Right below Gudrun and her allies, Kurt thought. He still found it hard to believe that his sister - his *sister* - had managed to crack the *Reich* in two, but it was undeniable. *And what happens to her if we lose?*

"I hope you're right," Loeb said. He shook his head. "Too many men are about to die either way."

"I know," Kurt said. The lead helicopter settled to the ground, its escorts swinging around the town as they watched for trouble. "But defeat means the end of the world."

CHAPTER SEVEN

Berlin, Germany
3 September 1985

"I trust you had a pleasant flight?"

"It was smooth," Gudrun said. She'd never flown before the uprising, but she'd discovered she enjoyed it. "If there hadn't been so many delays, we would have made it back to Berlin before nightfall."

"I dare say it doesn't matter," Volker Schulze said. "What did the French have to say?"

Gudrun hesitated. She wasn't sure *how* to react to Schulze, these days. He would have been her father-in-law if she'd married Konrad, a glowering presence at family meals…she thought she could have endured it. Some of her friends *hated* their in-laws, but Schulze wasn't a bad man. But now…he was Chancellor of Germany, ruler of the western half of the Third *Reich* and it had been *Gudrun* who'd started the chain of events that had put him in the big chair. She wondered, sometimes, if he blamed her for Konrad's death…or if he still thought of her as a little girl. He'd known her since she was in diapers.

"They're willing to keep sending supplies as long as we grant them political and economic independence," she said, flatly. "They also want the occupied territories back, but I did my best to dissuade them."

"I doubt they will accept it indefinitely," Schulze said, gravely. He turned his chair, slightly, so he could peer out of the window into the distance. "No requests for military or technological support?"

"No," Gudrun said. "All they want is the *Gastarbeiters* back."

"That may cause some problems, in the short term," Schulze mused. "But we will have to learn how to handle it."

He turned back to look at her. "How long do you think Jacquinot can hang on to power?"

"I'm not sure," Gudrun said. She looked up at Horst. "Do you have an opinion?"

"It depends," Horst said. "If the SS retakes power, I imagine Jacquinot will get down on his knees for them and stay there until he dies. Ouvrard and his friends will be quietly removed, along with every other nationalist they can find. There will be no hope of resistance."

He shrugged. "But if we win, or if the civil war bogs down, it will become a great deal harder to make predictions," he added, after a moment. "They may offer troops to us in exchange for more concessions."

"Or make use of the time to build up their own armies," Schulze said.

"I imagine they are already working on expanding their forces," Horst said. "But they'll be very careful about picking a fight with us."

"So they probably won't try to go for Alsace-Lorraine," Schulze said.

"I don't think so," Horst agreed. "We wouldn't let that pass - and they know it."

"So they know we are weakened, but not too weakened," Schulze mused. "As long as they stay quiet for the moment…we'll honour our side of the bargain."

Gudrun nodded. "Has there been any news from the east?"

"The flood of refugees has been slowing down sharply," Schulze said. "I don't know if that means they're clamping down on population movements or if everyone who wanted to flee the SS has managed to leave already. We may never know for sure."

"True," Horst agreed. "The SS has always been pretty popular in the east."

"So you keep saying," Gudrun said. Hardly anyone knew that *Horst* had once been an SS agent, a spy who'd switched sides. "I think I got the message."

"You have to remember it," Horst warned. "You may think that Holliston is a lunatic and his followers madmen, but there are plenty of people in the east who will see him as the second coming of Adolf Hitler. I don't think they'll crack under the economic crisis any time soon."

"Of course not," Schulze agreed. "The east can feed itself."

He took a breath. "Right now, all we can do is muster our forces and prepare to fight - to the bitter end, if necessary," he added. "I'd like you to visit the recruit training camps just outside the city, if you don't mind. Let them see what they're fighting for."

"Of course," Gudrun said. She rather suspected that Schulze didn't quite know where to put her, but she understood. "Has there been any word from the Americans?"

"They're making approaches to us, but it's very quiet," Schulze said. "It would not do for anyone to get wind of them."

Gudrun nodded in agreement. Every last schoolchild in the Third *Reich* was told, time and time again, that the United States was a capitalist nightmare, a melange of interracial and incestuous breeding, a place where women led men and children ran riot in the streets. She was sure that was a lie - discovering that Jews weren't misshapen monsters had shocked her to the core - but far too many Germans believed it without question. The mere *suggestion* that the Americans were backing the provisional government would cripple the government's legitimacy. And it wasn't as if it *had* much legitimacy.

"And they will certainly be considering their own interests," Horst warned. "They will probably not be displeased if the *Reich* split into two pieces."

"Or more," Schulze agreed. "Germany North is tightly tied to us, but Germany South and Germany Arabia *might* manage to go their own way. I doubt either we or Germany East have the ability to force them back into line."

"And they would become far more powerful, relatively speaking," Gudrun said. International politics, she'd discovered, had a great deal in common with playground skirmishing. "They would prefer us broken and weakened."

"Yeah," Schulze said. "They may help us, but they'll look to their own interests first."

Gudrun nodded and rose. "I'll see you at the meeting tonight?"

Schulze, thankfully, didn't look surprised to hear she was intending to attend the *Reich* Council meeting. Gudrun was fairly sure that *some* of the councillors - particularly Arthur Morgenstern - thought she should be playing with dolls or looking for a suitable man, rather than involving herself in politics. It was infuriating, given that none of them would hold the positions they did if it wasn't for her. But then, Morgenstern had an excuse, of sorts. His daughter was no older than Gudrun and *she* had a tendency to be silly.

So does her mother, Gudrun thought. *But no one can deny she's effective.*

"It starts at seven," Schulze said. "Be seeing you."

Gudrun glanced at Horst as they walked out of the office, passing the pair of armed guards and heading down the corridor. No one was taking chances, these days; everyone believed that the SS could drop a second commando team onto the roof at any time. Gudrun had been told that the SS would have to get very lucky to sneak an aircraft through the growing network of air defence radars covering the *Reich*, but the SS had planned and carried out far more daring dangerous operations in the past. The guards - and clerical workers - were all armed, ready to fight at a moment's notice. She couldn't help wondering if that meant they would accidentally wind up firing on each other if there actually *was* an attack.

"He seems distracted," she mused, as soon as they were out of earshot. "Is that normal?"

"He was a factory worker only a few months ago," Horst reminded her. "Now he's lost his son, seen his government overthrown and found himself forced to fill a pair of very big shoes."

Gudrun nodded, feeling a stab of guilt. It had been *her* fault, after all. She knew she was being stupid - she knew the *Reich* would have had problems with or without her - but she couldn't help feeling guilty. Hundreds of people had already died - perhaps thousands, in Germany East - and it was all her fault. *She'd* started the ball rolling.

"You need a bigger portfolio," Horst added, as they walked down the stairs. "I imagine everyone else on the council is already jockeying for position."

"I know," Gudrun said. It was a minor frustration - and, she suspected, a bigger one for Schulze. He had a very mixed cabinet and almost *all* of them were trying to build power bases of their own. "But apart from representing the students…what can I do?"

"Probably aim for the interior ministry," Horst said, after a moment. "You don't have much experience, but the people underneath you would know what to do. You'd only have to set policy. And you wouldn't be warped and twisted by years spent climbing up the ladder."

Gudrun shook her head. "It might be better to run for a seat on the *Reichstag*, when we finally hold elections," she said. "I'd have a reasonable chance of winning."

"A *reasonable* chance," Horst repeated. "I'd say very few people would dare to stand against you."

"Hah," Gudrun said.

She shook her head in irritation. She *was* famous, true. But a sizable percentage of the population refused to believe that a young *girl* - a *girl* - could possibly start an underground political movement. As far as they were concerned, Gudrun was nothing more than a latter-day Irma Grese; a woman, true, but not one who did anything for herself. There were quite a few people who claimed that the *true* originator of the movement had been killed by the SS - or had simply been too cowardly to reveal himself. They certainly didn't give any credit to *Gudrun!*

"I'm serious," Horst said. "But tell me. How long will it take for the various power blocks to outmanoeuvre the *Reichstag?*"

Gudrun scowled. She hadn't known much about the inner workings of the *Reich* a year ago, but she'd always been a fast learner. The *Reichstag* had been nothing more than a rubber stamp for years, ever since Adolf Hitler had claimed supreme power for himself. Its members barely even met, save to engage in pointless ratification of laws and budgets hashed out by the *Reich* Council. Most of them had surrendered their posts without a fight almost as soon as it became clear the provisional government wasn't going to collapse overnight.

And the Reichstag has no independent means to pressure the government bureaucracies, she thought, sourly. *Their approval or disapproval is largely irrelevant.*

"Not long," she said, finally.

"Exactly," Horst said. They reached the bottom of the stairs and entered the garage, walking across to the nearest government car. "The *Reichstag* doesn't control anything, *ergo* the *Reichstag* is powerless. You need to fix that problem or our government will eventually collapse - or explode into chaos."

Gudrun sighed, inwardly, as she climbed into the car. Horst was right, she told herself, as the engine roared to life. But she didn't *want* to take a post she didn't understand. It would be easy for her subordinates to outmanoeuvre her too, just as easily as the ministries could outmanoeuvre the *Reichstag*. The only way she could think of to give the *Reichstag* some clout was to put it in charge of distributing taxes, but the Finance Ministry wouldn't give that up in a hurry. Hans Krueger might have been the closest thing to a moderate on the old *Reich* Council - he'd switched sides in a hurry - yet that didn't make him a pushover.

It would mean giving up some of his power, she thought, rubbing her eyes.

She shook her head in irritation, mainly directed at herself. She'd dared hope that they'd bring lasting change - and they had - but she'd never thought she might have to keep working afterwards. And yet, what *was* she? A young woman who would become nothing more than a wife, a mother and a grandmother, while leaving the politics to the men? Or did she want to wield power and influence policy in her own right?

"I can be an idiot at times," she muttered.

"Everyone can be an idiot at times," Horst pointed out. "The only real question is just how well you cope with it when you realise your mistake."

Gudrun nodded, then held his hand as she peered out of the window. It felt odd to be driving around the city in a government car, staring out of the tinted windows and knowing that the people couldn't see her. She knew, all too well, that much of the city *hated* the government cars, hated how they could push everyone else off the road as they roared to their destinations. Now, she'd even heard reports of stones being tossed at government cars as they passed, even though the old government had fallen. Far too many repressed hatreds had started to come out…

"We have to win the war," she said, as the car turned into a parking lot and stopped. "After that, we can worry about the politics."

"Everyone else will be thinking differently," Horst warned. "But if we don't win the war, we'll all wind up dead anyway."

Gudrun nodded as Horst opened the door and helped her out of the car. She had no illusions about her fate if the SS captured her for a second time, particularly as they knew - now - that she'd been deeply involved in the movement, even if they *didn't* believe she'd been the founder. She'd be tortured, then probably raped to death. The SS loved handing out gruesome punishments to traitors and terrorists. And *her* death would probably be displayed in cinemas all over the *Reich*, just to make it clear what fate any future rebels could expect.

Sickening, she thought.

She felt an odd twist in her belly as she walked towards the sports field. She'd had too much experience with them as a young girl, when the BDM matrons had forced her to run and play games until she'd been on the verge of collapse. She might have enjoyed some of the games, she admitted privately, if the matrons hadn't taken them so seriously. The winning teams were always feted, but the losers were punished…as if they'd *meant* to lose.

And a great many matrons have been killed or forced to flee, she thought, nastily. No one was interested in protecting the bitches, not now. If only one in ten of their former victims had both the desire and nerve to take revenge, *none* of them would be safe. *Serve the monsters right!*

"They're just warming up," Horst said. "But at least they have enthusiasm."

Gudrun nodded. The sports field was dominated by men, ranging from sixteen to twenty-five, who were being put through their paces by a handful of military veterans. Most of them, at least, would have a fairly good grounding, thanks to the Hitler Youth; a handful, she couldn't help noticing, seemed to have let themselves get overweight since leaving school and entering the work-force. The veterans seemed to be working hard to separate out the ones with true promise from everyone else, she noted; the former would be amongst the first to be given guns and put on the walls.

If the SS reaches Berlin, she thought. *If…*

"Councillor Wieland," a middle-aged man said. He reminded Gudrun of her father, although he didn't have the iron sternness she'd come to associate with the man who'd sired and raised her. "Welcome to the madhouse."

Gudrun smiled and shook his hand. "Thank you," she said. He didn't seem anything like as formal as her father either. "And you are?"

"*Oberfeldwebel* August Sattler," the man said. "Recently called back into service after five years out of the *Heer*."

"Thank you for your service," Gudrun said, and meant it. "How are they shaping up?"

Sattler smiled as he turned to indicate the groups of men. "The ones with real military training - anything past the Hitler Youth - have already been forwarded to more advanced training cadres," he said. "Everyone else… well, we're getting there. Half of them are at the shooting range, learning how to put a bullet within a couple of metres of the target; the other half are doing PT here. There's a handful that need more focused training, but realistically we don't have the time to give them the care and attention they need."

Gudrun frowned. "How bad is it?"

"Oh, there's a handful of idiotic malingers in every batch of recruits," Sattler said, dispassionately. "Little princes, mostly, who learned the wrong lessons in the Hitler Youth and never bothered to master discipline. Normally, we'd just send them for shit duty if they refuse to grow up; here, it's a little harder to deal with them."

"Send them to help build defences," Horst suggested.

"It might come down to that," Sattler said. "But realistically I wouldn't trust them to dig a trench, let alone do anything more complex than carrying junk here and there."

He shrugged. "Basic training normally takes at least three months, Councillor," he added, bluntly. "I've been told that we may expect an invasion at any moment, so we're cramming as much as we can into a single training period. They're not going to be up to normal levels, no matter how hard we push them, but hopefully we can get some advantages that will balance those problems out."

Gudrun frowned. "Like what?"

"Fighting in a city gives the defenders a great many advantages," Sattler said, bluntly. "We can wear the enemy down, although at a very high cost."

"Very high," Horst said.

Gudrun nodded. She'd have to discuss it with him afterwards. "I understand," she said, slowly. "What are the odds?"

"Impossible to calculate," Sattler said. "Our contingency plans for defending Berlin, I have been told, are years out of date. *Nothing* is what it was back in 1960. We're having to improvise defences and ready ourselves for a major offensive."

"I know," Gudrun said. She'd been told the same, by Voss and his comrades, but it was nice to have independent verification. The *Wehrmacht* was a power bloc in its own right. "Can you introduce me to some of your trainees?"

"Of course," Sattler said. "If you'll follow me…?"

CHAPTER EIGHT

Berlin, Germany
3 September 1985

Horst kept his opinion to himself as *Oberfeldwebel* August Sattler introduced Gudrun to a dozen trainees, reassuring her - in a manner Horst found quite irritating - that the new recruits would keep the *Reich* safe. Privately, Horst was much less impressed. The recruits might have been in the Hitler Youth, but it was alarmingly clear that their tutors hadn't prepared them for the rigours of war. The training forced upon children born in the east - who knew they were in a war zone from the moment they were old enough to walk - was rarely given to their western counterparts. To them, the Hitler Youth was just another imposition from their ultimate superiors. It was an attitude that could not be tolerated in the east.

Gudrun had grown better at politics, he thought, as he followed her around the training field and listened as she chatted briefly to some of the trainees. Most of them eyed her with open awe, although a handful appeared doubtful that she'd managed to play a leading role in overthrowing the previous government. *That* was an attitude that wouldn't have lasted long in the east, either. Women on farms could be just as tough as their male counterparts and often had to drop tools and pick up weapons to fight for their lives. They might be barred from front-line combat units, but that didn't keep them from having to fight. Horst's own mother had had to fight to defend herself several times.

But it's a great deal safer here, Horst thought, ruefully. *The Westerners have forgotten that their stability comes with a price.*

He kept his face expressionless as Gudrun finally finished speaking to the recruits, then went on a walking tour of the growing defence lines. Berlin was huge, easily the largest city on Earth; Horst wouldn't have cared to be the general who had to capture it against even minimal opposition. But at the same time, the population was so vast that starving the citizens out was a very real possibility. The SS might not have the *time* to wait for Berlin to surrender, yet if they did Horst doubted they would try an offensive at all. Why expend thousands - perhaps tens of thousands - of lives if they could get the city for minimal expense?

They can't leave us alone indefinitely, he reminded himself. *We're a direct challenge to their view of the universe.*

He had no illusions about just how ruthless the SS was prepared to be. He'd worked for them, after all. Starving out the population - forcing them to bend the knee - would work wonders, particularly given the growing contempt for the soft westerners among the easterners. Horst had heard, more than once, mutterings that the westerners should be brought to heel, a long time before the uprising had begun. The easterners could not allow themselves to go soft, knowing it would mean their destruction. But the westerners had forgotten that the world was red in tooth and claw. Those who had the strength and the will made the rules, while those who lacked one or both were doomed.

Gudrun nodded to him as the walking tour finally came to an end. "Shall we go back home?"

"If you wish," Horst said, pensively. Most of the recruits were enthusiastic, he had to admit, but Sattler had been right. It would take months, months they didn't have, to smooth out their rough edges and turn them into soldiers. He couldn't help wondering just how many of them were going to die in the next month. "Your meeting is tonight, right?"

Gudrun nodded as they walked back to the car, the driver starting the engine at once and taking them back onto the roads. Horst eyed the traffic in grim disapproval, unable to keep from wondering just how many of the drivers truly *needed* to drive. They were wasting fuel, he knew, fuel that needed to be stockpiled for the military. And yet, the provisional government's ability to coerce the population was very limited. They'd set the precedent for defying and overthrowing the government themselves. Horst knew Gudrun had been right - the previous government had been dragging the *Reich* into an early grave - but he couldn't help fearing for the future. A government that was weak was just as bad, in many ways, as a government that was too strong.

"You're very quiet," Gudrun observed. "What are you thinking?"

"Far too many people are about to die," Horst said.

He shook his head, grimly. He had no illusions about the *Waffen-SS* either. They drew most of their recruiting base from the easterners. There was no way they'd be *gentle* as they sliced into the defence lines, even when dealing with unarmed civilians. Anyone who didn't take up arms against the provisional government, as soon as it was announced, would be a traitor as far as the stormtroopers were concerned. The *Waffen-SS* would unleash a nightmare of blood, rape and slaughter on Germany Prime. Holliston might seek to prevent atrocities - although Horst doubted that very much - but he would probably find it impossible. His servants wouldn't see any profit in covering the iron fist with the velvet glove.

And they'll be worried about their settlements too, he thought, as the car parked below the *Reichstag* and they walked up to their bedrooms. *That will only make them more determined to smash us into a pulp.*

"I wish we had more time," Gudrun said, once they were in her room. "But…"

Horst nodded, ruefully. Sex was definitely one of the best ways to keep from thinking about the future, but they didn't have time. Gudrun needed to shower and change before she went to the meeting or the old goats would refuse to take her seriously. Horst would have cheerfully strangled any of the bastards who insulted her to her face, but there was nothing he could do about hidden or not-so-hidden contempt. He gave her a kiss on the lips, then hurried out of the room before his passion could overwhelm him. They'd shared so much together that he knew there was nothing that could drive them apart.

He sighed to himself as he entered his room, shaking his head at how some of the social *mores* had remained firmly in place. Gudrun was a Councillor, yet she could not be seen to share her bedroom with a young man. Horst would have been surprised if the staff *didn't* know, but so far most of the Councillors appeared to be unaware. And Gudrun's father didn't know either - or did he? He was a policeman, after all. Gudrun had once admitted that neither she nor any of her siblings had ever been able to lie to their father.

And he probably doesn't know how to handle her any longer, Horst thought, closing the door firmly behind him. *Getting pregnant is one thing, but living in sin…*

He stopped, dead, as he saw the note on his bed. He'd made it clear to the staff - very clear - that they were not to enter his rooms. The small collection of weaponry he'd stockpiled under the bed, along with a handful of very useful tools, would only have upset them. And some of the other pieces of equipment would have raised questions he would have preferred not to answer. But the note had definitely not been there when he'd left the bedroom in the morning…

Cursing under his breath, he donned a glove and picked up the note. The SS had been known to use contact poisons, some of which had no known cure. He might have had to slice off his own hand, if he'd touched the paper with his bare skin…. if, of course, he realised he'd been poisoned before it was too late. His instructors had admitted, after discussing several interesting ways to booby-trap a desk drawer, that poisons spread very rapidly through the body. And the most dangerous of them had no antidote.

There was nothing on the paper, save for a handful of code phrases. Horst recognised them instantly; they looked innocuous, but only a handful of people could have written them, let alone known to send the note to him. His blood ran cold as he realised the implications. An SS stay-behind unit was operating in Berlin…and at least *one* of the people in the *Reichstag* was a traitor. Probably a servant, he thought numbly, as his heart began to race. No one would have questioned a servant coming in or out of a bedroom suite. It wasn't as if the *important* people would be expected to do their own housework.

He smiled, rather wanly, at the thought, then sat down to have a think. The note specified a time and a place, a bare thirty minutes away. Had that been deliberate? Or was it merely a coincidence? There was certainly no time to contact Gudrun and tell her where he was going…if he went at all. He'd pretended to have been duped, the last time he'd been questioned by his former superiors, but that excuse would probably no longer hold water. There was no disputing - now - that Gudrun was deeply involved in the provisional government. *And* that the SS had had her in its claws, only to let her go.

And that was my fault, he thought. *If I go to this meeting, I may walk right into a trap.*

Gritting his teeth, he ran through the possibilities as he donned his great-coat and checked his holstered pistol. There was no denying that there *was* a stay-behind cell in place, a cell that could do a great deal of damage if allowed to operate unmolested. He could *not* let the chance to locate the cell pass, whatever the risk. And if they wanted to kill him…he added a handful of other weapons, burying them within the greatcoat, then scribbled out a quick note for Gudrun he could put in her room. She, at least, would know that *something* had happened to him.

Horst walked out of the building, passing the guards at the gates without trouble, then removed and folded the greatcoat as soon as he was in the near-est alleyway. It was pathetic, compared to some of the disguises he'd used dur-ing his training, but it was amazing how many people missed the obvious. He looked like another trainee, heading home after a hard day prancing around the sports field, rather than an SS officer or a policeman. No one would pay much, if any, attention to him.

He kept a wary eye on his surroundings as he walked further into the residential part of the city. The apartment blocks were massive, intended to house young men and women who had travelled to Berlin in hopes of a better life. Some of them looked like nice places to live, others looked like homes he would have preferred not to visit without armed backup. A handful of older men were sitting by the roadside, drowning their sorrows in cheap booze and shouting obscenities at passing cars. They'd have been arrested by now, a year ago, but the provisional government had other problems than the growing number of homeless on the streets. There just wasn't the manpower to deal with it.

The landlords started kicking them out, Horst thought. There had been laws, once upon a time, about kicking veterans out of their homes, regardless of who actually owned the building. Landlords had *hated* the laws because it left them stuck with tenants who could neither pay nor be evicted, tenants who lowered the tone so much it made it impossible for them to attract ten-ants who *could* pay. *And no one gives enough of a damn to take them in.*

He couldn't help feeling a flicker of sympathy as he reached the safehouse and paused outside the door. Gudrun's grandfather had been a disgusting old drunkard, but his family had never given in to the temptation to dump him onto the streets. But not everyone was so patient, not everyone was willing to give their parents a home. It was depressing, really, to think that *he* might end up like that, had things gone differently. And yet, if he treated his family like servants, how could he really blame them?

The door opened. A hand beckoned him inside.

Horst braced himself, keeping his hand in position to draw his pistol if necessary and stepped through the door into the darkened building. Someone had taken the advice offered by the provisional government literally and covered the windows in newspapers and tape to keep even a *chink* of light from shining out into the darkness. And yet, the only source of light in the building was an open door at the end of the corridor. He kept his face expressionless as he walked into the room, only to be caught by strong hands that frisked him expertly and removed the weapons before letting him go.

"He's clean," an unfamiliar voice said.

"Good," a *very* familiar voice said. "Horst, my boy, perhaps you have an explanation?"

Horst kept his face under tight control as *Standartenfuehrer* Erdmann Schwarzkopf stepped into the light. He'd lost track of Schwarzkopf after the uprising had begun, although a handful of Schwarzkopf's spies - his laughably ill-prepared spies - had been brutally beaten to death. Horst had hoped that Schwarzkopf had gone the same way, but the damned *Standartenfuehrer* had clearly managed to go underground before his first safehouse could be torn apart by the mob. Schwarzkopf had always been good at covering his ass.

"At last," Horst said. He pushed as much enthusiasm into his voice as he could. "I've been waiting for you."

Schwarzkopf lifted his eyebrows. "You have?"

"Of course," Horst told him. "I put myself close to the traitors and waited."

"You have been *very* close to one of the traitors," Schwarzkopf said. "I hear you have been in *bed* with her."

His voice hardened. "A traitor *you* told us was *not* a traitor."

"I do not believe she was, at the time of her arrest," Horst said, carefully. If they realised he'd lied to them, back before the uprising, he'd never leave the building alive. "She was pushed into treason by the way she was handled, after her arrest."

"She is hardly the first person to have been arrested and then released," Schwarzkopf observed.

"That is correct," Horst said. "She was merely the right person at the right time."

He paused, then went on. "When I realised she had become entangled with the traitors, it was far too late to do anything about it," he added. "Therefore, I attached myself to her and waited for you to make contact. I knew you would have *someone* within the *Reichstag*."

"You could have used one of the dead-drops to make contact," Schwarzkopf pointed out, darkly. "Why didn't you?"

"A number of files were captured by the traitors," Horst said. "I knew they were watching for signs of treason. There was no way I dared trust any of the dead-drops."

He held himself immobile, meeting Schwarzkopf's eyes without flinching. If Schwarzkopf bought it…he knew the man well enough to know that telling him what he wanted to hear was never a waste of time. And yet, Schwarzkopf had probably had a truckload of shit dumped on him by his superiors after Gudrun had become the public face of the student movement. It wouldn't be out of character for him to suspect that Horst was either an idiot or a traitor himself. God knew he had good reason to be furious.

"And you spent your time having your knob sucked," Schwarzkopf said. "I do trust you enjoyed it?"

Horst had to fight to keep his face expressionless. No true German youth would allow such a sally to go unpunished, not if he had genuine feelings for the girl. Insulting a girlfriend was the easiest way to start a fight, even better than a suggestion that a young man's mother might have been an *Untermensch*. And yet, he knew Schwarzkopf was probing. If he suspected that Horst *did* have feelings for Gudrun…

And he has someone watching us, he thought, grimly. They'd thought they were being discreet, but someone who kept their head down and merely watched might have a very good idea of what they did together. *How much does he know?*

"I know my duty, *Herr Standartenfuehrer*," he said, stiffly. He couldn't allow himself to get angry, not now. "It is my job to do whatever is necessary to insert myself into their innermost councils."

"I'm sure you hated every last minute of it," Schwarzkopf said. His face twisted into an ugly smile. "How long can you remain here?"

Horst checked his watch, wondering just what sort of answer he could give. Schwarzkopf had a source within the *Reichstag*. Horst wouldn't have bet a single forged *Reichmark* that he didn't have a good idea of Horst's schedule already. Getting caught in a lie would be very dangerous.

"At least an hour, perhaps two," he said, finally. He forced himself to leer. "I normally seduce her after the council meetings, so we can discuss matters in a pleasant haze. She might be suspicious if I am not available as soon as she leaves the council chambers."

"An hour," Schwarzkopf mused.

He cleared his throat. "I have a number of questions for you, then we will set up contact procedures," he said. "You will be expected to play your part in the triumphant restoration of the Third *Reich*. If you serve well, your previous mistakes will be forgiven; if you blunder again, you will be executed. *Heil Holliston!*"

"*Heil Holliston*," Horst echoed. He would have to be very careful when he answered, but he had no choice. "I will not fail you."

"Very good," Schwarzkopf said. "And now we begin."

CHAPTER NINE

Berlin, Germany
3 September 1985

Gudrun had wondered, from time to time, why her father hadn't actively sought promotion in the police. Given his career - he'd been a military officer - and some of his connections, he should have been kicked up a level or two long before the uprising. But when she'd asked, as a younger girl, he'd told her that he hated being trapped behind a desk, having to deal with bureaucratic meetings. She'd thought he was just making excuses, but now - after three hours of largely pointless blether - she was starting to see his point.

She sighed, inwardly, as she walked slowly back to her bedroom. Volker Schulze was eminently practical, thankfully, but both Finance Minister Hans Krueger and Admiral Wilhelm Riess were experienced bureaucratic infighters who seemed to be prepared to argue for hours rather than concede anything to their rivals. She'd hoped for better from Arthur Morgenstern - Hilde's father - but he seemed unwilling to do anything apart from sit in his chair and drink coffee. Gudrun had only met him a couple of times, before the uprising, yet she'd never realised just how much of a milksop he was. Promoting him to the *Reich* Council might have been a mistake.

A pair of serving girls jumped to one side as she passed, their eyes going wide. Gudrun smiled at them both, unable to keep from feeling sorry for them. She'd talked to a few, back when she'd moved into her bedroom, only to discover that they'd been treated badly by the old council. They'd even been expected to provide sexual services to the councillors! And to think they were good German girls.

She pushed the thought aside and stepped into her bedroom. Horst was sitting on the bed, as she'd expected, but his face was grim rather than welcoming. Gudrun felt a chill running down her spine as she closed and locked the door, then swore inwardly as she saw the device in Horst's hand. Portable bug detectors were vanishingly rare in the *Reich*, almost unknown outside the intelligence services. And if Horst had been searching the room for bugs…

"We have to talk," Horst said. He rose from the bed and sat down in the comfortable chair, a sign that he wasn't interested in making love. The world had to be coming to an end. "There have been…developments."

Gudrun sat down on the bed, feeling cold. "What happened?"

"My old…associates contacted me," Horst said. He ran through a brief explanation, then leaned forward. "They managed to get a message into my bedroom."

It took Gudrun a moment to realise the implications. "They have a spy in the *Reichstag*?"

"Perhaps more than one," Horst warned. "If they can get access to my bedroom, then nowhere is safe."

He rubbed his forehead. "If they have two spies, neither one will know about the other. The SS was quite fond of placing observers in the government and military, reporting back to their superiors."

"Observers like you," Gudrun said.

She still shivered in horror when she remembered Horst telling her, rather apologetically, that he was an SS officer. He could have betrayed her at any moment, if he'd remained true to his oaths. She'd never suspected, even with the benefit of hindsight. And she'd invited him to the very first meeting! They could have been quietly arrested and dispatched to a concentration camp at any moment, along with their families. Horst…she knew, all too well, that she owed him her very life.

"Yes," Horst said. "I doubt they will be easy to catch."

"We have the files," Gudrun said. "Don't we?"

"I would be surprised if the files we recovered from the *Reichssicherheitshauptamt* include anyone who works in such a role," Horst said. "There were no files relating to me or any of the others I knew. As far as the *Reichssicherheitshauptamt* was concerned, I was just another student with a pure-perfect record."

Gudrun nodded, shortly. The university had prided itself on selecting the best and brightest young Germans to be its students, but *none* of them would have been allowed to pass through the doors if their families and bloodlines hadn't been pure. Horst *had* been qualified, as well as an SS officer; he'd certainly blended in perfectly. The same couldn't be said for the other spies. They'd been so obvious that Gudrun doubted that *anyone* had been fooled.

"So the files will say they were just…ordinary people," she mused. "How do we catch them?"

"I don't think we can," Horst said, after a moment. "A full-scale hunt for a spy will tip them off, I think. And that will prove to the bastards that *I* can't be trusted."

Gudrun swallowed. If Horst hadn't spoken up for her, she doubted she would have been allowed to return to Berlin. Her father had been furious, but she would sooner endure her father's anger than a concentration camp. The files had made it very clear - all too clear - just what the camp inmates had had to endure, before they died.

"I see," she said. She took a long breath, calming herself. "What do they want from you?"

"Right now, they just want me to keep an eye on you and the rest of the councillors," Horst said. "But I expect that will change in short order."

"They'll want you to kill us," Gudrun said, flatly.

"Probably," Horst agreed. "The defences around the *Reichstag* are good, even if they are a little crude. Inside help will make it easier for them to get a second kill-team into the building."

"We're not going to be staying here for long, anyway," Gudrun reminded him.

"No," Horst agreed. "And the confusion caused by the move, I think, will make it much easier for them to accomplish their goals."

Gudrun swallowed, hard. "Can we track down the stay-behind team?"

"I don't think it will be easy," Horst said. "Standard procedure is to hold meetings with untrustworthy assets well away from the base of operations. Even if we capture my contact, he's unlikely to break in time to allow us to capture the remaining commandos. They'll have procedures in place to deal with a sudden upset."

Gudrun cursed. "So all we can do is wait to be hit?"

"We make some very quiet precautions," Horst said. "But otherwise...we have to wait for them to move first."

He paused. "And they know about us."

Gudrun coloured. "Everything?"

"I think so," Horst said. He looked embarrassed. "We *could* get married, you know."

"I'm not pregnant," Gudrun said, automatically. She *did* love Horst, but she wanted to be something more than a wife. If she was married, everyone would assume that Horst was pulling her strings. "And wouldn't that be a *little* too revealing to your superiors?"

Horst smirked. "There was a spy in America who was married to an American girl and, as far as anyone could tell, he was the perfect American," he said. "It didn't stop him from stealing a bunch of secrets one day and fleeing back to the *Reich*, leaving the poor girl and his family behind."

Gudrun shuddered. Americans, she'd been told, regarded marriage as something that could be made or broken in an instant, but Germans took a more conservative view. For a husband to betray his wife in such a manner...it was unthinkable. Even having an *affair* could make a husband a pariah in his community, while a wife could face criminal charges for defiling her marriage. But then, in America, women had *rights*. Certainly, they had more rights than any German woman would have, once she entered a marriage...

She pushed the thought aside. "I think you should tell the Chancellor," she said. "He has to know the truth."

Horst frowned. "Won't that cause problems for you?"

"Probably," Gudrun said. If things had been different, she would have been Volker Schulze's daughter-in-law. But if things had been different, she would never have become Sigrún and *he* would never have become Chancellor. "I think we have worse things to worry about right now."

"I know," Horst said. He shook his head, slowly. "It goes against the grain to have so many people *know*."

Gudrun nodded, although she thought he was wrong. Schulze - and his son - had both been in the *Waffen-SS*. There were some people who would question Horst's loyalties, after hearing that *he'd* been in the SS too, but she doubted Volker Schulze would be one of them. Besides, Horst had had ample opportunity to nip the uprising in the bud if he'd wanted to, a point that was firmly in his favour.

"I think he will keep it to himself," Gudrun said, as she rose. "Are there likely to be agents in the *Wehrmacht* too?"

"Everywhere," Horst said. "Disloyalty can come from anywhere and anyone, as my former instructors put it."

"Including the SS itself," Gudrun said.

Horst shrugged, then rose and gave her a tight hug. Gudrun was tempted, just for a long moment, to pull him onto the bed, but there was no time. Instead, she kissed him once and led the way towards the door, careful to keep a distance between them. It was probably futile - there was no hope of keeping their relationship a secret now - but she wanted to keep it from her parents as long as possible. Her father would go through the roof when he discovered she was practically living with someone before marriage.

Volker Schulze, she knew from past experience, worked late. His wife and daughter - his sole remaining child - often nagged him to come home early, but Gudrun had heard that Schulze often worked until midnight. There was just so much for him to master, before the war began, so much he needed to learn to keep more experienced political movers and shakers from outmanoeuvring him. And yet, Gudrun couldn't help wondering what sort of strain it put on his married life. *Her* mother hadn't been too happy when her father had started to come home late at night, after being given unpaid overtime by his superiors.

"Councillor," Schulze's secretary said. He was a middle-aged man, easily old enough to be Gudrun's father, someone who'd worked in one of the factories before Schulze had asked him to work for him personally. "The Chancellor has asked not to be disturbed."

"Please tell him that this is urgent," Gudrun said. She wondered, suddenly, if Schulze was taking advantage of the servants, then dismissed the thought. It was unthinkable. "We need to speak with him."

The secretary nodded curtly, rose and hurried through the door. Gudrun rather suspected he didn't like the idea of taking orders from a young girl - his daughter was only a year or two younger - but his dislike was the least of her concerns. She waited, as patiently as she could, until the man returned. He didn't look pleased.

"You may enter," he said.

Gudrun thanked him and stepped through the door, into the *Reich* Chancellor's office. It was striking, she had to admit, even though Schulze had removed some of the more ornate decorations that had lined the walls. Some of the paintings on the lower levels had been stolen from France, Gudrun had been told, even though the official line stated that the French had nothing worth stealing. She wondered, absently, just what the provisional government should do with them. Return them to the French…or hide them away?

"Gudrun," Schulze said. He stood from behind his desk, looking tired. It was a bitter reminder that he was actually seven or eight years older than her father. His eyes flickered across Horst for a long moment, then locked on her. "What can I do for you?"

"We have a problem," Gudrun said. She glanced at Horst. "Tell him."

————

Volker Schulze kept his expression blank - with an effort - as Horst Albrecht outlined his story. He hadn't paid too much attention to the younger man, seeing him as nothing more than one of Gudrun's fellow students. Indeed, their closeness could easily be explained by shared struggles against the world, rather than a romantic relationship that might predate Konrad's death. But to hear that Horst Albrecht was actually an SS observer…it was maddening. It was enough to make him wonder what else had escaped his notice over the last two weeks.

He wasn't inclined to condemn Horst merely for being an SS officer. It would be hypocritical. Volker had been a paratrooper himself before his retirement; he'd certainly seen nothing wrong with encouraging his son to follow in his footsteps. A tour or two as a stormtrooper would leave Konrad perfectly positioned to become a paratrooper or a commando himself, if he hadn't been critically wounded on his very first tour. How could he condemn Horst for serving the SS?

But he could - and perhaps he would - condemn the younger man for being a spy.

"So they made contact with you," he said, when Horst had finished. "Do they not doubt your loyalties?"

"I tried to convince them I was fooled," Horst said, bluntly. "They have little reason to doubt me."

Volker scowled. He hadn't had much to do with the observers, back when he'd been a paratrooper, but he had the distant feeling that Horst's superiors would be watching him with a very jaundiced eye. They *had* to wonder just how much Horst had known - or suspected - before the uprising took place. At the very least, they would be questioning his competence and wondering just how far he could be trusted. And, at worst, they would be stringing him along while preparing their own surprise. If they had other sources within the *Reichstag*, why would they need Horst at all?

He rubbed his forehead. If they had no sources, they might try to bluff Horst into thinking they had...but if they *did* have sources, they could try to manipulate Horst into doing something stupid...he felt his head start to pound, reminding him that he had been surviving on caffeine since six o'clock in the morning. He just couldn't think clearly now.

"You made sure Gudrun wasn't kept in prison," Volker said, flatly. "They are certainly going to be doubting your competence."

"Better that than my loyalties," Horst said.

Volker wasn't so sure. If the SS believed that Gudrun and Horst were lovers - and their body language betrayed them - they would wonder just who had seduced who. Would they think Horst had seduced Gudrun to remain close to the provisional government...or would they believe that *Gudrun* had seduced *Horst* to distract him from his duty. Volker was no innocent. He *knew* just how often sex was used to bribe or corrupt government officials, from bureaucrats handing out ration cards to policemen who caught unescorted women on the streets after dark. The SS would know it too.

"They wouldn't have contacted you if they hadn't felt they needed you," he mused. He cleared his throat. "I expect to know about it the moment they make contact, again."

"Understood, *Herr Chancellor*," Horst said.

"And we clearly need to reshuffle everything when we move to the underground bunker," Volker continued, after a moment. "Their spies can be reassigned elsewhere."

"As long as it looks natural," Horst said. He didn't sound enthusiastic. If there were any major changes before the war actually began, his superiors might start thinking he'd tipped off the provisional government. "I'll keep you informed."

"And I'll decide what you can give to them," Volker added. "I don't want any surprises."

He rubbed his forehead, again. "Wait outside," he said, addressing Horst. "I want a word with Gudrun in private."

"*Jawohl, Herr Chancellor*," Horst said.

Volker watched him go, then looked at Gudrun. He couldn't help thinking that she looked alarmingly like a schoolgirl who had been unjustly sent to the headmaster, torn between the urge to protest and the certain knowledge that protests would be worse than useless. He shook his head, tiredly. Gudrun really *was* too young for any of this. She was still idealistic, in a world where the idealistic were always betrayed and abandoned. It wasn't fair…

…But it was the way of the world.

"You should have told me about him," he said, flatly. It was hard, very hard, not to snap at her. "I understand why you didn't, but you should have done."

Gudrun nodded, not meeting his eyes. "I…"

Volker cut her off. "I expect you to make sure that the *only* things his superiors hear are things we have already decided they *should* hear," he added. He'd have to discuss the matter with Luther Stresemann and hope to hell that the Head of the Economic Intelligence Service was trustworthy. The *Abwehr* had more experience, but the *Abwehr* had worked too closely with the SS. "We don't need more leaks."

"No, sir," Gudrun said, quietly.

"Good," Volker said.

He studied her for a long moment. Her arrest - and near-death - hadn't left any scars on her face, although her eyes were harder than he remembered. Gudrun had lost some of her innocence, back when she'd learned just what had happened to Konrad. She wasn't the girl he'd met, not any longer. He couldn't help wondering, deep inside, just what would have happened to her if Konrad had survived. The *Reich* could not have kept itself going indefinitely.

"Get some sleep," he ordered, quietly. "And we'll discuss the matter further in the morning."

"I understand," Gudrun said. "And thank you."

Volker lifted his eyebrows. "For what?"

"For trusting him," Gudrun said. "It means a lot to me."

"Does it?" Volker said. He didn't trust Horst *that* far, even though the young man had come clean as soon as he'd returned to the *Reichstag*. "You can't trust anyone completely, Gudrun; you can't even trust yourself. All you can do is hope, when the betrayal comes, that it won't be fatal."

"That's a grim attitude," Gudrun said, bluntly.

"It's life," Volker said. "*Everyone* has a price."

CHAPTER TEN

Berlin, Germany
7 September 1985

"Is it safe out here?"

Andrew Barton shrugged. Nazi Germany had *never* been a safe place, even if one *did* have diplomatic immunity. There were quite a few horror stories about embassy staffers who'd been arrested and subjected to humiliating and degrading procedures before they'd been reluctantly released with an insincere apology. Indeed, one of the reasons that most of the staffers had rooms at the embassy itself, rather than hiring accommodation outside the building, was the prospect of being picked up by the SS and harassed for the next few hours…

And, of course, the certainty that your rooms would be bugged, he added, silently. *A room in Berlin that isn't bugged is probably used for immoral purposes.*

"I wouldn't say so, Penny," he said. "But risk is our business."

Penelope Jameson gave him a nasty look. She was a CIA agent, true, but she specialised in economics rather than dirty underhand spy work. Andrew wouldn't have brought her along at all, if he hadn't felt it would be better to pretend to be a young couple out for a stroll rather than a single young man. Berlin's sexual values remained firmly conservative, but the uprising and the prospect of being invaded by the SS had convinced hundreds of couples that it was better to bite the bullet and get married before all hell broke loose. Apparently, even the police had started ignoring couples making out in the parks.

Andrew sighed. "There's no more risk than usual, perhaps less," he said. "But we can't account for every eventuality."

It was hard to sound reassuring. The provisional government couldn't be trusted completely - they were Germans, after all - yet they had good reason not to want to piss off Uncle Sam. They might return a pair of wandering Americans to the embassy, but they probably wouldn't have them humiliated, tortured or killed. Or so he hoped. It was quite possible that an SS officer would do just that, in the hopes of souring relationships between the provisional government and the United States.

He kept that thought to himself as they strolled up the road. The people who lived in *this* part of Berlin were amongst the richest and most powerful civilians in the *Reich*, a mixture of wealthy industrialists and government ministers who'd been careful to keep one hand in the till while they did their jobs. Even now, with the police having more important things to do, it was rare to see any of the *hoi polloi* enter the district, knowing that anyone caught there without a valid reason would be lucky if they saw freedom again. Nazi Germany's elite wanted nothing to do with the peons, Andrew thought. The real question was just how much the peons wanted to do with - or to - them.

"Nice house," Penelope said, as they stopped outside a pair of wrought-iron gates. "How much do you think it cost?"

"It would be priceless," Andrew grunted. He nodded at the guard, who opened the gates and pointed towards the mansion. "Money alone would not be enough to buy this house. The buyer would need a shitload of political influence."

He felt a stab of sympathy for the provisional government as they strolled up the driveway, trying to ignore the handful of peacocks pecking at the ground. Arthur Morgenstern was staggeringly wealthy, by the standards of the average citizen, but he wouldn't have amassed quite so much wealth if he hadn't had connections at all levels. And yet, even *he* had been at the mercy of the SS. Andrew knew that America wasn't perfect, that his country had its flaws, but he would sooner have been a poor man in the United States than a rich man in Nazi Germany. The price for such staggering wealth was far too high.

And sorting out the mess - and building a proper economy - will take years, if they can do it at all, he thought. *There are too many people who know how to work the current economy to their advantage.*

The butler - a German, rather than a *Gastarbeiter* - opened the door when they approached and motioned them into the hallway. "*Herr* Morgenstern will see you in the drawing room," he said, as he took their coats. "With your permission, I will escort you there."

Andrew nodded and allowed the butler to lead the way down a long corridor. A pair of girls in maid uniforms appeared at the end, gazing at the two Americans with wide eyes. *They* were very definitely Slavs, Andrew noted; their skins and eyes darker than the average German. He couldn't help noticing that they flinched back when he met their eyes - and that their skirts were far too short for common decency. Technically, raping *Gastarbeiter* women was illegal, but it was unlikely that anyone would bother to prosecute Arthur Morgenstern, if it came out into the open. He'd had far too many friends in high places even before the uprising.

And he's probably had them spayed too, he thought, darkly. *The bastards just wanted to make sure that no German genes blended with the Untermenschen.*

He felt sick as the butler showed them into the drawing room, a splendid chamber that wouldn't have been out of place in Buckingham Palace. The United States had dismissed the idea of eugenics long ago, but the *Reich* pursued it with an unblinking zeal that had always creeped him out. God alone knew how many women - including many Germans - had been sterilised for having impure bloodlines. A woman who came to work in the *Reich*, even on a short-term contract, would be lucky if she could have children after she left. And the amount of effort the *Reich* had wasted on its search for a homosexual gene…

At least it wastes their resources, he thought. *Who knows what else they could have done with the money?*

"Mr. Barton," Arthur Morgenstern said, as he stepped into the room. "I apologise for the delay."

"It was barely worth noticing," Andrew assured him. He shook Morgenstern's hand firmly, unable to avoid noticing that Morgenstern had a very weak handshake. "This is Penny. I think she would appreciate a stroll around the gardens."

"My wife is currently occupied, but my daughter would be happy to assist," Morgenstern said. He rang the bell for the butler, then sat down and motioned for Andrew to take one of the comfortable seats. "She is quite looking forward to going to America."

"I'm sure she is," Andrew said, as Hilde Morgenstern entered the room. "Penny will be happy to answer any questions she has."

He shot Penelope a sharp look - he'd warned her that she would be sent out of the room - and then studied Hilde thoughtfully. She didn't *look* happy to be going to America. Andrew had no difficulty in recognising the sullen petulant look of a spoiled teenage girl. It was a pity, really. Hilde would have been quite pretty if she'd taken a little more exercise. But then, very little of her life was truly *hers*. Caught between a milksop of a father and a dominant mother, Hilde had hardly any chance to develop a personality of her own.

She went to the university, Andrew reminded himself, as Hilde practically marched Penelope out of the room. *She's not an idiot.*

"I suppose that leads to the first point," Morgenstern said, once the maids had served coffee and left the room. "When can she leave?"

"We hope to be flying back all non-essential personnel on Sunday," Andrew said. "The Brits will be dispatching a large aircraft for both sets of embassy staff. I was going to suggest that Hilde accompanied them, with her luggage sent on afterwards. Once she was in London, she would be flown to Washington and then fostered with a suitable family."

"One that meets our requirements," Morgenstern said, hastily.

Andrew nodded, careful to keep his distaste off his face. He could understand Morgenstern demanding a wealthy foster family for his daughter, but he'd *also* stipulated that the family had to be white, ideally of Germanic origin. Andrew had a private suspicion that Hilde was in for a shock, if she *did* go to a wealthy Germanic family. Several of them were Jewish, while almost all of them hated the Third *Reich*. She'd be better off with a family that had roots leading all the way back to the War of Independence.

"It shall be arranged to suit her," Andrew assured him. "Has she picked a university?"

"I'm afraid not," Morgenstern said. "She...has been reluctant to go."

Hah, Andrew thought. He'd read that on the girl's face. *And what have you told her?*

He put it into words. "How much have you actually told her?"

"That it would be better for her if she was on the other side of the world," Morgenstern said, shortly. "Her mother agrees with me. But she is rather less keen to leave her friends and go."

Andrew sighed. "Have her delivered to the embassy on Saturday night and we will make sure she gets on the plane," he said. If worst came to worst, Hilde could be handcuffed to a chair and transported to the aircraft. It wasn't something he cared to do - it would definitely raise eyebrows in London and Washington - but it was possible. "Now, how does the provisional government intend to respond to the growing threat from the east?"

Morgenstern frowned. "We're going to fight, of course," he said. "Troops are already being deployed to block the threat."

Andrew had his doubts. The *Wehrmacht* was no longer the smooth fighting machine it had been, back in the days it had crushed Poland, France and Russia. If some of his sources were to be believed, too many experienced officers had retired to make it *easy* for the provisional government to pull the military back together. But Morgenstern had access to the very highest levels of power.

Which doesn't mean anything, he reminded himself. *The Mexican Government didn't realise how bad things were becoming until it was far too late.*

He leaned forward. "And what are your chances?"

"Uneven," Morgenstern said. "Some of the military officers profess high confidence, others are rather more concerned. In any case, our industrial base is in trouble."

Andrew nodded in agreement. At least two of the German industrial belts lay within easy reach of the SS forces, massing on the far side of the border. They were already being stripped of everything that could be moved, according to satellite observation, but far too much of the machinery wasn't easy to transport elsewhere. The SS would have problems replacing the trained manpower - the *Reich* had been running short of trained manpower for years - yet it could be done. If, of course, they had the time.

He kept his opinions to himself as Morgenstern chatted, silently wondering if the provisional government *knew* the United States had a hold on its Minister of Industries. Volker Schulze was a complete unknown, as far as OSS was concerned; CIA and MI6 didn't know much more, if anything, about the new Chancellor. Perhaps Schulze was happy to keep a backdoor channel open between America and the provisional government…or, perhaps, he would react badly when he found out that Morgenstern was effectively committing treason. No, there was no *effectively* about it. Morgenstern *was* committing treason.

"The United States is ready to offer a loan to the provisional government," he said, once Morgenstern had finished. "Naturally, we are unwilling to take sides in your internal dispute, but we are prepared to loan you money on *very* favourable terms."

Morgenstern frowned. "The Chancellor is unwilling to approach you to ask for assistance," he said, after a moment. "He does not want Germany to wind up like Argentina."

Andrew frowned. Argentina had run into colossal problems paying her debts to America, to Britain and even to the *Reich*. Her government had launched the Falklands War in a desperate attempt to keep their people from noticing their empty bellies, only to lose the war and - very quickly - their heads. Argentina had yet to recover fully from her economic collapse, a problem made worse by American refusal to forgive their debts. He couldn't really blame the provisional government for refusing to fall into the same trap.

"I understand," he said. "What do you think he *might* agree to?"

"Very little," Morgenstern said. "He does not want to appear your patsy."

He frowned as he peered out of the window. "Hilde appears to be showing your escort our gardens."

"It will keep them both out of trouble," Andrew said. He shrugged. "Can you arrange a contact for me with the Chancellor?"

Morgenstern looked down at the floor for a long chilling moment. "Direct contact between his office and your embassy will be used against him," he said. "But covertly…a meeting could be arranged."

"Then tell him that we can offer assistance, all under the table," Andrew said. "And there are no strings attached to it."

"Indeed?" Morgenstern asked. "That will be a first."

"My government would infinitively prefer to do business with you, rather than the SS," Andrew said, truthfully. He opened his briefcase and removed a folder, which he placed on the table. "And even if you are unwilling to ask for direct help, there are quite a few things we can do to assist you."

He smiled to himself as Morgenstern opened the folder and began to study the pages, one by one. God, he *loved* playing at spies. The risk of being arrested, interrogated and perhaps killed only added to the thrill. He might be playing Morgenstern or Morgenstern might be playing him…not knowing *precisely* where everyone stood was part of the fun. Penelope didn't understand, he knew…he wondered, inwardly, if Morgenstern did. People became spies because they liked the game, when they didn't want to spy on their fellows. He had a nasty feeling that far too many of the SS's agents were really nothing more than voyeurs.

"I shall discuss it with him," Morgenstern said, finally. "And you are sure there is no price tag?"

"Just win the war," Andrew said. "Like I said, we would prefer to do business with you."

———

Herman watched, dispassionately, as the buses drove through the growing defence line and straight into the courtyard. They were *crammed*; older men, women and children, all pulled from the towns and villages along the defence line and dispatched straight to Berlin, where they would be allocated to trains and buses heading further west. It would have made more sense, he was sure, just to send them directly to Hamburg, but no one - not even Gudrun - had asked his opinion.

Maybe it does make a kind of sense, he conceded, reluctantly. *They need to know how many they're sending before they can decide where to send them.*

"All right," someone shouted. "Come out, collect your luggage, then move straight into the barracks!"

Herman braced himself - there had been a number of fights amongst the refugees - but this lot seemed surprisingly quiet. The children looked nervous, picking up on the concern and fear on adult faces; their mothers - and a handful of fathers - looked worried. Herman didn't really blame them, either. They had been uprooted from their homes and dispatched westward, suddenly at the mercy of a bureaucratic system that was on the verge of breaking down completely. The older children and teenagers - ranging from ten-year-old boys to twenty-year-old girls - didn't look any better. For some of them, it was perhaps the first true awareness that their parents were not all-powerful.

We exist to keep these people safe, Herman thought, as he saw a blonde-haired girl holding her mother's hand as they walked towards the reception point. She couldn't be any older than twelve; hell, she might still be in classes with the boys instead of being segregated when she entered the older school. *They don't deserve to have their lives torn apart.*

He shook his head, morbidly. He'd still been a child when Britain signed an armistice, bringing the war to an end, but he still remembered the shortages and privations his family had endured. They'd been nothing special, either. *Everyone* had faced the same problems, ranging from minor but irritating shortages to having to move house after the British bombers scattered high explosives over various cities at random. Having to share his house with several other families, all of whom were related to him in some way, had taught him more than a few lessons. But he'd thought those days were long gone.

I'm sorry, he thought. *But they're coming back.*

He sucked in his breath as he saw a teenage boy, almost certainly only a month or two away from adulthood, running away from a tired-looking woman who had to be his mother. It was easy to read her story, just from her posture; her husband dead, a growing teenage lout without a strong male role model…and probably no real hope of finding another husband either. There was a *reason*, after all, that it was rare to have a female teacher tutoring male students after they entered their teenage years. Boys *needed* a male role model.

They clearly missed this one, Herman thought. One of the policeman caught the boy and dragged him back over to his mother. *And when he's conscripted into the military, he'll probably get himself beaten to death by his first sergeant.*

He looked away, then frowned as he saw a blonde woman stepping out of the bus. There was something about her that puzzled him, something that nagged at the back of his mind. What was she…?

And then the teenage boy started to shout, distracting him.

"Get him cuffed up," Herman snapped, leaving the odd woman behind. "And give him a good kicking if he causes more trouble."

He shook his head as the boy started to shout out words he shouldn't have known, not at his age. It was going to be a very long day.

CHAPTER ELEVEN

Near Warsaw, Germany Prime
12 September 1985

Oberstgruppenfuehrer Alfred Ruengeler allowed himself a moment of relief as the helicopter dropped to the ground, then grabbed his knapsack and ran, keeping his head down, towards the building he'd turned into a makeshift Command Post. The CP wasn't much, compared to the installations he'd used in Germany East and South Africa, but it would have to do. No one had seriously expected having to fight a civil war, not in the middle of Germany. Behind him, the helicopter rose back into the darkening sky, heading away from the CP. It would be refuelled at the nearest airbase, twenty miles east.

"*Herr Oberstgruppenfuehrer,*" *Sturmbannfuehrer* Friedemann Weineck said, as Alfred strode into the command room. "I trust you had a pleasant tour?"

"Things are as well as can be expected," Alfred said, bluntly. "The Panzers are *finally* ready to march."

He kept his face impassive as he gazed down at the map, ignoring the handful of operators in the chamber. He trusted Weineck as far as he trusted anyone, which wasn't very far in the *Waffen-SS*. True, the *Waffen-SS* wasn't the *Gestapo* or the *Einsatzgruppen*, but no one could be considered truly reliable these days. The merest hint of disloyalty would have him hanging from a meat hook in the heart of Germanica, like countless others who had been purged in the aftermath of the uprising. It bothered him - there was a difference between reasonable doubt and open disloyalty - but there was nothing he could do about it.

"I received a message from *SS-Viking,*" Weineck said. "They're finally ready to move."

"Glad to hear it," Alfred said. There were four SS Panzer divisions on the border, but it had taken longer than he'd expected to whip them into shape. None of the troops had seriously expected a full-scale deployment, certainly not one that had to be put together in less than a fortnight. As it was, Alfred was surprised it hadn't taken longer to get everything in place before the offensive began. "I trust that the officer commanding has been read the riot act?"

"He has, *Herr Oberstgruppenfuehrer*," Weineck said. "I warned him that he would be relieved for cause if he didn't shape up in future."

Alfred sighed. There was always *someone* who had been promoted above their level of competence, either through political connections or sheer bad luck. He'd been tempted to relieve *SS-Viking's* commanding officer the moment his problems had first shown themselves, but he had no idea what would happen if the asshole made a fuss or complained to the *Führer*. There was no way to know what Karl Holliston would do.

"Good," he said.

He studied the map for a long moment. A handful of commando teams had already crossed the border - there had been a number of shooting engagements between them and the defenders when they encountered armed patrols - but the remainder of the invasion force was hanging back, making the final preparations to advance. Four Panzer divisions, backed up by thirty infantry divisions - ranging from light armoured units to footsoldiers and mountain troops - and well over two thousand aircraft. The enemy might have an advantage in jet fighters, Alfred reluctantly conceded, but they didn't have anything like as many CAS aircraft as the *Waffen-SS* could bring to bear. It would be a different story if they brought back the forces in South Africa, but the *Fuhrer* had been confident that those forces would remain out of play until the war was over, one way or the other. Alfred hoped he was right. There was no way to know which way those forces would jump either.

"The offensive is scheduled for 0600," he mused. "Have the security precautions been maintained?"

"Yes, *Herr Oberstgruppenfuehrer*," Weineck assured him. "Our men have been very careful."

Alfred snorted, rudely. He'd been one of the few officers allowed to review the vast collection of documents recovered from the Kremlin, after Moscow had fallen. It had been clear that there had been *hundreds* of leaks, in the run-up to Operation Barbarossa, ranging from men deserting their units and crossing the border to spies in high places within the *Reich*. If Stalin hadn't been so intent on refusing to believe that Hitler intended to attack, the invasion of Russia might just have ended badly. No, *someone* would have leaked, whatever his officers said.

And even if they didn't, the traitors know we're coming, he thought. *We're running out of time to launch an offensive before winter.*

"Then contact Germanica," he ordered. "I want to speak to the *Fuhrer*."

"*Jawohl*," Weineck said.

Alfred watched him head to the secure telephone, then turned his attention back to the map. There had been no time to carry out a detailed study of the invasion plan, no time to run the troops through a whole series of exercises designed to identify weaknesses and deal with them before the fighting actually started. His men were a curious mixture of experienced - and tough - counterinsurgency fighters and reservists with varying levels of experience. Very few of them, outside exercises, had ever fought on a modern battlefield.

And some of them will treat the civilians as the enemy, he thought, morbidly. He'd already reprimanded two of his senior subordinates for encouraging hatred and contempt for the westerners. They'd been talking about giving the westerners a beating they would never forget, as if the westerners were nothing more than Slavic *Untermenschen*. *And that will make it easier for the traitors to rally the rest of their population against us.*

He shook his head, bitterly. Avoiding atrocities made good tactical sense, but very few units in the *Waffen-SS* gave a damn about civilian casualties. Indeed, they'd been *trained* to machine gun *Untermensch* women and children, just to keep them from breeding the next generation of insurgents. But what worked in the depths of Germany East would be a public relations disaster, if the outside media got hold of it. No one in Germanica gave a damn about *American* public opinion - not about massacres in South Africa - but they had encouraged the Americans to flatly refuse to sell anything to either the South Africans or the *Reich*. He couldn't help wondering just how badly American sanctions had hurt the *Reich*.

"*Herr Oberstgruppenfuehrer*," Weineck said. "The *Fuhrer* is on the line."

Alfred nodded, strode over to the table and took the handset. "*Mein Fuhrer*."

"*Herr Oberstgruppenfuehrer*," Karl Holliston said. "Is everything in order?"

"Yes, *Mein Fuhrer*," Alfred said. "We are still working to integrate Category B and Category C reservists, but the main body of the invasion force is ready to go."

"Excellent," Holliston said. "And the troops have been briefed? They have a complete list of traitors to arrest?"

"Yes, *Mein Fuhrer*," Alfred said.

He kept his face expressionless. Personally, he thought it would be better to win the war before starting the mass purge of traitors, but Holliston had had years to build up a very detailed enemies list. The traitors, their families and their friends were already marked down for death, if they were caught. Alfred rather suspected that most of them wouldn't be stupid enough to let themselves be taken alive. They had nothing to look forward to, if they were caught, apart from humiliation, torture, public confession and death. And then *their* bodies would be left hanging from meat hooks too, just to remind the *Volk* that public dissent would not be tolerated.

"Very good," Holliston said. "I shall expect your forces to be entering Berlin within the week."

"We will proceed with as much speed as possible," Alfred assured him. "But we have to be prepared for the worst."

He sighed, inwardly, at the explosion of irritation on the other end of the line. There was no way it would be anything like as easy as Holliston seemed to believe. The traitors had a number of good officers working for them, as well as much of the *Luftwaffe* and almost *all* of the *Kriegsmarine*. Getting to Berlin within a week would be difficult, if the traitors played it smart. They'd attended the same tactical schools, after all. They *knew* what to expect; an armoured thrust, mechanized infantry bringing up the rear and consolidating the gains as the armour prepared itself for another thrust…

And they have space to trade for time, he thought. *And the more time they have at their disposal, the more force they can bring to bear against us.*

"Very well," Holliston said. "I shall leave the conduct of the war to you."

"Thank you, *Mein Führer*," Alfred said. He knew better than to take Holliston's assurances at face value. The man was a hopeless micromanager. Indeed, he'd even volunteered to take command of the South African War personally. "Do I have your permission to launch the offensive as planned?"

"You do," Holliston said.

"*Heil Holliston*," Alfred said. He did his best to inject a note of confidence into the discussion. "I will see you in Berlin."

There was a click on the other end of the line. Alfred returned the phone to its cradle, then looked at Weineck. "Send the signal," he ordered. "We move as planned."

"*Jawohl, Herr Oberstgruppenfuehrer*," Weineck said.

Alfred nodded, then sat down at the table as the operators started to work, picking up their phones and issuing the orders that would set one of the most powerful military machines in the world into action. The Panzers would start warming up their engines, the aircraft would start preparing for takeoff, additional supplies of live ammunition would be issued…he hoped, desperately, that their logistics held out for the duration of the war. Their contingency planning had been focused around relieving firebases and settlements within Germany East, not supplying a military advance towards Berlin. He'd rounded up every truck within the region, ignoring all objections, but he had no idea if they would be enough. No one had launched such a powerful offensive since 1947.

"*Herr Oberstgruppenfuehrer*," Weineck said. "The commandos are receiving their orders now."

"Good," Alfred said.

He cursed under his breath. The steady barrage of patriotic music, interspersed with exhortations to join the legitimate heirs of Adolf Hitler rather than a rabble of traitors in Berlin, had been going out over the airwaves since it had become clear that the provisional government had survived the decapitation strike. Alfred rather doubted that anyone was paying attention to it - none of the people who'd crossed from west to east had mentioned the broadcasts during their debriefings - but it served a useful purpose. Now, specific songs would be played, informing the commandoes that the time had come to go to war. There was no stopping the war now.

Sighing, he rose to his feet and headed for the door. There was nothing for him to do now; nothing but wait for the first reports from the front. He pushed the door open and stared into the darkness, looking up at the stars overhead. The towns and settlements to the east had been ordered to go dark, for fear of attracting bombers. There was almost no light pollution at all. He leaned against the wall and removed a packet of cigarettes from his pocket, lighting one up and puffing on it gratefully. Far too many Germans were about to die.

And whatever happens, the Reich will never be the same, he thought. He'd been a very junior officer when Adolf Hitler had died, but he'd been aware - far too aware - that the different factions in Berlin had nearly come to blows. *A civil war will tear us apart.*

He cursed, again, wishing he could talk openly to his subordinates. He was loyal - of course he was loyal! And yet, he knew all too well just what would happen when the war started in earnest. A military machine that had dominated the entire continent would be badly weakened, even if the war lasted no longer than Holliston expected. Rebuilding the economy would be very difficult, ensuring that the panzers and aircraft lost in the war could not be replaced quickly. The Americans would move ahead - far ahead - and the *Reich* would no longer be able to keep up.

But the merest whiff of disloyalty will get me killed, he thought grimly, as he looked up at the stars. *And who will take command then?*

The stars offered no answer. But then, he hadn't expected one. He gazed at the twinkling lights, reminding himself that not all of them were natural. Some of them would be orbiting satellites: German and American. The battle for control of the satellites had been savage, with both sides trying to lock the other out. In the end, neither side had really won.

He dropped the cigarette on the ground and trod it into the dirt with his toe. There was nothing to be gained from worrying himself, not now. The offensive was due to kick off in less than seven hours, once the troops had moved up to their final jump-off positions. And then…who knew? Maybe the war *could* be ended quickly.

Sure, he told himself, as he walked back into the complex. *And maybe Untermenschen will learn to fly.*

———

Leutnant Kurt Wieland couldn't help feeling a shiver running down his spine as he toured the darkened town, even though he knew he should be catching some sleep before he had to go back on duty. The sentries were awake - they would have regretted it for the rest of their careers if he'd caught them sleeping - but the entire town was so silent it was almost eerie, as if he was walking through one of the monster-infested villages of legend. He'd read all of the *Beowulf* stories when he'd been a child and the memories lingered, even after he'd learned that the worst monsters in the world walked on two legs.

He stopped at the edge of town, peering into the distance. There was a minefield there, along with a handful of traps that probably wouldn't slow down a panzer for very long but give an infantry force a very nasty surprise. Several of his men had competed to produce the nastiest trap; digging trenches, filling them with broken glass and then camouflaging them with artistically-placed trees and bushes. A couple had even been filled with flammable material, harvested from a couple of the houses. Kurt didn't feel right about stealing items from the former inhabitants - he'd already put four of his men on punishment duties for stealing ladies underwear - but there was no choice. He rather doubted the town would still be standing when the *Waffen-SS* had finished with it.

"*Herr Leutnant*," Loeb said. "Can't sleep?"

Kurt shook his head. He'd worked all day - he *should* have been able to sleep - but he hadn't been able to keep his eyes closed. It was frustrating, after mastering the old trick of sleeping whenever he had a chance, yet perhaps it was understandable. He'd never had so much responsibility in his career. The men under his command were going to war, a war none of them wanted. And very few of them were truly *ready* for the war. Kurt was hardly the only combat virgin in the platoon.

You did fire on the SS in Berlin, he reminded himself. *But they weren't expecting you to open fire.*

"The waiting is never easy, *Herr Leutnant*," Loeb said. "But you really should sleep."

Kurt gave him a ghostly smile. He *knew* he should sleep. But lying in his cot wouldn't make him feel better, not when time was slowly running out. Everyone knew the big offensive couldn't be far off, not when it was already growing colder. No one in their right mind would want to fight in the eastern winter, after all. The SS would want to get as much of the fighting over with as possible before winter started to hamper their operations.

"We should get some warning of their advance, *Herr Leutnant*," Loeb reassured him. "They can't just drop in on us."

"They did drop in on Berlin," Kurt pointed out.

"And it cost them a number of highly-trained commandos, for nothing," Loeb said. "I don't think we're important enough to risk another commando unit."

"I hope you're right," Kurt said.

He sighed, inwardly, as he peered into the darkness. They were only twenty kilometres from the border, which was hardly a solid line. There had been enough outbursts of firing between patrol groups to keep everyone on their toes. A Panzer division could cross the border and reach the town within an hour, perhaps less, if nothing slowed them down. It was quite possible the war would end, for him, on the day it started.

"We're only a handful of soldiers," Loeb pointed out. "Their commandos are worth far more than any of us."

Kurt shot him a sharp look. "Thanks."

But it was true, he knew. SS Commandos went through absolute *hell* to qualify. Indeed, if the more striking rumours were true, a third of each class of volunteers didn't survive the training program. The survivors were tough, willing to do anything for the *Reich*, but they couldn't be expended lightly. There were nowhere near enough commandos for them to be treated like ordinary soldiers.

"Get some rest, *Herr Leutnant*," Loeb advised. "It won't be long now."

Kurt nodded and took one last look into the darkness. It was unbroken; there wasn't a single light for miles, not after the military had declared martial law and threatened to arrest anyone who showed a light. He couldn't help wondering if they'd gone back in time, to the days before electric light and other modern conveniences. Fredrick the Great would have told him he was being an idiot, if they'd spoken. *His* men had campaigned under far more disagreeable conditions.

"I know," he said. "They'll be on their way soon."

CHAPTER TWELVE

Near Warsaw, Germany Prime
13 September 1985

Obergefreiter Hugo Stellmann hated to admit it, but he was bored. He'd hoped for an exciting assignment when he'd joined the *Heer*, yet so far the only real excitement had come from marching up and down in front of Hamburg's Town Hall. Even the uprising hadn't brought him any excitement, save for an assignment to the border and orders to guard one of the *autobahn* bridges over a river. He'd found himself checking refugees as they headed west, ordering them to wait until they could be processed and entered into the system, but it hadn't been particularly exciting. And even the trickle of refugees had dried up, over the last four days.

He scowled as he glared eastwards. He'd never liked the SS, although - if he were being honest with himself - it had more to do with their success with women than any moral objections. There wasn't a blonde-haired girl his own age or near it who hadn't done her duty with one of the black-shirted men, marrying him and bearing his children while Hugo himself remained without a wife or a girlfriend. They were overrated, he felt; they had hundreds of little blessings from the government while men like Hugo, the ones who did all the work, had nothing. Surely, a wife wasn't too much to ask.

At least the bastards won't be chasing women over here any longer, he thought, as he peered into the darkness. The first hints of sunrise were slowly rising above the horizon. *They can ravish their way through Germany East for all I care.*

He lit a cigarette, shaking his head slowly. His father had died when he was very young, leaving his mother struggling to bring up four children on their father's pension. She didn't have the connections to organise marriages for her children, even if she'd wanted to. It was yet another reason to hate the SS. Everyone *knew* that SS dependents not only received bigger pensions, they were regularly introduced to prospective partners as soon as they reached marriageable age. And the SS made sure that their men were rewarded for marrying and bringing more black-shirted brats into the world.

And they blew up the economy while they were doing it, he thought. *They just couldn't pay for all their children.*

He snorted to himself. It would have been funny, if he hadn't been so sure that men like him were going to get the shaft as a result of their gross carelessness. He didn't pretend to understand basic economics - he'd never done very well at school - but it was evident, to him, that one couldn't spend more money than one earned. God knew the bank managers had laughed at him when he'd gone, cap in hand, for a loan. *They* knew better than to loan money that probably couldn't be repaid.

The sound of engines echoed in the air. He glanced up, one hand reaching for the pistol at his belt, then relaxed as he realised they came from the west. Their relief was due early in the morning, thankfully. They'd be rotated back to the inner defence lines, where they'd probably wind up digging more trenches…it was unlikely they'd have any hope of actual *leave*. But who knew? Perhaps some enterprising bastard had set up a brothel near the front lines and started charging soldiers for entry. Hugo didn't like the idea of dipping his wick in some *Untermensch* bitch on a work-contract, but it was better than nothing. And there was no hope of a little Hugo popping out, nine months later. The bitches in the brothels were always sterile.

He turned as the truck approached, a simple troop transport. There were literally hundreds of thousands, perhaps *millions*, of them in the *Reich*. Many were sold to civilians, allowing the factories to make a profit while keeping careful track of where the transports could be found, if there was a sudden demand for additional logistic support. The driver waved cheerfully to Hugo as he parked on one end of the bridge, then beckoned him forward. Hugo nodded and walked over to the cab…

…And found himself staring straight into the barrel of a gun.

"Shout and you're dead," a voice hissed. He looked up into a pair of merciless eyes. "Do as I tell you and you *will* live this day."

Hugo swallowed, hard. He felt liquid trickling down his legs as his bladder gave way. He was dead. He was *so* dead. He'd been watching for trouble from the east, but it had never occurred to him that he should be wary of *anyone* approaching the bridge. The man covering him *had* to be a commando. He would shoot Hugo down without hesitation if Hugo gave him the slightest excuse. And there was nothing he could do.

The back of the lorry opened, revealing a dozen men wearing standard grey urban combat uniforms. They moved like trained professionals, their eyes scanning the bridge for signs of trouble while holding their weapons at the ready. None of them paid much attention to Hugo save for brief glances to confirm he was no threat. For once, Hugo was almost grateful. The SS would kill him in a moment if they believed otherwise.

"Call your men," his captor ordered. "Now!"

Hugo wanted to refuse, but he knew it would be pointless. His men were already trapped within the guardhouse. Resistance would last as long as it took the commandos to roll a grenade into the tiny room…he'd been a fool, allowing them to remain in the concrete guardhouse. It would have been smarter to have an Observation Post established near the bridge.

He cleared his throat. "Out, now," he shouted, hearing fear in his voice. Maybe one of his men would realise that something was wrong and…and do what? There was nothing they *could* do. "Come out…"

The commandos caught the handful of guards as they came out, searched them roughly and then bound their hands with plastic ties. Hugo's captor did the same, grunting in distaste as he inspected Hugo's sodden trousers, then marched Hugo over to the wall and positioned him against it. The charges affixed to the bridge, the charges Hugo was supposed to detonate if it became clear the bridge was about to be lost, were rapidly removed. He watched, helplessly, as the truck moved past them, crossed the bridge and vanished into the east.

He heard the dull rumble of engines and knew, with a sickening certainty that admitted of no doubt, just what was coming his way. Moments later, he recoiled inwardly as the first panzer came into view, a giant tank easily large enough to knock down his house without ever noticing the impact. Its main gun traversed threateningly as it hunted for targets, the smaller machine guns mounted on each side of the turret passing over the helpless captives before ignoring them. Hundreds of other tanks followed, their crews waving cheerfully at the commandoes as they headed westwards. Hugo closed his eyes in bitter pain, unable to shut out either the growing racket or the terrifying awareness that he had failed. The door was open, the SS was on the march…

…And it was all his fault.

His captor leered down at him as another lorry parked near the bridge and unloaded two platoons of heavily-armed soldiers. "I shouldn't worry, *Mein Fraulein*," he said. He patted Hugo on the shoulder, then hauled him to his feet and pushed him towards the lorry. "For you, the war is over."

———

Marlene Johan kept her face expressionless as she peered into the squadron ready room, where thirty-two young men were laughing, talking or trying to get some sleep while they waited for the call to action. Four of them were already aloft, flying their ME-347s in Combat Air Patrol over the border between east and west, but the others knew they might have to grab their jackets and rush to their planes at any moment. There should have been four more men in the room, yet they were missing. Marlene had a feeling that they'd successfully managed to seduce some of her staff and talk them into the private bathrooms.

They'll be in deep trouble if they're caught, she thought with dark amusement, hearing the noise from one of the closed doors. *And they will be caught, if they keep making that racket.*

She smirked at the thought as she made her way into her office. The pilots were on duty. They weren't *supposed* to be caught diddling the cleaning staff. She might even feel sorry for them, after the base's commander finished tearing strips off their hides and threatening them with instant dismissal - and perhaps castration - if they allowed themselves to be distracted again. *She* would have had a word with her staff too, under other circumstances. No one really cared *what* the pilots did when they were off-duty - their uniforms were enough to attract any number of women from the nearby town - but when they were on-duty they were supposed to *remain* on-duty. If someone was shot down and killed because one of his comrades was late to his plane, they'd never hear the end of it.

Yes, they will, she thought, as she carefully removed the assault rifle from her locked cupboard and slotted the ammunition into place. *None of them will survive this day.*

She shook her head as she put the grenades into her pocket, wondering just why the guards hadn't bothered to search her office. A pistol would have been hard to explain, let alone an assault rifle. But then, she'd been inside the wire - part of the furniture - long before the uprising had cast the shadow of civil war over Germany. Too old and unattractive to interest the pilots, too female to be considered dangerous…she'd kept an eye on the young men for disloyalty, even as she'd cleaned up the mess they left behind. They thought nothing of her, if they bothered to think of her at all. She'd take a certain delight in showing them the error of their ways.

If you survive the day, her own thoughts reminded her. *And the odds are not in your favour.*

She picked up the rifle, then opened the door and glanced outside. The noise of two bodies slamming together was growing louder, but there was no one in sight. Marlene smirked as she hurried out of the door towards the ready room, one hand taking a grenade from her belt and removing the pin. None of the pilots had bothered to think about the fact - it was hardly a secret - that she'd been born in Germany East. She might be a woman - old and ugly to them - but she'd been using weapons since she was nine. An assault rifle was nothing more than a tool to her.

Opening the door, she tossed the grenade into the room and braced herself. There was a shout - the pilots were sloppy, more used to showing off in the air than fighting for their lives - before the grenade detonated, shaking the building. *Everyone* would have heard the blast, including the guards. Marlene hefted the rifle and stepped into the room, her eyes scanning for pilots who had survived the blast. She put the handful of lightly-wounded survivors down with single-shots, ignoring the badly-wounded men. They'd be a drain on resources, if they were left alive…

She heard the sound of a door banging open behind her and hurried back out into the corridor. Isabel was standing there, her bare breasts bobbling as she looked from side to side in shock; behind her, one of the more odious pilots was trying to draw his pistol from his belt. Marlene shot him down without hesitation, then aimed at Isabel. The dark-haired girl crumpled to the ground, fainting in shock. Marlene was tempted to put a bullet through her head anyway - Isabel was too stupid to be allowed to breed - but thought better of it as she heard the sound of running footsteps. The guards were finally coming to stop her. No doubt they thought that one of the pilots had turned on his fellows.

Bracing herself, she took another grenade, removed the pin and hurled it down the corridor as the guards came into view. They were on the alert; two of them threw themselves to the ground as the grenade detonated, while another one hurled himself backwards. Marlene fired a long burst of bullets towards them, then turned and ran, using another grenade to cover her tracks. The explosion shook the building, sending pieces of debris crashing towards the floor. There were a handful of shots behind her, but none of them even came close.

No training for an internal assault, Marlene thought, gleefully. The guards had trained hard, she recalled, but all their training had been based around an external assault on the airbase. It hadn't seemed to occur to them that one of the charwomen might be an SS operative, ready to turn on them when she received the signal. *They're not ready for me.*

She ran through the door and onto the tarmac. It was dark - the sun wouldn't be peeking above the horizon for at least another hour - but it was light enough for her to see the line of aircraft waiting for pilots. The ground crewmen turned to stare at her as she ran out, then ducked for cover as she opened fire, hurling the last of her grenades into the nearest cockpit before it could detonate. She'd hoped for a chain reaction - she'd imagined the line of planes exploding into fireballs, one by one - but only one plane caught fire. Someone was shouting behind her…

A hammer struck her shoulder, sending the assault rifle flying as she fell forward and slammed face-first into the tarmac. The impact dazed her; it took several seconds for her to realise that she'd been shot. She heard the sound of running footsteps as she tried to struggle to her feet, discovering to her horror that her body was no longer working. Blood - her blood - was pouring out of her wound.

"Damn bitch," someone growled. She gasped in pain as he kicked her in the side, hard, then turned her over. The pain was so agonising that she almost passed out. "Damn you…"

Marlene looked up into the face of one of the guards, a young man she recalled helping to write a letter to his girlfriend after their relationship had hit a nasty bump in the road. It had been easy to slip into the role of mother-substitute, to keep him from thinking of her as a potential threat. And it had worked. He wouldn't be staring at her with so much hatred if he hadn't been completely fooled.

She felt blood welling up in her mouth and choked. He made no move to help her, instead just staring down and drinking in the sight as she died. She wasn't too surprised, she thought, as a dreadful numbness settled over her body. She'd betrayed them all, after all; she'd killed at least thirty men in her brief rampage and sowed the seeds of a distrust that would kill hundreds more.

Heil Holliston, she thought, as she fell into the darkness. *And…*

———

The observation post was hidden near the bridge, close enough to keep an eye on what crossed the river, far enough to pass unnoticed if - when - someone decided to search for watching eyes. Both of the soldiers assigned to the post were experienced woodsmen, capable of making sure that neither of them were detected, let alone caught. It wasn't a job they enjoyed, but it was necessary. The defenders, after all, had known the bridges would be overwhelmed very quickly.

"There wasn't even a fight," Ott Wild muttered, as he watched the endless line of panzers crossing the bridge. "They overwhelmed the guards easily."

"It's been done before," Einhart Pusch reminded him. He picked up the phone, knowing it would set off an alarm at the command post. "The guards weren't expecting an attack from the west."

Someone picked up the phone. "Report!"

"Bridge Seven has been overwhelmed," Pusch said. They hadn't been told who they were calling, let alone where he was. No matter how good they were, they had to admit that capture and interrogation was a realistic possibility. "The bridge remains intact. I say again, the bridge remains intact. The panzers are crossing now."

"Understood," the voice said. "How many?"

"At least fifty, so far," Wild muttered.

"At least fifty, so far," Pusch repeated. "I imagine it won't be long before the regular troops start crossing too."

"Remain in place," the voice ordered, finally. "Continue to send reports as the situation develops."

Pusch nodded, coldly, as the connection broke. He hadn't expected anything else. If they were lucky, there would be some artillery pieces within range to shell the bridge, giving the SS a hot reception. But most of the heavy artillery was in Occupied France. Only a handful of weapons had been moved east before the war finally begun. They'd have to depend on the *Luftwaffe*.

"They're sending troop transports across too now," Wild commented. "And I can see engineers on the far bank. I think there's some mobile SAM units too."

"They'll have pontoons thrown up very quickly," Pusch agreed. The SS were bastards, but he had to admit they were good engineers. "And then they can double or triple the number of men advancing towards us."

"And then we're in trouble," Wild finished. They'd served together long enough not to need formality. "Let's hope the artillery or the air force gets up here before it's too late."

CHAPTER THIRTEEN

Berlin, Germany Prime
13 September 1985

"Sir, wake up," a voice snapped. "It's an air raid!"

Andrew snapped awake, one hand grabbing for the pistol he kept at his bedside before his mind quite caught up with what he'd been told. An air raid? It seemed absurd to think that *anyone* could strike at Berlin - he knew, all too well, just how tough ODIN'S EYE - the German Air Defence Network - was...but that had been before the uprising. Now, according to NORAD, ODIN'S EYE was in ruins. Half of the radar stations were in enemy hands and several more had been badly damaged by SS loyalists just after the provisional government took control.

"Crap," he muttered, silently relieved he'd worn pyjamas. "What do we know?"

The marine - he didn't look old enough to enter Camp Pendleton, let alone graduate - grabbed Andrew's arm and hurried him down the corridor. "We received a FLASH warning from NORAD, sir," he said. "Multiple missile launches were detected from Germany East. The preliminary analysis classed them as cruise missiles aimed at Berlin."

Andrew sucked in his breath. The Germans *claimed* that their latest cruise missiles were hypersonic, designed to smash American carrier battlegroups, but he didn't know anyone outside the *Reich* who actually believed them. Certainly, as far as he knew, neither American nor British intelligence had picked up any actual *proof* that the missiles were an order of magnitude faster than anything in America's arsenal. But 'merely' supersonic cruise missiles would be entering Berlin airspace within a matter of minutes, even if they were fired from Germanica itself.

He cursed as they hurried down the stairs, joined rapidly by the handful of remaining embassy staffers and marines. It was unlikely the SS would *deliberately* target the American Embassy, but accidents happened. German cruise missiles were blunt weapons, designed more for terror than actual precision. A missile aimed at the *Reichstag* might well hit the American Embassy instead. Even American weapons, far better designed than anything Germany was *supposed* to have, weren't completely reliable.

Ambassador Turtledove was sitting in the bunker, looking uncomfortable. He'd have been sent down the tube, Andrew reminded himself, instead of being forced to run down the stairs and into the bunker. He nodded to the ambassador, then calmed himself as the marines slammed the doors closed. In theory, the embassy bunker could stand off everything from a direct cruise missile strike to a nuclear blast, but in practice no one was entirely sure. It wasn't comforting to realise, deep inside, that even if they *did* survive a nuclear strike, no one was likely to come help dig them out. The Germans above them would have too many other problems.

"Direct uplink established to NORAD," a computer operator said. "They've updated the warning, sir; fifteen missiles will strike Berlin in seven minutes."

Ambassador Turtledove met Andrew's eyes. "They're not nukes, are they?"

"I don't think so," Andrew said. Intercepting a cruise missile was difficult, even for the most advanced American systems. And they were expensive. The SS wouldn't have wasted *fifteen* nuclear-tipped missiles on Berlin, not when one or two would be enough to inflict colossal damage on the city. "I think they're probably conventional warheads."

He kept the rest of the thought to himself. The Germans had a *very* well known chemical and biological weapons program. It was quite possible that one of those warheads had a chemical warhead, perhaps loaded with something nasty enough to kill half of Berlin. The SS would find such a solution appealing, he thought. They'd avoid the propaganda damage of destroying Berlin and, at the same time, exterminate thousands of rebels. They *did* have MOPP suits among the supplies in the bunker, he reminded himself, but some of the German weapons were supposed to be able to slip through protective garments. It struck him as unlikely, yet there was no way to know for sure...

"I ordered a warning to be flashed to the provisional government," Ambassador Turtledove said, quietly. "I just hope they take it seriously."

"So do I, Mr. Ambassador," Andrew said. "So do I."

———

Gudrun had never quite got used to sharing a bed, even though she'd known she would be expected to do just that after she finally tied the knot with *someone*. Having sex with Horst was one thing - and she'd grown used to *that* once she'd pulled him into her bed - but sleeping next to him was quite another. It left her torn between holding him at night and feeling as though she wasn't able to relax and sleep properly as long as he was there. She had never shared her bed before, not even with her siblings.

The alarms went off. Gudrun started, jerking upwards as Horst practically *threw* himself out of bed, one hand scooping up his pistol and swinging it round to cover the door. She could hear shouting outside; she hastily covered her breasts as she rolled off the other side of the bed, keeping low as Horst had told her. Someone might come crashing into the room at any moment...

"That's the air raid alarm," Horst snapped. He grabbed her dressing gown and threw it at her, then pulled his own on with terrifying speed. "We have to get down to the shelter."

Gudrun stared at him, her head spinning. "An air raid?"

"Yes," Horst shouted. He caught hold of her arm and pulled her to her feet, then yanked her towards the door. "Put your gown on and hurry!"

The alarms were getting louder. Gudrun had to fight to pull the gown on, uneasily convinced that Horst would pull her out of the room in a moment or two no matter how little she was wearing. She was a properly brought up young lady; she'd been taught never to be naked in front of a man unless he was her husband. There was no way she could run outside in the nude... Horst pulled her towards the door as soon as she was covered, holding his pistol in one hand as he opened the door. Dozens of men and women were running down the stairs, heading into the bunker as though the hounds of hell were in hot pursuit. Gudrun found herself pulled forward and into the crowd, leaving the door ajar behind them.

Someone could sneak into the room while everyone is panicking, she thought, as they ran down seven flights of stairs. Someone tripped, further down, only to be trodden on by a dozen others before she could crawl out of the way. *And someone might notice that we left the same room…*

She pushed the thought aside as they reached the bottom, Horst yanking her down the right-hand corridor as everyone else hurried down the left. She was too stunned to argue as they passed a pair of armed guards, then raced down a second stairwell she hadn't known existed. The bunker at the bottom was surprisingly luxurious, reminding her of Hilde's mansion in the heart of Berlin. It was where the *Reich* Council had intended to wait out the apocalypse, if nuclear war had broken out. She wouldn't be surprised to discover that it had cost more than an entire Panzer Division.

The door banged closed behind them, making her jump. Horst held her hand gently as she calmed herself, his blue eyes concerned. Gudrun couldn't help feeling touched, even though they might be in serious danger. He *did* have feelings for her! She told herself, a moment later, that she was being silly. This was no time to worry about their relationship.

"We're probably meant to be in the next room," Horst said, quietly. "Are you ready?"

Gudrun took a breath, then looked at herself in the mirror. Her hair was a mess, her dressing gown was barely decent and she'd left her slippers in the bedroom. She knew precisely what her mother or father would have said, once upon a time, if she'd walked around in such a state. She'd have been ordered to go back to her bedroom and changed before she was allowed out of the house, if she wasn't grounded for life…

The thought almost made her giggle helplessly. She *would* have giggled, too, if she hadn't been so tired.

"I think so," she said. "Let's go."

She followed him through a metal door - it reminded her of the aircraft carrier she'd toured, shortly after the uprising - and into a command and control chamber. Volker Schulze was sitting in a comfortable chair, watching a team of operators as they constantly updated a large wall-mounted display. Red icons moved around the display, blinking in and out of existence as new information flowed into the chamber. She was no expert, but she couldn't help noticing that there was a massive concentration of red marks along the border. Some of them were even heading to Berlin.

"It's like a giant television," Horst breathed. "I had no idea it was so advanced."

Gudrun nodded. Televisions were rare in the *Reich*, even though radios were so common that even the poorer households had two or three. She made a mental note to look up why that was actually so, then pushed the thought aside. No doubt someone had decided that kids should be doing something more useful - like joining the Hitler Youth - than watching television. Or perhaps the *Reich* simply couldn't *afford* to produce them. Who knew?

"Impact in thirty seconds," a voice said. One of the operators looked at Schulze, his face pale. "Trajectory places the impact point roughly in the centre of Berlin."

Gudrun squeezed Horst's hand as the countdown began. The bunker was supposed to be a secret, but the SS would probably know *precisely* where it was. Hell, it wasn't *too* hard to guess that there would be a bunker below the *Reichstag*. Nuclear war could begin at any minute, if propaganda was to be believed. A missile launched from Britain could reach its target within bare minutes, far too quickly for the council to move to a safer location.

"It should be fine," Horst muttered. She had to resist the urge to take him in her arms and hold him tightly. "I don't think they'll target this building."

"Zero," the operator said.

Gudrun braced herself, closing her eyes…but felt nothing. She'd expected everything from a dull rumble to the roof caving in on their heads, yet…there had been nothing. More red icons flared up over Berlin, warning her that several missiles had landed within the city limits, but she felt nothing. It was almost as if the missiles hadn't exploded at all.

"Target report," Schulze ordered.

"Two missiles came down on the Ministry of Economics, *Herr Chancellor*," the operator reported. "An additional missile struck the Schindler Barracks. Five more came down, seemingly at random; the remainder crashed outside the city. Their targeting was not particularly accurate."

"So it would seem," Schulze mused. "Damage reports?"

"None as yet," the operator said. "I have a report from one of the rooftop observers, who states that there are now several fires burning across the city, but nothing else."

"Make sure emergency teams are prepped for chemical weapons," Schulze ordered. "Do you have a direct link to the front?"

Gudrun looked at Horst. "I felt nothing."

"This is the safest place in the *Reich*," Horst muttered back. "I read through the specifications while you were taking your place on the council. A nuke couldn't scratch the protective layers over our head, let alone harm us. And they're unlikely to strike at the *Reichstag* in any case."

He smiled, rather dryly. "And if we get *trapped* in here, we have tunnels that connect us to the underground, giving us a dozen options for escaping," he added. "The *Reich* Council was determined to make sure it could remain in control, even during a nuclear war."

"Oh," Gudrun said. She looked at one of the operators. "What's happening?"

"Let them work," Horst told her, quietly.

"The war has begun," Schulze said. He rose and strode over towards them, just as one of the phones started to ring. An operator picked it up and began speaking in a low voice, trying not to disturb the others. "We've had reports of enemy panzers crossing the border, missiles and long-range artillery strikes and a number of…incidents…at various military bases."

Gudrun met his eyes. "Incidents?"

Schulze looked back at her. She felt her cheeks heat as he studied her outfit, yet she refused to look away. Maybe he *would* have been her father-in-law, if things had been different, but it no longer mattered. Their lives had taken very different paths.

Horst leaned forward. "Shootings, unless I miss my guess," he said. "Some of their observers will have been told to go on the attack."

"Correct," Schulze said. He didn't seem angry with Horst, something that puzzled Gudrun until she realised that Schulze must have been aware of the possibility long before they'd told him about Horst's past. "We don't have a full set of reports yet, but they've already hampered our ability to launch counterattacks."

Gudrun paled. "Are we going to lose the war?"

"Early days yet," Schulze said. He sounded as tired as she felt. "There's no real danger here, at least at the moment; I suggest you take a bedroom and get some rest. We should have a better idea of what's going on in a few hours."

"I understand," Gudrun said.

"Come on," Horst said, gently. "I'll take you to bed."

Gudrun blushed as Schulze cleared his throat, then turned and walked back towards the waiting operator. Thank *God* that hadn't slipped out during a council meeting. The old men would never have taken her seriously... those of them that didn't already consider her too young, too female or too rebellious to be worth their time. She took one last look at the display - there were more red icons to the east - and then allowed Horst to lead her out the door and through a maze of corridors. If she hadn't already *known* they were in a bunker, she wouldn't have believed it. She'd expected concrete walls and dank smells, but the interior was *designed* to look surprisingly pleasant. The only downside were the complete lack of windows and the portraits of famous men lining the walls, ranging from Hitler himself to Himmler and Goering.

And Goering looks like a danger to shipping, she thought. The man had really been quite unpleasantly fat. Even a paid artist hadn't been able to disguise his bulk. *How did he even manage to walk around?*

"Get some rest," Horst ordered, once they reached her room. It was just as luxurious as the rest of the complex. "I'll be waiting outside."

Gudrun pulled him into the room before he could escape. "Is there anything you can do here?"

"I doubt it," Horst said. "There's certainly no hope of making contact with the stay-behind cell."

"Yeah," Gudrun agreed. Horst had kept a sharp eye out for any more notes, but none had appeared. She closed the door and grinned at him. "You may as well come to bed with me."

Horst blinked in shock. "But what about...?"

"Schulze knows," Gudrun said, flatly. She took his arms and pulled him, firmly, towards the bed. "And right now I really find it hard to care about the others."

"Ah, danger," Horst said. "That turns you on."

Gudrun snorted. "Horst?"

"Yes?"

"Shut up."

———

There had been no way *Hauptsturmfuehrer* Katharine Milch could have carried a radio with her, even though a handful of the refugees she'd joined as they made their trek westward had seemingly carried all of their possessions on their shoulders. They'd had them all confiscated as soon as they'd arrived in Berlin, before they'd been shown into a set of transit barracks that had clearly been designed for *Untermenschen*. Katherine had ignored the whining and moaning from her fellow inmates, concentrating instead on quietly picking up information from the guards and planning her escape. It hadn't struck her as particularly difficult. The transit camp *had* been designed as a prison, but the refugees weren't being treated *as* prisoners.

I got out of nastier prisons when I was a trainee, Katharine thought, as she heard the first cruise missiles flying over Berlin. Deep rumbling explosions followed moments later, telling her that it was time to kick off her blanket and leave the rest of the refugees behind. *And now it's time to leave.*

She smiled, rather unpleasantly, as she headed for the door. There were always a pair of policemen on guard, both of whom were young enough to talk more than they should to a pretty face and a very tight shirt. Katherine didn't mind; the more they looked at her chest, the less they looked at her face. She'd been taught a dozen simple ways to disguise herself - along with a whole series of skills that were rarely taught to eastern women, let alone western women - but the simplest tricks were always the best. She pushed the door open and glanced towards the guardpost. One of the policemen was clearly visible, while the other was out of sight. She hoped that meant he'd started the long walk around the transit barracks.

"You shouldn't be out here, *Fraulein*," the policeman said. He was desperately worried, so desperately worried that he barely even *glanced* at her chest. "The city is under attack."

Katherine nodded. Flames were rising up in the distance, casting unpleasant flickers of light over Berlin. She'd been told that a number of cruise missiles would be launched, in the hopes of decapitating the provisional government, but there had been no way to be *certain* that they'd hit their targets. But it was more than enough to tell her that it was time to go.

"I'm scared," she said, slipping closer. "I need comfort."

The policeman hesitated, just for a second. It was long enough for Katherine to draw her pencil from her pocket - they hadn't bothered to confiscate either her pencils or her notebooks - and ram it through his eye. He stumbled backwards, dead before he hit the ground. She took his pistol, glanced around for any sign of his partner, then hurried towards the open gate leading to the city. By the time the body was found, she'd be well on her way towards the rendezvous point.

And their record keeping is shoddy, she thought, as she walked onwards. *They may not even know who they're missing.*

CHAPTER FOURTEEN

Near Warsaw, Germany Prime
13 September 1985

"It's confirmed, sir. Bridge Seven has definitely fallen; Bridges Eight and Nine have come under heavy attack."

Generalmajor Gunter Gath nodded, coolly. He'd never expected the bridges to hold out for more than a few minutes, although he *had* hoped that the defenders would be able to drop them into the water before it was too late. Trying to make a stand on the river bank would probably have cost him more than he cared to lose, in the opening hours of the war.

"Order the gunners to start pounding the crossing points," he ordered, flatly.

"Jawohl."

He scowled as he turned his attention to the map, silently contemplating the developing situation. The SS would start counter-battery fire at once, but if he was lucky his shellfire might slow the enemy down for a few additional hours. He'd badly underestimated the SS's ability to cause trouble behind the lines, as well as their understanding of how his command network worked. They'd missed the command post, thankfully, but they'd sown enough chaos to make it harder for his forces to respond in a timely manner.

"The gunners have opened fire, *Herr Generalmajor.*"

"Very good," Gunter said. "And the remaining aircraft?"

"On their way," his aide assured him. "But their formations are a little ragged."

Gunter nodded, irritated. Pilots were easier to replace than planes; hell, the *Luftwaffe* had enough pilots held in reserve to crew the entire air force twice over. But the reservists would still need to be mated with their planes before they could be thrown into battle. He'd expected air superiority over the battlefield, if not air supremacy, but right now even *that* had been thrown into doubt. The SS, by killing over a hundred pilots, had disrupted half of his contingency plans.

And their own aircraft will be on the prowl too, he thought, grimly. *They do not have anything like as many supersonic jet aircraft, but that's not what they need right now.*

"Contact Berlin," he ordered, tersely. "Give them a status report."

He cursed under his breath as he sat back in his command chair. German officers - particularly middle-ranking officers - were meant to lead from the front, but there was no way he dared expose himself to enemy fire. The resignations and desertions had torn hundreds of holes in his formation, leaving very few high-ranking officers in position. He'd had to promote hundreds of junior officers to fill the gaps, officers who would have to learn on the job. And who knew how many of them could be trusted? A single officer working for the SS, in the right place at the right time, could do a hell of a lot of damage. Hell, a handful of workers had *already* done a great deal of damage.

And I'd sell my soul for an American battlespace command management system, he thought, morbidly. He'd laughed when he'd heard about the concept - it was a sign that the American faith in technology as a panacea to all ills had yet to fade - but right now he felt cut off and isolated, dependent upon his subordinates to push reports up the chain. His awareness of the battlefield - his fingertip awareness - was practically non-existent. *Right now, I'd be happy with the prospect of micromanaging the men.*

He pushed the thought aside, bitterly. There was no time for dwelling on pieces of equipment he'd probably never have, even if he truly wanted them. All he could do now was wait…

…And hope that the plan, thrown together in a flurry of desperate improvisation, would work.

––––––

Hauptmann Felix Malguth kept a wary eye on his radar screen, watching for potential threats, as the HE-477 raced towards the river. He knew he didn't dare let himself get bounced and shot out of the sky, certainly not when there were so few friendly aircraft in the air. The SS would already be on the prowl, he knew, and while he felt the SS pilots couldn't come up to the *Luftwaffe's* standards he had to admit they were pretty good. And besides, there *were* *Luftwaffe* bases in the east. Their pilots had probably joined the SS without even being *compelled*.

He shook his head in grim amusement as he pushed the aircraft forward. He'd worked with the SS a time or two, back in South Africa, and he had to admit the *Waffen-SS* were good soldiers. They never broke, they never ran… and they were never unappreciative of their CAS aircraft, unlike countless others in the *Reich*. Indeed, Felix had spent far too much time bloodying his fists while defending the honour of his HE-477 to *Luftwaffe* jet fighter pilots who thought their ME-346s were shinier and sexier than his workhorse. Perhaps they were, he conceded ruefully, but it wasn't *them* who came to the aide of troops cut off and facing annihilation on the ground. Their only role was defending the *Reich* from British and America intrusions…

Felix *had* been tempted to resign, when the officer commanding the unit had explained that anyone who didn't want to fight their fellow Germans could go, with no hard feelings. He wasn't quite sure why he'd stayed. On one hand, this *was* an opportunity to test his skills in a far more deadly field of combat - every pilot in his unit dreaded flying into the teeth of multiple SAM batteries - but on the other, the CO was right. They *would* be flying against their fellow Germans, even if they *were* easterners. He'd heard some of the pilots joking and laughing about finally showing the easterners what west-erners were made of, but Felix knew that such differences hadn't mattered in South Africa. East or west, Germans were Germans, the *Volk* united against the world.

And now that unity has been shattered, he thought, as his radar bleeped a warning. *And now we're going to war.*

He braced himself, his finger pressing lightly against the firing switch. He was coming up on the bridge…and a number of enemy radars, all far too close to the crossing. If the SS followed doctrine - and he had no reason to assume they would do anything else - there would be at least one or two mobile mis-sile launchers stationed at each side of the bridge, ready to engage any aircraft brave or foolish enough to fly into their sights. They couldn't afford to lose the bridge, after all. It would make it harder for them to deploy their forces into the west. Maybe they could drive their panzers across the riverbed - some tanks were practically amphibious - but getting the men across in fighting trim would be a great deal harder.

His heart started to race as the bridge came into view. It was a solid structure, built in the days when the *Reich* had thrust its network of *autobahns* further and further eastwards. The bridge had probably been *designed* to take panzers, even though everyone knew that driving a panzer division down an *autobahn* would rapidly render the road unusable. But the SS didn't seem to care. An endless line of panzers were crossing the massive bridge, while field engineers worked like demons to extend a network of pontoon bridges across the water; Felix couldn't help noticing that five of the pontoon bridges were already crammed with troops, advancing westwards. He hoped - prayed - that the men on the ground were ready for the nightmare coming their way.

He jammed his finger down on the trigger, firing a solid stream of cannon shells towards his targets. It was hard to say what his shells would do to the bridge - it *was* a very solid structure - but he had the satisfaction of watching one of the panzers explode into a fireball as he closed in on his target. *That* would delay them, at least as long as it took for one of the other panzers to push the wreckage over the side and into the water. And he knew from bitter experience that even the slightest delays could have significant knock-on effects.

His threat receiver screamed a warning as a missile flew into the air, launched by one of the mobile SAM batteries. Felix threw his aircraft to one side, hoping and praying that the launchers hadn't had time to lock onto his aircraft. Luck was with him. The missile flew past harmlessly and raced into the distance. He sprayed cannon fire over the forces gathered at one end of the bridge - a SAM unit exploded with staggering force - and then altered course, flying away as soon as his cannon was empty. Another missile rose up behind him, but fell back to the ground as he threw his aircraft through a series of evasive manoeuvres. The *Reich's* antiaircraft missiles had never been *quite* as good as the Stingers the Americans had produced and sent to South Africa. Felix knew pilots who had been blown out of the sky by the damned American missiles.

We could do with a few of them now, he thought. *The Americans will probably sell them to us, if we offer our firstborn children in exchange.*

He gritted his teeth as he headed back to the airbase, keeping a wary eye on the sky behind him. The SS would be sending jet fighters after him, now they knew there was at least one HE-477 in the sky. *They* wouldn't underestimate the danger he posed, not when they'd turned CAS into an art form. But intercepting a tiny - and slow - HE-477 with a jet aircraft was nowhere near as easy as it looked. He could fly through a forest road, barely above the ground, while a jet pilot who tried would wind up dead.

But there was no sign of enemy aircraft in the air, even when he approached the airbase and landed quickly. The fires he'd seen when he took off - set by a pair of SS commandos who'd killed nearly twenty men before they'd been stopped - had been put out, while four more aircraft were taking off from the runway. Felix allowed himself a moment of relief as the fuel and ammunition trucks raced towards his plane, then took advantage of the opportunity to relax. There was no point in unhooking himself from the seat and leaving the plane, even to piss. He'd wait until his plane was refuelled and rearmed, then he'd take off…

…And then he'd do it all over again.

———

"Pawn to king four," the radio squawked. "I say again, pawn to king four."

Major Jordan Beschnidt nodded once as he waited, trapped inside his panzer. The SS was on the march - and heading right towards his position. He hadn't been expecting to go to war, certainly not against the SS, but there was a part of him that relished the challenge. The *Waffen-SS* bragged of being the best panzer drivers in the *Reich* and Jordan would enjoy the chance to show them that wasn't the case, even if it *did* come with the very real possibility of getting blown up, burned to death or being captured and thrown into a concentration camp.

"No reply," he ordered. "We wait."

He felt sweat trickling down his back as the seconds slipped by, one by one. It had been sheer luck that he and his men had been anywhere near the east, particularly as no one had expected to have to fight a civil war in the middle of the

Reich. If he hadn't been stationed at the *Panzer Lehr* training camp…he smirked at the thought, then peered through his scope as the first SS panzer came into view. They would think - and not without reason - that the defenders had no panzers closer than Occupied France. And they were in for a terrible surprise.

"They're advancing fast," the driver muttered, as three more panzers appeared. "And they're alone."

Jordan nodded in agreement. There were no infantry, even though doctrine insisted that panzers should always be supported by infantry. But then, he knew - all too well - just how easy it was for the panzers to outrun their escorts. Getting through the defence line and into the rear had been part of German military doctrine for the last fifty years. The SS wouldn't want to slow the advance long enough to give the westerners a chance to reshuffle their forces and block their thrust.

He picked up the telephone - using a radio so close to the enemy would pinpoint their position for any marauding aircraft - and muttered a command. There were only four panzers under his command, all pulled from the training school…normally, he would never have dared send instructors into combat. They were good at their jobs, very good; replacing them would be a nightmare. But there was a shortage of crew - and besides, they wanted to show the SS what they could do too.

"Choose your targets," he ordered. Four *more* panzers were coming into view, bunching up as they made their way down the road. He'd have clouted any student who did that on exercise, although he was fair-minded enough to admit that combat rarely took place under ideal conditions. "And fire when we fire."

"Weapons locked," the gunner said. "They're closing…"

Jordan nodded, bracing himself. The closer the enemy came, the greater the chance of scoring two or more hits. But, at the same time, the greater the chance of the enemy realising they had walked right into a trap. The crews had camouflaged the panzers as best as they could, but the SS crews had plenty of experience in South Africa. They'd know what to look for, as they watched for unpleasant surprises; they might just spot the panzers lying in wait before it was too late. And if they did, they might just manage to slam a shell or two into *his* panzer before he realised he was under attack. A quick-thinking enemy commander could turn the ambush into a disaster in a matter of seconds.

"Fire on my command," he ordered. The enemy were coming closer…were their turrets starting to move? "Fire!"

The panzer jerked as it fired a shell into the leading enemy tank. At such close range, it was hard to miss; the shell punched through the heavy frontal armour and detonated inside the vehicle. It exploded into a fireball, the turret rising into the air as it was blown off. The crew, Jordan was sure, would have been killed instantly. He hoped, grimly, that they *had* been killed instantly. He'd seen enough men pulled from burning hulks, more dead than alive, to wish otherwise. No one, not even the worst of the SS, deserved such a fate.

"Pick the next target," he snapped. "Fire!"

He took stock of the situation as the gunner engaged a second target. Four enemy panzers had been destroyed; three more were rapidly targeted and blown apart while he watched. But the enemy were returning fire, hurling shells at random into the foliage. They hadn't got a solid lock on his panzers, he noted, but it hardly mattered. They'd score a lucky hit if they kept hurling so many shells in his direction.

"Move us," he ordered.

The panzer lurched to life, racing backwards. Jordan hung on for dear life, watching as the gunner sighted the main gun on another advancing panzer and opened fire. The shell struck the panzer's treads, disabling it; the crew hastily evacuated, seconds before another shell blew the panzer into flaming debris. The nasty part of Jordan's mind was tempted to mow them down with the machine gun, just to make sure they couldn't go back to the war, but he suppressed it firmly. Atrocities would only make the war more savage as both sides struggled to outdo the other in sheer beastliness. He'd heard too many horror stories from South Africa to take it lightly.

Where captured men are lucky if they're only castrated, he thought, darkly. It wasn't even the worst of the stories he'd heard. Savage tribesmen took delight in inflicting unspeakable wounds on their prisoners. *We don't want those atrocities here.*

He cursed savagely as one of his escorting panzers was hit and ground to a halt, smoke pouring from its turret. The crew bailed out hastily, running westwards without looking back. They'd link up with the remainder of the unit at the RP, assuming anyone else survived. Jordan muttered a command as the panzers kept moving back; the gunner put a shell into the disabled vehicle, ensuring that nothing could be salvaged from the wreck. The *Heer* engineers were trained to break down a disabled vehicle, stripping everything useful from the remains; he dared not assume that the SS would be any less competent. Killing one of his own panzers - and probably one that could be repaired - did not sit well with him, but there was no choice.

"They've given up pursuit," the gunner said. "We made it clear."

Jordan shrugged. He doubted it. The SS had taken a bloody nose, which would slow them down for some time, but it wouldn't stop them indefinitely. It was far more likely that they'd be calling for air support, demanding that a HE-477 plink his panzers from high overhead before they resumed the advance. It was what *he* would have done. Or maybe they'd be calling infantry and sending them on ahead to watch for a second ambush.

"Take us to the second firing position," he ordered. He was surprised they'd have a chance to use it. Indeed, he doubted there was much prospect of them surviving the day, but they were still in place to deal out a second bloody nose. The SS would have been slowed down and that was all that mattered. "And keep a sharp eye out for enemy aircraft."

"*Jawohl,*" the driver said.

CHAPTER FIFTEEN

𝕭𝖊𝖗𝖑𝖎𝖓, 𝕲𝖊𝖗𝖒𝖆𝖓𝖞 𝕻𝖗𝖎𝖒𝖊
13 𝕾𝖊𝖕𝖙𝖊𝖒𝖇𝖊𝖗 1985

Herman shook his head in grim disbelief as he stood near what had once been the Ministry of Economics. It had been a towering building, once upon a time, but now it was nothing more than a pile of rubble. The police and firemen who'd approached the building and set up lines to keep the public back weren't trying to do anything to recover bodies, he noted, even as the sun was starting to rise. They knew there was little hope of *anyone* surviving the holocaust.

"Quite a mess," a voice said. "Do you think it was deliberate spite?"

Herman turned, then straightened in alarm and snapped out a salute as he recognised Hans Krueger. He'd never actually *met* the man, not even after the uprising, but every policeman in Germany knew the names and faces of the *Reich* Councillors. A single word from one of them - even now, he assumed - would be enough to send a policeman to a very unpleasant duty station in Siberia or Germany South. But Krueger didn't look angry, merely contemplative.

"I do not know, *Mein Herr*," Herman said. He wasn't sure if Krueger knew who he was. It was unlike a *Reich* Councillor to confide in a mere policeman, even one with a *very* powerful relative. "It might have been a lucky shot."

"Holliston always hated economics," Krueger said. He sounded more as if he were speaking to himself, rather than to anyone else. "I would keep telling him we couldn't afford his grand projects and he would keep arguing, as if we could just print some more money and solve all of our problems."

Herman nodded. "How many people were in the building?"

"We evacuated most of the bureaucrats last week," Krueger said. "There shouldn't have been more than a skeleton staff."

"That's a relief," he said. A large percentage of the *Reich's* population would probably have cheered, if a few thousand bureaucrats were killed, but they *were* the ones who kept the *Reich* going. "Did he know that?"

"I have no idea," Krueger said. "But he wouldn't want to hit the *Reichstag* itself."

Herman frowned, inwardly, as Krueger strode off, a handful of armed bodyguards appearing from nowhere to escort him. No, the SS *wouldn't* want to target the *Reichstag*, but accidents happened. It was easy - all too easy - to imagine a missile going astray and coming down on top of the building, killing his only daughter. He hoped Gudrun would have had the sense to stay out of such an obvious target, but he hadn't heard anything from her since her return from France. She hadn't even found time to join the rest of the family for dinner.

He shook his head slowly as he turned his attention to the wreckage. Kurt was in danger too, somewhere along the border line, but Kurt was a young *man*. Kurt could handle himself. Herman had made sure of it, teaching Kurt how to take a punch and come up fighting. Gudrun, on the other hand, was a young woman, someone who needed protecting…and he felt helpless to protect her. He couldn't help wondering if he'd failed as a father.

"Get the buildings around the debris evacuated," he ordered, tiredly. He'd been on duty all night, but there was little hope of actually getting some sleep. "And then see if we can organise teams to drag the bodies out of the wreckage."

His radio buzzed. "Wieland?"

"Here," Herman said, lifting the radio to his mouth. "Go ahead."

"Take a car and go to the transit barracks," the dispatcher ordered. "There's been a murder."

Herman cursed under his breath as he passed command to one of the other policemen - the chain of command had been blown to hell by the uprising - and then summoned a driver to take him to the transit barracks. It was a relief - an immense relief - that the streets were almost deserted. Far too many young men and women had defied the curfew in the days following the uprising - and the police couldn't give them a good kicking any longer - but the bombardment had brought home the realities of war to Berlin. There were no cars on the streets. Most people, he hoped, would have the sense to stay inside.

He fiddled with the radio as the police car raced through the lightening streets, but heard nothing apart from patriotic music. *That* might be a mistake, he told himself; the provisional government needed to make *some* kind of statement before the rumours started to get out of hand. He made a mental note to discuss it with his superiors, then braced himself as the car came to a halt outside the transit barracks. The gates were wide open, with five policemen standing guard. None of them looked very happy to be there. He climbed out of the car and strode towards him. They stood to attention slowly, too slowly. It wasn't hard to deduce that they were retired policemen who'd been called back to the uniform.

"Report," he snapped.

"Karl was killed," one of them said. He sounded furious, yet scared. "Someone rammed a pencil into his eye."

Herman sucked in his breath as they led him towards the guardpost. The ordinary inhabitants of the transit barracks were watched at all times, but they hadn't had the manpower to keep an eye on the refugees, even if they *hadn't* been good Germans. And yet, if they'd murdered a policeman…he glanced towards the closed and locked door, then cursed mentally. The murderer was probably long gone.

"I assume you locked the door," he said. "Did you think to count the refugees?"

"There was never an accurate count," the spokesman reminded him. "We don't know who's missing."

Herman scowled. He'd *been* there when the refugees had been counted, but record-keeping hadn't been a priority. There had been so much chaos that he wouldn't have been surprised if a handful of the refugees hadn't been registered at all. And even if the murderer *had* been registered, he might well have given a false name. In theory, every citizen of the *Reich* was supposed to have a dossier; in practice, the registry system had broken down during the uprising and never recovered.

He knelt down next to the body, examining it thoughtfully. There was no reason to doubt the guard's deduction, not when the pencil was clearly visible. It had been driven through the poor bastard's eyeball and thrust straight into his brain, causing instant death. There was no sign of a struggle, suggesting that he had been caught by surprise. And yet, what manner of policeman let a complete stranger approach him without going on guard. The old fear was gone now. A civilian on the verge of being arrested might just try to fight back.

A refugee left the barracks, he thought. *And he wouldn't have left unless he had business somewhere within the city.*

A thought struck him. His frown deepened. *He…or she?*

It wasn't a pleasant thought, but it had to be considered. Someone had caught an experienced policeman - and former soldier - by surprise. It was unlikely that a hulking refugee - a *male* refugee - would have managed to do that, not when policemen knew and confronted all of the nasty tricks in the book. But a woman? A woman might be physically weaker than a man - Kurt was stronger than his father now, but Gudrun wasn't - yet she might just be able to surprise her victim. He'd told Gudrun to kick a man between the legs as hard as possible, if she felt threatened; there was no way she could trade blows with a man and survive the experience. It wouldn't be a fair fight, but life was not fair. Besides, only *idiots* liked the idea of a fair fight.

He sucked in his breath as he stood. A refugee had escaped, perhaps more than one. And, perhaps, a woman…there was no way to be sure, but the theory fitted the facts. And if the murderer *was* a woman, she *had* to be working for the SS. There was no other reason to kill a guard and make an escape in the middle of chaos.

"Keep the doors locked until we can get reinforcements," he ordered, finally. He would have to call his superiors and pass on his theory, assuming they didn't demote him for talking nonsense during a war. "And then we can speak to the refugees and find out who's missing."

"There might be more than one," the spokesman said.

Herman shrugged. "We'll find out," he said, as he reached for his radio. "And then we'll find the murderer."

———

Horst couldn't help feeling that the *Reich* Council - and he included Karl Holliston - had been slipping towards degeneracy long before they'd started hiding the truth about the number of soldiers killed or wounded in South Africa. Building a bunker network below Berlin was a sensible precaution - the

British had bombed Berlin repeatedly during the last war - but there was no need to decorate it like some perverse version of Buckingham Palace. His instructors had made him read about the Gates of Fire, back during his training, pointing out that the Spartans had survived on black broth while their Persian enemies had eaten countless fancy dishes at each meal. And each Spartan had been worth a thousand Persians…

And then the Spartans started eating like the Persians, he thought, morbidly. Their king had brought back a fashion for enemy cuisine, according to his instructors. It had been the chink that led to Sparta's inevitable fall. *And here, we are living like the British monarch.*

He turned his head slightly to look at Gudrun, sleeping next to him. Her breasts rose and fell with her breathing, perfect little handfuls that made Horst want to reach out and hold them with his hands. In her unguarded state, she was perfect, the epitome of Germanic beauty. Her mere appearance made him want to hold her, to protect her, to safeguard her from all harm. And yet, she didn't really understand just how hard life could become. The cruise missiles that had struck the city were merely the opening moves in a war that could last for years.

And you are being stupid, he told himself, tartly. *She wasn't born and raised in the east.*

It was an odd thought, one he perversely contemplated for a long moment. Gudrun *was* strong, although not in the way he'd been raised to respect. A weak woman who'd been arrested and held prisoner would have broken long before the strip search, just through not knowing what would happen to her. And Gudrun had kept going, daring the world to do its worst. Maybe she wasn't an eastern woman with one hand stirring the stew pot and the other near a loaded gun. She was still strong and determined to do the best she could, even if she wasn't quite sure what that was now.

The phone rang. He picked it up quickly, hoping it wouldn't disturb Gudrun. "Albrecht."

"*Herr* Albrecht," a voice said. Horst vaguely recognised it as belonging to one of the operating staff, one of the men he'd met when he was surveying the *Reichstag*. "Councillor Wieland is expected in the briefing room, one hour from now."

"Understood," Horst said.

He was tempted to order breakfast, but he had a feeling the staff had far too many other things to do with their time. Instead, he reached over and kissed Gudrun's forehead, gently tapping her until her eyes opened. She tensed automatically, then relaxed as she recognised him. Horst didn't blame her for feeling unsure of herself, even though she'd slept well as far as he could tell. She'd had quite a few nightmares over the last two weeks, after they'd started sleeping together. Now she'd actually overthrown the government - or at least started the ball rolling - she was all too aware of everything that could have gone wrong.

"It's time to get up," he said, quietly. "We have a meeting in an hour."

Gudrun sat upright, holding her arms over her breasts. Horst couldn't help finding it amusing - they were hardly strangers, after all the time they'd spent exploring each other's body - but she'd been raised to be modest. It wasn't as if girls in the east went around topless, he had to admit; they just knew there were worse things than being seen naked by a lover. There were more important things to be worried about.

"Joy," Gudrun said. She looked at him until he turned his back. "What time is it?"

Horst glanced at the wall-mounted clock. "Nine in the morning," he said. He was surprised they'd been allowed to sleep in so late, but circumstances were hardly normal. His old instructors would have roared with laughter at the suggestion that the trainees should be allowed to stay in bed until six in the morning, then sent whoever dared to suggest it on punishment duty. "Are you hungry?"

"Just feeling dirty," Gudrun said. She rose and headed for the shower; Horst turned, just in time to see her bare backside heading through the door. Her voice echoed back a moment later. "Can you order coffee?"

"Of course," Horst said. He picked up the phone and checked the number. "Do you want anything else?"

"No, thank you," Gudrun called.

Horst placed the order, then hunted for his pants and shirt while Gudrun showered herself thoroughly. He was tempted to join her in the shower, but time was definitely not on their side. He'd make sure to have a quick wash once Gudrun was finished, rather than escort Gudrun to the briefing smelling like a pig. He doubted *that* would go down well with the other councillors.

There was a knock at the door five minutes later, which he opened to discover a young dark-haired woman carrying a tray of coffee. He wasn't too surprised to discover that the bunker's kitchens had sent a plate of pastries too.

They must think we acquired a taste for them in France, he thought, as he took the tray and thanked the servant. *It's hard to get French pastries in the Reich without connections.*

He looked up as Gudrun stepped out of the shower, already wearing her bra and panties, then poured the coffee as she finished dressing. Gudrun had had a set of trousers altered to fit her, making her look surprisingly masculine despite her hourglass figure. Horst wasn't sure if it encouraged the other councillors to take her seriously or not - she hadn't sliced off her long hair - but he had to admit the outfit suited her. She definitely looked like someone who *should* be taken seriously.

"This is good coffee," Gudrun said, as she took a sip. "Where does it come from?"

Horst shrugged. "It tastes a bit thin to me," he said. The coffee he'd drunk in Germany East had been a great deal stronger, blacker than Karl Holliston's soul. "It probably comes from France."

Gudrun blinked. "The French grow coffee?"

"I have no idea," Horst admitted.

He contemplated the problem for a long moment. The *Reich* grew coffee in Germany Arabia, if he recalled correctly, but the *real* coffee connoisseurs spent hundreds of *Reichmarks* on imported coffee from South America. Argentina had even tried to flood the market after the country had been defeated in the Falklands War. Maybe they'd sold it to the French who then skirted import/ export restrictions by selling it onwards to Germany. And somehow he wasn't too surprised that the bunker had good coffee, at least by Germany Prime's standards.

There's probably a wine cellar somewhere below us too, he thought, darkly. *And I'd bet good money that the staff don't get to drink either the wine or the good coffee.*

"It doesn't matter," he said, instead. "All that matters is surviving the next few weeks."

He rose, leaving her to eat the pastries as he showered. They hadn't had the time to bring spare clothes down into the bunker, but one of the wardrobes held a selection of basic clothing in various sizes. It didn't take him long to find something suitable, even if it clearly *had* been designed for someone with a paunch. He made a mental note to bring more clothes down into the bunker, if they stayed where they were, then headed back to Gudrun. She'd wiped her hands and was now eying the clock nervously.

She glanced at him as they opened the door. "Is it wrong of me to be nervous?"

"Only a complete fool *isn't* scared," Horst said. His instructors had taught him that everyone - almost everyone - felt fear. It was how they coped with it, they'd warned, that determined what sort of man they were. But then, after weeks of running through hazardous death traps pretending to be tactical exercises, it was hard to feel fear in actual combat. "But you're not on the front lines."

Gudrun looked down, her face briefly stricken. Horst felt a stab of guilt - Gudrun's brother *was* on the front lines - and pushed it aside, savagely. She was at a loose end; she needed to find a purpose, now that the war had begun. And he had no intention of letting her fall back into bad old habits, after all she'd already done.

"There's nothing you can do about the danger," he added, after a moment. He had no idea just how many cruise missiles had been stationed in Germany East, but Holliston had quite a few bombers at his disposal. It wouldn't be long before they started hitting Berlin, unless the *Luftwaffe* kept them back. "All you can do is carry on as best as possible."

"Thanks," Gudrun said, dryly.

Horst smiled. "You're welcome."

CHAPTER SIXTEEN

𝔑ear 𝔚arsaw, 𝔊ermany 𝔓rime
13 𝔖eptember 1985

"The enemy have managed a handful of successful air attacks," *Sturmbannfuehrer* Friedemann Weineck reported. "They didn't manage to take out any of the main bridges, but a number of pontoons have been smashed."

"Then get them repaired," *Oberstgruppenfuehrer* Alfred Ruengeler snarled. "They're *designed* to be repaired quickly."

He scowled. The commandos had done good work, but they hadn't taken out *every* aircraft and some of those pilots were good, damned good. He was reluctant to admit it, yet it could not be denied that a couple of the HE-477 pilots were very definitely just as good as some of their SS CAS counterparts. They'd taken losses, of course - four aircraft had been shot out of the sky, one managing to slam into a pontoon bridge as it crashed - but they'd definitely slowed up the advance.

Not that I expected any differently, he reminded himself. *I planned on the assumption that there would be many more delays.*

The traitors were playing it smart, he had to admit. They weren't trying to stand and fight, even when they seemed to hold a local advantage; they were slipping into range, landing a couple of blows and then darting backwards to escape retaliation. It was costing him more time than anything else, but the more time he lost the longer it would be before he could reach Berlin. By now, the traitor government *had* to know the war had begun.

We dropped cruise missiles into Berlin, he thought, sardonically. *They'd have to be very stupid not to know the war has begun.*

"The gunners are reporting that enemy fire is continuing, but only on a sporadic level," Weineck stated. "They're trying hard to suppress enemy fire."

"Good," Alfred growled. He eyed the red telephone darkly, expecting it to ring at any moment. The *Führer* would want an update soon, he was sure. "And the forward units?"

"Moving forward carefully," Weineck informed him. "The coordinators are moving the second-line units forward now."

"Remind them to move additional AA units to the bridges," Alfred said. He'd earmarked those units for supporting the advance - he knew, all too well, that the *Luftwaffe* had several tactical advantages - but he'd underestimated their ability to threaten the bridges. "I don't want a single aircraft to get through our fire."

"*Jawohl,*" Weineck said.

Alfred sat back, trying to relax. His junior officers knew what they were doing, he told himself firmly. They were all experienced men, blooded in South Africa and the constant low-level war against the Slavs. They'd see whatever opportunities existed and take advantage of them, he knew. And yet, he wanted to watch through their eyes as they continued the advance. He needed to know what they were seeing.

And they don't need you looking over their shoulder, he reminded himself. Micromanaging would only make their task harder. *They'll do the job. You can count on it.*

The red phone rang. Alfred bit down a comment that would probably be reported, if he said it out loud, and reached for the phone. It was time to give his report. He just hoped the *Führer* was prepared to listen.

———

Obersturmfuehrer Hennecke Schwerk was tense, very tense, as he led his platoon down the road. The *Hauptsturmfuehrer* who had been in command had already been killed by a prowling aircraft, his vehicle targeted and blown into flaming ruins before he'd even known he was under attack. Hennecke had assumed command at once, as his training had dictated, but he couldn't help feeling as though he was badly unprepared for the task. This was not Germany East or South Africa. This was Germany Prime…

Hatred seethed in his gut as he prowled forward, listening carefully for the first *hint* of an enemy presence. How *dare* the westerners turn on the *Reich*? Didn't they *know* the fate that awaited the *Volk*, if the *Volk* grew weak? Hennecke had seen the aftermath of too many insurgent attacks - in both Germany East and South Africa - to have any delusions about what would happen if he fell into their hands. It was the kind of madness that could never be allowed to run free. Give an *Untermensch* a hint of freedom - as a handful of idiots had found out over the years - and he would stick a knife in your chest, castrate your sons and rape your daughters. He knew it, as surely as he knew his own name. The *Volk* could not allow itself to become weak or the *Volk* would be lost.

Sweat trickled down his back as he eyed the forest, wondering if the enemy were lurking within the shadows. He could hear explosions and gunfire in the distance, but there was no sign of anything hostile nearby. That proved nothing, he reminded himself, as they inched forwards. The insurgents in Germany East were masters at using the endless forests and mountains for camouflage, knowing that a single mistake would attract a prowling aircraft or a commando team. Those that weren't experts had been exterminated long ago. He tensed, again, as he heard something fluttering within the darkness, then sighed in relief as he saw a bird flying through the trees. But what had disturbed the bird...

He hit the ground, instinctively, as a shot cracked out. A soldier behind him wasn't so lucky; he crumpled to the ground, gasping in pain. Hennecke ignored him as he used hand-signals to deploy his men, ordering one section to lay down covering fire while a second section crawled off to the right, trying to outflank the enemy position. He took command of the third section and led it towards the enemy personally, even though he knew he should probably stay in the rear. The *Hauptsturmfuehrer* might have been able to lead from the rear, but Hennecke knew *he* didn't have that sort of authority.

The sound of shooting grew louder as the first section opened fire, bullets snapping through the trees and sending branches crashing to the ground. Hennecke would have been surprised if they actually hit anything - the enemy had had plenty of time to prepare their ambush - but it would certainly make it harder for the bastards to retreat. Unless, of course, they'd prepared their fallback position too. Hennecke disliked the idea of running from the enemy as much as the next *Waffen-SS* Stormtrooper, but there was nothing to be gained by sacrificing their lives for nothing. Their enemies *had* to know they wouldn't slow down the advance with a handful of shots…

He paused as he saw the enemy position come into view, a firing point that had clearly been prepared some time in advance. But then, securing one of the roads that led off the *autobahn* was clearly a priority for *any* attacking force. He paused long enough to signal his men, then unhooked a grenade from his belt and threw it towards the enemy. The enemy turned, too late, as the grenade exploded. Hennecke barked orders for the first section to stop firing as it detonated, then led the charge forward. A man turned, trying to bring his rife up into firing position; Hennecke shot him in the chest and watched him crumple backwards, feeling nothing. The traitor had gotten away lightly. A second man hurled his rifle to the ground and held his hands in the air. Hennecke kicked him down, searched him roughly and then kept a foot on his neck as the second section caught up with them.

"Two prisoners," he noted. "And four dead men."

He glared down at the prisoners, quietly accessing them. Very few of the stormtroopers had any respect for the *Wehrmacht*, but even *they* doubted that the *Wehrmacht* was composed of overweight soldiers. The basic training routines were largely identical, after all. No, the men who had barred their way were reservists, men called back to the colours to fight after a long spell in civilian life. He felt a sudden surge of hatred as he took in their condition. The prisoners had been living the easy life in Germany Prime, while he and his comrades had been fighting and dying to cleanse Germany East of its *Untermenschen* infestation. And now they had had the nerve to try to bar their way into Germany Prime…

Orders made it clear; prisoners were to be taken, if possible. But he would have to spare a couple of men to guard the prisoners, at least until an MP unit arrived to take them into custody and transport them to a detention camp on the other side of the river. He couldn't spare the men, he told himself; he was damned if he was risking the offensive for the sake of two traitors. Besides, he was sure no one would really care if the prisoners survived or not. They would never be released, not after taking up arms against the *Waffen-SS*; they'd spend the rest of their life in a concentration camp.

He cocked his pistol and pointed it at the first prisoner's head. The man's eyes went wide with fear and shock, even though he'd *known* that stormtroopers were rarely in the habit of taking prisoners. Hennecke smelt the tell-tale scent of urine as he took aim, then pulled the trigger. The prisoner jerked; his comrade opened his mouth to scream, but Hennecke shot him before he could make a sound. None of his men objected. They all knew what happened to prisoners, particularly insurgents. Indeed, Hennecke had given them an easier fate than they deserved.

Bastards, Hennecke thought.

"Leave the bodies," he ordered, as they scooped up the weapons. "Let's move."

———

"The advance is proceeding as well as can be expected, *Mein Fuhrer*," Alfred said. "We are advancing along the planned routes, slowly clearing out the enemy pockets as we encounter them."

"Good," Holliston said. "And the air defence of the bridges?"

Alfred kept his voice steady with an effort. *Someone* had clearly been telling tales to Germanica. He wasn't really surprised to know there was an agent or two within his command staff - although he supposed it could have been an officer attached to the bridges - but it was still annoying. Holliston was a born intriguer, with political skills that Alfred knew outmatched his own, yet he was no military officer. He might well demand something his men couldn't offer.

"The defences have been reinforced," he said, fighting down the urge to point out that he'd been *assured* that most of the enemy aircraft would be put out of service. "There will not be a second successful attack on the bridges."

"Good," Holliston said, after a long chilling pause. "And the enemy pockets?"

"They're behaving as we anticipated," Alfred said. If the traitors *had* managed to move hundreds of panzers from west to east, they might well have taken the risk of thrusting forwards and catching his forces as they tried to cross the river. "They're engaging us briefly, then falling back. I believe they are very definitely conserving their resources."

"Then continue the advance," Holliston ordered. "They are to have no time to prepare a tougher defence."

Alfred scowled. Holliston didn't see it, but the traitors *were* mounting a tough defence. Instead of lining up to be destroyed - that sort of idiotic behaviour was only seen in bad movies about French soldiers - they were slowing his panzers down, putting the offensive behind schedule while gathering their own forces. He'd assumed, right from the start, that there *would* be slippage, that matters would not proceed as fast as Holliston hoped. He had seen enough exercises to prove, to his own satisfaction, that timetables were nothing more than rough estimates.

But the *Führer* might think differently. It was less than two hundred miles from Warsaw to Berlin, as the crow flew. And a panzer could cover that distance in a few hours, if nothing happened to get in its way…

"I understand, *Mein Fuhrer*," he said. "The offensive will proceed as fast as possible."

"Very good," Holliston said. "Keep me updated."

Alfred sighed, inwardly, as the line disconnected. One of the operators was updating the ammunition consumption chart, warning him that stockpiles of ammunition were being used up faster than his worst-case estimates. There weren't any major shortages - yet - but it was only a matter of time before they faced serious problems. Germany East could produce millions of rifle rounds, if necessary…producing panzer shells and bombs was far harder.

But they will be in the same boat, he thought. *They'll have the same problem too.*

He sucked in his breath. The *Reich* had built up colossal stockpiles, after nearly running out of bombs and bullets during the last major war. But logistics had always been a secondary concern. Hitler had believed that Germans could muddle through, whatever happened, and had chosen to ignore how logistics constrained their operations. But it was growing alarmingly clear that all of the pre-war estimates had been badly inaccurate.

And we have been at war for less than a day, he thought. *What will happen if we keep expending ammunition at the same rate for the next two weeks?*

———

From his vantage point, Eduard Selinger could see the SS panzers as they advanced, one by one, down the *autobahn*. They'd clearly learned a few lessons, he noted to himself; the panzers were spread out, just to ensure that an air attack couldn't catch more than one or two of the vehicles before the aircraft had to beat a retreat. A pair of helicopters hung overhead, swinging from side to side as they watched for potential threats; high overhead, a pair of fast-jet fighters were clearly visible. In the distance, he could see a number of mechanized infantrymen, hanging back to allow the panzers to take the brunt of any ambush.

Makes sense, he told himself, as he peered through the scope. *But there isn't an antitank team waiting in ambush.*

He smiled, rather coldly, as he caught sight of the panzer commanders. They were perched on top of their panzers, their eyes scanning the horizon for significant threats rather than staying firmly buttoned down in their vehicles. Eduard didn't blame them - it was harder to keep track of what was going on inside a panzer - but it made them vulnerable. They'd be ready to duck down the moment something happened, yet…he'd still have the first shot.

I stalked insurgents in South Africa, he thought. Carefully, he took aim at the lead commander and squeezed the trigger. *This is easy…*

The rifle fired. He moved rapidly to the next target and pulled the trigger again, trusting that he had hit the first target. The third target was already ducking down, moving with commendable speed; Eduard fired a shot anyway, in hopes of winging him. It didn't look as though he'd succeeded, but at least he was sure his target knew he'd come very close to death. The panzers would be rather more careful about advancing now.

He rolled over, set the booby trap and headed for his escape route as the sound of approaching helicopters grew louder. They wouldn't know *precisely* where he was, but the pilots would be experienced enough to shoot at any hint of movement and ask questions later. He dived down the gully and held himself still, hoping that his camouflage was enough to keep him hidden from prying eyes. The rattle of gunfire sounded, moments later, but it didn't seem to be aimed anywhere near him. But as the helicopters passed overhead, he heard the sound of advancing infantry behind them. It was time to move.

Gritting his teeth, he crawled down the gully, reminding himself that he didn't dare be taken alive. The SS wasn't known for honouring the rules of war, but snipers rarely survived encounters with the *Heer*, let alone the *Waffen-SS*. He'd be lucky if they merely shot him in the head. Behind him, he heard a loud explosion as someone triggered the IED he'd placed near his hiding place. If he were lucky, the stormtroopers would slow down and advance carefully, suspecting that there were dozens of other IEDs in place. It was a common insurgent trick…

But not one I used, he reminded himself. There hadn't been time to lay a network of traps, even if he'd had the explosives. *And the moment they realise they've been tricked, they'll pick up speed.*

He glanced upwards as the helicopters started to return, willing himself to stay as still as possible. Someone on the other side had thought quickly, he admitted silently; the advancing infantrymen were the beaters, trying to force him to break cover, while the helicopters were ready to snipe him when he showed himself. He was tempted to remain still in the hopes the infantrymen would miss him, but it was too risky. The stormtroopers had been chasing insurgents for decades. They knew all the tricks.

Another burst of gunfire rattled out overhead, followed by an explosion. Eduard frowned, puzzled. He doubted the SS were firing missiles at random, not when each missile cost more *Reichmarks* than the average soldier earned in a year. And the explosion hadn't been anywhere near him…he glanced up, again, as a streak of light flashed across the sky, followed by a jet aircraft. He smiled openly as he realised what had happened. One of the patrolling ME-356s had seen the convoy and decided to attack.

A stroke of luck, he thought, as more gunfire echoed behind him. It was probably futile - jet fighters were faster than speeding bullets - but it worked in his favour. The advancing stormtroopers would be more interested in seeking cover than giving chase. Hell, the panzers would be in *real* trouble. A jet fighter's cannon could inflict significant damage. *Time to leave.*

Picking up speed, he crawled faster. Behind him, the sound of pursuit faded away.

CHAPTER SEVENTEEN

Berlin, Germany Prime
13 September 1985

"I'm sorry," the guard said. "Only councillors are allowed past this point."

Gudrun looked at Horst, who shrugged. "I'll get some of our stuff from the surface," he said, shortly. "Don't worry about it."

The guard looked uncomfortable. Gudrun couldn't help feeling sorry for him. On one hand, he had his orders; on the other, making an enemy out of a councillor could make his life very uncomfortable. *She* wouldn't send him to Siberia - assuming it was possible - but he had no way to know it. Shaking her head - she would have to do something to convince the guards that the provisional government wasn't as bad as the former council - she nodded to Horst and stepped through the door. Volker Schulze was sitting at the table, reading a detailed report; the remainder of the council was nowhere to be seen. Gudrun took a seat and waited, patiently, for the others to join them.

"The war has begun," Schulze said, once the entire council had been assembled and the doors firmly closed. "Field Marshal?"

Field Marshal Gunter Voss nodded from where he was sitting. "We just re-established contact with the front lines," he said. "The SS has launched a major offensive against us and is currently pushing into the teeth of our defences. My staff are still pulling the reports together, but it is clear that we severely underestimated their ability to disrupt our preparations. It may be some time before we are able to stop them."

If we can, Gudrun thought. She felt cold. *If they take Berlin, everyone in this room is doomed.*

"Right now, we are skirmishing with the advance elements as planned, bleeding them while preserving as much of our own firepower as possible," Voss added. "However, they have gained a number of advantages, including localised air supremacy. I do not expect to be able to stop them short of Berlin."

Kruger leaned forward. "Can't you speed up the process of moving troops from the west?"

"I was getting to that," Voss said.

He nodded towards the map on the wall. Someone had been marking the paper with red ink, each one - Gudrun assumed - representing a missile strike. She was no expert, but she couldn't help noticing that a number of strikes had taken place to the west. And yet, was she reading the map wrong? Why would the SS strike targets that were not in their way?

Voss explained. "My staff have reports of commando strikes and missile attacks targeting bridges to the west of Berlin," he said. "While those strikes have done relatively little damage, they *have* successfully delayed our movements. Getting panzers from the west eastwards will take weeks, more time - perhaps - than we have. We're currently working on reworking the operational plan to account for the lost bridges - we can throw up pontoons ourselves, if necessary - but it will take time."

"And perhaps allow them to secure the armoured forces without a fight," Schulze observed, darkly. "If we lose…"

"Yes, *Herr Chancellor*," Voss said. "It would be unrealistic of us to expect isolated units to continue to fight on after Berlin falls."

He took a long breath. "The offensive is only nine hours old," he added. "I expect we will have a clear idea of their true rate of advance by the end of the day, but such matters are always very variable. We will be targeting their bridges with as much enthusiasm as they targeted ours, for example. And they will need to stop and resupply their forces from time to time. Our stay-behind units may have a chance to give them another bloody nose."

"Thank you," Schulze said. He glanced at *Generalfeldmarschall* Markus Brandenburg, who looked grim. "What happened to the *Luftwaffe*?"

"We took a bloody nose," Brandenburg said. He sounded angry at his own words. "They attacked a number of airbases, killing or wounding well over three hundred pilots as well as destroying a number of planes. Our hopes of air supremacy were destroyed with them, *Herr Chancellor*. We may have to husband our remaining fast-jet fighters just to keep a protective shroud over Germany Prime."

He glared at the map, as if it had personally offended him. "The SS always controlled far too many CAS aircraft," he added. "They have a very definite advantage in that category."

"Because you refused to fly them for us," Voss snapped. "You never wanted the *Heer* to have its own air arm."

"It flies, it's ours," Brandenburg snapped back. "If that principle had been honoured, the SS wouldn't be anything like a major threat!"

Schulze slapped the table, hard. "*Enough*," he said, sharply. "There is no point in trying to refight the battles of the past. We must grapple with the situation facing us, rather than the situation we would wish."

Gudrun nodded in agreement. Her father had been a young man when the *Luftwaffe* had stubbornly insisted on hoarding all aircraft to itself, even though both the *Heer* and the *Kriegsmarine* had wanted aircraft of their own. She wasn't sure how the SS had managed to build up its own air force, but she had a feeling - reading between the lines - that CAS aircraft were seen as inherently less glamorous than fast-jet fighters. And yet, when fighting a counterinsurgency, fast-jet fighters were far less useful than slow but precise bombers.

"Yes, *Herr Chancellor*," Brandenburg said. He paused. "We are looking at ways to move support aircraft back from South Africa, but that will require some degree of cooperation from the French. Can we trust them to help us?"

Schulze looked at Gudrun. "Your thoughts?"

"The French aren't stupid," Gudrun said. It flew in the face of pre-uprising orthodoxy, but she didn't care. "I think they understand, deep inside, that an SS victory spells doom for France. Holliston is not going to let them get away with trying to take advantage of the *Reich's* problems for themselves. The panzers that roll through Berlin will *keep* rolling until they reach Vichy. I don't expect the French to do anything that might *prevent* us winning the war."

"Unless they're scared of Holliston," Foreign Minister Engelhard Rubarth grunted. "They won't want him to blame them for *anything*."

Kruger snorted. "Is there anything they can do," he asked rhetorically, "that will cleanse them of the shame, in his eyes, of being born *French*?"

Gudrun nodded. Holliston was not likely to show mercy to the French, not when the French had already played a minor role in setting the stage for the uprising. He'd need a foreign enemy to reunite the shattered *Reich* and the French would make excellent candidates. The German population was already conditioned to look down on them, while their ability to *resist* a panzer-led invasion was almost non-existent. Invading Vichy France and snuffing out their government would accomplish multiple goals for Holliston. Gudrun had never met him in person, but if what she'd heard was true, the simplicity would appeal to him.

"Then discuss it with them as a matter of urgency," Schulze said. He looked at Rubarth. "Is there anything new from the rest of the world?"

"The Italians have offered a couple of combat-ready divisions," Rubarth said. He didn't sound pleased. "The Turks have, so far, agreed to keep forces from transiting through their territory into Germany Prime, but that may not last."

"Italians," Voss said. "Do they want us to lose?"

"The Italian government may not last for much longer anyway," Rubarth said. "I don't think we can count on them."

"Of course not," Schulze said. "And economically?"

"Still pretty bad," Kruger said. "But we should be able to keep things fairly stable for the next few weeks. A long drawn-out war will kill us."

Gudrun nodded. Thousands of factory workers had been called to the colours, while others had founded dozens of new unions and were competing for increased wages, reduced hours and political accountability. Schulze must find it annoying, she suspected; he'd *started* the union movement, only to see it grow out of control. Cracking down on unions wouldn't be any easier for the provisional government than it had been for the *Reich* Council.

"Keep me informed," Schulze said, addressing Voss. "The rest of us...we carry on."

"We have no choice," Kruger said. "The future of the *Reich* itself is at stake."

"Yes," Schulze said. "And that leads to a question. Do we accept the American offer of covert assistance?"

"Out of the question," Voss said, immediately. "We would save the *Reich* from Holliston, only to become a suburb of Washington DC. The Americans will demand a high price for their help."

"Beggars can't be choosers," Morgenstern pointed out. "And we *are* beggars. What price our national pride if the nation itself is lost?"

Gudrun frowned, inwardly. Hilde Morgenstern had complained, loudly, about being sent to America. Indeed, she'd even talked about running off before reluctantly submitting to her father's insistence that she take the flight out of Berlin. For once, Morgenstern had shown actual *firmness* in dealing with his daughter, something that surprised and bothered Gudrun more than she cared to admit. She knew what would have happened if *she'd* talked back to her father like Hilde - she wouldn't have been able to sit comfortably for several days - but Hilde had always been a spoilt brat. Morgenstern was clearly more worried than he wanted to let on about the outcome of the war.

"Holliston will use it against us," Voss predicted.

"The Americans will soon be sending their spying aircraft overhead," Brandenburg predicted, dourly. "We may as well ask for copies of the photographs."

Schulze blinked in surprise. "You can't stop them?"

"It was never easy to stop those damnable planes while the air defence network was actually fully integrated," Brandenburg admitted. "The Americans would buzz our network from time to time, sending aircraft over the *Reich*… all of which were too high or too fast to shoot down. Even when we *did* hit an aircraft and bring it down, we never talked about it."

Gudrun frowned. No one had told her *that* before. But then, the *Reich* Council would not have wanted to admit that the Americans could fly through the *Reich's* airspace at will. Even shooting one or more of the aircraft down wouldn't be enough to make up for the humiliation of *knowing* the defence network could be penetrated. No wonder the *Reich* Council had never levelled *that* charge against the Americans. It was something that could easily rebound on them.

"They will make us pay an immense price," Voss predicted, sharply. "Does it not suit them to keep us fighting each other?"

"Yes, it does," Morgenstern said. He sounded oddly forceful. "But it does not suit them to have an SS-run government in Berlin. They can do business with us, Field Marshal, while they could not talk to Holliston."

"And bringing the arms race to an end can only benefit us," Kruger added. "It was pushing us towards bankruptcy even before the uprising."

"It will make us weak," Voss said. "And the Americans will take advantage of it."

"We will still have our nukes," Rubarth pointed out. "There will be limits to how far they can push us around and they will know it."

"Oh," Voss said. "Are you prepared to risk a nuclear war to keep France under our thumb?"

Rubarth looked back at him. "Are *they* prepared to risk a nuclear war to get France *out* from under our thumb?"

"Probably not," Schulze said. "We will talk to the Americans. And if they charge an unacceptable price, we will decline their assistance."

"We are not in a good position to bargain," Rubarth commented. "And they know that too."

On that note, the meeting ended.

———

Berlin was tense, Andrew Barton noted, as the car flowed towards the *Reichstag*. A couple of buildings had been blown into piles of rubble - a number of nearby buildings had been damaged by flying debris - but the remainder of the city was largely undamaged. And yet, Berliners seemed torn between fear and a growing hatred and defiance of the SS. The speakers he recalled from the days since the uprising were gone; instead, men were lining up outside recruiting offices and drilling with weapons, readying themselves for the coming onslaught. He smiled, despite himself, as he spotted a number of blonde-haired maidens studying battlefield medicine in one of the parks. They probably wouldn't be allowed to fight - the *Reich* rarely allowed women in the combat arms - but they'd be able to do their bit to support the men.

They would have had some practical first aid training in school, he recalled. *And all they have to do is build on it.*

He rolled his eyes at the thought. There were few advantages to German-style education, but he had to admit that German schoolchildren received a great deal of practical education in everything from cooking to basic medicine and first aid. Indeed, while there were puritans in the states who hated the idea of teaching children about sex, the *Reich* made sure its children knew the facts of life before they started having children of their own. And yet, none of the textbooks he'd seen discussed contraception. Even *condoms* were restricted, available only to housewives who'd already had at least four children.

The car rolled into the underground garage and came to a halt. Two armed men stepped forward as the driver opened the door, both wearing body armour instead of the ceremonial uniforms he was used to seeing. They frisked him as soon as he was out of the car, making sure he wasn't carrying anything dangerous. Security had always been tight around the *Reichstag*, but now the shooting had finally begun…they'd be twice as paranoid and four times as willing to do whatever it took to keep their leaders safe.

Not that we are any different, Andrew thought, as he was escorted into an elevator that headed upwards as soon as the doors hissed closed. *There's a ring of steel around the White House too.*

The doors opened, revealing that he'd been brought to the very highest level. Offhand, he couldn't recall anyone - even Ambassador Turtledove - who had been invited so high, a sign that the *Reich* took the matter very seriously. Normally, diplomatic meetings were held in a lower office specially set aside for that purpose. But now…he straightened up as he was shown into Chancellor Schulze's office. The man looked very tired.

"Chancellor," he said, in flawless German. "Thank you for inviting me."

"The invitation was a little vague," Schulze said. His English was badly-accented, but passable. He'd have been a child when English had practically been a mandatory second language in the *Reich*. "Am I to assume you are *not* a simple attaché?"

"Yes," Andrew said. Morgenstern would have taken his words to Schulze, he knew. There was nothing to be gained by pretending to be something he wasn't, not now. "I have authority to discuss certain matters with you."

Schulze's eyebrows rose. "And Ambassador Turtledove knows nothing?"

"Ambassador Turtledove understands that certain matters can only be discussed under the table, so to speak," Andrew said. He was surprised that Schulze hadn't picked a representative of his own, briefed him carefully and then ordered *him* to handle the discussions. He'd have to consider what that might mean later. "My presence here is completely deniable."

"One would hope so," Schulze said. He sat back in his chair. "I am no diplomat, *Herr* Barton, and I have no time to waste dancing around the issue. What are you prepared to offer and what do you want in exchange?"

Andrew took a moment to gather his thoughts. Schulze had thrown him off, deliberately or otherwise. There was no way to know if it was genuine or a deliberate attempt to appear either unconcerned…or naive. And yet, he had to respect Schulze's wishes. The United States was in a strong position, but it wasn't *that* strong. Failing to come to an agreement might just ensure that the SS won the war.

"What we have to offer depends on what you want," he said, bluntly. He had the feeling that Schulze wouldn't be impressed if Andrew tried to temporise. "At the very basic level, we can offer satellite imagery, as I showed Morgenstern; I believe you will find it superior to anything produced by the *Reich*."

Schulze showed no overt reaction, but he twitched very slightly. Andrew smiled. The NSA would be pleased to hear that the *Reich* was far behind them in orbital imagery, although it couldn't be taken for granted. There was a point beyond which the law of diminishing returns came into effect.

"We can also provide a certain level of logistical support," he added, after a moment. "Our President is unwilling to actually commit American forces to your war, but otherwise…give us a list of requests and we will try to meet them."

"I see," Schulze said. "And what do you want in return?"

Andrew sighed. The thorny issue of payment had been debated hotly in Washington and London, ensuring that he'd been sent several contradictory sets of orders. A number of politicians had wanted to try to ensure that the *Reich* was rolled back to a more manageable size, but several generals had pointed out that the provisional government would either refuse outright or go back on the agreement after the war. The price had to be something they could live with, afterwards.

"Two things," he said, bluntly. "First, we want an end to the war in South Africa. You pull your forces out, taking with you any South Africans who want to go."

"Finding living space for them won't be easy," Schulze said, flatly. He didn't seem inclined to refuse. "They will have to go to Germany South or Germany East."

Andrew nodded. "Second, we would want an end to tariff barriers and free trade," he added, carefully. *This* was likely to be the sticking point. "We want to be able to trade with France and the rest of Europe."

"That may be harder," Schulze said. He smiled for the first time. "We will have to haggle."

CHAPTER EIGHTEEN

Near Warsaw, Germany Prime
13 September 1985

"They're coming," the radio operator said. "I just picked up the warning."

Kurt nodded, shortly. The first reports had come in just before dawn, a series of commando and missile attacks all along the front. Only an idiot would have *failed* to realise that the war had just begun, even before the first flight of aircraft had screamed overhead, heading west towards the inner defence lines. The war was definitely underway.

He glanced along the defence line as the seconds ticked by, wondering just how long they had before the *Waffen-SS* reached the town. It wouldn't take long for a panzer to drive from the bridges to where he was lying in wait, but their way was blocked by snipers, antitank teams and dozens of carefully-concealed IEDs. Kurt doubted a handful of dead or wounded stormtroopers would be enough to stop the SS - the stormtroopers bragged of taking heavy casualties and yet carrying on the mission - yet it would definitely slow them down. The only question was just how *much* it would slow them down.

Not long, he thought, dryly. If they'd received the warning, the enemy was less than a mile away. *And soon we will know how well we've done our work.*

He walked from post to post, checking on his men and making encouraging comments as the seconds ticked away. It was the first taste of combat for many of them, even though they'd endured months of intensive live-fire training before they'd been inducted into the Berlin Guard. Some of them relished the challenge, some of them looked forward to testing themselves against the SS…and some of them were nervous, worried they would let their comrades down when the bullets started flying. They were all volunteers, Kurt reminded himself, but very few men would willingly leave when their comrades were ready to risk life and limb for the *Reich*.

And I wouldn't want them beside me if they were, he thought, as he returned to his post and started to scan the horizon for incoming threats. *They might break and run before I give the* order.

Sweat trickled down his back as he waited, feeling as though time was beginning to slow down. The ground was still, but he could hear explosions and gunfire in the distance; aircraft flashed overhead, briefly visible before racing either east or west. There was no way to determine which side was flying them, let alone what they were doing. He'd been trained to recognise the basic American designs - everything from A-10 Warthogs to F-16 Falcons - but both sides in *this* war used the same equipment. The SS's panzers were largely identical to the *Heer* panzers.

A gross oversight, he thought. An explosion flickered up in the distance, a plume of smoke wafting slowly into the sky. *If they used different aircraft…*

He sucked in his breath as the enemy panzers came into view, advancing forward with grim resolution. He'd known they were big - he'd trained alongside panzer crewmen - but he'd never understood what it meant to watch helplessly as a line of panzers charged a position, moving five abreast. Their main guns moved constantly, searching for targets; they crushed hedges and fences as they advanced, smashing them to dust beneath their treads. A tractor someone had abandoned, years ago, was crushed under the right tread of an advancing panzer, flattened into a pancake-like shape. Kurt knew, as icy fear gnawed at his heart, that he wouldn't last a second if a panzer ran over him. Indeed, *charging* an enemy insurgent with an RPG was regarded as a pretty smart target.

Behind the panzers, he saw a handful of men wearing combat uniforms and carrying rifles, keeping their heads down as they searched for what little cover they could find. There was hardly any, but it didn't stop them. Kurt had to admit they were good, even though they were exposed to his fire. They might well have a good chance of pushing him and his men out of the town, no matter what happened to the panzers.

He reached for the detonator and held it in his hand, silently counting down the last few seconds as the panzers advanced. One of them crashed through a stream as effortlessly as its partner had crushed the tractor, undeterred by the water or mud. Kurt hadn't expected the stream to delay any of the stormtroopers, let alone the panzers, but it was still disconcerting to watch. The panzers would crush the entire town beneath their treads if necessary.

Now, he thought.

He pushed the button, sending the command to the explosives they'd concealed along the approach to the town. The explosion shook the ground savagely, picking up one of the panzers and hurling it over and over until it came to a stop; two more were tipped onto their sides and left lying on the ground, like crabs that had been turned upside down and couldn't right themselves again. His missile crews opened fire seconds later, launching two missiles towards the remaining panzers as they started to lob shells into the town. It was far too late to keep his crews from picking them off, then engaging the advancing stormtroopers. Kurt saw a number of them drop to the ground before the remaining ones started to fall back. They'd be calling for reinforcements now, if he was any judge.

Pulling the whistle from his pocket, he blew it loudly and then hurried out of the post. The missile crews were already running, heading towards the other end of the town; the riflemen fired a handful of additional shots and then started running themselves. It was barely in time; Kurt threw himself down as he heard the aircraft approaching, then covered his head as cannon fire raked the spot where his men had been. The HE-477s retreated into the distance, leaving burning ruins behind. It wouldn't be long before the SS rallied and threw a second offensive into the town.

"Not bad, *Herr Leutnant*," *Oberfeldwebel* Helmut Loeb said, as Kurt reached the RV point. "We gave them a bloody nose."

"Yeah," Kurt muttered. The aircraft were coming back for another pass, their weapons glinting ominously on their wings. "Let's just hope we can get everyone out before they surround the town."

———

Someone had been a right devious bastard, *Obersturmfuehrer* Hennecke Schwerk thought, as he clung to the ground for dear life. Five panzers out of action - two of them would have to be righted before they could go back to war - and over a dozen stormtroopers dead or badly wounded. And getting into the town without being shot down would be far from easy, not when the enemy had near-perfect fields of fire. The town had been a trap and the panzers had driven right into it.

Idiots, he thought, as his radio operator called for help. *They didn't stop to think before advancing.*

The aircraft swooped overhead, engaging the enemy with cannon fire and then dropping a pair of bombs into the town. Hennecke shouted for his men to follow him, then led the charge towards the edge of the town. The enemy had been thoroughly pasted by the aircraft, he thought. They would need time to recover themselves, time he had no intention of giving them. He and his men would be amongst them before they realised that time was not on their side.

A shot cracked out as he reached the first building, narrowly missing him. Someone was hiding in one of the houses; he saw the rifle, just for a second, as the sniper took aim and fired at one of the stormtroopers. Hennecke pulled a grenade from his belt and hurled it towards the house, silently praying that it would smash the window and detonate inside the building. Luck was with him; the explosion blew out the windows, smashing through the interior of the house. The sniper was almost certainly dead or badly wounded, he told himself firmly. There was certainly no sign he was trying to fire again or crawl out of the damaged house.

He used hand signals to direct his men forward, warning them to throw grenades into every house as they moved past. The town would barely be standing, by the time he finished, but it hardly mattered. Any town that housed insurgents - and traitors now - was doomed, by the laws of war in the east. The provisional government should never have turned a good Germanic town into a strongpoint. Its devastation was firmly on their head.

A house exploded with surprising force, throwing a hail of wood and stone debris in all directions. Hennecke ducked low, frowning in puzzlement. The grenades were designed for clearing houses - they contained more explosive than standard grenades - but the house shouldn't have exploded like *that*. It had to have been an ammunitions dump, he decided, or an IED. A second house exploded moments later, catching two of his men in the blast. The bastards hadn't just set a trap, they'd rigged a number of houses to blow!

"Call in fire support," he ordered, tersely. The town was deserted - and marked for destruction. There was no point in risking his men clearing the town when it would be easier just to have the aircraft smash it to rubble. "Tell them we want this town gone!"

————

Kurt had been told - by Konrad - that SS stormtroopers were good, but he'd never really believed it until now. The stormtroopers had recovered from their shock, called in an effective air strike and then thrust forward once again, slamming into the eastern side of the town with staggering force. He'd hoped the IEDs would kill or wound a handful of the bastards, but it looked as though he was out of luck. The stormtroopers were flowing forward with practiced ease, some of them providing covering fire while the others slipped up to houses and threw grenades through the windows. They were systematically destroying the entire town.

Damn them, he thought.

He cursed under his breath as he heard aircraft approaching, then dived for cover as a flight of HE-477s passed overhead, dropping a hail of bombs on the town. The ground shuddered violently; he swore, cursing savagely, as he looked up and saw just how much devastation had been inflicted on the remainder of the town. Flames were rising rapidly, sweeping from house to house. The bombs had to have been more than mere high explosives, he told himself. He'd heard stories about the SS dropping napalm and poison gas to clear towns and villages in Russia, where no one gave a damn what happened to *Untermenschen*, but he wouldn't have thought they'd use such methods in Germany.

But you wouldn't have thought they'd fire on German citizens too, he reminded himself. *And you were there when they did just that.*

"They're pushing infantry around the town," Loeb warned. "We have to go."

"Sound the retreat," Kurt ordered. If the SS managed to seal off their escape route, they'd be in deep trouble. "And call in a strike."

"*Jawohl*," Loeb said.

Kurt took one last look at the burning town, then followed his men as they hurried westwards, leaving nine of their number behind. He hoped, desperately, that their bodies would receive a proper burial, if there was anything left of them to bury. But if the SS was prepared to burn a German town to the ground, they might just be equally willing to dump bodies in ditches or mass graves.

At least we hurt them, he told himself, savagely. He glanced up as he heard the sound of shells, whistling down towards the town. The gunners had orders to fire only a couple of rounds and then shift position, before the SS started trying to silence their fire, but they should give the stormtroopers a few nasty moments. *And if we keep hurting them, maybe we can make the bastards stop.*

———

"Incoming shells!"

Hennecke cursed under his breath as he hit the ground, trying to dig himself into the soil. A moment later, the first round of shells crashed down on the town, smashing what remained of it into rubble. He hoped that was the end of it, but a second barrage slammed down moments later. Aircraft roared overhead, heading west; he hoped, grimly, that they caught the gunners before they could shift position. The mobile gunners were causing problems up and down the line.

He stood, suddenly feeling very tired. The town had been devastated from end to end; there wasn't a single building that wasn't anything more than a blackened ruin. Even the church - which had looked old enough to predate Adolf Hitler - was a pile of debris. He had no qualms about destroying a town that had housed insurgents, but this...this was Germany.

Traitors, he reminded himself. *They deserve to lose everything.*

He lit a cigarette as he took stock of the situation. He'd lost nineteen men in all, not counting the panzer crews. Crushing the town had cost him badly, too badly. It was far too much...he wondered, absently, if he would be relieved for it. The upper ranks would be looking for a scapegoat and the panzer commander, the one who had driven right into the trap, was probably dead. Unfortunately, he'd probably had a chance to breed first...

"Orders from HQ," the radio operator said. "They want us to hold the town until they get reinforcements up to us."

"Understood," Hennecke said.

He shrugged. It wasn't as if the remains of the town were going anywhere.

We'll just have to bulldoze the debris out of the way, he thought, as he directed his men to start patrolling the outskirts. *And then we can start running supply lines down the road towards the autobahn.*

———

Kurt had expected trouble when they retreated, but he'd badly underestimated just how quickly the SS could throw a ring of steel around the town. Indeed, if he hadn't reacted quickly himself, punching through the stormtroopers and escaping into the countryside would have been impossible. He had no intention of seeing the inside of a POW camp - he'd be used against Gudrun, once his captors figured out who he was - but escaping had cost him two more men. By the time he reached the RV point, he was tired, drained and thoroughly sick of the war.

"Grab something to eat, *Herr Leutnant,*" the *Oberfeldwebel* running the RV point said. "The CO will be reorganising the formations over the next couple of hours."

Kurt nodded, too tired to argue. He wasn't blind to the implications, either. He'd hurt the enemy, but he'd taken heavy losses to do it. And the next engagement might be just as bad, costing him worse. And then…he shook his head slowly at the thought. They might run out of manpower before the SS reached Berlin.

He took a bottle of water and sipped it, trying to be optimistic. They'd met the SS and given them a bloody nose - and they'd never *planned* to hold the town. Five panzers destroyed or damaged was hardly a *small* bloody nose. But there was no denying that the enemy was still advancing, doing their best to push the defenders back. And the defenders *were* falling back.

We have more firepower, he told himself, firmly. *All we need is time to get it into position.*

———

Oberstgruppenfuehrer Alfred Ruengeler totted up the reports with a pronounced feeling of displeasure, mixed with a grim pride in his men. After the first set of victories - the bloodless capture of one of the bridges would definitely go down in the history books - his men had started to run into a wily and elusive enemy determined to make them fight for every last inch. Each encounter had cost him badly, forcing him to slow the advance as he ran more panzers and supporting vehicles over the bridges. Indeed, if he hadn't had air superiority, he suspected the offensive would have been stopped in its tracks.

He stood outside the command post, watching the sun sinking slowly in the west. Darkness was falling over the land, bringing the panzers to a halt…although he knew it wouldn't stop the fighting. His stormtroopers were trained and experienced at pushing forward under cover of darkness, keeping the enemy jumpy as the logistics officers struggled to keep the panzers fuelled and armed. They hadn't had a *real* war in far too long, he admitted. And smashing the joint logistics network into rubble hadn't helped either.

But we're advancing towards Berlin, he told himself, firmly. It *was* technically accurate, even though the advance was proceeding at a far slower pace than planned. *And we will reoccupy the city soon.*

He shook his head as he lit a cigarette. His troops were good, but their officers and NCOs were reporting increasingly harsh anti-westerner sentiments. So far, most of the towns and villages they'd stumbled across had been evacuated, yet it was only a matter of time before they encountered civilian populations. And then…he dreaded to think what would happen then. None of his men had been trained to *avoid* civilian casualties.

And the Führer won't give a damn, he thought. He dropped the cigarette on the ground, then stamped on it. *He's already got a list of men and their families he wants to purge.*

Alfred shuddered. There was no way they were going to be able to avoid an incident, no matter how harshly the men were disciplined. And then…if nothing else, the traitors would be able to use it to rally support. No one cared what happened to a bunch of *Untermenschen,* but good Germans? *That* was important.

And if they become committed to their cause, he asked himself, *what happens to us?*

CHAPTER NINETEEN

Berlin, Germany Prime
16 September 1985

Horst followed Gudrun through a hospital, silently marvelling at just how well she was able to connect with the wounded - civilians and soldiers - who had been brought to the building for treatment. She stopped and spoke to all of them, from the soldier who had been shot in the leg by a sniper to the little girl who'd been wounded when flying debris broke her arm, her words - perhaps - making it easier for them to believe that they hadn't been wounded in vain. Gudrun had worried over sounding fake, as if she didn't really care, but her hesitations and moments of silence only added to the effect. She wasn't a radio broadcaster, reading the script; she was someone trying her best to be *real*.

He kept his face impassive as a pair of wounded soldiers flirted cheerfully with her - they would never have dared flirt with anyone else on the council - and tried hard to resist the temptation to organise an extremely dangerous posting for both of them. They *had* been wounded in combat, true, and such wounds carried high status in the *Reich*, but they were flirting with *his* girl. And yet, they didn't *know* Gudrun was his girl. How could they? She wore no wedding ring, nothing to suggest she was anything other than an unmarried young girl. Someone who flirted with a married woman would be in deep shit, but not someone who flirted with an unmarried girl…

You're being an idiot, he told himself, sternly. *She's being nice to them and they are trying to keep themselves from falling into depression.*

Gudrun looked relieved as the tour finally came to an end and they made their way back to the car. Horst felt relieved too, even though they were out in the open without anything like enough security to suit him. Volker Schulze or Hans Kruger would have had a small army protecting them, if they left the bunkers, but Gudrun had only two bodyguards: himself and the driver. Maybe they didn't consider Gudrun *that* important, compared to the two older men...Horst knew, deep inside, that Gudrun *would* be a target. There was such a thing as malice and revenge. Holliston would definitely want Gudrun alive so he could make her death memorable.

"I think you need more security," he said, once the car doors were closed. "You're naked out here with only me."

"I'm not naked," Gudrun said. She glanced down at her jacket, which obscured the shape of her breasts. "Really..."

"You know what I mean," Horst said. Three days of fighting had seen the SS slowly advancing forward, pushing the defenders back. He'd heard nothing from the stay-behind cell, but his training told him that it was merely a matter of time before they got back in touch with him. "You need more security."

Gudrun shook her head. "I don't feel so close to people" - she nodded towards the hospital as they drove away - "when I have a dozen men surrounding me."

"It only takes one person to kill you," Horst said. He'd been nervous all the time they'd been outside the car, although really the car was no true protection. It was bulletproof, but a single RPG or antitank missile would be more than sufficient to turn it into scrap metal. Or a carefully-placed IED. "He might be posing as one of your admirers until the moment he stabs you with a knife."

He signed, knowing he was going to lose the battle. There was no way he could *force* Gudrun to accept more bodyguards, if she didn't *want* to accept more bodyguards, any more than he could force her to stay in the bunker. And she had a point, he had to admit. None of the common citizens had ever seen the *Reich* Council, not without hundreds of bodyguards, detailed security vetting and a strip search before they entered the dome. Gudrun, walking the streets without bodyguards, was far more capable of making a connection with the common citizens.

"I have to take the risk," Gudrun said, stiffly. "There's no choice."

Horst gave her a sharp look. Didn't she *know* the danger? But then, Gudrun had always been brave, sometimes to the point of recklessness. Her family connections wouldn't have saved her, if she'd been fingered as an underground leader, any more than they would save her now from a bullet through the head. A single sniper, perched on a nearby rooftop, could pick her off before anyone realised he was there. But hiding in the bunker would only undermine her connection to the rest of the city.

He said nothing as the car pulled into the underground garage and they made their way down to the bunker. The guards checked their names and faces, then waved them through without comment. Horst had hoped there would be a chance to pick up a briefing from one of the military officers, but the note waiting for them in their suite made it clear that there wouldn't be another formal meeting until later in the day.

"I know you worry about me," Gudrun said, once the door was closed. "But I owe it to myself to take some risks."

"You don't have to," Horst snorted.

"That's the point," Gudrun said. "I don't have to, but I'm going to take them anyway."

She did have a point, Horst conceded, reluctantly. He wouldn't have wanted to be a woman, not when a woman's opinions could be easily dismissed - and her life ruled by the men in her life - but there were *some* advantages. No one in the west expected women to actually fight, to stand and die in defence of the *Reich*. Gudrun might stand up and tell men to fight, yet she would never be asked to fight herself. And while a man would be called a coward if he shirked duty on the front line, a woman would be spared that particular insult.

But she needs to prove herself to the men, he admitted, silently. *Or they won't take her seriously.*

He gave her a quick kiss, then walked out of the bunker, up the stairs and into his bedroom, hoping his habit of checking the room each day hadn't gone unnoticed. The spy - whoever he or she might be - had to be keeping an eye on him. He worried, constantly, about finding the bastard, but a covert check of everyone in the building had turned up nothing. And yet, it wouldn't. The SS would hardly have failed to make sure that their observers had genuine covers. Horst himself was proof of that!

His blood ran cold as he saw the note, positioned provocatively on top of his bed. He sucked his breath in, sharply, as he picked it up, unsure if he should be damning the spy for sheer lack of tradecraft or not. Putting the message in such a blatant position was stupid, but it was also a warning that he was under observation. He'd already known that, of course, yet the message rubbed it in. He wondered grimly just what the observer - and his handler - was thinking, then opened the message. It gave a location, a date and a time, two days in the future. *That* struck him as more than a little odd.

He retrieved the street map of Berlin he'd obtained from the library and checked the location, hoping his memory had failed him. But it hadn't. The location the cell had selected was quite some distance from the *Reichstag*, a place where it would be easy for them to make sure that Horst was alone before he met them. Bringing a small army with him would be impossible, Horst conceded reluctantly. Even getting a pair of covert observers into position to watch proceedings would be fraught with difficulty.

Damn it, he thought. Schwarzkopf - or whoever had taken over, if Schwarzkopf wasn't in charge - had picked a very good spot. *And if I don't show, all hell is going to break loose.*

He sighed. It was time to talk to the Chancellor. Again.

———

Herman wasn't entirely sure why he had been called off duty and told to report directly to the *Reichstag*. Ordinary policemen were *never* invited into the *Reichstag*, even when they were in very deep shit indeed. Gudrun was the only person who might have called him, but he found it hard to imagine his daughter summoning him as though he was her minion. She would know better, surely. And yet, who *else* would call him?

It has to be something to do with the missing refugee, he thought, as he passed through security. *Someone has taken my concerns seriously.*

He watched the security guards, gauging their performance. The security procedures were admirably tight, although they were more concerned with removing his pistol than anything else he could use as a weapon. Given just how innovative some suspects could become, when it became clear they were going to spend the rest of their lives in a work camp - if they were lucky - he rather suspected the guards needed a crash course. But that, thankfully, wasn't his concern.

"*Leutnant* Wieland," a man said, when he was shown into a small room. Another man - it took Herman a moment to recognise him as one of Gudrun's friends - was standing by the window, watching Herman through bright blue eyes. "Thank you for coming."

"I wasn't aware I had a choice, *Mein Herr*," Herman said, tartly. Even now, with soldiers and reservists joining the police on the streets, Berlin remained uneasy. "Why did you call me off the streets?"

"You have an interesting record, *Leutnant* Wieland," the man said. He hadn't bothered to introduce himself, which in Herman's experience probably meant he was either SS or an intelligence officer. Hopefully, the latter. "You've moved from being a street cop to a detective and then back to being a street cop...may I ask why?"

"It's in my file, *Mein Herr*," Herman said.

"But I am asking *you*," the man said. "Why did you choose to return to the streets?"

Herman took a moment to formulate his answer. "I grew frustrated with being a detective, *Mein Herr*," he said, finally. "It was rare, very rare, to solve a case - and there were quite a few times when the perpetrator enjoyed political cover. There was no hope of bringing the guilty man to justice. I requested a transfer back to the streets and it was accepted without comment."

The man lifted his eyebrows. "Why?"

"Policemen, as they grow older, often try to get *off* the streets," Herman said. "An experienced officer who volunteers to return to the streets is a blessing."

"For his superiors, I imagine," the man said. "What did your wife say about it?"

Herman shrugged. "Kurt had joined the military by that point, so we didn't need so much income," he said. "But she wasn't too pleased about it."

He sighed, inwardly. *That* was an understatement. Adelinde had thrown a colossal fit, shouting and screaming in rage when she'd heard he was going back to the streets. A street policeman had a significantly higher chance of being injured or killed on duty than a detective, meaning that she would fear for his life every time he went on patrol. But he couldn't remain as a detective. The work had crushed his soul.

"I don't blame her," the man said. He sighed, then pointed to a chair. "Please, sit. We have a job for you."

He waited until Herman had sat, carefully not relaxing, then went on. "I read your report about the murder at the transit barracks," he added, slowly. "Do you stand by your conclusions?"

"Yes, *Mein Herr*," Herman said. Was this it? Was he about to be rebuked for writing an absurd suggestion into his reports? But surely his immediate superiors would have handled it, wouldn't they? "I believe they fit the facts."

The man frowned. "Why?"

Herman took a breath. "As I stated in my report, *Mein Herr*, an *experienced* police officer would not allow a male refugee so close to him without preparing himself for the possibility of a fight," he said. "The refuges have not been happy about being uprooted from their homes and there have been a number of violent incidents. A female refugee, on the other hand, would have seemed harmless until it was too late."

"And less worrying in general terms," the man agreed. He turned towards Gudrun's friend. "Horst?"

Horst stepped forward. Herman studied him, feeling the odd twinge of disquiet he'd felt when Konrad had asked his little girl out for the first time. Gudrun had been seventeen when she'd started to date Konrad, but Herman had found it hard to forget that she was no longer a child. He'd even had a stern discussion with Konrad, promising blood and pain if he hurt Gudrun in any way. And he'd *liked* Konrad. He wasn't quite so sure about Horst.

And he's been too close to Gudrun, he thought, darkly. Adelinde might not have noticed, but *Herman* had. The two youngsters had been standing far too close together, even in public, to be just *friends*. *Is he planning to marry her one day?*

"We have a problem," Horst said, bluntly. "There's an SS stay-behind cell somewhere within Berlin."

Herman's eyes narrowed. "A stay-behind cell?"

Horst nodded. "Their normal mission is to wait until the advancing spearheads have moved onwards to new targets, then come out of the shadows and engage the enemy," he said. "I suspect *this* cell intends to cause chaos within the city when the SS attacks from the outside."

"A reasonable suspicion," Herman said, carefully. Horst spoke with authority, but he was just a university student…wasn't he? No, there was something fishy about Horst's background. "How do you intend to track them down?"

"The uprising caught the SS by surprise," Horst said. "I…have reason to believe that their command network within Berlin was badly disrupted, perhaps fatally. They didn't have any contingency plans for actually losing control of the city, let alone the RSHA. The person responsible for the murder, the person who vanished into the city, may well be a commando sent to assist what remains of their network."

Herman eyed him for a long moment. "You have reason to believe…?"

Horst hesitated, then made a very visible decision. "I used to work for them," he said. "And they think - I hope - I still do."

The whole story spilled out, piece by piece. Herman stared. He was no stranger to crazy stories - he still smiled whenever he remembered the man who'd accidentally driven his car into the painting of a tunnel someone had placed on a wall - but this one was particularly absurd. Horst had been working for the SS all along? Except…he'd switched sides? Did Gudrun know?

"I told her," Horst said, when he asked. "It was right after I got her out of prison."

Herman scowled, torn between gratitude and a deep simmering anger. "And you didn't think to warn her that she could get into very real trouble?"

"She knew," Horst said, flatly.

He went on before Herman could muster a response. "We don't know how many people we can trust," he added. "The counterintelligence networks have also been shattered. I've done my best to go through the files, but an SS observer wouldn't be easily noticeable…we have to isolate and destroy the cell before it is too late."

"I understand," Herman said. "What do you want me to do?"

"I think we can trust you," Horst said. "Help us find the cell."

Herman nodded, although he knew the task would be far from easy. Berlin was hardly Paris or London, somewhere where a group of Germans would stand out like sore thumbs. An SS commando, even one from Germany East, would pass unnoticed in Berlin. Hell, the commando might even *be* a Berliner. As long as they were careful, they might just be impossible to locate.

"I'll do my best," he said. "Who can I call upon for help?"

"There's a handful of people who have been cleared," Horst said. "And if there's anyone you trust from the police, feel free to ask for them to be vetted."

Herman scowled. "How do you know you can trust me?"

"I imagine Gudrun would be dead by now or shipped off to Germany East, if you were working for the SS," Horst said. There was an airy tone to his voice that made Herman's temper flare. "And we're short of people we can trust."

"Only people who could have betrayed us are trusted now," the man warned.

"I see," Herman said. He scowled at Horst, daring the young man to look back at him. "Do you really think I would have betrayed my daughter?"

"You would not be the first, if you had," Horst commented. "A number of the women I knew in Germany East were exiled, after taking part in the feminist movement."

Herman scowled. He'd been a teenager at the time, but he remembered it all too well. The feminists had sought to change the eternal relationship between men and women, without realising just how far the *Reich* was prepared to go to maintain its power. Their cells had been broken, a handful had been executed for plotting against the state and most of the remainder dispatched to Germany East to become good little housewives. His mother had been on the fringes of the movement and its failure had made her very bitter…

"I would not have betrayed my daughter," Herman said.

"And there are some who would say you have betrayed the *Reich*," Horst countered. "And that's why I think we can trust you."

"Yes, you can," Herman said. "You can trust me on this. If you hurt her, I'll kill you."

"Good," Horst said. He sounded oddly relieved, rather than amused or fearful. "What self-respecting father could do more?"

CHAPTER TWENTY

Germanica (Moscow), Germany East
17 September 1985

"They made a deal with the Americans?"

"So it would seem, *Mein Fuhrer*," Reimer Wermter said. The intelligence officer leaned forward. "We only got the word now."

Karl growled, deep in his throat. He had grown far too used to modern communications, far too used to being able to get messages from Berlin to Germanica instantly. Now, with normal communications badly disrupted, it had taken several days for the warning to reach his intelligence staff. The traitors were in covert discussions with the Americans.

"The Americans will tear us apart and the traitors will *let* them," he snarled. "And that will be the end of us!"

He glared at the map, his eyes seeking out what had once been Japan. It was a hellish nightmare now, a territory where the races mixed freely and the once-proud martial culture had been almost completely eradicated. There were few pureblood Japanese left, he'd been told, and fewer still who cleaved to the old ways. The new generation of Japanese children were more American than the Americans. They treated democracy as though it were a god.

And that will happen to us, if the Americans win, he thought. *And they will win, if the traitors give them the chance.*

He could see the nightmare unfolding in his imagination. The steady collapse of authority, mirrored by the steady collapse of the family. Young girls breeding with *Untermenschen*, young men leaving their wives and families to support themselves; women working to earn money rather than taking care of their children, men treated as monsters by a depraved legal system. And young men running around without discipline, taking drugs and drinking heavily instead of serving their country and raising families of their own. Everything the *Reich* had built was in jeopardy.

The Americans don't know what's good for them, he thought, nastily. *And yet they may import their failures here.*

The thought tormented him. He'd once been reassured by the growing demographic crisis in America, although the Americans were alarmingly good at converting immigrants and *Gastarbeiters* - not that they used that word - into good Americans. Given time, he'd calculated, the American population would drop while the *Reich's* kept rising. But now…the civil war would tear the *Reich* apart before it could win the cold war by default. It had been a mistake, he knew now, to allow even a single American idea to enter the *Reich*. They should have closed their borders and waited, patiently, for the United States to collapse.

And now we are fighting each other instead of the Americans, he told himself. *They can just walk in afterwards and take over!*

He glared at Wermter. "What have they actually agreed?"

"The Americans are already sending them intelligence materials," Wermter said. He didn't look any more pleased than Karl felt. "They'll start shipments of MANPADS in the next few days…"

Karl swore. He hated to admit it, but the Americans had practically *invented* modern-day military logistics. They'd drowned the Japanese under a tidal wave of production that even the *Reich* had been unable to match. And yet, producing so many MANPADS and slipping them to the traitors in Berlin would be tricky, even for them. They'd have to draw down the stocks in Britain, unless…

He cursed under his breath. He'd suspected American involvement in the protests from the start. The Americans *liked* the idea of convincing people to change, rather than imposing change by force; they never seemed to see the downside, that the people might change in ways the United States neither expected nor wanted. If the Americans had planned to send MADPADS to the *Reich* from the start, could it be they'd planned the uprising and civil war all along?

Cold logic told him it wasn't likely. He'd had plenty of experience with intelligence work over the years. The more complex an operation, the greater the chance of failure. Surely, the Americans couldn't have planned the entire situation out from the beginning. And yet, they *were* moving to take advantage of the chaos. They had to be very sure the civil war wouldn't turn into a complete disaster.

"MANPADS," he said, out loud.

He snorted, rudely. American MANPADS were *good*. Stinger missiles alone had turned what should have been a relatively easy operation - to support the South Africans as they retook control of their country - into a bloodbath. CAS aircraft were uniquely vulnerable to American Stingers, which stripped the troops of their air cover when they needed it desperately. The blacks had used them, ruthlessly, to push the envelope and start attacking German troops, rather than the other way around. Introducing American-designed MANPADS into the German Civil War would only prolong the bloodshed.

Which is probably what the Americans want, he thought, darkly. *If we keep fighting each other, we will be in no position to resist when the Americans take advantage of the chaos.*

"Yes, *Mein Führer*," Wermter said. "They have promised over two thousand single-use missiles to the traitors."

Karl thought fast. The Americans had pretended that they hadn't been supplying the South Africans, but no one believed them. There was literally *no* other country on Earth, even Britain, capable of producing Stingers. Stripping all US markings off the missiles and their launchers was just pointless. And yet, the troops defending the traitors wouldn't know that, would they? They'd think the Stingers came from a *German* factory. The traitors wouldn't be keen to acknowledge that they'd received help from the archenemy.

"We have to find a way to use this against them," he thought. "Is our spy undetected?"

"I believe they do not suspect his presence," Wermter said. "However, they would be foolish to trust him completely."

"They'd be foolish to trust *anyone* completely," Karl mused. It was the old problem with revolutionary movements. The different factions tended to have different ideas about which way the movement should go. Even *Hitler* had needed to move against his former comrades, once the Nazi Party was in power. "But as long as he remains undetected…"

He frowned. He'd hoped the traitors would fragment into multiple factions, each one weakening the whole, but the growing pressure from the east probably ensured that any disputes would be put aside until the end of the war. The traitors knew they had to hang together or they would all be hanging together. He smirked at the pun, then turned his attention back to his subordinate. Wermter was looking distinctly uncomfortable.

"The Americans will not be giving them anything for free," he said. "What do they get in exchange?"

"A withdrawal from South Africa and free trade," Wermter said.

Karl swore, savagely. The withdrawal wasn't a problem - no doubt the traitors were already congratulating themselves on convincing the Americans to pay for something they'd been planning to do already - but free trade? It would be disastrous! He had no illusions about just how easily the United States could flood the *Reich* with civilian products, products that would be both cheaper and better than anything the *Reich* could produce for itself. And who knew what would come with it? Germans who should be doing their duty for the *Reich* would be asking questions, instead. They'd be demanding to know why *Germany* couldn't produce blue jeans and cheap televisions. And none of the answers they'd get would satisfy them.

And it would destroy our economy completely, he thought. *Who would buy one of our products when they could have an American product?*

"We have to stop this," he said. He glared at Wermter. "Get back to your other sources; find out what else they're planning to do. And then tell the advance teams I want them ready to move in on the *Reichstag* at a moment's notice."

"*Jawohl, Mein Fuhrer*," Wermter said.

Karl dismissed him, then keyed the intercom. "Maria, inform *Oberstgruppenfuehrer* Ruengeler that I wish to speak with him over the secure phone," he ordered. It would take time - Ruengeler had been spending far too much time at the front, getting a personal feel for the situation, rather than staying in the CP - but it would just have to be endured. "Inform me the moment he's on the line."

"*Jawohl, Mein Fuhrer*," Maria said.

Rising to his feet, Karl paced over to the window and stared out over his city. It was a towering monument to the dreams of the *Volk*, to what could be achieved if the *Volk* was bound together by a single movement. The gothic structures surrounding him were larger-than-life, the reflection of a pitiless will to dominate and reshape the world. It was magnificent; it was *always* magnificent. And yet, everything they'd built could be lost, if the war was lost. The traitors were playing games with the *Volk* itself.

He closed his eyes for a long moment, cursing the bastards under his breath. Didn't they *realise* what was at stake? The world was savage, red in tooth and claw. Their dominance had come at a price. Countless Germans had fought and died to build the *Reich*, from the men who had marched into Poland in 1939 to the men and women who fought insurgents in Germany East and South Africa. To give the *Untermenschen* a chance to harm the *Reich* wasn't just treason, it was…it was worse, yet he could think of no word for it. Karl understood the ebb and flow of politics, the complex series of moves and countermoves that sometimes left a knife buried in a comrade's back, but this was gambling with the future of the *Reich* itself. Karl would have sooner disbanded the SS than see the *Reich* collapse into rubble.

We had the will to dominate the world, he told himself. *But do we still have it?*

The secure telephone rang. He strode back to the table and picked it up. "Holliston."

"*Mein Fuhrer*," Ruengeler said.

"You need to push the advance forward." Karl said, bluntly. "Take whatever risks are necessary to reach Berlin."

There was a long pause. "*Mein Fuhrer*, the advance is already moving as quickly as possible," Ruengeler said. "I don't believe it can be pushed any faster."

Karl swore, inwardly, as he turned to stare at the map. The advance was grinding forward slowly, too slowly. He'd hoped for a swift strike towards Berlin, but the traitors were stalling his men and slowing them down. It was frustrating. Worse, perhaps, it was *costly*. If some of the reports were to be believed, replacing every lost aircraft, every lost panzer, would be a nightmare. He might win the war and purge all of his enemies, but the *Reich* would be so gravely weakened that the Americans would roll over them with ease.

"It has to be done," he growled. He didn't dare discuss everything over the telephone line. It was *meant* to be secure, but the Americans were very good at intercepting messages. He'd even read reports claiming that the Americans had actually found a way to hack into the telephone network without a physical connection. "I need you to have Berlin cut off, at the very least, within the week."

He forced himself to take a breath. "What is the current situation?"

"We're advancing, slowly but surely," Ruengeler said. "Unfortunately, they're holding back their airpower."

Karl frowned. "I was told that we were grinding their aircraft out of existence."

"They're holding them back, *Mein Fuhrer*," Ruengeler said. "And that worries me."

"That makes no sense," Karl told him, flatly. "If they had the airpower to take control of the skies, they would have used it."

"We haven't shot down anything like enough aircraft to weaken them, *Mein Fuhrer*," Ruengeler said.

"And yet they are allowing us to strike at Berlin," Karl sneered. Bombing the capital gave him no pleasure, but at least it made it clear to the citizens that the traitors had brought war to their city. "Why would they do that unless they were running out of aircraft?"

"They're conserving their strength," Ruengeler said. "I suspect they are preparing a counteroffensive of their own."

Karl snorted. "Take Berlin and it won't matter *what* they're planning," he snapped. "We can win the war and put an end to the traitors, then save the *Reich* from the Americans."

He went on before Ruengeler could say a word. "Push the offensive forward," he added, sharply. "And don't hesitate to relieve any officers who are insufficiently aggressive."

"*Jawohl, Mein Fuhrer*," Ruengeler said.

Karl put the phone down, hard. Ruengeler was starting to annoy him, even though he was one of the most experienced officers in the *Reich*. Couldn't he see that there was more at stake than simple military victory? A long drawn-out war would be disastrous, no matter which side actually won. They'd inherit a broken state. The satellites would be making a bid for freedom, the *Untermenschen* would be rising up against the SS. Everything the *Reich* had built over the past fifty years would be in doubt.

And I will not allow the Reich to collapse, he thought, as he tapped the intercom. *Whatever the cost, I will not allow the Reich to collapse.*

"Maria," he said. "I want to see Frank at once."

It was nearly five minutes before *Standartenfuehrer* Frank entered the chamber and saluted, smartly. He was a man who could easily have stepped off a recruiting poster: tall, blond, handsome and *very* muscular. Karl had wondered, back when he'd first met Frank, why he had never joined the *Waffen-SS*, but a glance in his file provided the answer. Frank's father had been a researcher who'd worked on nuclear weapons and his son, while lacking his father's intellectual gifts, had done his best to follow in his footsteps. Karl could hardly disapprove. His *own* father had been among the very first men to join the SS.

"*Mein Fuhrer*," Frank said.

"I need a progress update," Karl said. "Have you managed to unlock the nuclear warheads?"

"Not as yet," Frank said. His face was carefully impassive. "The Permissive Action Links have proved unpleasantly resilient to tampering."

Karl scowled. "And the missiles cannot be fired?"

"The missiles *can* be fired at their preset targets, *Mein Fuhrer*," Frank told him. "However, they cannot be *detonated*. The warheads cannot be detonated without the correct command codes. Even selecting new targets will be very difficult."

Karl scowled. "And the missile crews cannot help?"

"They were never trained to work on warheads, *Mein Fuhrer*," Frank said. "Their only task was launching the missiles, should the command ever come. Any maintenance work was handled by engineers who would be flown in from Berlin."

"And so the Americans have us over a barrel," Karl breathed.

"I don't believe so, *Mein Fuhrer*," Frank said. "If the Americans *did* fire on us, I'm sure we'd be able to get the arming codes from Berlin."

Karl snorted, rudely. The early-warning network was in shambles. If the Americans decided to gamble and launched a massive first strike, it was quite possible that their missiles wouldn't be detected until the nukes actually started to detonate. And by then it would be far too late. The *Reich* would have been utterly shattered. Hell, if they were lucky, the Americans would destroy the *Reich's* missiles on the ground.

And the traitors are already in bed with the Americans, he thought, darkly. *They might refuse to send us the arming codes.*

"We should never have placed so much faith in our system," he growled. "It never occurred to us that we would lose control of Berlin."

"The government didn't want anyone using nukes without their approval, *Mein Fuhrer*," Frank pointed out.

"I know," Karl growled. "They didn't trust us."

He shook his head. Deploying tactical nukes in 1950 might have been the only way to end the Arab Uprisings quickly - the *Reich* had been reeling after Hitler's death and really didn't need more problems - but it had come at a cost. The Americans, who had been going back to sleep, had started pouring money into defence, while the *Reich* Council had worked hard to ensure that no one could detonate a nuke without their blessing. No one at the time had realised that the *Reich* would be sundered in two. They'd known that unity was the only thing that kept the *Reich* from being ripped apart by its enemies.

"If you had a tactical nuke," he said flatly, "could you detonate it?"

"Perhaps, *Mein Fuhrer*," Frank said. "We are working on readying a number of tactical warheads now. However, the PAL system is designed to be extremely tamper-resistant, to the point of destroying the warhead if it isn't handled very carefully. It may be impossible to guarantee that the nukes will detonate."

Karl sighed. "And if we start building our own nukes?"

"It would take years, *Mein Fuhrer*," Frank said. "We may have a number of breeder reactors under our control, but assembly has always been done in Germany Prime. I think we would be starting from scratch. Building the machines to make the machines, if you will pardon the expression, will be costly - if we can do it at all."

"Another mistake," Karl said. Germany East's industry was limited. In hindsight, that had been a mistake too. "We can't get the tools without winning the war."

"Yes, *Mein Fuhrer*," Frank said. "Producing them for ourselves will take too long."

"Do a study, see if there's any way to speed up the process," Karl ordered. He didn't hold out much hope, but at least they could try. "Dismissed."

He watched Frank leave, then turned his attention to the map. His forces were advancing forward slowly, too slowly. Their gains would be worthless if they couldn't consolidate them by capturing Berlin, destroying the traitorous government. And yet, if they *couldn't* take Berlin…

I'll make the world burn before I surrender, he told himself, savagely. *And the traitors will pay for their crimes.*

CHAPTER TWENTY-ONE

Berlin, Germany Prime
18 September 1985

Horst wrapped his greatcoat around his body as he walked slowly down the darkened street, wishing he could wear a hood. A chilly breeze was coming from the east, sending shivers down his spine, but he needed to be recognised. The cell had picked an excellent spot for their meeting, he had to admit. A watcher lurking near one of the warehouses would be able to recognise Horst - and ensure he was on his own - long before Horst saw him. He'd worked through a dozen possible ways to have a police observer nearby - Gudrun's father had had quite a few good ideas - but none of them had been workable. The merest *hint* that he wasn't alone would be enough to get him killed.

He glanced up as he heard the sound of aircraft engines buzzing over the city, wondering if they were friendly or very hostile. Berlin had been bombed several times, the bombers dropping their bombs seemingly at random. Horst had never served in South Africa - or on any campaign, if he were forced to tell the truth - but some of his friends had insisted that the *Waffen-SS's* pilots could drop their bombs with startling precision. If that were true, the bombers had *definitely* been bombing at random, more to frighten the civilians than for any actual military value. They hadn't struck any targets within half a mile of the *Reichstag*.

And they might even hit their own people, he thought, feeling a flicker of grim amusement. *I doubt the pilots know there's an SS cell beneath them.*

He waited, ready to seek cover, but no bombs fell. The sound of aircraft engines slowly faded into the darkness. Horst allowed himself a moment of relief, then kept walking slowly towards his destination. The warehouses had long-since been stripped of anything useful, the guards and workers relocated elsewhere. There were quite a few homeless Berliners squatting in them, according to the police, but no one really cared. They weren't causing trouble - and, in any case, there was nowhere else to put them. He kept a sharp eye out for trouble as he kept moving, knowing that the crime rate had also skyrocketed in the less-pleasant parts of Berlin. The omnipresent fear of the police and the SS was gone.

And now people know they can change the world, he thought, as he reached the location and checked his watch. He was two minutes early. *Who knows what will happen the next time the government becomes unpopular?*

He pushed the thought aside as he leaned against the building and waited, feeling unseen eyes watching him from the shadows. Covertly, he checked around, but saw nothing. It didn't really surprise him. An experienced SS observer wouldn't let himself be seen, in any case, nor would they bother with any games. If they suspected his loyalties, he would probably have been picked off by a sniper as he walked down the road. Unless, of course, they thought he could be manipulated.

My life was much simpler before the uprising, he thought. *Back then, I thought I knew how the world worked.*

"Horst," a quiet voice said.

Horst tensed, then turned to see Schwarzkopf emerging from the shadows. The SS handler looked like a homeless man, smoking a homemade cigarette and wearing a tattered outfit that was too large for him. If Horst's experience was any guide, he'd be wearing something else underneath, something that would pass without comment anywhere in Berlin. Dump the clothes, lose the cigarette and comb his hair…he'd look very different. It wasn't a very clever disguise, but it didn't have to be. All it had to do was work.

"I came, as ordered," Horst said. He didn't like Schwarzkopf's surprising stealth. He'd always assumed that the handler was nothing more than a bureaucrat. But then, he'd presumably been a field agent himself before he'd been promoted. "I am at your disposal."

"Of course," Schwarzkopf said. Horst couldn't tell if he was being mildly sarcastic or stating a fact. "I have a great many questions for you."

Horst inclined his head, then waited.

"I have heard that the Americans have been reaching out to the provisional government," Schwarzkopf said, bluntly. "Is that true?"

"I haven't heard of any American contacts," Horst said. "But I am not allowed to attend the council meetings."

It was only half true. He didn't attend meetings, but Gudrun told him everything. And yet, *he* hadn't mentioned it to anyone else - and nor would any of the other councillors. The American contacts *had* to remain a secret. And yet...was Schwarzkopf fishing...or was someone playing both sides of the field? There were several councillors who might be able to switch sides - again - if they made themselves useful to Karl Holliston. They might be passing information to the east.

"I see," Schwarzkopf said. "And you heard nothing through pillow talk?"

Horst felt his cheeks turn red. "We don't talk about the war when we are in bed," he said, trying not to sound embarrassed. If Schwarzkopf suspected he had actual *feelings* for Gudrun, he'd be in deep shit. "We spend most of it trying to *forget* the war."

"Pump her, gently," Schwarzkopf ordered. "We need to know *precisely* what is going on."

"*Jawohl*," Horst said. What did Schwarzkopf know? There was no way, short of catching and interrogating the traitor, to find out. "But if I ask too bluntly, *Mein Herr*, she may suspect something."

"It is natural for a man to want to know what his woman is doing, is it not?" Schwarzkopf asked. He snorted, rudely. "Use your best judgement, but get us some answers."

"*Jawohl*," Horst said, again.

He sighed, inwardly. If Schwarzkopf was only guessing - or had only second or third-hand hints - he would be able to lie. But if Schwarzkopf knew more than he admitted, a lie could prove fatal. Unless, of course, he was able to convince Schwarzkopf that *Gudrun* had lied to him. And yet, even *that* would be too much for the man to swallow. He'd suspect that Horst was losing his touch, if he didn't *already* suspect it. Horst had fumbled the ball once already, as far as Schwarzkopf was concerned.

"Now," Schwarzkopf said. "What other developments have there been?"

"More and more refugees are pouring into Berlin," Horst said. "The provisional government has been trying to shift them westwards, but there's a shortage of food and drink, as well as towns and cities willing to take refugees. I think the council is considering drastic measures, yet they're worried about triggering off another civil war."

"A civil war within the civil war," Schwarzkopf said. He smirked, openly. "That's the price one pays for not having a strong government."

Horst was tempted to agree. Western cities weren't so keen on suddenly finding themselves responsible for hundreds of thousands of refugees, even if they *were* fellow Germans. And the provisional government didn't have the naked power to *compel* them to support the refugees. It didn't help that the military was trying desperately to shift forces eastwards, making it harder to control the growing refugee problem. He doubted it would end well.

"Quite," he said, flatly.

He paused. "Is there any other way I can be of assistance?"

"Not as yet," Schwarzkopf said. "We just want your intelligence from the *Reichstag*."

"I obey, *Mein Herr*," Horst said.

He had to fight to keep his face under control. There were over a hundred servants in the *Reichstag*, not counting the guards or personnel assistants. One of them - perhaps more than one - was reporting to the SS, but who? An extensive, if covert background investigation had turned up nothing suspicious. But then, he would have been disappointed in the SS if it had.

And now we have a second traitor, someone very highly placed, he thought. *And it has to be one of the older councillors.*

He considered it briefly. Gudrun and Schulze were obviously out - Voss too, given that the Field Marshal was in an excellent position to seize control of the city and surrender before he could be lynched. But after that... Kruger was unlikely, Horst had to admit, but all of the others had to be considered suspects. And they all had thousands of others under their control. Investigating them all was going to be a nightmare.

"There is a mirror in your bedroom," Schwarzkopf said, suddenly. "Isn't there?"

"Yes, *Mein Herr*," Horst said. "It hangs on my wall."

The question made him smile. He wondered if Schwarzkopf had ever sneaked into the *Reichstag* himself, then dismissed the thought as absurd. Dreary tradecraft might be tedious - nothing like the books depicting heroic

SS operatives - but it kept its practitioners alive. He doubted that Schwarzkopf would take the risk, even if he had the nerve. Unless Schwarzkopf *wasn't* the highest-ranking SS officer still in Berlin…

And we have at least one female commando out there, he reminded himself. *She is very likely to be extremely dangerous.*

"We want you to keep track of your girlfriend's schedule," Schwarzkopf said. "Write down her plan for the day, then place the papers behind the mirror. They will be collected."

"The schedule is rarely set in stone," Horst said. He was careful not to mention that it had been *his* idea. If Gudrun refused to allow herself to be surrounded by armed guards, she could at least keep her movements unpredictable. "I don't always know where we are going."

"Then you will do your best to find out," Schwarzkopf said. He leaned forward, his eyes glinting with menacing light. "I don't think I have to remind you that you are already in disgrace. This whole disaster could have been nipped in the bud if you'd done your job."

And if you knew just how true that actually was, Horst thought, *you'd have killed me by now.*

"You are required to prove your loyalty to the *Reich*," Schwarzkopf continued. "And if that means leading your girlfriend into a trap, that is what you will do."

He leaned back, then shrugged. "Remain here for ten minutes," he ordered. "And then slip back to her bed."

Horst fought down the temptation to punch Schwarzkopf - or shoot him in the back - as the SS officer turned and strode into the darkness. Another aircraft buzzed over Berlin, the sound moving from east to west…a bomber then, Horst decided, or a recon plane. But then, who would bother sending a recon plane over in darkness? Unless someone was parachuting men into the city…it was certainly possible.

He forced himself to remain calm as he waited, keeping an eye on his watch. There was no way to be sure if someone was watching him or not, but he could *feel* unseen eyes keeping an eye on him. And there was no shortage of cover. A sniper could be lurking nearby, watching him through a scope; he'd be ready to shoot Horst if he left a minute early. Or it could just be a bluff, his own imagination doing the rest.

No way to be sure, he told himself. Perhaps, in hindsight, he should have joined the *Waffen-SS* instead. It wouldn't have been hard to flub the tests he'd been given when he first applied to join. *And the bastard knows it.*

———

Gudrun rubbed her tired eyes as she looked at Horst. "We have *another* spy?"

"Probably," Horst said. "Schwarzkopf asked about American contacts."

Volker Schulze looked doubtful. "They might have noticed the American visiting the *Reichstag*," he said. "But that doesn't mean we've made a deal with them."

"There's no way to be sure," Horst said. "But if there is a very high-ranking spy…"

Gudrun fought down the urge to curse, wishing that she was alone. Volker Schulze was bad enough, but her father - sitting next to her - was a silent reminder of propriety. God alone knew what he'd say if she gave Horst a hug, let alone a kiss. She almost giggled at the thought. Technically, she out-ranked him…and yet she was still his daughter. Who knew which of them was really in charge?

Maybe we should get married, she thought. *But getting married would cause more problems than it would solve.*

It wasn't a pleasant thought. She'd contemplated it when her period had been a few days late and she'd feared the worst, but it *would* cause too many headaches. Ironically, getting pregnant before the uprising wouldn't have been a serious problem - even if her parents *had* exploded with rage - but now it would be disastrous. She wouldn't be taken seriously by the remaining councillors.

She pushed the thought aside and leaned forward. "If we do have a very high-ranking spy," she mused, "would he *have* to be a councillor?"

"No," her father said. "One of their trusted aides might be the *real* spy."

"They're not supposed to discuss such matters," Schulze said, flatly.

"They do," Horst said. "A single boastful fool could cause us all sorts of headaches, if one of his aides is a spy."

He sighed. "But someone on the council might think they could buy their own safety through helping the other side," he added. "They'd be ahead who-ever came out on top."

"At least they'd be alive," Gudrun muttered. *She'd* talked about such matters with Horst, after all. "And they might even be in a position of power."

"But we don't even know there *is* a spy," Schulze said. "The SS might just have gotten lucky."

"That's possible," Horst said. He paused. "And there's another possibility. They may be trying to test me, *Herr Chancellor*. It may not have occurred to them that there might have been *actual* contacts with America."

Schulze scowled. "So what do we do?"

"We keep telling them that you know nothing about any such contacts," Gudrun's father said, bluntly. "If they think there *have* been contacts, it's still a believable answer. And if this is nothing more than a fishing trip…well, nothing is betrayed. There's no reasonable excuse for you to be in possession of such knowledge."

Horst nodded.

"But we have to catch the spy in the *Reichstag*," her father continued. "And we have to track down the cell before it does something drastic."

Schulze nodded. "Any ideas?"

"The Easterners have been dropping bombs on us," Gudrun's father said. "It shouldn't be hard to make it clear to the staff that anyone who leaves the *Reichstag* should sign out of the building, like we do in the police station. There was enough chaos, wasn't there, the first time everyone had to run into the bunkers? We can use that as an excuse to build a list of who goes in and out of the building."

Gudrun nodded, seeing the sense of it. "Most of them live in the *Reichstag*," she said, feeling a flicker of pride. Her father might be strict, but he was no fool. "Anyone who leaves might be the spy."

"Or a spy," Horst said. "If I was in their shoes, Gudrun, I'd want more than one."

"Brilliant," Schulze said, sarcastically. "There might be more than one - or two - in the building."

"It's a start," Gudrun's father said. "Once we know who leaves regularly, we can start shadowing them."

"They may be trained to avoid pursuit," Horst pointed out.

"And if they were trying to avoid us," Gudrun's father said, "we'd know who we were looking for."

Gudrun sighed. "Why can't everything be simple these days?"

Horst smiled at her. "Life is rarely simple," he said.

"Make it happen," Schulze ordered. "But don't try to investigate the councillors."

Gudrun nodded in sympathy. *She* was the only councillor without a staff - and a small army of subordinates. Investigating the others would spark off discontent, if not paranoia. A man like Voss, far too used to watching his back for the SS knife, might see advantage in striking first, if he believed his life to be under threat. Or Kruger…fearful that he might be blamed for the economic nightmare gripping the *Reich*. Or…

Just one of them betraying us would be a nightmare, she thought. *Even if we found absolute proof, and we might, bringing them to justice would be impossible.*

"As you wish," her father said. He looked at Horst. "You are *not* to share Gudrun's schedule with them."

Horst didn't argue. "I'm planning to give them false information, then explain that the schedule kept changing on short notice," he said. "Which is what happens…"

"Too risky," her father insisted.

"If I don't give them something, they will suspect me," Horst said. "And if that happens, they will pull in their horns and disappear - right up until the moment they attack."

Gudrun held up a hand. "I don't mind the risk…"

"You should," her father growled. "Last time, when you were arrested, they didn't know who you were. This time…they will."

Gudrun shuddered, despite herself. She'd been stripped naked and locked in a cell for hours, exposed to the gaze of every passing male guard. And yet, that was tenderness incarnate compared to what they'd do now they *knew* who she was. She'd be lucky if she was *only* hung from meat hooks, after being tortured to death. The SS might normally hesitate to kill girls of good breeding, but in her case they'd probably make an exception.

"If there's a chance to lure them out on our terms," she said, "we should take it."

"But not at the risk of your life," Horst said. "It's too dangerous."

Her father nodded in agreement. "I forbid it," he said. "Your life is already in too much danger."

"So is Kurt's," Gudrun snapped.

"Kurt is a young man," her father said. His voice softened. "I don't want to see you dead."

Gudrun scowled, but said nothing.

CHAPTER TWENTY-TWO

Near Berlin, Germany Prime
21 September 1985

"They're coming into range, *Herr Leutnant*," Loeb warned

Kurt nodded. The SS had punched through the next set of defence lines two days ago, pushing forward despite taking increasingly heavy casualties. He would have admired their determination if they weren't breaking into territories where the evacuation program had barely begun, leaving hundreds of thousands of civilians stranded.

And we had to clear the roads just to keep moving, he thought, grimly. The roads had become snarled with refugees as they retreated west, forcing the soldiers to push them out of the way just to get into position to engage the SS again. *How many of them are about to die.*

He cursed under his breath. They'd taken up position near a town, a town that had barely even *started* to evacuate its population by the time the war reached them. There was no time to order an evacuation, even if it wouldn't have blocked their line of retreat. The hell he knew was going to break across the town was coming and there was nothing he could do about it. There was nothing *anyone* could do about it.

The sound of aircraft roared through the air as a pair of HE-477s raced westwards, hunting for targets. Kurt braced himself, fearing the aircraft might spot their position, but the two SS aircraft merely headed onwards. Behind them, a pair of helicopters held position over the advancing panzers, their weapons ready to engage any threat. Kurt muttered orders to two of his men, both of whom were carrying MANPADS. They were nowhere near as good in combat as he'd been told - they'd found that out the hard way - but at least they'd force the helicopters to back off. The SS wouldn't have an unlimited supply.

And we don't have an unlimited supply of weapons either, he reminded himself. It had practically become a mantra as the *Waffen-SS* continued its advance. *Get in, land a blow and then get out.*

"Take aim," he ordered, quietly. The lead panzer was slowing as it approached the town, its main gun shifting position to cover the buildings. They'd already hurled HE shells into houses snipers had tried to use as firing positions, if rumours were to be believed. *Kurt* had no trouble believing them. "Brace yourselves…"

He tensed, silently timing it in his head. It was the same problem, one that had played itself out time and time again. The closer the panzers, the greater the chance of scoring hits…and the greater the chance of being discovered ahead of time. A hail of fire from the panzer's machine guns would be more than enough to slaughter his entire command before they could fire a single shot. But if they fired too soon, the missiles might not kill their targets.

"Now," he snapped.

Loeb fired the antitank missile. It lanced through the air and struck the lead tank, burning through its armour and exploding inside the hull. The second missile took out the second tank; the third missile struck its target, but glanced off and exploded harmlessly. One of the helicopters was hit at practically point-blank range and exploded into a fireball, the other jerked back so hard it nearly stood on its tail.

"Run," Kurt snapped. The third panzer was already rolling forward, machine guns spitting fire. "Move it, now!"

He turned and ran for his life, hoping desperately that their escape route remained clear. The SS stormtroopers behind the panzers would be already jumping out of their transports and advancing forward - and there was nothing to stop them. Perhaps, in hindsight, they should have targeted the trucks instead…but taking out the panzers would do more to blunt the advance than killing random stormtroopers. He heard shots behind him, but none of them came near to his men. The SS had *definitely* been caught by surprise.

And yet we're still falling back to Berlin, he thought, as they slipped out of sight. *And they're still advancing.*

"We hurt them," Loeb said.

"Yeah," Kurt said. He heard more aircraft high overhead, but they didn't seem interested in dropping bombs. Rumour had it that Berlin was being bombed savagely, yet rumour was known to lie. "But did we hurt them enough?"

———

Obersturmfuehrer Hennecke Schwerk cursed savagely as he rolled out of the transport, rifle at the ready, then ran forwards, past the ruined panzers. Two of them were nothing more than scrap metal now, he noted, while a third had a nasty scorch mark on the hull. His squad followed him as he charged the enemy firing position, then slowed as it became clear that the enemy had made their escape. They'd run into the undergrowth, skirting the town and then headed west. Chasing them down would be futile.

The panzers rumbled forward again, heading into the town. Hennecke and his men followed, keeping their heads down, but no one tried to bar their way as they drove through the puny barricade and down the road into the town square. It was a typical town; a town hall, a church, a few hundred homes and shops... the sort of place that would be ideal, if one wanted a quiet life. But not now.

A shot cracked out. He ducked, instinctively, as a bullet pinged off the side of the nearest panzer, then looked towards the source. Someone was lurking in an upper bedroom, aiming a gun towards them. A panzer fired, a second later. The shell detonated inside the house, blowing it into rubble. Hennecke heard, just for a second, someone screaming before the sound cut off abruptly. Dead, injured or silenced? There was no way to know.

"Clear the houses," he bellowed, as more stormtroopers flooded into the town. The town was in revolt and he knew how to deal with it. "Get the population into the damned church!"

He kicked open the nearest door and led the way into the house. An old man - probably old enough to remember the days before Hitler - stared at him in shock. Two younger women looked terrified; behind them, a handful of children lay on the floor. There were no boys older than fifteen, Hennecke realised, even though there was a photograph of two boys wearing military uniforms on the mantelpiece. They'd have joined the traitors, he thought, if they weren't serving in South Africa.

"Get out," he snarled at them. "Now!"

The old man met his eyes with a kind of dignified resignation that had Hennecke's blood boiling in rage. He lived in a town that had dared to stand against the SS, that had dared to allow one of its buildings to be used against them...how dare he show anything other than complete and total submission? Growling, he caught the old man and thrust him towards the door, silently daring him to make a fuss. The women followed, both looking even more terrified. They were older than he'd thought, he realised. They'd be daughters or daughters-in-law, not teenagers. And perhaps they were mothers too...

He bit off that thought as he glared at the children. The admiration he'd always received from children in the east was lacking; instead, they stared at him in fear. They hadn't deserved to be raised by traitors, he tried to tell himself, but he was too angry to care. It was his duty to ensure they were passed to the *Lebensborn* officers for transfer to a new family, where they would be raised properly...he shrugged. They were at war. The normal rules could go to hell.

The children hurried out, following their mothers; he ordered his men to search the house and then hurried back outside. Hundreds of civilians - old men and women, younger women, children - were being marched out of their homes and ordered into the church. Behind them, their homes were ransacked and anything incriminating - weapons, stashes of money or treacherous propaganda - was removed. The panzers moved through the town and back onto the road as it became clear there would be no more resistance, leaving Hennecke and his men in charge of the town.

"They're all in the church, *Herr Obersturmfuehrer*," the *Strumscharfuehrer* said. "Orders?"

Hennecke glared. He knew precisely how to treat towns and villages that supported insurgents and terrorists. It was what he'd done, time and time again, in Germany East, where the Slavs took advantage of every *hint* of German weakness. Doing it here, in Germany Prime, bothered him more than he cared to admit, but the townspeople *had* supported the traitors. They didn't deserve to live.

"Lock the doors, then burn the church," he ordered, shortly. "Kill them all."

He watched, grimly, as his men carried out his orders. They'd done it before, in Germany East. The doors were sealed, then incendiary grenades were hurled through the windows, triggering a firestorm. Hennecke shuddered, despite himself, at the screams as the flames lashed out, the wooden church catching fire with terrifying speed. The trapped inhabitants battered on the door, but it was already too late. Moments later, the building started to collapse into burning debris. There were no survivors.

"We could have saved a few of the girls," one of his men muttered. "And had some real fun."

Hennecke frowned. Raping Slavic girls was strictly forbidden, even if the girls were killed afterwards. Quite apart from the simple fact it was bad for discipline - and it was - it ran the very real risk of introducing Germanic blood to the Slavs. But here…he doubted there was a single girl in the town who had a trace of non-German ancestry in her blood. Most half-castes had been removed or killed a very long time ago. His superiors wouldn't be able to object on racial grounds.

But it was still a disciplinary issue.

"No," he said, firmly. "If we have to kill them, we have to kill them. But we are not going to abuse good German girls."

He turned and marched towards the edge of the town. As tired as they were, they would have to do it again and again until they reached Berlin, where things would get harder. His superiors had insisted that Berlin would fall without a fight, but Hennecke wasn't so sure.

Grandfather fought in Stalingrad, he reminded himself. *And he had nightmares for the rest of his life.*

It was a bitter thought. His father had often rebuked Hennecke's grandfather - his father-in-law - for telling Hennecke stories of the war. And yet, *he'd* been a soldier too, fighting and eventually dying to protect Germany East. Hennecke had never really understood the man, or the odd admiration his grandfather had had for the Slavs. It wasn't as if he'd ever treated the servants any better than the rest of the family.

It probably made sense to him, he thought. *And now we have to proceed onwards.*

———

180

"This is confirmed?"

"Yes, *Herr Oberstgruppenfuehrer*," *Sturmbannfuehrer* Friedemann Weineck said. "It was reported through the network and confirmed by the MPs."

Oberstgruppenfuehrer Alfred Ruengeler sucked in a breath. He'd known that anger and frustration was burning through the ranks - his men were hardly used to encountering foes that could slow them down, let alone stop them - but this was a nightmare. Slaughtering vast numbers of *Untermenschen* was one thing; killing over a hundred men, women and children from Germany Prime was quite another. There would be no peace if this went on.

He looked up. "We know who did it?"

"*Obersturmfuehrer* Hennecke Schwerk," Weineck said. "He's actually in line for promotion to *Hauptsturmfuehrer, Herr Oberstgruppenfuehrer*; his former commanding officer was killed on the first day of the war and since then Schwerk has been holding down his responsibilities. Before then...he had a honourable reputation as an infantryman in the east."

"Where he picked up a few bad habits," Alfred growled.

He looked at the map, thinking hard. There had been quite a few incidents as the advancing stormtroopers mingled with the civilians - a number of civilians killed for being on the roads, several more killed in the crossfire, a couple of young women raped - but this was by far the worst. And yet it wouldn't be the last. Alfred *knew* his men were getting frustrated, both with their slow progress and with the German civilians. Far from being welcomed as liberators, they were being ignored or defied when they weren't being attacked.

But the Fuhrer will approve, Alfred thought. *He won't give a damn about the dead civilians, will he?*

He groaned, inwardly. It would be easy to send a pair of MPs to arrest Schwerk and transport him back to the CP for a quick court martial, followed by execution, but the *Führer* would not like it. He'd see Schwerk as a hero, as the man who taught a bunch of cowardly fence-sitters the cost of defying the SS. And he wouldn't give a damn about just how badly it would cost them, in the long run. Hell, killing more westerners - even ones of good blood - would make it easier for him to reshape the west in his own image.

And I can't even put a ban on future atrocities, he told himself. *The Fuhrer wouldn't like that either.*

Weineck leaned forward. *"Herr Oberstgruppenfuehrer,* how do you wish to proceed?"

Alfred scowled. Punishing Schwerk was out of the question. The *Fuhrer* was already breathing down his neck, insisting that he relieve a number of officers for being inadequately aggressive. Karl Holliston simply didn't realise that charging forward, firing madly, was not a good tactic, not when it meant getting panzers impaled on antitank guns and blown into flaming debris. The logistics were already a nightmare; he dreaded to think what would happen if they started to run short on panzers too. And then there was the puzzle over just what the enemy was doing with their air force...

"Promote him to *Hauptsturmfuehrer,*" he ordered, curtly. "And make sure he has a chance to practice his skills - put him at the tip of the spear."

"Jawohl, Herr Oberstgruppenfuehrer," Weineck said.

And hope the bastard gets killed on the front lines, Alfred added, silently. It wasn't much, but it was all he had. *There's nothing else I can do to him.*

He turned back to the map. "Are the enemy trying to stiffen their resistance at any point?"

"It looks as through their main units are still retreating towards Berlin," Weineck said. He seemed relieved that the subject had changed. "They just won't stand and fight."

"Of course not," Alfred said, tiredly. They'd been over it before, time and time again, as the frustration started to bite. "They know they will lose in a straight fight."

He shrugged. The *Fuhrer* would want an update soon, he was sure. And if he didn't, it was only because the *Fuhrer* was getting his updates from someone else...

And if that happens, he thought grimly, *I'm going to be the next officer to be relieved.*

———

Generalmajor Gunter Gath cursed under his breath as he read the report. A pair of snipers near an insignificant town, waiting for a chance to put a bullet through an SS officer's head, had watched helplessly as the population was herded into the church and burned to death. It would have been unbelievable, Gunter was sure, if there hadn't been so many other reports of SS atrocities as their advancing spearheads began to cross paths with innocent civilians.

And I believe it, he thought. He would have liked to deny it, but he'd seen too much to do anything of the sort. *Now what?*

He cursed under his breath. The laws of war, insofar as the Third *Reich* admitted they existed, allowed retaliation, an eye for an eye. But against what? Bombing a random town in Germany East wouldn't upset the SS, let alone deter them from carrying out more atrocities of their own. Shooting prisoners was likely to be more effective, but they just hadn't taken enough prisoners to make the effort worthwhile. And besides, if they *did* start shooting prisoners, the SS would probably do the same.

And they have far too many of my men prisoner, he thought.

He glared at the map, noting the arrows denoting the advancing spearheads. Hundreds of his men had died - or been captured - after being overrun by the panzers. They'd been marched off into captivity, transported eastwards across the river and out of his ken. Even the orbital photographs someone in Berlin had managed to coax out of the satellites hadn't shown him where the prisoners had been taken. Gunter hoped - desperately - that they hadn't simply been killed, but he had to admit it was possible. The SS had machine-gunned prisoners in South Africa, after all...

But they were Untermenschen, he thought. *They deserved to die.*

His own thoughts mocked him. *And what were the men, women and children who were burned to death in the church?*

He shook his head, slowly. Dealing with SS atrocities would have to be a political decision, but he couldn't see many *good* options. Deploying anything from poison gas to tactical nuclear weapons would only encourage further retaliation, while slaughtering prisoners would only lead to the SS doing the same. Hell, they might even be *relieved*. The bastards had far more prisoners, all of whom needed to be fed, than *he* did. And they'd even have an *excuse* for mass slaughter.

We did it to them, he thought, *so they can now do it to us.*

Cursing, he reached for the phone. He'd never liked being micromanaged, but this was one hot potato he was happy to drop into someone else's life. Let the provisional government decide what to do. *They* could have the responsibility…

…And the blame, if it only made the bloodshed far worse.

CHAPTER TWENTY-THREE

Berlin, Germany Prime
22 September 1985

"I cannot believe they'd *do* this," Gudrun protested, honestly shocked.

"Don't be naive," Horst said. He sounded irritated - and exhausted. She would have been annoyed at his tone if she hadn't known he'd been up for most of the night, working with her father and his handpicked team to try to track down the SS spy. "They wouldn't hesitate to kill whoever got in their way, if it suited them."

Gudrun shook her head, slowly. She'd known - intellectually - that the SS had carried out thousands, perhaps millions, of atrocities. Grandpa Frank had even admitted to having served in the *Einsatzgruppen*. But to casually burn over a hundred men, women and children, all of good German blood, to death, just because a sniper had used a house in the town…it was appalling.

She looked at the photographs, cursing under her breath. She'd never been particularly religious - religion was officially discouraged at school, although the *Reich* had never tried to stamp it out completely - but even *she* knew a church was supposed to be holy. And yet, the SS had herded up the townsfolk, crammed them into the building and set it on fire. Over a hundred people were dead…and it was all her fault.

The guilt struck her like a physical blow. *She'd* started the ball rolling, but she hadn't realised - not really - just how high a price the *Reich* would pay for what she'd done. Overthrowing the *Reich* Council couldn't have brought matters to a conclusion, could it? This wasn't a neat little story where every single plot thread was tied up in the final chapter. The villain had escaped to the east and started a counterattack. God alone knew how many people had died in the fighting, the fighting she'd started…

"My fault," she muttered, bitterly.

She closed her eyes in pain. She'd thought she'd known the risks when she started, she thought she'd known - and accepted - what would happen to her if she was caught. And she'd done her best to make sure that her friends knew too, even though they'd been compromised just by listening to her. They'd all known the risks…

…But the townsfolk hadn't. They hadn't been involved in the protest movement, as it grew and diversified; she would have been surprised if they'd even *heard* of the protest movement before the *Reich* Council crumbled into dust. And yet, they'd paid a steep price for her decisions. The town was dead, save perhaps for a handful of young men who'd joined the military and left before the advancing SS stormtroopers captured the town. She knew, deep inside, that they would never forgive her for what she'd brought upon their families.

Horst wrapped an arm around her, gently. "It wasn't your fault."

Gudrun pushed him away. She didn't feel like being cuddled, not now.

"It wasn't your fault," Horst repeated. "You heard Kruger, didn't you? The *Reich* was heading for a fall long before you were born. You may have started the protest movement, Gudrun, but it would have happened with or without you."

Gudrun snorted. Even in the university, political debate had been almost non-existent. She knew - now - that thousands of people had seen the cracks in the state, the hundreds of tiny problems that spelt looming disaster, but very few had dared to speak out and prove to the others that they were not alone. It had been *her* who had worked up the nerve, *her* who had made those people see that there were hundreds of thousands of others who felt the same way too. And if it hadn't been her, who *would* it have been? She still found it hard to believe that *she* had had the nerve to do it.

She sighed, bitterly. If Konrad had been unharmed - or even if she and his family had *known* what had happened to him - she would never have dared to start the protest movement. She would have married Konrad, after graduating from the university, and done her best to balance her career with life as a married woman. If, of course, he *allowed* her to have a career. Her husband could have forbidden her from working, if he'd wished. It had been one thing she'd sought to change at once, as soon as she'd taken her seat on the council, but the demands of war had pushed social reform aside.

And if I hadn't started the movement, she thought, *what would have become of me?*

Horst tapped her shoulder, firmly. "Gudrun, you can't blame yourself for this," he said. "The war is bringing out all the old nightmares."

"I can blame myself," Gudrun said, tartly. "I *do* blame myself."

"Blame Holliston," Horst said. He scowled. "If the so-called *Fuhrer* was angry about what happened to the poor bastards, he would have made his feelings clear by now. Or blame Voss and Gath for failing to evacuate the town, even though it would have clogged up the roads with even more refugees. Or blame the *swinehund* who ordered the people killed. You cannot be blamed for what they chose to do, of their own free will."

He paused. "And Holliston was willing to kill hundreds of his fellow Germans before the *Reich* Council fell," he added. "You didn't make him do that, did you?"

Gudrun shook her head, then looked up at him. "Did *you* do anything like that? In the east, I mean?"

Horst met her eyes, evenly. "No," he said. "But the war out there is merciless. We all knew it happened and we all applauded it."

"Monsters," Gudrun said.

"What would you have them do?" Horst asked. "You can't live and let live with *Untermenschen* who want to kill you. And you can't move millions of people out of their homes in the hopes of keeping them safe. What would you have them do?"

"Maybe I wouldn't have turned Russia into Germany East," Gudrun snapped.

Horst cocked his head. "Maybe not. So what?"

Gudrun blinked. "So what?"

"So what?" Horst repeated. "You cannot change the past. There is no way you can go back in time and convince Adolf Hitler not to invade Russia, or force the *Reich* Council not to hand it over to the SS. You have to deal with the situation you have, not the situation you want. And, right now, what you have is an endless insurgency that demands the harshest possible measures to bring it to an end."

"Which have now been exported westwards," Gudrun said.

She shook her head. "I don't know what to do," she added. "Can you leave me alone for a while."

Horst frowned. "You do have an appointment at the transit barracks…"

"Cancel it," Gudrun snapped, sharply. She knew she was hurting him, but she found it hard to care. "Just leave me alone."

She wondered, just for a long moment, what Horst would do. Shout back at her? Part of her would have welcomed a shouting match, even if they'd probably be overheard by everyone in the bunker. Or hit her? It wasn't uncommon, but she would have hit him back…and who knew what would happen then? And yet, the pain would have dulled her fears…

"I'll get some rest," Horst said, rising. "And I would suggest you get some rest too."

Gudrun snorted. It wasn't easy to sleep alone, now. She'd grown far too used to having a warm body in her bed, even though her father would definitely notice something - if he hadn't noticed already. There had been the odd tension between him and Horst, after all. She watched Horst leave, his back stiff and felt a flicker of a very different guilt. She'd practically chucked him out of the room they shared. But she needed to be alone for a while, alone with her guilt.

She looked at the final photograph - the remains of the church, surrounded by armed guards - and then picked up the list of known townsfolk. Records were a mess now, she knew; it was unlikely that *everyone* on the list was dead. It was quite possible that some of the smarter townsfolk had seen what was coming in their direction and driven westwards, trying to stay with relatives in Hamburg or Kiel. And yet, she knew that *most* of the people on the list were dead. Older civilians with nowhere to go, children too young to get married or join the military…and women, married to men who were currently serving in South Africa. It would be months, perhaps, or years before their husbands learned they'd been widowed.

Something has to be done, she thought, numbly. *But what?*

She sighed. Perhaps it was time to learn how to pray.

The unmarked aeroplane looked, to the civilian eye, to be identical to the other aircraft on the tarmac. It was large, easily forty metres from nose to tail; indeed, the only obvious difference was the complete lack of markings. And yet, to Andrew, it was easy to tell that the aircraft was American. There was a *smoothness* to the aircraft that was lacking in the *Reich's* designs. It touched down neatly, the pair of escorting fighters flashing over the airfield and heading into the distance. Andrew couldn't help hoping that they found a pair of prowling easterner aircraft on their way home. The bombing of Berlin was growing more intensive as the front lines moved closer.

"That's the fifth shipment," General William Knox said. "You think they're not going to try and take them apart?"

Andrew shrugged as the aircraft came to a halt, the ground crew already running forward to open the hatches and start unloading before the airfield came under attack again. The *Reich* might consider the airfield to be a state secret - despite being close to Berlin, it wasn't shown on any official map - but the SS knew about it. They'd even tried to bomb it twice before, although it had cost them a pair of long-range bombers. He'd seen the wreckage as they'd driven towards the airfield.

"I think they've already captured a few," he said. It had been a concern - a very valid concern - back when the US had started shipping Stingers to South Africa. If the Germans captured a missile launcher, the doubters had said, they might be able to reverse-engineer the technology and start supplying it to *their* clients. "And in any case, the risk is acceptable."

Knox smiled. "Is that your choice to make?"

Andrew grinned. "It was the President who made the final call," he said. "If the provisional government wins the war, we find ourselves talking to a government that owes us a favour - and, just incidentally, might be better for Germany than their old government. But if the SS wins the war, we go straight back to the days when nuclear war seemed a very real possibility."

"I am aware of the reasoning," Knox said, a little tartly. "But the *Reich's* long-term health isn't our concern."

"It is," Andrew said. "If they get desperate, they might do something stupid in hopes of getting out of the trap."

He shook his head, then watched as the first set of pallets were unloaded and transported towards the warehouse. The Stingers were designed to be idiot-proof, even though he knew that some idiots could be very clever indeed when it came to breaking things. If they could be used by illiterate tribesmen from somewhere with an unpronounceable name, they could be used by German soldiers who were both literate *and* aware of the importance of following instructions. The handful of printed instructions attached to each of the missiles - in German - would be more than enough for them.

And it might just convince most of the soldiers that the weapons were produced in the Reich, Andrew thought. The days when German weapons had dominated the world were long gone, but he had to admit that some of their designers were quite ingenious. Their general technological base had been falling behind America's for quite some time, yet they sometimes came up with ideas the US had missed. *Hopefully, that will make it harder for them to believe that the provisional government is talking to us.*

"I'm due to go to the front tomorrow," Knox added. "They were quite keen on warning me about the dangers."

Andrew nodded. "You could be killed," he pointed out. "Or captured."

Knox made a rude gesture with his hand. "I didn't join the marines to sniff flowers," he said, sarcastically. "Or to count trees in Siberia."

"If you get killed, there won't be any official protests," Andrew reminded him. "And if you get captured…"

He scowled, allowing his words to trail away. A handful of covert intelligence operatives - and observers - *had* been captured by the *Reich*, only to vanish without trace. God knew the United States had done the same, with German agents captured in Latin America, but it still pained him. The US promised its defenders that none of them would be left behind, even to the point of threatening a major conflict with Mexico, yet pushing the *Reich* around was far more risky. If Knox were captured, there would be no demands for his return. His widow would be given a sealed coffin and told her husband had died in the line of duty.

This is a shitty world, he thought, grimly. *Poor Marian doesn't deserve to lose her husband like that.*

"I know the risks," Knox said. "But when are we ever going to get a better chance to see our foes in action?"

Andrew nodded, curtly. Orbital and high-altitude reconnaissance had told the United States a great deal about the *Reich*, ranging from flaws in the latest panzers to the limitations of German antiaircraft weapons, but they needed more. Knox was right. A US observer, embedded with the provisional government's defenders, would be able to learn a great deal about how the *Reich* actually worked. And such data would come in handy, Andrew knew, if the US ever had to go to war. Just knowing that the armour on the panzers was weaker than they'd supposed was a titbit of information that was worth its weight in gold.

"Be careful," he said.

He would have gone himself, if he hadn't been ordered to stay in Berlin. Given how much he knew about ongoing covert operations, his bosses didn't want to take the slightest chance of him falling into enemy hands. Knox would probably get a noodle in the back of the head - SS slang for a bullet through the brain - but they'd take their time with Andrew, if they knew who he was. They'd drain everything he knew, then dump whatever was left in a mass grave...

The alarms began to howl. Andrew glanced up sharply, then swore as he realised the aircraft was far from completely unloaded. Knox grabbed his hand and dragged him towards the nearest shelter, the ground crews dropping whatever they were carrying and following the Americans as they ran. Three tiny dots appeared, low in the sky; they hugged the ground as they raced towards the airfield. A missile launcher swung around and opened fire, blasting one of the aircraft out of the sky, but the remaining two kept coming, their cannons spraying explosive shells into the grounded aircraft. Andrew had barely a second to turn and watch helplessly as the American aircraft exploded into a colossal fireball, a wave of heat scorching his face as he dropped to the ground. The easterner aircraft swooped around, dropping a pair of dumb bombs on the runways, then fled back towards the east.

Should have ringed the airfield with defences, Andrew thought bitterly, as he picked himself up. Four American aircrew were now dead, along with at least a dozen Germans. *But they didn't want to draw attention to the airfield.*

"Damn," Knox said. "Now what?"

"They'll just have to send more aircraft," Andrew said. "And we'll have to lie about the pilots."

He contemplated the problem, briefly. Shipping the Stingers into the *Reich* would be far harder than flying them in. The *Reich* rarely allowed British or American ships to dock, particularly in naval bases. Someone would certainly start asking questions if that changed in a hurry. But there might be no choice. His superiors were unlikely to authorise more flights to Berlin…

He ignored Knox's angry stare as he looked at the flaming wreckage. There was no help for it, not if they wanted the operation to remain covert. The pilots would be recorded as having died in training accidents, with a carefully-manufactured paper trail to back it up - if anyone checked. OSS would make sure the families received a hefty payout in exchange for their silence, even though they might never know what had happened to their husbands and sons.

It galled him, more than he cared to admit. Intelligence - and covert operations - work called for secrecy, demanded secrecy. He'd had to lie to girlfriends, in the past; he'd have to lie to his wife, if he ever married. Knox's scorn was quite understandable. There was something inherently *honest* about the Marine Corps, while far too much intelligence work was dishonest by nature. Manipulating someone into betraying his country was far too much like trying to seduce a married woman. And the pilots, men who had only been in the fringes of the operation, would never be applauded for their work. Their deaths would pass unremarked. There would certainly be no threats of retaliation.

Perhaps the whole story will be declassified, one day, he thought. He knew too much of his own work would never see the light of day - he'd seduced too many foreigners into working for the United States - but the pilots weren't true intelligence operatives. *And then their families can be truly proud of them.*

CHAPTER TWENTY-FOUR

Berlin, Germany Prime
27 September 1985

"Their advance spearheads are within five kilometres of the city limits," Field Marshal Gunter Voss said, "and we have reports of recon units on both sides of the city. It won't be long before they have Berlin completely surrounded."

Volker Schulze barely heard him. They were standing on the roof of the *Reichstag*, staring into the darkness. A handful of fires could be seen within the city - and a couple more in the distance, outside the city - but otherwise Berlin was as dark and silent as the grave. The criminal element was slowly growing out of control, he knew; the police and security forces were badly overstretched. They were lucky, very lucky, that starvation hadn't begun to bite - yet. When it did, he feared, Berlin - and the provisional government - was finished.

"They'll have complete air superiority over the city tomorrow," Voss added. "Even with the...special weapons" - Volker concealed his amusement at how Voss couldn't quite admit, even in private, that the weapons came from America - "we're going to have trouble enduring the bombardment."

He paused. "We could call back some of the other aircraft."

Volker shook his head, without turning his gaze from the darkness surrounding his city. The plan would work, he told himself firmly; it would work because it *had* to work. Move forces eastwards, get them into position to launch a two-prong counterattack *after* the *Waffen-SS* had over-committed itself...assuming, of course, that they could keep the SS from using its own airpower to knock out the advance. He'd pulled back nearly all of the remaining fast-jet fighters, *Luftwaffe* and *Kriegsmarine*, to cover the gathering forces.

And, in doing so, I have left Berlin naked, he thought, grimly. *The air attacks we have faced so far will be a pinprick, compared to what's coming.*

He turned to look at the Field Marshal. "And the retreating forces?"

"Most of the infantry have fallen back into the outer defence lines," Voss said. "I've pulled a handful of the logistics units further back, just to support the main counter-offensive when it begins. The SS is now in control of far too much territory outside the city."

Volker nodded. The American flights had been reduced - sharply - after one of their aircraft had been destroyed, then stopped altogether after the airfield had come under heavy shelling from the advancing forces. Getting even a handful of people out of Berlin now would be difficult, even though a couple of roads were still open. The SS had even started driving more and more refugees into the city, forcing him to choose between feeding them or leaving them outside the defence lines to starve. All his plans to move the poor bastards further to the west had come to nothing.

"They'll try to take the city," he said, quietly.

"It depends," Voss said. "They may feel that starvation will do the job for them."

Volker had his doubts. Stalingrad had been a nightmare, according to his father. The Russians had fought for every inch of ground and *kept* fighting, even when it had become clear that the battle was lost. In the end, they'd bled the *Wehrmacht* badly, although nowhere near badly enough to keep it from taking Moscow the following year. The SS's generals would know the perils of fighting in a city…

…And yet time was not on their side. It was already growing colder, with reports of frost and snow further to the east, but that wasn't the *real* problem. The longer the *Reich* remained sundered, the weaker it would become. Karl Holliston might inherit a broken state - a *more* broken state - when he finally marched into the *Reichstag* and planted his ass in Volker's chair. No, the SS would launch an offensive into Berlin as soon as it felt it could actually win. And then…who knew what would happen?

He might win the battle, Volker thought, *but he might lose the war.*

"I've relieved Gath and dispatched him to take command of the counter-offensive forces," Voss said, into the silence. "I'm not going to abandon Berlin as long as you're here."

Volker gave him a brief smile. He'd never liked Voss - the Field Marshal was too much of a Junker for his tastes, heir to a tradition that had endured fifty years of Nazi rule - but he had to admit the man had nerve. He could have taken command of one of the counteroffensive forces - either in person or from the field HQ - and no one would have said a word against him. Staying in Berlin as the noose tightened was the mark of a good man.

"Thank you," he said, quietly.

"You're not leaving either," Voss pointed out. "Have you made preparations for the future if…if the worst happens?"

Volker nodded, although he hoped none of them would be necessary. The provisional government couldn't hope to survive for long if it lost Berlin. Germany, already starting to fragment, would shatter. The bonds holding the *Reich* together would come apart. Towns and cities would start operating independently, while each and every military officer with substantial firepower under his command would become a warlord. Holliston couldn't hope to hold the *Reich* together through anything, but force. After what he'd done…

No one trusts the SS any longer, Volker thought. *But then, no one in the west trusted them anyway.*

He sighed. He'd made no attempt to conceal what the SS had done, either the handful of significant atrocities or the hundreds of tiny crimes, each one representing a blow at the German people. The refugees shot down for being in the way, the men dragged out and executed for not being in the military, the women and young girls who had been brutally raped…And yet, making them public might have been a mistake. It had fired up anger and hatred, true, but it had also made people fearful. It was impossible to tell just how many of them would remain willing to fight, after Berlin fell.

"We will have to do our best to stop them here," he said, sternly. "I hope - I pray - that the soldiers are catching their breath."

"They are," Voss said. "Do you wish to address them?"

Volker concealed his amusement with an effort. He'd *been* a *Waffen-SS* paratrooper, after all, and he'd always *hated* it when a headquarters officer, someone who wore a clean uniform that had clearly never seen war, took time out to address the tired and grimy soldiers as they returned from their last operation. They'd all wanted nothing more than a bite to eat and a place to rest, but the uniformed politicians had never seemed to realise it. Volker was damned if he was making the same mistake.

"I'll press the flesh once they've had a chance to recuperate," he said, firmly. "I trust you made sufficient preparations for their accommodations?"

"Yes, *Herr Chancellor*," Voss said. He paused. "There's also the issue of medals and awards for the soldiers. And a handful of battlefield promotions that need to be confirmed."

Volker sighed. Medals came with financial rewards - or they had, before the economic crisis started to bite. Give a man the Knight's Cross and he'd expect a boosted pension, if he didn't take the money and spend it on drink and whores. It had been one of the many - many - problems facing the *Reich*.

"Confirm the promotions, unless you feel there's something that should be looked at more carefully," he ordered. "But don't grant any medals. We're going to have to make sure that there aren't any additional costs involved."

Voss looked disappointed. "The men try to earn medals for the rewards," he said. "They need them."

"And we don't have the money," Volker reminded him. "Paying the troops is going to be a nightmare."

————

"Kurt," a voice called. "*Herr Hauptman!*"

"I haven't had the promotion confirmed yet," Kurt said, as he turned to face his old friend. "And I see you've been promoted too."

Hauptman Bernhard Schrupp puffed out his chest. "They finally had to give me a promotion," he said, catching Kurt by the arm. "My natural beauty eventually overcame them."

"I think it was the scraping noise as you tried to get your head through the door," Kurt said, deadpan. "Who did you have to kill to get promoted?"

"They were asking for volunteers to block a couple of roads and I didn't jump backwards in time," Schrupp said. "And we did the job, so we were rewarded."

He elbowed Kurt, non-too-gently. "Did you get a day of leave?"

"Technically," Kurt said. He'd been given strict orders to stay within a kilometre of the makeshift barracks, which meant that going home to see his parents or siblings was out of the question. "But only technically."

"You mean you are tied to the barracks with a piece of string," Schrupp said. "Honestly! You'd think we were dogs!"

"Of course not," Kurt said. "Dogs are fed better."

"You got that right," Schrupp said. He caught Kurt's arm and pulled him forward. "Come with me."

Kurt pulled back. "Where are we going?"

"To a place we can now go," Schrupp said, with a wink. "You'll love it."

Kurt frowned, torn between curiosity and the urge to disagree. Schrupp might have found something interesting - a bar perhaps - or it might be something he'd be forced to disapprove of on principle. But he *was* technically on leave…he glanced up at the dark sky, then followed Schrupp down the road and past a pair of armed guards, standing outside a mid-sized building that was completely blacked out. The guards glanced at the rank insignias and let them through without comment. Inside, a middle-aged woman wearing a long sleeveless dress smiled cheerfully at the two young men.

"Hah," Schrupp said. "Who's available tonight?"

Kurt stopped, dead. "Is this a brothel?"

"Better than that, Kurt," Schrupp said. "This is an *officers* brothel. None of your two-mark tarts here! The girls actually know how to do interesting things with their mouths."

He elbowed Kurt, then tugged him towards the peepholes. "We can't eat or drink, but at least we can be merry," he added. "For tomorrow we may die."

Kurt felt his cheeks reddening as he peered through the peepholes. A dozen girls were on the far side, wearing nothing more than their underwear. The youngest looked to be a year or two younger than him, although it was hard to be sure. They had covered themselves with cosmetics to hide any imperfections. He found himself staring at them, despite his embarrassment. He'd known the brothels existed, but he'd never dared go. The stories he'd heard had put him off.

"Choose a number," the woman said, cheerfully. "Or two numbers, if you wish."

"Two in bed," Schrupp hissed. "Doesn't that sound fun?"

Kurt found himself unable to speak. He'd always assumed that he wouldn't lose his virginity until he got serious with a girl, although his father had promised to beat him black and blue if he got someone pregnant before he married her. Kurt had wondered, despite himself, if *his* parents had had to marry in a hurry, even though it was hardly unusual in the *Reich*. But that wouldn't be a risk in a brothel. The girls would have been treated to make it impossible.

"Pick one," Schrupp urged. "Or I'll pick one for you."

Kurt glared at him, then looked back through the peephole. There were blonde girls, brown-haired girls, dark-haired girls…all Germanic. It made him wonder how they'd managed to wind up in the brothel, although he supposed the pay would actually be quite high. The officers wouldn't want a *Gastarbeiter* woman who'd been thrown out by her masters and sold to a brothel. And one of the dark-haired girls was quite pretty…

"Number twelve," he said.

"Right this way, *Mein Herr*," the woman said. She glanced at Schrupp. "I'll be back in a moment for your choice, my dear."

Kurt could feel his heart racing in his chest as the woman opened a door and showed him into a room. It was larger than his bedroom at home, dominated by a giant four-poster bed that looked as though it had been dragged out of a museum. The sheets looked clean - he hoped, desperately, that they were changed between visitors. A side door opened into a small bathroom, with a shower, a toilet and a notice warning him to be careful how much water he used. It was so out of place that it made him smile. But then, water supplies to the city were in danger of being cut off.

The door opened. He turned, just in time to see the girl step into the room. She'd donned a silk dressing gown that clung to her curves in all the right places, hinting at the shape of her body rather than revealing bare skin. She carried a tray in one hand, holding a small bottle and a pair of glasses. Kurt found himself staring helplessly as she placed the tray on the mantelpiece and then turned to smile at him. It made him feel as though he wanted to melt.

"Well," she said. "Is this your first time?"

"Yeah," Kurt stammered. He wasn't ashamed of being a virgin, even though he *had* had girlfriends in school. His father had been right. He had been in no position to marry until after he'd completed his education. "Here and...and everywhere."

She smiled. "I understand," she said. She patted the bed with one hand. "Please, sit. We have all the time in the world."

Kurt sat, feeling conflicted. She - he didn't even know her *name* - was beautiful, the most beautiful girl he'd seen. He hadn't been close enough to any of his girlfriends to do more than kiss them; he'd certainly not been allowed to touch their breasts or slip his hand into their panties. The recruits at the barracks had bragged, when the lights were out, of their exploits, but he'd just remained silent. His father had also told him that most men lied through their teeth about sex.

The girl leaned forward and kissed his lips, her dressing gown coming undone and falling open to reveal her bare breasts. Kurt stared, his hands jerking forward to touch them. He'd never seen bare breasts, not outside a handful of magazines his father had beaten him for possessing. They certainly hadn't been *real*. But now...they felt soft and warm against his hand, welcoming...

"You have all night," the girl whispered, as she started to undo his shirt. "Lie back and enjoy it."

———

"Start setting up the defence lines," *Hauptsturmfuehrer* Hennecke Schwerk ordered, as they slowly took up position outside Berlin. "And keep a close watch on our approaches."

"*Jawohl, Herr Hauptsturmfuehrer.*"

Schwerk smirked as his subordinates scurried to do his bidding. The company under his command might have been thrown together in a hurry - the remains of his former unit combined with two others - but he found it hard to care. He'd been *promoted*! None of his family had ever been promoted in combat, let alone been given command of a scratch unit in the middle of a war. The company might be far from perfect - very few of the men had trained together - but they'd learned fast as they continued the march towards Berlin.

They're pleased with me, he thought, as he touched his new rank insignia. *And I won't let them down.*

He peered through the darkness towards Berlin. Even in the darkness - the city had blacked out most of its lights - it was clear that Berlin was far larger than any city he'd seen, far larger than Germanica itself. A sprawling nightmare, according to the map; a maze of government buildings, residential areas, factories, transit barracks and everything else a modern city needed to remain alive. Berlin had never been rebuilt, unlike Moscow; there was no order to the city at all. And yet, the defenders had already started to dig into the city. Fighting their way into Berlin was going to be a nightmare.

We can do it, he thought, coldly. He was damned if he was conceding anything to the enemy, not now. *And they won't be able to stop us.*

A gunshot cracked out, far too close to him for comfort. He ducked down, drawing his pistol with one hand as he searched frantically for targets. The westerners weren't *good* at sneaking around, not like the men and women who had grown up in a war zone, but a number of them had taken the risk of engaging the stormtroopers at night. Schwerk had rapidly come to learn that nowhere could be trusted completely, not even a seemingly-deserted campsite that looked perfect for a night. The sniping and IEDs were taking their toll on his men. And they, in turn, had taken it out on the civilians. Schwerk had watched, dispassionately, as prospective insurgents were hung; he'd turned a blind eye when a couple of his men had marched a female prisoner away from the camp for some fun. The insurgents and those who sheltered them deserved no less.

He stayed low as he peered into the darkness, but no more shots echoed through the air. The bastards were just trying to keep his men awake, rather than catching some desperately needed sleep. Chances were that whoever fired the shot was already well away from the camp, but no one would know for sure. Unless, of course, they stumbled across his body...

Bastard, he thought, as he rejoined his men. Tomorrow, the enemy would have nowhere to run. The stormtroopers were already surrounding Berlin, cutting off all routes in and out of the city. *And you'll soon be dead.*

CHAPTER TWENTY-FIVE

Berlin, Germany Prime
28 September 1985

"You really should not be up here," Horst said, as Gudrun scrambled to the top of the ladder and peered into the distance. "There are snipers out there."

"I owe it to my conscience to take *some* risks," Gudrun snapped. They'd made up after their last argument, but even repeated lovemaking hadn't been able to hide the fact that their first disagreement had never been fully resolved. "And I'm not in the front line."

She ignored his snort as she peered towards the enemy lines. The SS had crept close to Berlin under cover of darkness, laying out their positions and digging trenches with a thoroughness she could only admire. Voss, from what she'd heard before they'd left the *Reichstag*, had admitted that the defenders didn't have a hope of making a successful sally without being torn to ribbons. The SS lines were too strong. And the handful of shells they'd hurled into Berlin - already - was merely a taste of what they could do, if the city refused to surrender.

"Get down," Horst ordered, sharply. "If they see you, they'll take a shot at you."

"They couldn't hit anything at this distance," Gudrun said. "And..."

She yelped as Horst grabbed her foot and pulled. Her fingers lost their grip on the ladder and she fell, straight into his arms. She struggled, pulled herself free and found her footing, then whirled around to glare at him. She'd never been so tempted to slap a man since one of her distant relatives had visited and spent the whole time staring at her chest. And the little bastard had had the nerve to ask her out afterwards...

"They are already sniping into the city," Horst snapped. "I don't want to lose you too."

"They couldn't hit me…"

"They can and they will, if they think it's worth taking the shot," Horst snarled. "What happens if you die?"

Gudrun glared. "You think I'm *that* important?"

"I think you're very important," Horst snapped back. "Who is going to stand up and tell the Chancellor that he's in the wrong? And who is going to make damn sure that the *Reichstag* actually lives up to its title?"

"I don't think I'm the only idealist out there," Gudrun said. She wanted to yell and scream, but she knew it would be pointless. The hell of it was that he had a point. Germany had no real tradition of political debate, of the give and take that characterised democracy. And it would be easy to slip back into fascism. "And do you care more about me than about the *Reichstag?*"

"You," Horst said. He leaned forward and kissed her forehead, very lightly. "I don't want to lose you."

Gudrun shook her head in silent frustration. She loved Horst, but his over-protectiveness got on her nerves. And yet, he was better than many other boyfriends or husbands…who knew what would happen when they got married? Perhaps he'd change, or she'd change, or everyone else would change. And if they didn't get married…

Father would go mad, she thought, as they slipped away from the ladder. *He'd expect me to marry someone sooner or later.*

She smiled, despite herself, as she heard aircraft buzzing over the city. A missile - an *American* missile - lanced up towards one of them, blowing the aircraft out of the sky. Its comrades scattered, dropping bombs at random as they fled. The bombing didn't seem to be very effective, but it would definitely add to the fear and panic threatening the city. All of a sudden, getting married - or living in sin - no longer seemed a real problem.

Horst caught her arm. "Gudrun, I want you to stay inside from this moment on," he said, firmly. "You're in great danger."

"No more than anyone else," Gudrun said. They reached the car; the driver opened the door for them, then carefully ignored their argument as he started the engine. "We're all in danger, aren't we?"

"Yes," Horst said. The reports of refugees being raped and murdered had continued to flow into the city, as if the SS had decided to simply take off the gloves. "And yet you're definitely one of the people the SS *really* wants. Everyone else…has at least a reasonable chance of survival."

Gudrun snorted. She'd read the reports from Stalingrad, the reports that had been deemed too sensitive to be published. The Russians had come very close to fighting the *Wehrmacht* to a standstill. If the stormtroopers chose to press into Berlin, the bloody slaughter would catch thousands of civilians as well as soldiers. The provisional government had even asked the SS to allow the refugees and civilians to leave, but the SS hadn't even bothered to reply. Voss had noted that the refugees actually weakened the defenders. Either the defenders refused to feed the refugees - which would cause riots - or they fed the refugees and ran out of food quicker, ensuring that the SS could take the city without a fight.

"*No one* has a reasonable chance of survival," she said.

"You certainly don't," Horst said, flatly. "And nor does anyone else on the purge list."

"I know," Gudrun said. "How many names do they know?"

"They'll be settling old scores as well as merely purging the provisional government," Horst said. "I expect they'll kill just about every high-ranking military and civil official in the west."

Gudrun couldn't disagree. The SS had carried out a number of random atrocities, but they'd also rounded up and arrested - or killed - hundreds of government bureaucrats in captured towns. They'd even arrested mayors, policemen and a number of soldiers who'd resigned, rather than fight their fellow Germans. Gudrun had no idea why the SS had considered them suitable targets for a purge, but she couldn't deny the results. Hundreds of other officials, caught in the path of the SS's advance, had deserted their posts, making the evacuation efforts - already badly strained - completely impossible. And, from what little she'd heard, the SS's replacements were more concerned with political reliability than getting the occupied territory running again.

"The country will fall apart," she protested, weakly.

Karl Holliston had to be mad. Gudrun knew - whatever Horst might say - that she wasn't particularly important. She had no true power base of her own. But Hans Kruger and Field Marshal Voss *did* have power bases, power bases that were part of the system that held the *Reich* together. Murdering every last senior bureaucrat in the *Reich* might make the SS popular again - Gudrun had heard her mother grumbling about filling in form after form just to get a driving licence - but without them the system would simply collapse.

"I don't think Holliston cares," Horst said. "He just believes that purging the rot from the *Reich* will be enough to purify it."

"And he thinks I'm the rot," Gudrun said.

"Yes," Horst insisted. "Which is why you need to take very good care of yourself."

He paused. "If nothing else," he added, "don't give him the satisfaction of dancing a jig on your grave."

Gudrun nodded. "I…"

"Shellfire," the driver snapped. He yanked the car to one side as shells crashed down on the city. "Get ready to jump if necessary."

The ground shook. Gudrun braced herself, but the shells hadn't landed *that* close to their position. She breathed a sigh of relief, then looked backwards to see flames and smoke rising from the impact point. God alone knew who had been caught by the shells, if *anyone* had been caught by the shells. The SS seemed to like hurling bursts of shellfire into the city at random.

"That was alarmingly close," Horst said. He slapped the partition. "Get us back to the *Reichstag* as quickly as possible."

"*Jawohl*," the driver snapped.

Gudrun caught Horst's arm. "We're going to the hospital!"

"Not this time," Horst said. "Those shells could have been aimed at you."

"I doubt it," Gudrun said. "If they knew where I was, surely they would have sent a commando team after me."

"We're not taking the risk," Horst said. "I'm taking you home."

Gudrun saw the grim look in his eyes and decided that further argument would probably be futile. Horst was determined to keep her safe, even from herself. At least he wasn't trying to tell her she couldn't stay on the council… she scowled at him, then sat back in her seat and crossed her arms. Was it normal to feel so mad at someone who was actually trying to help, she asked herself, or was it just the strain getting to her? There was no way to know.

She rose as soon as the car slipped into the underground garage and came to a halt. "I need to talk to my mother," she said. "I'll see you in the bunker?"

Horst gave her a concerned look. "I'll walk you to her apartment," he said. "And then I'll wait outside."

Gudrun opened her mouth to argue, then nodded reluctantly. There was at least one spy in the *Reichstag* itself, perhaps two. And if there was a spy on the council itself…that spy wouldn't be connected to any other spies. He'd be too valuable to go sneaking into Horst's bedroom to leave notes and instructions.

"Very well," she said.

Her mother had moved into the *Reichstag* almost as soon as she'd been asked, after a brief show of reluctance. Gudrun had been relieved, even though it meant she'd be living far too close to yet another pair of prying eyes. It ensured her mother's safety even in such trying times. But, at the same time, her mother couldn't be protected completely. She'd become far too involved with the various female protest groups.

"Gudrun," her mother called, when she entered. "How are you?"

Gudrun swallowed as Horst checked the room, then left, closing the door behind him. Her mother had been just as inflexible as her father, although in a very different way. Gudrun had never been the ideal daughter; indeed, they had never really understood one another. And yet, being the only two women in the house had brought them together more than either of them might have wished.

Her mother eyed her for a long moment. "Problems with him?"

"A few," Gudrun said. Hadn't her life been so much simpler last year? "Is that normal?"

"Yes," her mother said. She waved Gudrun to a chair. "Why don't you sit down and we'll talk about it."

———

Oberstgruppenfuehrer Alfred Ruengeler had been to Berlin more times than he cared to recall, although he'd never really *liked* the city. It wasn't something he could put his finger on, a sense - perhaps - that there were just too many different attitudes clashing together in close proximity. Germanica was cleaner and simpler, the work of an architect who'd built on the ashes of a dead city. Berlin…was a dark city.

And it would be hell to take, he thought, as he surveyed the growing defences through his binoculars. The last contingency plans to defend Berlin had been drawn up in the 1960s, back when there had been a major disagreement between the *Reich* and America that could have easily led to war, but that had been before the sprawling had just exploded out into the countryside. Now, Berlin was *huge*, far larger than any city the *Reich* had had to take by force...and most of his men would be utterly unprepared for the role.

"They don't seem to have any panzers," *Sturmbannfuehrer* Friedemann Weineck pointed out, thoughtfully. "Just...antitank weapons."

Alfred snorted, rudely. If there was one thing he'd learned during the war, it was that the Panzer XI - the finest tank in the world, according to the designers - had a number of nasty little flaws. Someone had sold the *Reich* a bill of goods, he'd concluded, after reading the umpteenth report of missiles punching through the panzer's forward armour plating; someone was going to die, when he got his hands on them. But it was something that would have to wait until the end of the war.

"The panzers will be torn apart if they get into Berlin," he said. Panzers were rarely useful in close confines, as the *Waffen-SS* had found out more than once. "It will be primarily an infantry operation."

He closed his eyes in pain. His stormtroopers *did* have advantages, they'd discovered, but the *Wehrmacht* soldiers were hardly *weaklings*. They'd managed a successful series of engagements, followed by quick retreats, that had bloodied his forces while denying him a shot at a quick victory. He'd hoped to crush one or more of their forces as they attempted to retreat, thrusting armoured spearheads forward, but the enemy had managed to escape the noose before the infantry caught up to finish the job.

And our logistics have been pushed to the limit, he thought. *The bastards have stripped everywhere bare.*

He turned and walked slowly back towards the new CP, established in what had once been a farm before it had been captured. The farmer and his two teenage sons had put up a brief fight, but hadn't managed to do more than wound one of the attackers before they were captured, beaten and hung. Thankfully, at least for Alfred's conscience, the farmer's wife and three daughters - their existence clearly indicated by the photos on the wall - had made themselves scarce before the stormtroopers arrived. He hoped, as he stepped into the living room, that they'd made it safely to the west. A farmwife would have no trouble finding work on another farm.

"*Herr Oberstgruppenfuehrer*," an aide said. "The *Fuhrer* is on Line One."

Alfred nodded. "I'll take it in the secure room," he said, walking towards the door. "Get me a complete report from *SS-Volk* and remind her CO that I don't want any more of his games."

"*Jawohl*," the aide said.

The secure room was anything but, certainly when compared to the facilities in Germanica or Berlin itself. His communication staff had moved a pair of telephones into the room and installed guards outside, but there was no way to render it anything like as secure as he wanted. The enemy might well already know where they were and, if they did, they might take advantage of the situation to intercept his calls.

But there was no choice. He picked up the phone and put it to his ear. "*Mein Fuhrer.*"

"*Herr Oberstgruppenfuehrer*," Karl Holliston said. He sounded pleased, something that worried Alfred more than he cared to admit. He'd dared to make a mild protest about the increasing number of atrocities as his forces advanced, but the *Führer* had ignored him. "I trust that all is in readiness to attack Berlin?"

"Not as yet," Alfred said. "I need to bring up more supplies and get the men rested before launching an invasion of the city itself."

"Time is not on our side," Holliston said. The *Fuhrer's* voice hardened. "You do know that, don't you?"

"Yes, *Mein Fuhrer*," Alfred said. "I understand the problem facing us."

He scowled. He'd stared at the map so much it was burned into his brain. The traitors were playing it smart, shipping panzers eastwards from Occupied France - despite dropped bridges and ruined railway lines - and massing them somewhere to the west of Berlin. It was hard to be sure where because the remainder of the *Luftwaffe* - and those never-to-be-sufficiently-damned American-made missiles were defending the area with savage intensity. The last four recon aircraft that had been sent in that direction had never come back, which told him things he didn't want to know about its defences. And no one would expend so much effort on defending areas of no tactical or strategic value.

No, he told himself. The traitors were massing their forces, preparing a counterattack. He had every faith in his men, but they were already tired, their faith in their panzers shaken and their logistics operating on a shoestring. The traitors, if they could throw an offensive into the field at the right time, would smash his men and send them reeling all the way back to Germany East. It would be disastrous.

This is what the Russians wanted to do to us at Stalingrad, he thought. The records had been quite clear, although the Russian ambitions had far outstripped their capabilities. Even the emergency aid the Americans had sent after it became clear that Moscow was at risk of falling hadn't been enough to save them from the consequences of their own stupidity. *I wonder if Field Marshal Voss read the same reports.*

"We have to take Berlin," Holliston said. "How soon can you launch the attack?"

Alfred took a moment to think, but in truth he already knew the answer. "Four days, perhaps five," he said. "We can weaken them through shelling and air attacks while building up our forces. Right now, we just don't have the reserves to take advantage of any chink in their defences."

"Understood," Holliston said. "But no more than five days."

"*Jawohl, Mein Fuhrer*," Alfred said. *That* was surprisingly accommodating. He'd expected to have to launch the offensive in two days, despite the risks. "It shall be done."

He heard the click on the other end of the line, then sighed. They *could* weaken the enemy, but nothing short of a nuke - perhaps more - would be enough to allow them to walk into Berlin without a fight. And *that* was off the table. He had no idea if *any* nukes were usable - yet - but destroying Berlin would shock the entire *Reich*. Holliston might be on the verge of going mad, yet he wasn't *insane*.

Yet, his own thoughts pointed out. *What will you do if he does nuke Berlin?*

But there was no answer. What *could* he do?

CHAPTER TWENTY-SIX

Berlin, Germany Prime
29 September 1985

Undisciplined wretches, Hauptsturmfuehrer Katharine Milch thought, as she strode along under cover of darkness. *You should all be cleared off the streets.*

It was annoying, she had to admit, even if it *was* helpful. The tidal wave of refugees heading into Berlin - as if they thought there was some kind of safety in the city - made it easier for her and her team to operate without being detected. And they would consume more and more food, forcing the traitors to decide between stamping down hard on refugees or allowing themselves to be starved into submission quicker than they'd planned. But it was annoying, a sign of the wishful thinking and soppy sentimentality that had plagued the west since the death of Adolf Hitler. A *true* government would have taken steps to remove the refugees before it was too late.

She clung to the shadows, keeping her distance from the refugees as she led her team towards the target. There were a couple of policemen in view, both of whom looked cold and nervous. Several policemen had been killed on the streets over the last few days and, so far, no one had tracked down their killers. Katharine had killed two personally, she knew; the remainder had either fallen to her team or had been picked off by criminals or people with private scores to settle. The Order Police had never been popular and, now the *Reich* had been badly weakened, the fear was gone.

Should have cracked down hard, Katharine thought, nastily. *And then put the refugees to work.*

The thought made her smile as she skirted yet another clump of refugees. In the east, people who had been forced to flee their homes - like she had, when she'd been seven - were put to work at once, earning their keep. She still shuddered at the thought of cooking, cleaning and washing for her adopted family, even though they'd been very kind to the orphaned girl. And they'd even sponsored her when she applied to the SS, even though only a handful of women were ever accepted for training. They'd known she wanted revenge on those who had killed her family. But the traitorous government didn't seem inclined to force the refugees to work.

They could hew wood, draw water and build barricades, if nothing else, she thought, glancing into one of the makeshift tents. *And the girls could help move weapons and supplies to the men.*

She allowed no trace of her feelings to show on her face as their target finally came into view. A warehouse, protected by four armed policemen and a single armoured car. They must have taken it out of storage, she decided; the thin-skinned vehicle wouldn't last a second on a modern battlefield, even if pitted against a Panzer III from the war. And yet, it was more than intimidating enough for a bunch of unarmed refugees. Katharine couldn't help wondering if its machine guns were actually loaded, although she wouldn't assume that was the case until the vehicle refused to engage the attackers. The defenders protecting the edge of the city wouldn't be keen on releasing ammunition to the guards *inside* the city.

Keeping her footsteps even, she strode past the warehouse, covertly circling the building and checking to ensure there were no other guards hiding in the shadows. There were no other entrances, save for the big doors at the front; health and safety had never been a particular concern of the *Reich*, certainly when the workers had been *Untermenschen*. She smiled at their conceit, then used hand signals to tell her team what to do. And then she walked forward, right towards the policemen.

They reacted with surprising speed, the moment she made a beeline towards them, lifting their weapons into firing position. But it was already too late. Katherine yanked up her machine pistol and opened fire, gunning all four of the policemen down, while one of her men hurled a grenade under the armoured car. It exploded into a fireball, the heat scorching Katherine's face as she hurried towards the doors. The grenade was designed to take out tougher vehicles than a single outdated armoured car.

The doors crashed open, revealing a colossal stockpile of everything from ration packets to industrial equipment. Katherine puzzled over it for a long moment, then decided that the traitors must have stripped food supplies and anything else that might be useful from the towns and satellite cities surrounding Berlin. It wasn't a bad move either, she had to admit, but it was going to cost them She was tempted to call for the refugees, to offer them the chance to loot the warehouse, yet she knew the traitors would probably arrive in time to keep the refugees from stealing everything. They'd have reinforcements already on the way.

"Burn it," she ordered.

She unhooked the grenade from her belt and hurled it into the warehouse. It detonated seconds later, sending out a wave of fire that ignited everything it touched. The SS had designed the grenades to burn Slavic hovels to the ground, tiny huts built of wood, mud and makeshift brick. They were tougher than they looked, according to her instructors, but the same couldn't be said of the warehouse's contents. The flames were spreading faster and faster, burning everything to a crisp.

"Time to go," she said.

She turned and led the way back along the streets, hearing the sound of approaching cars. It was tempting to set up an ambush, to engage the policemen as they approached, but she had a feeling that it would prove pointless. She had only four men under her command, apart from the handful of SS operatives; she didn't dare risk losing even one of them if it could be avoided. Besides, there would be soldiers on the way too. Her men were good, but they would be massively outnumbered.

The police cars roared past, followed by a pair of red fire engines. Someone had seen the blaze then, she noted; she wondered, absently, just who had managed to call in a report so quickly. Unless they'd anticipated an attack on the warehouse…but surely, if they had, they would have made sure the building was actually secure. Clearing the nearby buildings and setting up a line of checkpoints would have made her job much harder.

It might be better to target the fire engines next, she thought, as she watched more police cars racing past. *And make it harder for them to put out any other fires.*

She glanced behind her - the inferno was still blazing, a towering pillar of flame rising into the air - and then smiled. It wasn't much - four men, a single armoured car and a shitload of supplies - but it would hurt the rebels. Now the city was under siege, they would have no hope of replacing the destroyed supplies before the *Waffen-SS* attacked. And they would have to cover the other warehouses by drawing men from the front lines.

"A good day's work," she said, as they reached the hideout. "Get undressed, then get into bed and catch some sleep."

She smirked as she walked into the bedroom and started to undress. As far as anyone knew, they were a family that had remained in Berlin since the uprising - and they had the papers to prove it. Katherine had expected to have to infiltrate London or Washington - she could pass for either British or American, at a pinch - but slipping into Berlin and operating within the city had been almost disconcertingly easy. Her instructors had told her never to break cover, never to do anything that might reveal her true nature…and yet, Berlin was hardly a *challenge.*

Don't get complacent, she reminded herself, sternly. *If they search this place, our cover will be thoroughly blown.*

Closing her eyes, she went to sleep.

———

"Six men dead," Herman said, tartly. "One armoured car destroyed. Half the supplies in the warehouse burned to a crisp and the rest probably of dubious value."

He scowled at the mess in front of him. The warehouse was a blackened shell, the walls caved in and the steel girders looking as if they were on the verge of collapsing into a pile of debris. A hundred firemen had worked desperately to salvage what they could, but there just hadn't been the time to get *everything* out of the building. He had no idea what sort of chemicals the strike team had used, yet - whatever it was - it had burned hot enough to set fire to almost everything in the building.

"A very basic strike team," Horst commented. "Why weren't there more guards in place?"

Herman felt his anger deepen. "Where would you have us leave unde-fended," he snapped, "so we can cover a single building?"

Horst showed no visible reaction to his words. The former SS agent had been oddly distracted, when he'd met with Herman to discuss the ongoing investigation; Herman would have bet good money that it had something to do with Gudrun. And yet, he didn't have the time to worry about it. Losing so much food would cause panic all over the city, once it sank in that rations - already small - would have to be reduced still further. Starvation - or the threat of starvation - might be enough to set off a riot that would tear Berlin apart.

"There just isn't the manpower to cover everywhere," Herman added, tartly. "It isn't as if we can pull troops off the wall."

"We might have to," Horst said. "Taking out the food supplies…it's always been part of the SS commando doctrine."

Herman sneered. "Know a few commandos, do you?"

"I did," Horst said. He sounded oddly nostalgic for a long moment. "They were the sort of men who would think nothing of crawling for hours, just to get to a target, then poisoning the wells."

He swore. "We need to keep a careful watch on the water supplies and power stations too," he added. "They'll come under attack soon."

Herman cursed. He'd gone without food for a couple of days, during his military service, but humans couldn't live long without water. Three days, his instructors had said, if the person going without was in reasonably good health. The old and the young would need water far more frequently…the thought of being without water was definitely enough to spark off more riots. If the SS managed to cut or reduce the water supplies, Berlin was doomed.

He took one last look at the ruined warehouse, then glanced up in alarm as he heard an aircraft flying over the city. These days, with the *Luftwaffe* badly weakened, it was a dead certainty that it wouldn't be *friendly*. The SS bomb-ing raids were pinpricks, compared to the sheer immensity of the largest city in the world, but they did *some* damage and wore down morale. He couldn't blame the civilians for slowly losing their cool under the constant sniping, shelling and bombing.

"We need to go back to the *Reichstag*," he said. "And see if we can speed up the detective work."

"I would be surprised if we cracked their cover so quickly," Horst admitted, as they headed for the car. "They'll have been trained for *far* more unfriendly places."

"We have to try," Herman said. He'd need to put forward recommendations, too. Random searches would annoy the population, but they might just uncover something of value. At the very least, it would warn the SS cell that they might have to be prepared to move at any moment. "Who knows? Maybe their cover will be too perfect."

Horst snorted, sitting back in his chair. "Their papers will be perfect because they'll have come from the official producer," he said. "There won't be any obvious forgeries to find."

Herman smiled. "You mean, like yours?"

"I passed the entry exams for the university," Horst said, flatly. "There was *no* fakery."

Herman was reluctant to admit it, but he was impressed. Gudrun had almost worked herself into a coma, preparing for the exams. He'd even seriously considered withdrawing permission for her to attend the university when he'd realised it was affecting her health, unlike the exams he and the boys had taken when they'd left school. And yet, he knew she had done well. He wished, suddenly, that he'd told her just how proud he was…back before she'd turned into a politician. It might not have been *traditional* for a girl to go to university - it made it harder for her to find a husband - but he'd been proud of her. Those exams had been nightmarishly hard.

And that means that Horst is smarter than he looks, he reminded himself. *He couldn't have passed for a student if he wasn't.*

Horst leaned forward and closed the partition, ensuring that the driver couldn't eavesdrop on them. "*Herr* Wieland," he said, formally. "I have a question."

Herman kept his amusement off his face. He had a feeling he knew *precisely* where this was going. But he merely nodded, inviting Horst to continue. There was nothing to be gained by making life *too* easy for the younger man.

"I would like to marry your daughter," Horst said, after a moment. He sounded nervous, too nervous. Herman found himself torn between amusement and concern. "I…I believe I could make her happy."

Herman considered it, carefully. He knew that Horst and Gudrun had *some* kind of relationship, if only because he wasn't blind. They inclined towards each other, particularly when they thought they weren't being watched. They'd been careful, he had to admit, but nowhere near careful enough to conceal the truth from him. And, even a mere *year* ago, it would have been cause for a number of pointed questions.

And yet, the thought bothered him. Gudrun was hardly his youngest child, but she *was* his only daughter. Putting her into the hands of an unworthy man would torment him for the rest of his life, if the marriage went sour. Divorce was almost unheard of in the *Reich*, if there were children. He'd been called out to far too many domestic battlegrounds where the husband had beaten the wife, or the wife - desperate and unable to escape - had mortally wounded the husband. He was damned if he would allow Gudrun to remain in such a household...

"I see," he said, carefully. He kept his face carefully blank. At least Horst was doing it properly, seeking his approval before formally popping the question. There were no shortage of horror stories about young couples, fancying themselves in love, who ran away when their parents rejected the match. "Is she pregnant?"

Horst flushed bright red. "Not...not to the best of my knowledge."

Herman allowed himself a moment of relief. Everyone joked that a blushing bride could deliver a baby in six months, rather than nine, yet it wasn't something he would have wanted for Gudrun. Most people would politely ignore the proof that a happy couple had been sleeping together before exchanging vows, but Gudrun was a politician. She had enemies, he suspected - and if she didn't have them already, she'd have them soon enough. One of them would be happy, no doubt, to call her out for sleeping with her husband before the actual marriage.

And then he frowned. If Horst and Gudrun had been sleeping together, she might already be pregnant and not know it.

He met the younger man's eyes. "And how do you plan to support her?"

Horst looked back at him, evenly. "Right now, I am drawing a salary from the *Reichstag*," he said, simply. "If I lose that position, for whatever reason, I *am* a trained commando and covert operative. I should have no difficulty volunteering my services to the *Wehrmacht*."

He smiled. "Technically, I am also entitled to an SS stipend, but I suspect that won't be paid."

Herman had to smile, despite his concern. "And how will you treat her as a wife?"

"I recognise that she has a career," Horst said. "And I will do nothing to interfere with it."

"Really," Herman said. "And will you be a house-husband?"

"If necessary," Horst said.

Herman frowned, inwardly. House-husbands were vanishingly rare in the *Reich*, more common in dramas about the horrors of living in America than in the real world. A man was expected to work to support his family, leaving the wife to take care of the home and raise the children. Indeed, the only house-husband he'd ever met had been a cripple, whose wife worked as a secretary to pay the bills. And no one could have denied he was unable to work.

But for a young man, barely out of school, the humiliation would be unbearable.

He put that thought aside for later consideration, then glanced out of the window and nodded towards a destroyed building. "One would argue that this is hardly the time to get married," he pointed out. "You might both be dead tomorrow."

"We are aware of the dangers," Horst said, stiffly.

Herman nodded, considering it. He had no reason to dislike Horst personally, even though the young man had been in the SS. At least he'd done the right thing at the right time, saving Gudrun's life before she'd ever realised it had been in danger. And he'd been willing to approve Konrad as a prospective husband…

"I must discuss the matter with my wife," he said, finally. Adelinde would *kill* him, perhaps not metaphorically, if he made the decision without consulting her. "But then you will have to convince *Gudrun* to marry you."

"I know," Horst said. He looked relieved. If Herman had said no, it would have made his life very awkward. "But I wanted your approval first."

CHAPTER TWENTY-SEVEN

Berlin, Germany Prime
29 September 1985

Horst found it hard to keep the relief off his face as the car pulled into the underground garage and came to a stop. He'd done a number of hard things in his life, but asking Herman for his daughter's hand in marriage had to be the hardest. And yet, perhaps, it would soon be the second-hardest. Herman might have approved the match - he certainly hadn't said no - but asking Gudrun would be the hardest of all. She might say no, or insist that they waited until the end of the war, or...

He shook his head. It wasn't going to be easy, but if he'd wanted an easy life he would have stayed on the farm. He could have avoided joining the military or the SS, simply by being in one of the protected categories of jobs. And yet, if he hadn't, he knew the uprising wouldn't have taken place. The spy who was sent in his place might not have been so inclined to listen to Gudrun, let alone decide to join her.

Herman had a point, he admitted silently as they made their way up to their office. A pair of trusted guards stood outside, with strict orders not to admit anyone unless they had been cleared by Herman personally. There *was* a war on...and Gudrun was almost certainly at the top of the list of people Karl Holliston intended to purge, if he won the war. And Horst himself might not be on the list now, but he certainly would be if Holliston ever found out just how badly he'd betrayed his masters. Horst knew the SS too well to imagine they would ever be satisfied with vague reassurances and evasions, not after the uprising. They would strip him down to the bedrock, then shoot whatever was left for the single greatest act of treason since Von Braun had fled the *Reich* for the United States.

And so we may as well live while we can, he thought, morbidly. *Enjoy the war, for the peace will be terrible.*

A handful of reports sat on the desk. Herman sat down and started to go through them while Horst poured two mugs of coffee. The coffee was already starting to run out, he'd heard, although the *Reichstag* had a huge cellar crammed with everything from fancy French wines to imported food from America. It wouldn't have done for the *Reich* Council to be deprived of the good things in life, even though the rest of the *Reich* was slowly starting to starve as food prices went up. Volker Schulze had ordered half the food handed out to the civilians, keeping them alive...in hindsight, that might have been a mistake. They'd have done better to start rationing from the very beginning.

"Police coffee," Herman commented, as he took a sip. "You do very good coffee."

Horst kept his expression carefully blank, suspecting he was being nee-dled. The coffee was as dark as Karl Holliston's soul, with no milk nor sugar to lighten it. Gudrun had winced, the first time he'd made coffee for her, although he did have to admit she'd drunk it anyway. But then, such coffee was intended to keep the drinker awake, rather than anything else. The sour taste was a bonus.

"Over the last week, seventeen staff went out of the *Reichstag*," Herman said, when Horst didn't deign to reply. "As you can see" - he held out the papers - "fifteen of them were absent for more than three hours, two of the remainder only returning to start their shifts the following morning. And yet all seventeen of them sleep in the building!"

"That doesn't prove anything," Horst pointed out. Indeed, he was tempted to dismiss the two who'd clearly spent the night elsewhere. The SS wouldn't want to run the risk of having their agents dismissed, just because they'd gone to a bar or a brothel. "They may have friends or family within the city."

"Some of them do," Herman said. "But they're very much in the minority."

Horst nodded. The *Reich* Council had been reluctant to hire Berliners to work in the *Reichstag*, although he'd never been sure why. Indeed, there were nearly five hundred staffers in the building and only fifty of them had been born and raised in Berlin. But it hardly mattered now…unless, of course, the Berliners could be dismissed from consideration because they stood out like sore thumbs. Or was that what they were supposed to think?

"So we have seventeen possible suspects," he mused. And he knew that he'd given three intelligence packets to the spy, all of which had been removed. "How many of them went out more than once?"

"Five," Herman said. "One staffer stayed out overnight twice, according to the records; the other four went out five times in the past week."

Horst scowled. If there was one spy, logically it had to be one of the five suspects. And he could see why a spy's handlers would want him to stay out overnight, allowing them to be pumped for further information, even though it *would* raise eyebrows. But if there was more than one spy, they could be rotating courier duty…which meant that all of the original seventeen had to be considered possible suspects.

He looked at Herman. "A battlefield is far simpler, isn't it?"

"Yeah," Herman said. "But there's also a greater chance at being blown away by a random shot."

Horst had to smile. He doubted he would have the patience for detective work, let alone the mindset of a street policeman. Patrolling the streets in Russia was deadly dangerous, but Berlin was well on the way to turning into a nightmare in its own right. Even without the SS commando cell - or whatever - that had burned down the warehouse, the city was slowly collapsing into chaos. And with an army just outside the city, sniping at everyone who showed his face, a major riot might just be enough to give the city to the SS.

And if that happens, I grab Gudrun and run, Horst promised himself. *There will be no hope of savaging the situation.*

Herman cleared his throat. "I'll have all seventeen shadowed, if they try to leave the *Reichstag* again," he said. "It isn't as if this is a dangerous place to be."

Horst nodded. None of the shells had landed within a kilometre of the *Reichstag*, accounting for the growing number of refugees squeezing into the magic circle. Karl Holliston, it seemed, wanted to recover the building intact, although Horst had a private suspicion that he wanted to ensure that the provisional government could actually surrender. Killing the only people who *could* order a full-scale surrender would be very unwise.

But then, he thought, *who would want to surrender?*

He sighed as he started to pace the room. The reports were very clear, even if some of the details had been hidden from the general public. Soldiers, sailors and airmen who fell into enemy hands were being marched eastwards to an uncertain fate. Horst would not have cared to put money on their survival. The SS might not be machine-gunning surrendered prisoners, but they could easily be kept in concentration camps and starved to death. Hell, the SS had even started shipping women and girls eastwards too. Horst had a nasty feeling he knew what *that* meant.

They're of good blood, he thought. It was rare for German women to be executed, although he suspected the women might wind up wishing that they *had* been allowed to die. *And in the east, they can be turned into brood cows without anyone giving a damn.*

Herman was saying something. Horst flushed. He hadn't been listening. "I'm sorry," he said. "Can you repeat that?"

"I said that the *Reichstag* is the safest place in Berlin," Herman said, patiently. "Who would want to leave?"

"It is the safest place until they actually storm the city," Horst replied. "And far too many of those refugees" - he nodded towards the wall - "are going to be ground up like sausage when the shit finally hits the fan."

———

Gudrun had had a busy day, even though she hadn't left the *Reichstag*. Her mother hadn't been able to offer her much advice, but she *had* urged Gudrun to spend time talking to the older women who had taken over the Woman's Institute. Gudrun hadn't enjoyed the experience - the older women seemed torn between clucking in disapproval and being pleased that a female had finally climbed into a position of power - but she had to admit that *Frau* Morgenstern was a formidable advocate. Under her command, the Woman's Institute had swallowed up its rivals and was plotting reform…after the war was finished, of course.

She looked down at the list of proposed legal amendments and sighed. Some of them were ones she wanted for herself, ranging from the right to refuse a suitor to guarantees for protection if a marriage broke down, while others were troublesome and contradictory. The older women might want some degree of freedom for themselves, but they were reluctant to extend such freedom to their daughters. Gudrun *definitely* felt sorry for Hilde, even though she'd been more than a little spoilt. Having *Frau* Morgenstern run her life couldn't have been fun.

And she's now in America, she thought. *I wonder if she'll want to come home.* There was a tap on the door. "Come in!"

She looked up, her eyes widening as she saw her father stepping into the room. He looked tired - he would have been woken at the same time as Horst - but his face was under careful control. Gudrun rose to her feet, unsure quite why he'd chosen to visit. He'd never visited her office before, not even after she'd invited him. She had a private suspicion that his mind had separated her into two people, Gudrun-The-Daughter and Gudrun-The-Politician. Maybe it was the only way he could cope with having a daughter who outranked him.

He wouldn't be so stuffy if Kurt was promoted to Field Marshal, she thought, feeling a flicker of resentment. *But then, father would still be the head of the household.*

"Father," she said, carefully.

Her father closed the door. "We need to talk," he said, firmly. He'd used the same words, she recalled with a shiver, when he'd approached her about Konrad. Had her mother spoken to him? Or...or what? "Please, sit down."

Gudrun sat, irked. It was *her* office.

Her father sat facing her, his eyes meeting hers. "Your boyfriend spoke to me today," he said. "Did you know he was going to do it?"

"No," Gudrun said. She found herself torn between joy and fear. On one hand, there was only one thing Horst could have said to her father that would have brought him to her office, but - on the other hand - her father might be inclined to say no. "What did he say to you?"

"He asked for your hand in marriage," her father said. He cocked his head, slightly. "Are you pregnant?"

Gudrun flushed, angrily. "No," she snapped. She was already feeling her body's warning signs. Her period was due within a day, perhaps two. "And I know for sure, *father*."

Her father showed no visible reaction, somewhat to her disappointment. Mentioning female issues in her house had always caused male deafness, as if they didn't want to admit that they were real. Gudrun's mother - and her teachers, on the other hand - had been brutally frank, but most of them had been women. The male teachers hadn't discussed the matter at all.

"Very good," her father said. He studied her for a long moment. "Do you want to marry him?"

"I love him," Gudrun said.

"That isn't an answer," her father pointed out. "Do you *want* to marry him?"

Gudrun closed her eyes for a long moment. She'd often thought that having a policeman for a father wasn't *fair*! He'd always been able to pick up on her lies, or half-truths, or when she'd been unwilling or unable to tell him everything. And he'd even told her, more than once, that he met more experienced liars on the streets. He'd certainly had no trouble detecting her own doubts and concerns.

"I don't know, father," Gudrun said, honestly. There was no point in trying to lie - or mislead. "I do love him...if things had been different, I would have agreed at once."

"If things had been different," her father pointed out, "you would have married Konrad."

Gudrun winced in pain. "Konrad is dead," she snapped. "If things had been different...yes, I *would* have married Konrad. And I would have done my best to be a good wife for him."

"He would have liked that, I think," her father said, dryly.

"But right now, I don't know if I want to marry," Gudrun admitted. She was too upset to care about what she was saying. "Why *can't* we have a relationship without getting married?"

"Because, sooner or later, you will get pregnant," her father retorted. His voice was surprisingly even, which worried her. "And what will you do then?"

Gudrun cringed. If she could have, she would have jumped out of the window or made herself vanish in a flash of light. Her father...her father couldn't know what Horst and she had been doing, could he? And yet, he'd been a young man too. Gudrun - and her siblings - were living proof that their parents had slept together at least four times. She didn't want to think about her parents being intimate, but there was no way to avoid it.

"Marriage exists to ensure that children are raised in a safe and loving home," her father continued, when she said nothing. "If you are not married when you give birth...people will raise eyebrows."

It would be worse than that, Gudrun knew. If there had been a strong promise to marry - which had been broken, through no fault of the woman - she might just be regarded as untainted. But if there had been no promise... she knew it would reflect badly on the woman, her parents and everyone else. It didn't seem fair, somehow, that it was always the woman who suffered for a mutual sin. A man who slept with many girls, outside marriage, would be given a slap on the back by his friends, while everyone scorned the women...

"I do want to marry him," Gudrun said. "But at the same time, I worry about all of this."

Her father's lips twitched. "Your mother has started to move into politics, too."

Gudrun met his eyes. "What do you think of that?"

"I think it would be unwise to object," her father said, dryly. He smiled. "One thing you will learn, when you start married life, is that while your husband is always meant to be in charge, you will have a great deal of influence behind the scenes."

"Unless you get a very bad husband," Gudrun said.

"Unless you do," her father agreed.

He leaned forward, resting his hands on her desk. "I approve of Horst," he said, flatly. "He did...he did a great many things to keep you safe, before and after the uprising. He's smart, he comes from a good family, he has prospects..."

"So do I," Gudrun said.

"Yes, now," her father said.

He cleared his throat. "I have discussed the matter with your mother," he said, firmly. "We have agreed that we will approve the match, when Horst works up the nerve to ask you. It may take some time."

Gudrun blinked. "He's brave..."

"There are many kinds of bravery," her father said, cutting her off. "Charging into the teeth of enemy fire is one thing, I suppose. Asking a girl to marry you...that's a very different kind of bravery."

"He approached you," Gudrun said.

She shook her head. It was hard not to feel that Horst should have approached *her* first, even though law and custom demanded that her father be asked for his approval before the girl herself was asked. His refusal would have put an end to the whole affair, unless the happy couple ran off and married secretly…a difficult task, when the law demanded that both sets of parents needed to be present when the marriage took place. She knew girls who had only found out by accident that their parents had rejected a number of prospective suitors. Some of them had been very hurt, but what could they do? They had no recourse if their parents turned down the match.

"That isn't quite the same," her father said. "The fear of being rejected by a girl is so much greater."

He paused. "Give him time to work up the nerve," he warned. "You don't want him to feel pressured into it, not when marriage is fraught with emotional hazards. And when he asks…well, you shouldn't make him wait *too* long before you say yes."

"If I do say yes," Gudrun said.

Her father met her eyes. "Marriage will change your life," he warned. "If you are not sure that you want to marry him, say so now. I will be quite happy to refuse the suit for you, if that is what you wish."

"But I don't want you to refuse the suit," Gudrun said. "I just don't know if I want to marry him *now*."

"Make up your mind," her father said. He nodded towards the window as a pair of explosions echoed out in the distance. "You may not have much time left."

"I know," Gudrun said. And yet…she sighed. Perhaps *she* should broach the topic with Horst, rather than waiting for him. "I'll make up my mind soon."

CHAPTER TWENTY-EIGHT

Berlin, Germany Prime
3 October 1985

"The advance forces are in position," *Sturmbannfuehrer* Friedemann Weineck reported, briskly. "Aircraft and gunners are standing by."

"Order them to open fire in ten minutes," Alfred ordered. "The advance forces can move forward five minutes after that."

"*Jawohl*," Weineck said.

Alfred nodded, never taking his eyes off the looming city. There were no cracks in the city's defences, no hidden tunnels that would take the stormtroopers directly into the *Reichstag*. A handful of tunnels *had* existed, he knew, but a cursory examination had told him that they'd all been collapsed. The provisional government wouldn't have missed *that* trick, not after underground tunnels had been used to move commandoes into Moscow during the war. It was impossible to avoid the simple fact that the only way to break into Berlin was through naked force.

This is going to cost us, he thought. He'd used all of the five days Holliston had allowed him to muster his men and resources, but he still felt as if he needed more time. And yet, Holliston had a point. Germany East had to win the war quickly or she would never win at all. *Far too many of my men are going to be killed.*

He cursed under his breath. The scouts had reported back, but none of their messages had been very reassuring. There were row after row of defences, ranging from basic trenches to fortified houses. Breaking through one defence line would only expose his men to fire from the *next* defence line. There was little hope of ramming a spearhead through the defence and then pushing reinforcements into the gap before the enemy could rally and counterattack. It would be disastrous if he tried. There just wasn't the room to manoeuvre his forces. No, he would have to clear the defence lines one by one in a full-frontal assault. And it was going to cost him dearly.

A nuke would clear the way, he thought. *But that would open up Pandora's Box.*

Berlin was just too large, he noted, as he finally turned his attention to the map. The reports from inside the city hadn't been very detailed, but between them, the aircraft and the recon reports he knew more than he wanted to know about the defences. Even trying to break through to the *Reichstag* would be a nightmare, particularly if the rest of the city was used as a base for the enemy to recuperate before launching a counterattack. About the only advantage he had was that the *Fuhrer* had told him that it didn't matter if Berlin was reduced to rubble. The capital would be rebuilt after the war.

"The aircraft are taking off now," Weineck reported. "They'll be over their targets in five minutes."

Alfred nodded, not trusting himself to speak. They'd moved every aircraft they could westwards, ranging from single-propeller hunters that had served in the counterinsurgency to fast-jet fighters that were normally charged with guarding the seas between Kamchatka and Alaska. Drawing down their airpower across Germany East was a calculated risk, one that could easily backfire if all hell broke loose. No matter who won the war, the *Reich* would be badly weakened for years to come. It was on the tip of his tongue to cancel the airstrike, but he knew it would be a waste of breath. The odds of winning the battle quickly were in no way improved by withholding the aircraft.

"Order the gunners to watch their targeting," he said, instead. "We don't want to accidentally hit the *Reichstag*."

He scowled as Weineck turned away. He'd argued to leave the *Reichstag* alone until the battle actually began - there was no point in hoping for a surrender that was never going to come - and then shelling it into a pile of rubble, but the *Fuhrer* had overruled him. Karl Holliston wanted to sit in the *Reichstag* once again, as her lord and master - her *Fuhrer* - and he didn't give a damn how many stormtroopers died to return him to Berlin. Or how many civilians…Berlin had had over three *million* citizens before the uprising. Now, with hundreds of thousands of refugees streaming into the city, the population could be a great deal higher. And far too many of them were about to die.

Shaking his head, he looked back towards Berlin as the flight of aircraft roared overhead, blocking out the sun. The Berliners were about to be exposed to the first full-scale airstrike since the Arab Rebellions had been brutally crushed…

…And, somehow, he knew it wasn't going to be enough.

Too many men are going to die, he thought. *And I can do nothing.*

———

"Radar reports that hundreds of aircraft are inbound," the young messenger gasped. "They're coming!"

"You don't say," Kurt snapped. The aircraft were already in view, advancing towards the defence lines with stately malice. His ears were starting to hurt from the racket. He raised his voice, knowing the NCOs would pass on the warning. "Get down!"

He scowled at the messenger, who was staring around like a gormless idiot, then pulled him into the trench as the bombs started to fall. Darkness fell over him as the aircraft passed overhead, the droning rising and falling as a handful of aircraft were picked off by guided missiles and blown out of the air. The bombs started to detonate seconds later; he covered his ears, praying desperately that none of the bombs would find targets. If they didn't land on the trench directly, he told himself, there was a good chance of survival…

The sound of explosions faded away as the aircraft banked, trying to avoid flying over the city. Several aircraft had been shot down over the last few days, their pilots bailing out only to drop down to a welcoming committee composed of angry civilians. They'd been lynched, the police idly standing by as the civilians tore the pilots asunder. After reading some of the horror stories from the east, as the SS brutally trampled its way westwards, Kurt found it hard to care.

"Shit," the messenger breathed. "They destroyed the line."

"Shut up," Kurt ordered. A number of buildings *had* been knocked down, but the defence line was still largely intact. Hell, the rubble would make better barricades than flimsy warehouses that had been put together by the cheapest possible contractor. "Get back to the CP and tell them we're still alive."

He shoved the messenger towards the edge of the trench, then peered eastwards as the shells started to rain down on the city. This time, the shells were crashing down with terrifying force, rather than a handful of shells hurled into Berlin at random. The ground shook, time and time again, as the barrage crawled over their position and headed west. He heard someone scream, so loud he could hear it over the constant rumble of exploding shells, and knew one of his men had been hit. But there was no way to get him to a field hospital until the shellfire had finally come to an end.

"Mines," someone shouted. "They're dropping mines!"

Kurt swore under his breath. "Careful where you put your feet," he bawled. The SS might not be planning to attack his position, then…unless they just didn't give a damn about their own people. "Don't go near one of the damned things!"

He swallowed, hard. Shell-dropped mines were absolute nightmares, although they didn't tend to bury themselves automatically. The ground would have to be swept carefully before it could be declared safe. They rarely carried enough explosive to kill, but a soldier who lost a leg in combat would be rendered useless, even if he did get rushed hastily to the field hospital. Surely, if the SS was reduced to dropping the tiny weapons on his position, they weren't actually planning to attack…

"Incoming," Loeb shouted. "We have incoming!"

Kurt turned, hefting his rifle; he swore out loud as he saw the grey-clad figures moving slowly towards him. They were good, he noted; one section moved forward while two more covered them, using every last chunk of debris to keep themselves hidden from watching eyes. And they didn't seem to be firing too…hell, the bombardment had tailed off completely, as if the enemy had run out of shells.

Or as if they don't want to kill their own people, he thought, darkly. *That would be very bad for their morale.*

He felt a surge of hatred as the stormtroopers advanced closer. Konrad had been alright - for a young man who was courting Kurt's sister - but far too many other SS stormtroopers were bastards. Kurt wouldn't forget any of the atrocities in a hurry, or what it meant for the civilians caught in the city. Half the population was female…they'd be raped and then murdered by the SS, if they were lucky. The remainder, if rumour was to be believed, were being taken east. He didn't want to *think* about what would happen to them there.

"Take aim," he ordered, choosing a target. The SS man was sneaking closer, using his helmet to hide his face. A rapist, perhaps? Or merely one of the monsters who'd slaughtered the population of dozens of towns and villages. "Fire on my command."

He forced himself to remain calm, thinking hard. None of his superiors had expected the line to last indefinitely, not when the SS would bring overwhelming force to bear against any prospective weak point. Their orders were to give the enemy a bloody nose and then fall back, something that reminded him far too much of their earlier orders. But Berlin was huge and they had plenty of space to trade for time. Let the SS have the outer edge of the defence lines, if they wished. The mortars already had the area firmly targeted.

Gritting his teeth, he took aim at his target. "Fire!"

There was a ragged burst of firing. Four stormtroopers fell; the remainder, their skills sharpened by constant combat, dropped to the ground and started to crawl for cover. A handful fired back, but their shots went wide. Loeb tapped his radio, calling in a mortar strike, as the soldiers kept firing, trying to hit the stormtroopers as they hid. For a second, the advance seemed to come to an end…

…And then the stormtroopers resumed their crawl, pushing forward with icy determination.

Assholes, Kurt thought. He picked off another stormtrooper, then ducked hurriedly as a bullet cracked through the air alarmingly close to him. Two of his men were dead, a third badly wounded. *You'll just keep coming until we stop you.*

The mortar shells crashed down, shaking the ground and stopping the advance for a few brief seconds. Kurt rose, blew the whistle as hard as he could and then followed his men down the path they'd planned for their retreat. Another explosion, a smaller one, told him that one of his men had stumbled over a mine; he glanced left and swallowed, feeling his stomach heave, as he saw the victim lying on the ground, his legs completely missing. Blood was pouring from his thighs…Kurt didn't want to think about what had happened to his *manhood*. Even if he could be saved - and Nazi Germany led the way in transplants - there was no way he'd ever be complete again.

Loeb scooped the man up, blood pouring down and staining his uniform. "Run," he snapped, loudly. Behind them, shots echoed in the distance. "Move it!"

Kurt nodded and ran. More mortar shells crashed down, concealing their escape until they reached the next set of trenches. A machine gun opened fire, riddling a pair of stormtroopers who had pushed too close to the defences. Kurt jumped down into the trench, then turned to help Loeb. But the *Oberfeldwebel* was staring down at his charge with a bitter expression.

"He's dead, *Herr Hauptmann*," he said. "There's nothing we can do."

"We can keep fighting," Kurt snarled. He'd never hated anyone quite as much as he'd hated the SS, not now. A man had died in screaming agony because he'd put his foot on a tiny little mine, then been carried to a nearby trench. He hadn't deserved to die. And the hell of it was that Kurt couldn't even remember the man's *name*. "That's all we can do."

He thought bitterly of Marie, the girl he'd met at the brothel. She'd been sweet, warm and loving...and though part of him knew it was an act, he would have preferred to be with her than on the battlefield. He watched grimly as Loeb placed the body to one side, his expression making it very clear that the poor bastard would probably never have a proper burial. It was unlikely they'd be able to hold the trench long enough to get the body to the nearest graveyard.

Poor bastard, he thought. *But at least he's at peace.*

Turning, he took up position and watched as the enemy readied themselves for another thrust.

———

Hauptsturmfuehrer Hennecke Schwerk kept his head down as he crawled slowly towards the enemy position, the position he knew had to be directly ahead of his squad. The shellfire had made a mess of the ground - they'd already overrun one trench that looked to have been dug in a hurry - but that actually worked in their favour. They'd assumed that their enemies would have an intimate knowledge of their own territory, yet the shellfire had torn it up so badly that their knowledge was almost worthless.

Bastards, he thought, as he heard the crash of incoming mortar fire. *They have all the trenches zeroed in.*

He clung to the ground as the shells exploded, one by one, then took the risk of lifting his head and peering ahead of him. The enemy had converted a large blockhouse-like building into a strongpoint, ringing it with barbed fire and placing a number of machine guns in position to cover all the approaches. It looked tough enough to shrug off shellfire, but he could see a problem with the design. There were no protective grills over the murder holes.

"Get one of the antitank rockets up here," he ordered, as he deployed his men to snipe at the enemy and keep them from mounting a counterattack. "I want to put a rocket right into that blockhouse."

"*Jawohl*," the *Strumscharfuehrer* said.

Hennecke smirked, then fired a handful of shots towards the enemy. If they were smart, they'd already be calling in more mortar fire to catch his squad on the hop, but it was just possible they didn't have the ammunition to open fire. Or that their mortars were being redeployed to provide fire support to another strongpoint. Either way, no shells crashed down on them as the *Strumscharfuehrer* reappeared, carrying a basic antitank missile launcher in one hand. Hennecke had used them before, in Germany East, to clear strongpoints. The Berlin Guard, lacking real experience, might not have anticipated such an attack.

It's in the manuals, he reminded himself, sharply. *Even if they never took part in counterinsurgency operations, they will have read the damned manuals.*

The *Strumscharfuehrer* fired. The wire-guided missile roared forward and crashed right through the murder hole, detonating inside the strongpoint. There was an entire series of secondary explosions, the final one shattering the building beyond repair as it crashed down into a pile of rubble. Hennecke shouted a command to his men, then rose and led the charge towards the debris. A handful of shocked defenders had no time to run before they were shot down, one by one. Moments later - far too late - mortar shells slammed down on where Hennecke had been, leaving his men unscathed.

"*Herr Hauptsturmfuehrer*," one of his men shouted. "Two of them are alive!"

Hennecke blinked in shock, then turned to walk over to where the two prisoners were standing. One of them was an older man, probably a reservist who had been called back to the colours, while the other was young enough to be barely out of basic training. He was shaking with fear, blood pouring down from a cut on his forehead and staining his uniform, while his older comrade was merely staring at the stormtroopers with a cold expression that sent shivers down Hennecke's spine. The man didn't expect to survive the coming hours.

His orders were clear, but contradictory. On one hand, he was to continue advancing forward until he found something that forced him to stop; on the other, he was to send all prisoners back to the intelligence staff to be interrogated. And yet, he didn't have the manpower to do both. If he detached a couple of men to escort the prisoners, he wouldn't be able to push so far into the defences…

He shrugged as he drew his pistol and pointed it at the younger man's head. It wasn't as if either of the prisoners was going to survive the winter in any case. He'd heard rumours about what lay in wait for the prisoners - and he knew that medical treatment wasn't going to be provided. Really, he was doing them a favour.

The older man glared at him, but said nothing as Hennecke pulled the trigger. Hennecke felt an odd chill running down the back of his neck at such silent hatred, even though it was useless. The man wouldn't survive more than a handful of seconds. And yet, he'd seen such hatred before, on the faces of Russians forced to dig a mass grave before the firing squads put them in it. He'd seen their faces in his nightmares until he'd finally reminded himself - and believed it - that they were *Untermenschen*. Their opinions and feeling didn't matter.

But the man in front of him was no *Untermensch*…

Gritting his teeth, he pointed the pistol at the second prisoner and pulled the trigger. The man made no sound as his body tumbled to the ground.

"Come on," Hennecke ordered, savagely. He was damned if he would show weakness in front of the men. "Let's move!"

CHAPTER TWENTY-NINE

Berlin, Germany Prime
3 October 1985

Gudrun could hear the fighting in the distance as she made her way slowly down to the bunker, the dull thunder echoing over the city. It grew quieter as she passed through the first security checkpoints, then vanished altogether once the doors were closed, but she could still feel it in her bones. Two hours of increasingly savage fighting had made it clear that, whatever else happened, there wasn't going to be much of a city left when the war finally came to an end.

She looked up at Horst as they reached the final checkpoint. Somewhat to her disappointment, he hadn't managed to work up the nerve to ask her to marry him - and she hadn't had the nerve to ask him either! Part of her mind insisted that that was his job, the rest of her thought that *she* should be able to ask the question first. And yet, her father's warning hung in her mind. To push a man to commit himself, before he was *ready* to commit himself, would only end badly.

"I'll see you afterwards," she said, quietly. If the guard hadn't been standing outside the door, she would have kissed him. "Take care of yourself."

Horst smiled, rather tiredly. "We have far too much to do to worry about taking care of ourselves," he said. "Good luck."

Gudrun nodded - she knew that both Horst and her father had been working hard to catch the spy, then turned and stepped through the door into the war room. Volker Schulze was sitting at the head of the table, looking grim, while the other councillors were slowly taking their seats. Gudrun looked from face to face, wondering which one of them was the spy - if there *was* a spy. Horst had pointed out that the SS could simply be fishing for incriminating information, if only because the *Reich* wouldn't have hesitated to meddle if the *Americans* had had a civil war. Anything that kept the planet's other superpower busy - and weakened it badly - would have suited the old council just fine.

Which raises the question, Gudrun thought, as she took her seat. *What would happen if the Reich became too weak?*

She contemplated the prospects grimly as the doors were closed and servants served coffee, then looked up as Schulze called the room to order. He looked tired, she noted; he knew, all too well, that several of the men before him were plotting to betray him. They might not be working for the SS, Gudrun knew, but they'd all risen to power through careful manipulation of the system. Reducing Schulze to a figurehead, just like Adolf Bormann - the *Fuhrer* who had been so unimportant that no one had bothered to kill him - would have been ideal. They could continue to master their separate power bases, while discussing matters that affected them all in committee.

Which is stupid, Gudrun thought, tartly. *If he wins the war, Karl Holliston will have every last man in the room shot, if they're lucky.*

"The battle has finally begun," Schulze said, quietly. "Field Marshal?"

Voss leaned forward. He was old enough to be Gudrun's father, but she'd always found him a little impressive, even if she didn't like him very much. Quite apart from a genuine military record, he'd stayed in Berlin when he could have easily taken command of the relief force and escaped the city. Schulze had stayed, of course, but he hadn't really had a choice. Voss, on the other hand, could have left easily. Instead, he'd chosen to put his life on the line.

Not that he could have escaped anyway, Gudrun reminded herself. The reports from the east were horrifically clear. *Anyone who does not support Holliston enthusiastically will be counted as an enemy.*

"The *Waffen-SS* launched a major incursion into the city two hours ago, following a major bombing raid," Voss said. "So far, as predicted, we have lost the outer edge of the defence lines, yet the remainder are still firmly in place. Fighting has been savage, hand-to-hand in some places, but we have more than held our own. There has been no mass collapse, nor have we had to send in the reserves."

Kruger snorted. "So the *Waffen-SS* isn't as good as they claimed?"

"They're attacking a city," Voss reminded him, calmly. "All of their usual advantages are weakened, perhaps lost. Their airpower isn't as effective when they have to worry about antiaircraft missiles and their shelling isn't as accurate as they might have hoped. And we have nowhere to run. There's no hope of a breakthrough they can use to wrench our legs open and thrust inside."

He nodded at Gudrun. "Begging your pardon, of course."

Gudrun kept her face impassive. She knew when she was being needled.

Schulze didn't look impressed. "Can we hold out long enough for the relief force to arrive?"

"It depends on a number of factors," Voss said, flatly. "We stockpiled vast amounts of ammunition in the city prior to the invasion, but expenditure has been an order of magnitude over any pre-war predictions. Fortunately" - he smiled, rather dryly - "they probably have the same problem. I would expect them to be having problems shipping supplies to the front."

His smile grew wider. "And they certainly *will* have problems once our stay-behind cells come out of hiding."

Gudrun took a moment to put it all together. "Won't that encourage atrocities against the civilian population?"

"Yes," Voss said, flatly. "Would you rather lose Berlin? And, with it, any hope of preserving your revolution?"

He is not my father, Gudrun reminded herself, sharply. The tone - the voice he used to address a silly little girl - was far too close to her father when he was in a bad mood, but her father was...well, her *father*. It was his job to keep her from making stupid mistakes, even ones as minor as adding two and two together and getting five. *And he should not be talking to me like that.*

She leaned forward, speaking in an icy tone she would never have dared use to her *real* father. "And would you prefer to see countless civilians killed?"

"I would *prefer* to see the SS vanish," Voss said. He sounded oddly amused - and, for a second, she saw a flash of *respect* in his eyes. "But we have to deal with the reality we have, not the reality we want. And the reality we have is that failing to make life difficult for the SS's logistic officers is going to cost us badly. Allowing them to mass their firepower against Berlin will be disastrous."

"I understand the costs," Schulze said, quietly. "And we have no choice."

The hell of it, Gudrun knew, was that they were right. Horst had taught her enough about logistics for her to understand their argument. But, at the same time, she knew what would happen to any innocent civilians caught nearby. The reports from the east were an endless liturgy of horror. They'd be tortured, raped and finally killed. If the SS had ever hoped to win hearts and minds - and she found it rather unlikely - that hope had long since faded.

She closed her eyes in pain. Horst had explained, more than once, that the easterners regarded the westerners as soft, but she'd never really understood it. The *Reich* had never been noticeably more liberal in Germany Prime. Indeed, the only place where there had been any real *hint* of liberalism had been Germany South…and, even there, saying the wrong thing at the wrong time was more than enough to get someone sent to a concentration camp and brutally murdered. But it didn't really matter. Whatever the cause, the easterners held the westerners in contempt. And that contempt was pushing them to commit atrocities.

Voss cleared his throat. "I don't promise victory," he said. "But as long as they don't make a major breakthrough, we should be able to hold the line."

"Except that we already have rats within the walls," Admiral Wilhelm Riess said. The head of the *Abwehr* scowled at Voss. "They have at least one team of commandos in Berlin, perhaps more."

"We have doubled security at all vulnerable points and mounted a number of raids on suspect households," Voss said, sharply. "There is little else we *can* do."

"They are already spreading SS propaganda," Riess announced, loudly. He pulled a folded sheet of paper out of his briefcase and unfolded it, holding it in the air so they could see the words. "This was found near a recruiting station."

He gave Gudrun a sharp look. "They clearly learned a few things from you."

Gudrun scowled as she read the poster. It wasn't much, merely a reminder that the SS was coming and all those who stood against their advance would be branded traitors, but the mere fact that someone had managed to put it in place was worrying. And yet, it would be easier for the SS than it had been for her, back when the underground movement had been starting out. There were fewer policemen on the street and a growing tradition of questioning uniformed authority.

"And this isn't the worst of it," Riess continued. He reached back into his briefcase. "My men caught a handful of brats distributing these!"

Gudrun frowned as Riess produced a handful of leaflets and placed them on the table. She took one and read it, quickly. The basic message was identical to the poster, but there was an offer of conditional amnesty for anyone who deserted the provisional government or simply turned on their comrades, when the main offensive began. She had no idea how many people would be tempted, yet - as the noose tightened around Berlin - she had a feeling that far too many people would be very tempted indeed.

"I see," Schulze said. "And what did the distributors have to say?"

"Very little," Riess admitted. "They were refugee children, already on the verge of starvation. Their families were to be given additional foodstuffs if their children distributed the leaflets around Berlin. We have rounded up and interrogated the families, but they don't seem to know anything useful. We need tighter security."

"Which we do not have the manpower to provide," Voss snapped. "If we put more soldiers on the streets, we take them away from the front lines."

"Then we need to expand our counter-intelligence network," Riess snapped back. "The SS handled all such matters and the SS is gone!"

Gudrun groaned, inwardly, as the pieces fell into place. It was a power grab. The *Abwehr* - military intelligence - had long resented its subordination to the SS, although - unlike the *Gestapo* - it had managed to retain a separate identity. Expanding the *Abwehr's* counter-intelligence responsibilities would give Riess far more power, which he could use to push himself into prominence. Why not? Himmler had done the same and, before the uprising, the SS had been one of the most powerful factions in Germany.

And if we let the Abwehr grow in power, she thought numbly, *how long will it be before we have a new master?*

She shuddered at the thought. She'd always had mixed feelings about the SS, but after reading some of the files she'd discovered just how far the SS had worked its way into the warp and weft of German politics. Politicians, military officers and bureaucrats had been steadily brought under the SS's sway, bribed or blackmailed into supporting its decisions and enforcing its rules. She'd been taught to fear the informer from a very early age - like all German children - but she'd never imagined that high-ranking politicians could feel the same way. It had simply never crossed her mind.

"This is not the time to expand the *Abwehr's* responsibilities," Voss said. "We need to locate and remove other SS informers within the ranks."

"And someone within the ranks may be helping them," Riess pointed out. "Tracking down the commandos within Berlin might lead us to the informers."

"I highly doubt they will allow themselves to be taken alive," Voss sneered. "These men are trained to avoid capture."

Schulze tapped the table. "This is a decision for another time," he said. "Right now, the police are attempting to track down the commandos."

"The police," Riess said. He sounded scornful. "The Berlin police couldn't organise a drunken rampage in a brewery, let alone find an experienced SS commando cell!"

"Nonetheless, they are all we have," Schulze said. "Training your people to serve an expanded counter-intelligence function would take too long."

Riess sat back, looking cross. Gudrun eyed him, wondering just what was going through his head. Irritation at having his power grab shot down so quickly, frustration at failing to take advantage of the chaos to benefit himself...or genuine concern? There was no reason why Riess couldn't be worried about the SS commandos, even if he was inclined to use their existence to benefit himself. The SS and the *Abwehr* had been enemies for so long that Riess didn't have any hope of survival if Berlin fell.

Karl Holliston will purge everyone who isn't willing to pledge themselves to the SS, she thought. *And he won't trust the military at all.*

Schulze cleared his throat. "Are there any other matters of concern?"

"The food stockpiles are under pressure," Kruger said, flatly. "Right now, there is no hope of bringing in food from outside the blockade. Assuming that our remaining warehouses do not come under attack, we have enough food to feed the city for roughly one month at current rations. I believe we can stretch that out to two months if we cut rations to everyone, but the men on the front lines."

"That will certainly cause problems within the city," Gudrun said, quickly.

"Yes, it will," Kruger acknowledged. "Quite apart from riots, there will be long-term health problems. Cutting food supplies to pregnant women, for example, may damage the babies in the womb. Cutting food supplies to children will cause other problems."

Gudrun shuddered. She had a feeling she knew *exactly* what the SS would do, faced with the same situation. Round up everyone who was nothing more than a useless mouth - the old, the infirm - and execute them. No, *murder* them. Grandpa Frank had been a horror, a blight on his family, but she recoiled in horror at the thought of murdering him. He'd died a hero, perhaps making up for the sins of his past…how many others would be denied the same chance, if they were killed out of hand. There was no way she could condone such a solution.

And yet, the nasty part of her mind whispered, *is it not better that they should die, so that the rest of us may live?*

She told that part of her mind to shut up and leaned forward. "What will happen if we cut rations later - say two weeks from now?"

"Impossible to tell," Kruger said. "The only real case study we have comes from Leningrad, where the city practically starved itself to death before the defences finally collapsed. I have no idea just how long the public will remain calm, particularly since we don't have enough manpower to squash any riot before it gets out of hand. Right now, with the population already aware that governments can be overthrown…"

Gudrun had no trouble filling in the blanks. A starving population, desperate for succour, rising up against the provisional government. Soldiers, forced to choose between shooting their families and turning on the government, attacking the *Reichstag*. And the SS watching the chaos from a safe distance, then stepping in to restore order and impose its own peace once the infighting came to an end. It had happened before, after all, when Kurt and his men turned their weapons on the SS stormtroopers before the *Reichstag*. And if they were unlucky, it would happen again.

It isn't fair, she told herself, sharply. *We wanted to change the world.*

And you did, her own thoughts replied.

"We will lower rations for those who can handle it," Schulze said. His voice was very flat, betraying no emotion. "And we will go on short rations too."

Voss leaned forward. "Do you think the public will believe us if we *say* we're on short rations?"

"We have to try," Schulze said. "And we are not going to be holding banquets when people are starving in the streets."

Gudrun wondered, darkly, just how many other politicians were going to follow his example and go hungry. The black market had been a feature of Berlin life for decades, run - she hadn't been surprised to discover, after the uprising - by a number of high-ranking politicians and bureaucrats. It wouldn't be long before *someone* started trying to sell off government supplies, even if there *was* a war on. Hell, she wouldn't be surprised to discover that someone was *already* doing it.

There will be families trading everything they own, just for a can of preserved meat, she thought, bitterly. *And girls forced to prostitute themselves for a bite to eat.*

"Warn your people," Schulze added, addressing the whole room. His voice was firm, warning them that there were limits. "I will not tolerate anyone breaking the united front in any way. The only thing keeping the people from turning on us is the awareness that we are suffering too."

Except we are down in the bunker and the people upstairs are not, Gudrun thought. *And the snipers are still looking for targets.*

"The people of Berlin haven't known privation in a very long time," Voss pointed out. Horst had raised the same concerns, Gudrun recalled. "Do they have the drive to hold out?"

"Let us hope so," Schulze said. He smiled, rather dryly. "Because if they don't, we are all about to die."

CHAPTER THIRTY

Berlin, Germany Prime
8 October 1985

Gudrun felt a stab of guilt, despite the gnawing pain in her stomach, as she walked towards the car, Horst following her. The hospital was crammed with casualties, soldiers wounded in the ongoing battle for Berlin. Their words haunted her, leaving her wondering if she had done the right thing after all. How many young men were dead - or crippled - because of her? And how many wives and girlfriends were never going to see their menfolk again - or would wish, afterwards, that their menfolk had died rather than returned as cripples?

She shuddered, bitterly. Some of the men had cursed her, others had been so lost in their pain that it was hard to tell who - if anyone - they were talking to. She'd heard a young man - younger than her, she thought - screaming for his mother as the doctors fought to save his life, watched helplessly as an older man begged to be killed rather than be forced to live without his legs. And the nurses - and the young girls who had volunteered to assist in the hospital - slowly giving into despair as more and more wounded flowed into the hospital.

I thought it was bad when Konrad was in hospital, Gudrun thought, fighting down the urge to start crying. *But this is far worse.*

"It isn't your fault," Horst said, quietly. The car lurched to life, the driver steering them onto the road. Civilian traffic had been banned the day the SS finally surrounded Berlin, leaving the streets clear. "It wasn't you who decided to invade Germany Prime."

Gudrun shook her head slowly, blinking away tears. *Kurt* was on the front lines; *Kurt*, her bigger brother who had alternatively tormented her and protected her. *Kurt*, who had helped her sneak into the hospital…had it really only been a few scant months ago? It felt like an eternity had passed between the girl she'd been and the woman she had become. And if *Kurt* was wounded or killed, she didn't know what she'd do. The thought of being responsible for her brother's death was horrifying.

"I know," she breathed. Horst wrapped a warm arm around her, heedless of the driver's presence. "But it doesn't feel that way."

She leaned into his arm, but said nothing as the car finally reached the *Reichstag* and passed through two checkpoints before driving into the garage. Security had been tightened, again, as the fighting wore on. The SS commando cell hadn't launched any big attacks, thankfully, but a handful of policemen had been killed on the streets and a pair of soldiers badly wounded by a makeshift bomb. Gudrun's father had said that the attacks might not be the work of trained professionals - there was an amateurish feel about the incidents that suggested inexperience - but there was no way to be sure. Either way, the original group of commandos hadn't gone away. They would be planning something.

And Horst hasn't heard anything since the fighting began, she thought. *Who knows what that means?*

She tossed possibilities around in her mind as they walked up to her bedroom. They might assume that Horst couldn't sneak out of the *Reichstag* without being noticed…or they might have finally realised that Horst had turned against them. If the latter…Gudrun wouldn't have bet on his survival, if he fell into their hands. The SS regarded betrayal as the worst of all sins. Horst would be executed, once they knew he was guilty. And who knew if anyone would be told what had happened to him?

It was hard to care, in her state, just who saw Horst following her into the room. The staff had probably noticed something, by now; they knew she'd shared both the upper bedroom and the bunker suite with him. Her father would be furious if rumours got out, she knew, but she was too tired to worry about it. And besides, her parents approved of her prospective marriage. That, at least, was a weight off her mind.

"It isn't your fault," Horst said, as Gudrun sat down heavily. "The SS made its own choices."

He moved behind Gudrun and began to massage her neck. "None of this is your fault."

"I don't feel that way," Gudrun said. She felt too hungry to do anything, but sit. She'd noticed how the price of food was slowly rising, long before the uprising, yet she'd never really been *hungry*. Little flickers of hunger, caused by turning down school food, were nothing compared to the gnawing pain in her chest. "How many people are going to die because of me?"

"It would have happened anyway," Horst said. He let go of her neck and walked around the chair, kneeling in front of her. "The *Reich* was heading for a fall long before you were born."

Gudrun swallowed. She found it hard to imagine what it had been like in 1944, when the *Reich* and the British Empire had finally signed a truce. Or in 1940-41, when panzers had rolled into France and Russia. Or even in 1919, when Germany had been unfairly blamed and penalised for all the woes of the world. Her history teachers had told her that Germany had been betrayed, from within and without, but now...the *Reich* might have built a towering edifice, yet they'd built on very shaky ground.

"Kruger said as much," she said. "But I don't believe it."

Horst reached out and took her hands, holding them gently in his. "Gudrun," he said, very quietly. "Gudrun...will you marry me?"

Gudrun stared at him, feeling her heart starting to race. A flurry of conflicting feelings ran through her mind; delight, fear, relief, terror...marriage would change her life, no matter who or what she was. It would be a change for the better and a change for the worse. She would be expected to be a mother as well as a politician - or, perhaps, a mother *instead* of a politician. It was hard to imagine staying at home - or within the restrictive circle of other married women - and preparing dinner for the moment Horst came home from work. Her life had expanded too far, too fast, for her to step back into a traditional role.

Horst was looking back at her, his blue eyes...vulnerable. It was a surprise. She'd never seen him vulnerable before, not when he'd confessed the truth or even when they'd slept together for the first time. But then, perhaps she wasn't his first. Girls might be expected to remain virginal before marriage - or at least maintain a convincing pretence that they'd only ever had premarital sex with their future husband - but boys had far more latitude. Sex was one thing, marriage - to a boy - was quite another.

She hesitated, trying to think of an answer. A year ago, if they had been in a relationship, she would have answered yes without hesitation. Horst would have been a great catch, an up and coming SS officer…she would have been his wife, borne his children and shared his life, taking a payout from the government for every single child she brought into the world. But now…her life had changed too much. She *couldn't* go back to where she'd been, before the uprising.

"I won't try to stop you from being a politician," Horst said, quietly. She wondered, suddenly, just what had happened to his remaining family. The SS wouldn't have let them live if they knew Horst had betrayed them. "I understand you'll want to continue being…being a councillor. There's no need to have children."

Gudrun swallowed. She did want children, one day. Most married women had their first child within a year or two of the wedding, if they weren't already pregnant when they marched to the altar. Two little boys, perhaps; or two sweet little girls. She didn't want more than two children…

…But that wasn't the concern, was it? She was honest enough to admit the truth, if only to herself. Girls practically *defined* themselves as daughters, then wives. Or society made that definition for them. By marrying Horst, she would give up the independence she had won, at least in the eyes of the world. Her father hadn't attempted to pull her back to the house, after the uprising, and she had no idea what would have happened if he'd tried. But by marrying Horst, she might be expected to resign…

…And if he changed his mind, if he decided he wanted her to stay at home, the law would be on his side.

And if I have children, she thought, *taking care of them is going to consume my time.*

"It won't be easy," Gudrun warned. "You'll have to get used to the idea of having a politician for a wife."

"It could be worse," Horst said.

Gudrun shrugged. Her mother had pointed out, in some detail, that men rarely liked it when girls beat them, even in something as minor as a maths competition. She'd wondered, at the time, if the segregated school system - there had only been a handful of mixed-sex classes after she'd turned twelve - was designed to keep the boys from feeling inferior to the girls, rather than the other way around. Her mother had even advised Gudrun to hide her intelligence, just in case it provoked resentment. A teenage boy could be ignored...

...But a grown man - and a husband - could not.

Horst looked up at her. "I know it won't be easy," he said. "Not for either of us. But I am prepared to accept whatever it brings."

Gudrun felt touched. She *knew* she wasn't pregnant. Horst could have walked away, without consequences. And, with a little ingenuity, she could probably have avoided consequences for her too. If, of course, she decided to have another relationship. Instead, he'd approached her father and gained his permission to take the next step. She had to admit it, even if it had taken him several days to work up the nerve to speak to her.

And we may be dead in a month, she thought. *And if that happens, it won't matter if we are married or not.*

She sucked in her breath. The reports made it clear that the SS was inching forward, even if every last building was taken and retaken time and time again before it was finally cleared. They would hardly be the only couple getting married quickly - she'd heard from two of her friends who were trying the knot, just so they could live with their partners before the city fell. If, of course, the city *did* fall.

And if it doesn't, she told herself, *we will just have to live with it.*

She leaned forward, pulling him to his feet. He was big, taller and stronger than her, yet he'd never made her feel unsafe. Indeed, she hadn't been wary of him even *after* he'd confessed the truth. Even when they'd argued, she'd never feared that he would hit her, beating her into submission like far too many wives. And that, perhaps, was all the answer she really needed.

"I will," she said, meeting his eyes. A sudden surge of energy blazed through her as his eyes stared back at her. "I *will* marry you."

Horst kissed her, pulling her into a tight hug. Gudrun wrapped her arms around him, kissing him back with all the intensity she could muster. His hands pulled at her dress, bunching it up around her waist as he fumbled with her panties; she undid his trousers and allowed them to fall to the floor as he half-pushed her towards the bed. She leaned back, allowing herself to land neatly on the bed, then pulled him down on top of her…

And then there was nothing in her world, apart from him.

———

Horst lay on the bed afterwards, feeling tired and yet almost deliriously happy at the same time. Gudrun lay next to him, her eyes closed; her deep even breathing was enough to tell him that she was sleeping properly. She'd had too many nightmares over the last few days, nightmares that had jerked her awake time and time again. Horst knew she wouldn't be the only one - some of his bunkmates had had nightmares during training - but she had more reasons than most to feel guilty.

The Reich was definitely heading for a fall, Horst thought. *But without her, things might have been very different.*

He doubted, deep inside, that they would have been *peaceful*. The SS was too strong, too determined to maintain its perfect state. Mass protests, peaceful or not, would have been broken up, with machine gun fire if necessary. He'd watched, helplessly, as dozens of protesters *had* died…it would have been far worse, he was sure, if Gudrun hadn't been involved. But there was no way to know.

Gudrun shifted slightly, pressing against him. She looked…happy, Horst decided, a faint smile crossing her lips even in her sleep. Her clothes were torn; they'd probably have to be replaced, if they couldn't be repaired. Gudrun's mother was probably going to have a few things to say about that, if she was anything like Horst's mother and auntie. Clothes were not to be wasted, the women had said. They could be handed down to the next generation, if they weren't passed aside to someone with a greater need for them. The family had a stockpile of baby clothes that were shared amongst the mothers, who would return them to the stockpile once their child had outgrown them…

The thought caused him a pang. His parents were dead. There would be no father, standing next to him, the day he and Gudrun were married. His aunt and uncle would be better served by staying as far from him as possible, although there was little point in trying to hide. He'd sent them a warning, when the uprising had finally begun, but he'd heard nothing from them, no hint that they might have escaped Germany East. And they'd been far enough from the border to need travel permits to head west.

They might be dead, he thought, grimly. *Or held somewhere in Germanica.*

There was nothing he could do about that, he knew. Certainly not now, not when the civil war was well underway. There was no way he could protect the man and woman who had taken him in, after his parents had been killed. All he could do was work as hard as he could to bring the civil war to a victorious end.

A low rumble echoed through the air, shaking the building. He shuddered, despite the girl curled up next to him. The *Reichstag* had remained safe, thankfully, but that wouldn't last forever. Given time, the defences would eventually be worn down and the SS would break into the city. But would they be held off long enough for the relief force to arrive?

A race, he told himself, as Gudrun's eyes flicked open. *And whoever gets there first wins.*

"They're hammering the city," he said, quietly.

"I know," Gudrun said. Her moods had always swung erratically after sex, something that perplexed him. His uncle might have been able to offer advice, if he hadn't punched Horst in the face for daring to run the risk of getting a nice girl in trouble. "When do you want to get married?"

Horst hesitated, considering the question. Gudrun was brave, the bravest woman he'd ever met. And to think she'd been born and raised in Germany Prime! Once she'd committed herself, she didn't hesitate to move forward. The SS had very good reason to regret letting her go, after she'd been arrested. Her death would have solved all sorts of problems.

"Soon," he said. "Do you want a church wedding?"

Gudrun shook her head. Horst felt a flicker of relief. He'd never been religious, even though he'd heard rumours of cults within the SS, cults dedicated to Odin, Thor and the other Norse gods. The idea of having the marriage solemnised in a church didn't sit well with him. But if she'd wanted it, he would have accepted it. He wanted to keep her happy.

He kissed her, gently, then sat upright and climbed off the bed. It would be wonderful to stay in bed with her, but he knew he had work to do. And she had to approach her parents and tell them that she'd accepted his offer, pretending - all the time - that Horst hadn't asked her father first. The tradition had always puzzled him, until now. It was far too easy for a girl to be pushed into marrying someone her father wanted, rather than someone she would have chosen for herself.

Not that Gudrun would have surrendered so easily, he thought, as he beckoned her to follow him into the shower. *She wouldn't have married someone she didn't want.*

He smiled at the thought, then turned on the water and washed himself quickly as she stepped into the shower. Water ran down her body, drawing his attention to her breasts and the tuff of hair between her legs. Desire rose up within him, but he forced it down savagely. There was no time, not any longer. When he looked back at her, she was smiling. She felt the same way too.

"There will be time later," he promised, as he hugged her. Her bare breasts felt tantalisingly warm against his skin. It was all he could do not to make love to her again. She wanted it as much as he did. "But for now…"

And when he finally made his way down to *his* bedroom, he found another note waiting for him.

CHAPTER THIRTY-ONE

Berlin, Germany Prime
10 October 1985

Stay very quiet, Hauptsturmfuehrer Hennecke Schwerk told himself, as he inched forward though the house. *Stay very quiet and listen carefully.*

The sound of the constant bombardment was growing louder, making it harder for him to hear anything over the racket, save for his own heartbeat. Sweat trickled down his back as he listened, hoping to hear something - anything - that would tell him if the building was occupied. It was a simple house, built for a couple who might be expecting their first child; the possessions and kick-knacks surrounding him suggested that they'd had their first child and were probably expecting a second. There was a faint - a very faint - sound in the distance, but he couldn't make out what it was…

There might be someone here, he thought. *Or it might be empty…*

He kept moving forward, peering into what had once been a neat kitchen. It looked to have been stripped of anything edible or useful, then abandoned. The gas cooker had been disconnected, the pipe closed; the water pipes to the entire suburb had been turned off after the population had been evacuated, further into the city. He wondered, absently, as he heard a faint tapping sound, if the owners had made it west or if they were trapped somewhere towards the heart of Berlin. There was no way to know.

His breath caught in his throat as he moved into the next room. His gaze swept the room, taking in the sofa, the comfortable chair, the portraits of Adolf Hitler and Adolf Bormann hanging from the walls…the owner would be a low-level party functionary, then. Too intimately involved with the party to avoid hanging portraits on the walls, too low on the pecking order to be able to afford better decorations or a home nearer the *Reichstag*. He kept his rifle at the ready as he crept towards the door, wondering if the home could be declared secure and then left empty. There was no love lost between the *Waffen-SS* and the millions of bureaucrats who kept the *Reich* running, but he had to admit they were necessary. Maybe the owners would return, with the wife looking after the kid while the husband went back to work…

He turned the corner and practically ran into the enemy soldier. For a second, they stared at each other in mutual shock, then tried to bring up their rifles. Hennecke realised, in a flash of insight, that his enemy had the advantage; he hurled himself forward, trying to draw his knife from his belt as he slammed into the enemy soldier. But the enemy knocked the knife from his hand as they crashed to the floor, both men desperately trying to kill the other before he was killed instead. Hennecke got on top, then was thrown back as the enemy pushed forward, grunting in pain. He was a good fighter, Hennecke had to admit; his training was different, but none the less thorough.

Hennecke glanced around for his knife, but it was nowhere to be seen. He didn't have the time to draw his pistol without losing it too. His opponent knocked him backwards, drawing back a fist to slam Hennecke in the face; Hennecke punched him as hard as he could in the groin. His fist met something hard - the soldier was wearing protection - but it still hurt, distracting the enemy soldier long enough for Hennecke to punch him in the jaw, snapping his neck back. And then Hennecke slammed him again, as hard as he could. The enemy soldier tottered backwards, his neck broken, and hit the ground with a dull thud.

Hennecke could only stare at the body for a long moment, torn between relief and a peculiar kind of excitement as his enemy breathed his last. He'd had unarmed combat skills hammered into his head during training, his instructors drilling the recruits mercilessly until even the least of them was deadly with or without a weapon, but it was the first time Hennecke had ever killed a man with his bare hands. It had simply never been necessary, not for all of his career. And now he'd done it, he found himself unsure what to feel.

He sucked in his breath as he heard the sound of running footsteps, then hastily picked up his rifle. Losing it would be a good way to get in trouble. He checked the body as a *Strumscharfuehrer* entered the room, rifle at the ready. Hennecke didn't recognise him, but that hardly mattered. Far too many units had been chewed to pieces as the fighting raged on, the enemy refusing to fall back to their next line of defence until they had taken out as many stormtroopers as they could. But it hardly mattered. The assignment - clear the suburb - had to be completed, whatever else happened.

Shaking his head, he checked the body for anything useful, but found nothing that might interest his superiors. Jokes aside, the enemy weren't stupid enough to put copies of their battle plans on the corpses of ordinary soldiers. And if he had found something that claimed to be a battle plan, he would have been reluctant to pass it on to his superiors. It would almost certainly be a fake. He removed a half-empty packet of cigarettes and a lighter, then led the way back out of the house. The sound of shelling grew louder as he stepped into the open and peered towards Berlin. Great clouds of smoke were rising in the distance, obscuring the city.

But the aircraft will still be able to find their targets, he thought, nastily. *And as long as they're not dropping bombs on us, who cares?*

He took a moment to study the squad as it slowly reformed. He'd lost too many men from his original company, but his superiors had supplied replacements - the survivors of other units that had lost too many men to remain viable. They'd have to be rebuilt from the ground up, if the war ever came to an end. Hennecke had been fighting for seven days, barely finding the time to get a few hours of sleep in between attacking, counterattacking and counter-counterattacking. He felt perpetually hungry and increasingly deaf.

And his men looked ragged. They were all experienced - even the least of them had spent months marching over Russia, chasing insurgents - but none of them had experienced a hellish nightmare like Berlin. Hennecke knew, as little as he wanted to admit it, that they needed to be pulled out of the line and given a few days to rest. But it wasn't going to happen, not when their superiors were demanding results. The best they could hope for was good food and warm drinks and it didn't look as though they were going to get either of them.

He sighed, feeling torn. There was a part of him that loved the fighting, that loved testing himself, that loved showing the westerners that treason had consequences. The dumb bastards had never really believed in the *Reich*, let alone committed themselves to doing whatever was necessary to ensure that the *Reich's* dominance. They deserved, every so often, a reminder that the universe was cold and harsh, red in tooth and claw. And yet, he hated to think just how many stormtroopers had died. The battle to break into the suburbs had cost *him* over twenty men, suggesting that over five *hundred* men had been killed in a single bitter skirmish.

And that meant…

He shook his head. They were committed, now. The SS would either fight or die; the war would be won or lost. But there was no way to back off, to live together. West and east could not coexist. Only one could be supreme.

Bracing himself, he hefted his rifle. There were more buildings to clear before night fell.

———

Andrew kept his face impassive as he strolled through Berlin, even though he knew it was quite possible that he would be mistaken for an easterner, rather than an American. Quite a few pilots had been brutally torn apart by angry mobs, he'd been told. He was rather tempted to believe that, if anything, the stories were underrated. Berlin hadn't been bombed since 1944, when the British had launched a handful of air raids before the end of the war. And the Berliners were angry.

"The SS are pushing hard," his escort said. "But we are holding them."

"You're doing well," Andrew said. "But how much of a city will you have left when time finally runs out?"

His escort - a young military officer - didn't bother to answer. Andrew shrugged and turned his attention to the buildings as they walked past. Berlin was a huge city, but more and more buildings were badly damaged, even knocked down, by the fires of war. Broken windows were everywhere, despite advice from the provisional government warning homeowners to board up their windows or cover them with plastic. Makeshift tents were scattered everywhere, offering very limited comfort to the refugees and Berliners who had been driven out of their homes. Andrew had even heard that thousands of Berliners were even flocking into the city's underground stations, just as the British had done during the Blitz. It provided more protection than they were likely to get elsewhere.

His lips thinned as they passed a soup kitchen. A dozen German women, all wearing trousers rather than the party-approved long skirts and blouses, were handing out soup, bread and something that smelt faintly unappealing. Andrew's nose wrinkled as he took in the desperate refugees and, behind them, Berliners who were starting to look pale and wan as hunger took its toll. It was a sight he'd never seen in America or Britain; it was a sight that wouldn't be out of place in the refugee camps in South Africa, the townships where black civilians were clustered as the military fought to exterminate the insurgents.

This is the beginning of the end, he thought. *And the start of hell itself.*

He looked past the refugees to the poster on the wall, feeling a flicker of concern that no one had bothered to take it down. A signal, perhaps, to anyone who might be watching that they weren't *totally* opposed to the SS? Or a simple sign of apathy? There was no way to know, but it concerned him that none of the passing policemen or soldiers had cared enough to rip it from the walls. Perhaps, just perhaps, there were more rats within the provisional government's walls than it wanted to admit.

"We could stop for soup," he said, just to see what his escort would say. "I could pay, you know."

"We're expected at the front," the escort said. He wasn't quite experienced enough to hide the anger - and the shame. "They will be upset if we're late."

Andrew nodded, wondering just how *he* would have felt if Washington, D.C. had become a battlefield. There had been countless attempts by the *Reich* to resurrect the Confederate States, attempts so pitiful that the FBI had wondered if they'd been a joke, an attempt to distract the Americans while the Germans got on with the *real* plan. But Andrew, who had spent more time than he'd wanted to in the *Reich*, suspected that the *Reich* had genuinely believed that the Confederate States of America was just waiting to be reborn, just as they believed that a non-Nazi government would surrender Germany to chaos and madness. It seemed hard to grasp, but they had very little under-standing of the outside world. They judged all others as treacherous because *they* were treacherous themselves.

Don't pity the bastards, he told himself, as they walked past a gaggle of teenage girls wearing knee-length skirts and giggling loudly. They would prob-ably have been marched home by the police, before the uprising; their parents would have beaten them for acting in such a lewd manner, if they weren't too relieved that their daughters had returned at all. *Pity instead their victims.*

The sound of shooting grew louder as they approached the front lines, passing a handful of men in police uniforms manning a barricade. His escort took him through the lines, then nodded towards a man standing in a CP. Andrew recognised him instantly, even though he'd exchanged his normal uniform for a field tunic and cap. But then, the SS had hundreds of snipers prowling the battlefield. A man wearing the grand uniforms the *Wehrmacht* designed for its senior officers would make a very tempting target. Andrew had attended exercises, conducted at Fort Hood, where a couple of snipers had snarled up a military advance for *days*, just by taking out a handful of officers. The *Wehrmacht* would be foolish if it didn't realise the danger too.

"Field Marshal," he said, as Voss dismissed the escort with a wave of his hand. "Thank you for allowing me to come."

"It's nothing," Voss said. Andrew didn't know him as well as he knew his predecessor, but it was easy enough to see the irritation under the affable exterior. And yet, was it real? Voss had learned his trade in a political snake pit. He might well know how to conceal his innermost feelings, then project a false front. "The Chancellor wanted you to see what was happening."

Andrew nodded, looking past Voss to the map mounted on the wall. A pair of operators, their ears permanently pressed to phones, were constantly updating it, adding red arrows as the *Waffen-SS* pushed further and further into Berlin. Andrew was no expert, but General Knox had told him that the Battle of Berlin was turning into an absolute nightmare. A building could be declared secure, only to become very insecure indeed as the defenders sneaked back into it and opened fire on the SS from the rear. And, as the SS kept moving, they were smashing more and more buildings. Andrew couldn't help wondering if they were doing their best to make sure that no one could survive in the wreckage.

We had to destroy the village in order to save it, he thought. An American officer had said that, back during the Mexican War. The communists had been too deeply entrenched, he'd argued, for the limited American forces on hand to clear the village. And so he'd ordered it firebombed to ashes. *And now the SS is doing the same to an entire city.*

He looked at Voss, sensing - for the first time - the growing concern beneath the facade. The German was a Junker, heir to an established military tradition that long predated the United States of America, a tradition that even Hitler and Himmler hadn't been able to destroy completely. And yet, the man was on the brink of despair. He had more than enough firepower to halt the offensive, if only he had the time to bring it to bear on his foes...

And he might not have the time, Andrew thought. *Whoever takes Berlin takes the Reich.*

"It's bad," he said, finally. "But it's always darkest before the dawn."

Voss snorted, rudely. "You Americans," he said, as he turned to walk towards the door. "So *sentimental.*"

———

Hauptsturmfuehrer Katharine Milch kept her expression carefully blank as she listened to the dozy cows manning the soup kitchen, silently grateful for the intensive training she was forced to undertake before she was cleared for duty. The SS might have a role for female agents, but it was no more inclined to take the average woman and turn her into an operative than the *Wehrmacht*. A seductress was one thing, a woman willing and able to use her natural charms to seduce someone into saying something incriminating; an operative was quite another. Katharine had had to work hard from the day she'd determined what she wanted to do with her life, while the women surrounding her had been given their freedom on a platter.

And not much of that, she thought, as a woman in fine clothing started ladling out the pork and leek soup. *They may be upper-class bitches, but their husbands are the ones with real power. There's no true freedom here and they know it.*

She watched the refugees carefully as they trudged in and out of the kitchen, each one taking a bowl of soup, a piece of bread and a glass of pure water. They looked broken, perhaps pushed beyond endurance by having to leave their homes...Katharine snorted at the sheer foolishness of believing that was the worst that could happen. *She'd* endured worse, even before joining the SS. The refugees still had their lives, they still had their beauty...

they could rebuild, if they wished. But instead they were moaning about how unfair it was that they only got a small portion of food.

"I heard that the policemen and their families get more food," she said, when an opportunity arose. The silly women were twittering away, repeating and embellishing rumours as though they were facts. Such foolishness would never be tolerated in Germany East. Stupid women - or men - didn't last long out there. "And that some of them are selling ration cards to their friends."

"Of course not," one of the older woman said, indignantly. "My husband is a policeman and he would never do such a thing!"

Katharine concealed her amusement as two of the other woman started wittering, questioning the first woman closely. They were fools, but such foolishness had its uses. No matter how much the first woman might deny it, the seeds of doubt were planted and would grow rapidly into more and more rumours. By the time they reached the ears of someone in authority, the entire city would have heard the rumours…

…And a certain percentage would believe them.

She shrugged and returned to her work, content to allow the women to carry on the conversation alone. She'd leave as planned, knowing that the rumours would spread - and, like all rumours, grow in the telling. And no one would be able to trace them back to her.

It isn't quite the same as direct action, she thought, as she finished up. *But it may be just as effective in the long run.*

CHAPTER THIRTY-TWO

Berlin, Germany Prime
14 October 1985

Kurt leaned against the stone wall, feeling tired and worn.

The fighting had lasted for eleven days, he knew, but it felt as though it had been longer, much longer. Endless attacks and counterattacks, losing and recapturing buildings, only to lose them again when the enemy launched yet another thrust against the weakening defences and punched through. Berlin, the city of his birth, was being steadily destroyed and he could do nothing. His unit had been so badly weakened that his superiors were slotting in troops from other units that had come off even worse.

He struggled to catch his breath, half-tempted just to put a gun to his temple and pull the trigger. Several soldiers had already done just that, unable to endure the constant fighting combined with the near-complete lack of sleep. Others had wounded themselves, either unaware or uncaring that there was no hope of medical evacuation. The system that had prided itself on airlifting wounded soldiers to a field hospital had broken down, if it had ever worked at all, in the flames consuming Berlin. None of the men could expect anything more than a mattress, if they were lucky. Rumour had it that every last hospital in Berlin was running short of just about everything, to the point that the doctors had to use alcohol to disinfect wounds. He honestly had no idea just how long the city could continue to hold out.

"*Hauptmann* Wieland," a voice called.

Kurt looked up, suppressing a flicker of irritation when he saw the speaker. The boy - Kurt would have been astonished if he was actually old enough to enlist, in a more rational age - looked as tired as Kurt felt, although it didn't look as though he was doing anything more dangerous than taking messages forwards and backwards across the battlefield. But then, Kurt had to admit, that *could* be very dangerous. The SS snipers were advancing forward, ready to put a bullet in anyone foolish enough to show themselves too openly. He would have bet half his salary, if he thought he had a hope of collecting it, that a number of other messengers had died running through the lines.

He scowled, inwardly, as he waved the boy over. Johan - Kurt's younger brother - definitely looked older than the messenger. Kurt had no idea where Johan was - he'd volunteered to join the military shortly after the uprising - but he hoped his brother was safe. And yet, safety was increasingly an illusion in Berlin. SS shellfire had knocked down hundreds of buildings, trying to disrupt the defenders as the stormtroopers pushed forward.

"*Herr Hauptmann*," the boy said. His eyes were alight with *something*. It took Kurt a moment to recognise that it was hero-worship. "I have a message for you."

Kurt sighed, inwardly. Hardly anyone used paper messages these days, not when a messenger's body might be retrieved by the wrong side. It was a shame that the field telephones were unreliable, too. The damned SS had known *precisely* where to aim their guns to do maximum damage. He met the young boy's eyes and nodded impatiently, silently urging him to get on with it. His body was just too tired to curse the youngster for not giving him the message at once.

"You are to report to the *Reichstag*," the young boy said. "Your CO has already approved the transfer."

Kurt felt his eyes narrow. There was nothing for him in the *Reichstag*, certainly not as far as he knew. Gudrun wouldn't have called him out of the front lines, would she? She certainly hadn't arranged his promotion when she'd had the political power to do almost anything, although he knew that abusing the power would have been a good way to lose it. And yet, why would anyone else call him to the *Reichstag*. He was a mere *Hauptmann*, not a Field Marshal! Orders would normally pass through several higher ranks before they reached him.

"I understand," he said, taking a look at his men. Two-thirds of them were trying to catch some sleep, too used to the endless bombardment to allow it to keep them from resting; the remainder were trying, hard, to entertain themselves before they went back to the war. "I'll be on my way in two minutes."

He sighed inwardly, then waved to Loeb. If he was lucky, this - whatever it was - could be resolved quickly, allowing him to return to the front. The men under his command were *his* men. He shared their trials and tribulations and, in exchange, they respected him. He'd worked *hard* to build up that rapport, damn it! He didn't want to lose his connection to his men, simply because he'd been called to the *Reichstag*. Unless he was in deep trouble, of course.

Not likely, he thought. *They'd have sent the MPs to arrest me if I was in trouble.*

"I've been called out of the line," he said, bluntly. Loeb nodded, his face showing no visible reaction. "I'll be back as soon as possible."

"We're due to rotate back into the front lines in two hours, *Herr Hauptmann*," Loeb reminded him. "Do you think you'll be back by then?"

"If I'm not, take command yourself," Kurt ordered. Loeb had more experience than his entire graduating class put together. He was damned if he was allowing a green officer to take command of his unit, not when they were fighting for their lives and freedom. "Don't let the bastards get any closer."

Loeb nodded - they both knew it was a tall order - then saluted as Kurt turned and walked away, following the messenger towards the rear of the lines. He kept his head down, trying to ignore the handful of bodies on the ground. No one had yet had time to draw them to one of the mass graves, let alone give them a decent burial. Standard procedures were to dispose of bodies as quickly as possible, just to keep disease from spreading, but procedures were steadily breaking down under the onslaught. The bodies might have to wait until nightfall before they were finally recovered and buried.

He shuddered as they reached the edge of the lines and hurried into the city itself. The streets were almost deserted, save for emergency vehicles; the windows were boarded up or covered over to minimise the danger of flying glass. He saw a handful of civilians on the streets; he winced, inwardly, as he saw a pair of young girls, no older than Gudrun. Once, he might have tried to strike up a conversation, but he didn't have the energy. And they barely even noticed him as they staggered home. They looked alarmingly thin for girls who should have had more than enough to eat before the uprising.

The fear on the streets was almost palpable. Berlin had always been a city of fear - he didn't understand how Gudrun had found the nerve to challenge the government on its own territory - but this was different. The fear of the police, of ever-listening ears, of schoolmasters who watched for the slightest hint of independent thought was gone, replaced by the fear of incoming shells and the coming holocaust when the SS finally breached the defences and stormed the city. Hundreds of buildings were damaged, dozens more lay in ruins, struck by shells and collapsed into rubble. He hated to think of just how many people had died in the fighting so far. It was possible that no one would ever know for sure.

"The guards will see you though the checkpoints," the messenger said, as they finally approached the *Reichstag*. Kurt didn't know if he should be relieved or angry that most of the buildings around them were intact, save for one that had been struck by a cruise missile in the early days of the war. "And they'll tell you where to go."

Kurt nodded, tartly, as he strode up to the first checkpoints. He'd expected headquarters troops - wearing clean uniforms, shiny boots and unearned medals - but the troops guarding the building were very clearly experienced soldiers. They wore urban combat outfits and carried their weapons at the ready, clearly unconcerned about threatening high-ranking visitors to the *Reichstag*. Kurt kept his expression carefully blank as they checked his ID, then searched him so thoroughly he couldn't help wondering if they planned to strip him naked. It was a surprise when, after passing through three separate checkpoints, they returned his service pistol to him. The remainder of his weapons would be held in storage until he left the building.

"Kurt," his father said, as he was shown into a room. "Welcome back!"

Kurt blinked in surprise as his father enfolded him in a tight hug, then drew back long enough for Kurt to see that his mother and youngest brother were also in the room. *That* was a surprise. Kurt had known that his parents had rooms in the *Reichstag* - they couldn't remain in their old home, not after the uprising - but he'd never visited. There just hadn't been time.

"You stink," Siegfried said, with all the wit of a twelve-year-old. "Really, you stink."

"Thank you," Kurt said, sarcastically. Clobbering his youngest brother in front of their parents was probably not a good idea. "It comes of not being able to shower for years."

He turned back to his father before he could give in to the urge to tell his brother off, rather sharply, or smack him on the head. Siegfried had always been a prat. It came of being the youngest, Kurt supposed, but he found it hard to care. Siegfried had always been spoiled, in *his* view. Even Gudrun, the sole daughter, hadn't been allowed as much latitude as her younger brother.

"Father," he said. "Why am I here?"

"We couldn't tell the messenger," his father said. He smiled, a curious mixture of emotions crossing his face. "Gudrun is getting married."

Kurt blinked in surprise, then put the pieces together. "Horst?"

"Horst," his father confirmed. "And if you have any good *reason* to object, say so now."

"Gudrun would kill me," Kurt said. He'd occasionally thought that it was lucky for the *Reich* that Gudrun had been born female, rather than male. A man with her drive and daring would have probably wound up running the state, instead of tearing it down. "I wouldn't dare."

"He's a prat," Siegfried said. "Getting married…ugh."

Kurt reached out and tousled Siegfried's hair. He knew his younger brother hated being treated like a child, even though he *was* a child.

"Just you wait until you're older," he said. "It will all make sense then."

He glanced at his mother. "When's the wedding?"

"Tomorrow," his mother said. "But we will hold a more formal ceremony after the war."

Kurt kept his expression carefully blank. Getting married so quickly would have been unthinkable, once upon a time, unless Gudrun was pregnant. But quite a few soldiers he knew had gotten married over the last few weeks, determined to share their lives with *someone* before they went out on the battlefield. Maybe Horst and Gudrun felt the same way themselves. Marriage might be for life, but their lives might last less than a month, if the SS broke into the city. Kurt could only hope that Gudrun had the sense to kill herself before she fell into their hands.

And besides, he told himself, *she will kill me if I dare object.*

"That's good," he managed finally. "And I look forward to welcoming him into the family."

———

"So," Schwarzkopf said. "I hear you are to wed."

Horst tensed, despite himself. Only a handful of people knew that Gudrun and he were getting married, but that included the entire council. Gudrun's family wouldn't have told the SS anything - they certainly didn't work for the SS - yet someone on the council might have leaked the information. It was confirmation, of a sort, that there was indeed a traitor on the *Reich* Council.

Unless someone was careless at some point and blabbed, Horst thought. *And one of the staff overheard it.*

His mind raced. If Schwarzkopf doubted his loyalty, he would have waited to see if *Horst* brought the matter up himself. *Not* telling his handler that he was planning to marry Gudrun - that he was *going* to marry Gudrun - would have been more than enough proof that his loyalties no longer lay with his former masters. Indeed, it was why he had carefully prepared an outline of what had happened that would uphold his claim to be merely manipulating Gudrun. But it didn't seem necessary.

He pushed the thought aside with an effort. "It is a way to solidify my grip on her," he said, lightly. "A wife finds it hard to disagree with her husband, even when the man is clearly in the wrong."

Schwarzkopf snorted, rudely. "You've never been married, have you?"

Horst frowned. "No," he said. "Have you?"

His handler ignored the question. "How many guests are you inviting to the wedding?"

"Just her family," Horst said. He'd had very few true friends in Berlin, even before the uprising. Friendship could be very dangerous if one was trying to maintain a cover story. "I won't have anyone to stand beside me when I sign the papers."

"She'll hate that," Schwarzkopf said. He sounded perversely amused. "Just a simple registry wedding. No ceremony, no speakers, no famous guests. And to think you could probably get most of the council in one room."

"They vetoed that idea," Horst said, flatly. It was true enough. Any security officer worth his salt would go ballistic at the thought of gathering hundreds of important people in a single location. "It will have to wait until after the war."

"And won't happen at all," Schwarzkopf said. "I trust you *do* recall your duty?"

"I have never forgotten my duty," Horst said, stiffly. "What do you wish of me?"

"We require more precise scheduling details," Schwarzkopf said. "Particularly of your lovely wife."

"She isn't my wife yet," Horst said, feeling ice trickling down the back of his neck. The limited pieces of information he'd sent them had probably been useful, but he knew they would be keeping him in reserve until they finally needed him. He was just too well-placed to risk. And yet, the sound of gunfire and explosions echoing over the city made it clear that time was running out. "What sort of information do you want?"

"Just her routine schedule," Schwarzkopf said. "We'll give you more information nearer the time."

Horst thought fast. Assassinating Gudrun was a very real possibility, but - as far as Schwarzkopf was concerned - he had an agent who literally slept next to her. Snapping Gudrun's delicate neck while she slept would be easy. There was no point in trying to sneak a kill-team into the *Reichstag* when Horst could do the deed and then make his escape, hours before anyone realised that something was wrong. And if they doubted his loyalty, it would be an excellent test.

They want to kidnap her, he thought, numbly. *Taking her out of the Reichstag would be impossible, but grabbing her off the streets would be far easier.*

"Her schedule changes frequently," he said. He carefully did *not* mention that altering her plans at a moment's notice had been his idea. "I can give you the schedule I know, but I cannot guarantee that it won't change."

Schwarzkopf leaned forward. "You cannot ensure your wife is in the right position at the right time?"

Horst knew he should probably make a crude joke, something to make it clear that he thought nothing of Gudrun, but he couldn't muster the determination. Instead, he met his superior's eyes.

"She generally has a handful of places to choose from," he said, carefully. "And while I can *try* to propose a particular destination, I don't think I can guarantee that she will go there."

Schwarzkopf lifted his eyebrows. "Indeed?"

"She is flighty," Horst lied. "Four days ago, she went to a hospital and chatted to the wounded men; three days ago, she decided she would be going to the hospital again, then changed her mind and insisted on visiting a school instead. I think she enjoyed terrifying her old schoolmasters."

"I'm sure she did," Schwarzkopf said.

Horst nodded in agreement. It was an article of faith in the west, he'd discovered, that girls had an easier time of it at school than boys. But he had a feeling that it wasn't particularly true. Girls who failed to conform could expect little better than boys who failed to conform, even though girls had less use for educational certificates than boys. And their parents might eventually be told to make them conform or else.

And now Gudrun is in a position to seek revenge, he thought. He would have smirked, if he hadn't been trying to keep his face blank. *I bet that upset quite a few of her old teachers.*

"I can give you a provisional list," Horst added. "And I can try to slant it, but there will be no guarantees."

"So you keep saying," Schwarzkopf said. "Do the best you can. We will act as we see fit."

"I know," Horst said.

"And congratulations on your wedding," Schwarzkopf added. "I trust you will have a pleasant honeymoon?"

Horst laughed. "We can't get out of the city," he said. It was traditional for newly-weds to go off for a honeymoon, but leaving Berlin was impossible. "We'll just have to take a day or two off and pretend we're in Bavaria."

"Pathetic," Schwarzkopf said.

"There's no way to leave," Horst said. He moved quickly to dismiss the next possibility, before Schwarzkopf could suggest it. "Even finding a hotel is impossible, these days."

"What a pity," Schwarzkopf said, dryly. A hotel would have made an ideal spot for a quick kidnap, although getting Gudrun out of the city afterwards would have been tricky. "You'll hear from us after the wedding, no doubt."

"No doubt," Horst agreed.

CHAPTER THIRTY-THREE

Berlin, Germany Prime
15 October 1985

Gudrun stood in front of the mirror and slowly disrobed, removing her clothing piece by piece until she was as naked as the day she was born.

She studied her body as dispassionately as she could, despite the churning morass of emotions that threatened to bubble up into her mind. It was a good body - both Konrad and Horst had said so - and she knew it was satisfactory. Her skin was pale, with barely a blemish; her long blonde hair hung down to brush against the tops of her breasts. She'd been lucky not to have darker skin or anything else that would have suggested that there had been a non-Aryan somewhere within the family tree. There had been a handful of girls who *had* been darker, she recalled all too well. They'd had papers proving that they met the standard definition of Aryan - no hint of non-Aryan blood for at least four generations - but it hadn't been enough to keep them from becoming social outcasts. In hindsight, she admitted quietly, she'd treated them as cruelly as everyone else.

Because you didn't want to be an outcast yourself, she told herself. *It was safer to pick on the girls who were.*

She cursed the younger person she'd been, then continued to scrutinize her body, her eyes trailing down her legs to her feet. Her arms were strong, but she was nowhere near as muscular as Horst or her father. She would never be, she knew, no matter how hard she exercised her body. Horst had warned her, bluntly, that girls needed to learn to fight dirty, if they wanted to fight at all. A man would almost certainly be stronger and faster than any woman. The only way to win was to fight dirty.

There was a knock at the door. "Gudrun," her mother called. "It's me."

"Come in," Gudrun said. There was no one else in the suite, but she still tensed when the door opened. "Did you bring the dress?"

"I did," her mother said, briskly. "Did you have a quick shower?"

"I showered this morning," Gudrun said, rather disdainfully. Water rationing was starting to bite, even in the *Reichstag*. A five-minute shower was nowhere near long enough to wash her hair. Some of the maids had even started cutting their hair short to make it easier to wash. "I don't want to shower again."

Her mother looked her up and down, then nodded. "You look very much like I did at your age," she said, as she passed Gudrun her undergarments. "I was expecting shortly afterwards."

Gudrun coloured. "I'm not expecting, mother," she said. "Really."

"You soon will be," her mother predicted, bluntly. "A virile young man like yours? He'll want to share your bed all the time."

"Mother," Gudrun said, cringing. "*Please.*"

Her mother gave her a droll look. She'd been remarkably informative after Gudrun had discussed Konrad with her, even though Gudrun still winced at the thought of her parents actually having sex. Gudrun knew she should be grateful that her mother was willing to tell her anything - what she'd learned in school hadn't been particularly informative - but there were details she hadn't wanted to know. Man-management was apparently a science all of its own in the *Reich*, with secrets passed down through successive generations of mothers and daughters. But she really hadn't wanted to know about some of the problems her parents had faced.

Gudrun sighed, heavily. She was twenty years old. And yet, far too many of her old classmates from school were already married. They hadn't gone to university, they hadn't dreamed of an independent career…she'd looked them up, out of curiosity, and discovered that twenty-seven out of thirty girls had married within six months of leaving school. A number even had children of their own now, children who would be entering nursery school within two years. And of the remaining three, two of them were practically old maids.

Twenty years old and yet no husband, she thought, morbidly. *Their parents will be pushing them to accept the first man who comes calling.*

She pulled her undergarments on, then closed her eyes as her mother lowered the wedding dress over her head. Gudrun had been offered her mother's old dress, one that had been in the family for five generations, but she'd declined, pointing out that it wasn't a formal ceremony. Her mother hadn't objected - Gudrun knew she was quietly planning a huge ceremony for after the war - yet the dress they'd selected in its place was whiter than Gudrun would have preferred. But then, white wedding dresses were often nothing more than polite fictions within the *Reich*.

"You look good," her mother said, as she fussed around the dress, loosening some of the seams and tightening others. "Very like a bride on her way to the registry hall."

"Oh *good*," Gudrun said. She knew her mother wanted a formal ceremony, but that wasn't going to happen until after the war. "That's the look I was trying for."

Her mother snorted.

Gudrun hid her amusement with an effort, then glanced at the door. Normally, it took at least a week to get a marriage certificate, but the flood of couples trying to get married had done the impossible and forced the bureaucrats to speed up the process. Horst and her father had flatly refused to allow her to go to the registry hall herself - there was too great a risk of being assassinated or kidnapped - and the register had, reluctantly, been escorted to the *Reichstag*. The wedding itself would be held in a small room on one of the lower levels…

"This is your last chance to back out," her mother said. "Are you sure you want to marry him?"

"Yes," Gudrun said.

She shook her head. Her mother's words were just as much a polite fiction as the white wedding dress. A relationship that had come so far simply could not be cancelled and forgotten, not after both sets of parents had paid for the marriage certificate and what other pieces of paperwork were required. Maybe a girl who got cold feet could run, but it would be a major scandal and tongues would be wagging for years. Her family would probably disown her, just to make it clear that they didn't condone her actions.

And if I was pregnant, she thought, *I could never leave.*

She looked at her mother, wondering if she dared ask a question that - on any other day - would probably get her slapped. But her mother had been open with her - disconcertingly open with her - after she'd started making her plans…

"Mother," she said. "Do you ever regret marrying father?"

Her mother's lips thinned, just for a second. "Marriage is…*different* to being a daughter," she said, finally. "This morning, you are a daughter; tomorrow morning, you will be a wife."

"That doesn't answer my question," Gudrun said.

"Marriage…is two people learning to live and work together," her mother said. "It has its ups and downs. We have fought, sometimes quite badly, over everything from the household budget to your education. And yet…I have learned to be supportive of him and he has learned to be supportive of me. Gudrun…you'll find you won't truly *know* your husband until you have spent years with him, sharing his life."

She shook her head. "No, I don't regret it. I have four lovely children and a husband who does his very best for them - and me. There are worse husbands out there, but few better ones. Your father is a good man."

Gudrun cocked her head. "Even if he did have shouting matches with Kurt?"

"That's what happens when a young boy grows into a man," her mother said. "He starts clashing against the older man in the house."

She smiled, rather tiredly. "The sooner Kurt gets married, the better."

"I'll see if I can find anyone who might be interested," Gudrun said. "I owe him that much, I think."

She finished dressing and checked her watch, then allowed her mother to lead her out of the door and down towards the wedding chamber. It was bare, save for a single desk placed at the rear of the room. A man stood behind it, wearing the drab uniform of a bureaucrat; he gave her a single look, then nodded to himself as she entered the room. There was nothing obviously wrong with her, Gudrun guessed. It would have been a different story if she'd had dark skin or anything else that marked her out as - perhaps - not being racially pure.

"Gudrun," her father said, as he stepped into the chamber. He held a brown envelope in one hand. "Are you ready?"

"Yes, father," Gudrun said.

She looked back as Horst entered the room, flanked by Kurt, Johan and Siegfried. Horst wore a simple *Heer* uniform without any rank badges, very unlike the black dress uniform he would have worn as an SS stormtrooper - as *Konrad* would have worn, if things had gone differently. She felt a sudden stab of guilt, as if she was betraying his memory, even though she knew it was absurd. Konrad wouldn't have wanted her to spend the rest of her life alone, no matter what else happened. And yet...

Kurt and Johan wore their uniforms, she noted, while Siegfried wore a simple black suit that had been tailored to fit him. He hadn't yet entered his final growth spurt, but he was already tall and muscular for his age. He'd thrown a colossal fit when his father had banned him from joining the boxing club and then sulked for days before finally subsiding. Gudrun hoped that he hadn't said anything nasty to Horst. But then, Kurt would have walloped him if he had. Horst was alone, his family on the far side of the border. And there was no way to know if they were even alive.

"I love you," she mouthed.

"I love you too," Horst mouthed back.

Siegfried made gagging motions, which stopped abruptly when their father turned his gaze on him. Gudrun allowed herself a moment of relief, then looked at her father, wondering just what thoughts were going through his head. His little girl was getting married, leaving the family home for the last time. Gudrun hadn't set foot in her home for nearly a month, now, but it hardly mattered. Her relationship with her father would never be the same again.

Her father cleared his throat. "Shall we begin?"

The register looked up at them as they approached the table. Up close, he had a bland featureless face that seemed completely unremarkable. His eyes flickered over Horst, then moved to Gudrun. Her father put the brown envelope on the desk; the register opened it with a knife, then pulled out the documents and checked them, one by one. Gudrun felt her heart beginning to race as time seemed to slow down, even though she *knew* it was an illusion. The slightest mistake with the paperwork would be enough to get the ceremony cancelled, at least until the mistake could be sorted out...

He'd have to be an idiot to say no now, she thought, with a flicker of amusement. *Doesn't he know who we are?*

"Everything appears to be in order," the register said, finally. He looked at Horst. "Your documentation is very limited."

"That was covered when we obtained the marriage certificate," Horst said, flatly. "The original copies of my documents - my file - are in the east."

The register nodded. "Understood," he said. "And now…"

He spoke casually, almost as if he were bored. "This ceremony will make you husband and wife in the eyes of the *Reich*," he said. "From the moment you sign the documents and take the marriage certificate, you will be married, whatever ceremony you plan to hold afterwards."

Gudrun nodded. This was it, the end of her life as a daughter, the start of her life as a wife…

"I must ask you both to swear, now, that you carry no taint of non-Aryan blood within you," the register said. "Do you swear?"

"I swear," Horst said.

Gudrun nodded, not trusting herself to speak. She had a pure-perfect record from the Race Classification Bureau, one she'd had written out for her when she started planning to marry Konrad. And there was a copy in front of the register. He *knew* they were both pureblood Germans. There was no need to demand a final oath in front of so many witnesses. And yet, there was no point in making a fuss.

"I swear," she said, finally.

The register pulled three certificates out of a folder on his desk, their names and details already filled in. Gudrun took the first one and read it carefully, checking every last detail, before taking a pen and signing her name at the bottom. She passed it to Horst, then read and signed the remaining two certificates. Her father, her guardian, was the last person to sign his name. Without his signature, it wouldn't be valid.

"You are now husband and wife," the register said. His tone hadn't changed at all. "I wish you both a long and happy marriage."

Gudrun fought down the urge to giggle, then turned to Horst and lifted her lips, allowing him to kiss her gently. She heard Siegfried say something rude behind them, then grunt in pain, but she didn't care. Horst held her for a long moment, then released her, his eyes shining with…*something*. They were married now. Their lives had just been bound together, for better or worse…

her emotions were a mess. Part of her was tempted, far too tempted, just to start crying.

Her father paid the Registrar, then marched her family out of the room. Gudrun followed, holding Horst's hand as they walked into the small dining room. There wasn't much to eat - Gudrun was damned if she was feasting while much of the population was starving - but there were two bottles of expensive wine and some sweets from France. It wasn't how she'd envisaged her wedding, when she'd thought about what she'd wanted as a young girl, yet the lack of ceremony didn't matter. All that mattered was that they were together.

She glanced up at him, then giggled as he started trying to feed her. Siegfried made even more rude noises, then quietened down as Kurt glared at him. Gudrun sighed, wondering what his problem was, before deciding it didn't matter. Siegfried was already far too spoilt simply by being the young-est. Their parents weren't *quite* as strict with him as they'd been with their older children.

"Don't drink too much," her father advised as he passed her a glass of wine. "You are already very emotional."

Gudrun nodded. Now the ceremony was over, part of her had doubts. She had - technically - promised to obey Horst...and the law would back him up, if there was a dispute. And yet, she was damned if she was just submitting to him. Even her own mother, however quiet she might be in public, was hardly submissive in private. And yet...she took a sip of the wine, silently grateful that her mother had forbidden her from drinking more than a glass on special occasions. The boys could have their drinking contests, if they wished, but it wasn't something she cared to allow herself. It was too dangerous.

She ate enough to keep herself going, then watched as her parents escorted her siblings out of the room. If there was one thing to be said for such a simple ceremony, it was that Horst and she were left alone within two hours of the wedding. A more complex ceremony would take far longer...

"Mrs Albrecht," Horst said, quietly.

Gudrun nodded. She'd already determined that she would use her maiden name for her professional life, but she would be Mrs Albrecht in private. And yet, even acknowledging it made her feel strange. They were together now until one of them died. Divorce was practically unthinkable. If they had children, it would become completely impossible.

Horst rose and held out a hand. "Shall we go?"

"Yes," Gudrun said. She stood and kissed him, as hard as she could. "Let's go."

———

"I trust you had a few words with Siegfried?"

"Kurt already gave him a lecture," Herman said, as he stepped into the room he shared with his wife. Adelinde was already sitting on the bed, her blonde hair shining under the harsh electric light. "He's quite protective of Gudrun."

"He'll have to be protective of someone else soon," Adelinde said, curtly. She sounded annoyed. "And Siegfried needs to grow up."

"He's twelve," Herman reminded her. "It's going to be a while before he grows into a man."

"I know," Adelinde said. "But he's too old not to know when he's being rude."

Herman nodded. His youngest son had always been a handful. Herman had had less time for him, while Johan had been four years older than Siegfried and Kurt had been in military training, depriving Siegfried of a true playmate or someone to look up to. And Gudrun had been a girl...

He sighed as he sat down next to his wife. He'd given his daughter away to a man she'd chosen, surrendering her to another man. It felt wrong, even though he'd *known* that Gudrun would eventually move out from the moment she was born. His daughter was no longer his little girl, but a grown woman. Their relationship would never be the same.

And if Horst tries to boss her around, he thought, *I'll...*

He smiled in genuine wonderment. It was odd, but Gudrun - perhaps - was the only one of his children who really took after him. If Horst tried to boss her around, or beat her, Herman was sure he'd regret it very quickly - if he survived. Gudrun had brought down a government! A single man wouldn't present a real problem...

Adelinde gave him a sharp look. "What's so funny?"

"Gudrun is very like me," Herman said. "And that's odd."

"Hah," Adelinde said. She stuck out her tongue. "I've been trying to tell you that for a very long time."

CHAPTER THIRTY-FOUR

Berlin, Germany Prime
20 October 1985

"The reports are clear, *Mein Fuhrer*," Alfred said. "I just heard back from the scouts."

He paused. Bad news was rarely welcomed by his superiors. "The traitors are massing to the west," he added. "They should be ready to move within the week, perhaps ten days at the most."

"So it would seem," Karl Holliston said. The *Fuhrer* sounded oddly calm, something that worried Alfred more than he cared to admit. "What are they trying to do?"

Alfred turned to look at the map his staff had pinned to the wall. "Depending on the timing, *Mein Fuhrer*, they either intend to punch open a relief corridor to Berlin or trap our forces against the city," he said. "It was what the Russians intended to do in Stalingrad."

"The *Untermenschen* failed," Holliston snapped.

"Yes, *Mein Führer*, but we are not facing *Untermenschen*," Alfred said. "The traitors have successfully rallied a large percentage of fighting men to their banner."

He took a breath. "I would like permission to lift the siege and withdraw from the city," he added, carefully. Holliston was *not* going to take *this* calmly. "I do not believe we can break into the city without taking hideous losses."

"Out of the question," Holliston snapped. "To lose Berlin - again - would be disastrous."

Alfred braced himself. "The situation is grim," he said. "We have lost thousands of men in the battle and we will lose thousands more if we push onwards. I believe we can take Berlin, but then we will lose it again when the traitor relief formations arrive. Our logistics network is shot to hell and far too many of our units have been chewed up. We need time to put our forces back on a secure footing."

He cursed under his breath. No one had ever anticipated a civil war. Even the disagreements in 1950, after Hitler's death, hadn't threatened all-out war. Naturally, very few precautions had been taken to prepare for such a war. The *Waffen-SS* was in the odd position of being an elite force that didn't have as much of the latest equipment as it would have preferred. Many of the vehicles it deployed in Germany East wouldn't have lasted more than a minute on a modern battlefield, not against the massed power of the *Heer*. They needed to trade space for time, time to get production started, time to learn from the battles they'd already fought...

"Time is the one thing we do not have," Holliston said. "If they force us away from Berlin, we risk losing everything."

"We may lose everything if we stay in position," Alfred said. "*Mein Fuhrer*, our ability to handle the coming storm is very limited. And staying in one place will only pin us down..."

"There are plans afoot to strike at the very heart of their power," Holliston said. "That will distract them, will it not?"

Alfred took a moment to calm himself. The *Reichstag* should never have been left untouched. His gunners could have pulverised the building and the surrounding area, destroying - or at least crippling - the traitor government. It would have proved, beyond all doubt, that the government couldn't even protect itself. And yet, Karl Holliston had flatly refused to allow the gunners to shell the *Reichstag*. He'd made it clear, very clear, that the entire region was to be left strictly alone. Even his spiteful destruction of the Ministry of Economics had been made after some soul-searching.

But we could rebuild, Alfred thought, bitterly. *Rebuilding the Reichstag would hardly be a major problem.*

"It might," Alfred said. "But their fighting men have nowhere to run."

He sighed as he glared at the secure phone. He'd studied the great campaigns in Poland, France and Russia and all three of them had one thing in common. There had been room for both sides to manoeuvre, room for the defenders to break and run...when they hadn't had that room, they'd tended to fight harder. The Russians at Leningrad, Stalingrad, and Moscow hadn't been able to run and they'd fought like mad bastards. He'd read the campaign records, including diaries that had been deemed too inflammatory to release to their families; if anything, he'd come to realise, those long-dead German soldiers had understated the nightmare of fighting in a city. Berlin was being held so strongly that he doubted his ability to take the city…

And if we do take the city, he thought morbidly, *we may lose the war.*

"It will not matter, if we can retake the *Reichstag*," Holliston said. "Prepare your men for a final savage push."

Alfred winced. "*Mein Fuhrer*," he said. "Can your forces within the city take the *Reichstag*?"

"Yes," Holliston said. "And they can do much else besides."

There was a pause. "Prepare your men. There is one final battle that must be fought."

Alfred closed his eyes in pain. Resistance - further resistance - would be worse than futile. A single word from Germanica would be enough to ensure his death, either at the hands of an SS security force or a covert operative hidden within his staff. He knew, beyond a shadow of a doubt, that there *was* someone keeping an eye on him. If he resisted Holliston, if he ordered a retreat or even a redeployment to face the oncoming storm, his life and those of his family would be forfeit.

And if I retire, he asked himself, *who will take my place?*

He shuddered at the thought. The SS commanders ranged from enthusiastic to outright fanatical, the kind of fire-breathers who should never be in command of anything larger than a company. There was something to be said for aggression on the battlefield, he had to admit, but it needed to be tempered with due care and long-term thinking. An SS panzer division wasn't an assault troop and couldn't be treated as one. And those who did couldn't be allowed to take command of the entire army.

"It shall be done, *Mein Fuhrer*," he said, finally. "When do you want the offensive to begin?"

"Four days," Holliston said. "Do whatever you have to do to make it work."

"*Jawohl, Mein Fuhrer*," Alfred said.

The line disconnected. Alfred stared at the phone for a long moment, then returned the handset to its cradle, thinking hard. The *Fuhrer* had told him to do whatever he had to do to make the offensive work, an order that gave him a great deal of latitude. Karl Holliston probably wouldn't approve of just how far he intended to take the order and run with it, but Alfred found it hard to care. If taking Berlin was the only thing keeping him - and his family - from ending their lives hanging from meathooks in a cellar under Germanica, he would do everything in his power to make sure the final offensive was actually *final*.

Rising, he strode into the next room and nodded to Weineck, who made his way over to stand beside his superior as Alfred studied the map. The endless fighting might have overrun parts of Berlin, but none of them were particularly important. A couple of suburbs had been completely worthless, save for the opportunity to wear down the defenders by forcing them to fight for the territory.

And expend their ammunition, he thought. If *his* ammunition consumption calculations had been so badly off-base, surely theirs had been too. *They can't have much left, can they?*

Weineck glanced at him. "*Herr Oberstgruppenfuehrer?*"

Alfred frowned, without taking his eyes off the map. Was Weineck receiving secret orders from Germanica? Or would it be one or more of the communications techs, the men whose names he barely knew? Or some of the guards? Or perhaps his orderly, who had been with him for the last decade? There was no way to know, no way even to *guess*.

"The *Fuhrer* wishes us to make one final push towards the *Reichstag*," he said, flatly. There was no point in worrying about it, not now. "We need to make some preparations."

"Of course, *Herr Oberstgruppenfuehrer*," Weineck said. "This time we will be victorious."

And are you saying that for my benefit, Alfred asked himself, *or for the edification of any listening ears?*

He pushed the thought aside as he looked up at his aide. "Pull all of the Category A units out of the front lines," he ordered. "Give them a day or two of rest, then prepare them for a final thrust. We'll mass our forces and advance under heavy shelling."

Weineck frowned. "Our stockpiles of shells are quite low…"

"Then we need to bring in more," Alfred said. "And I want you to inform the gunners, when the offensive begins, that they are not to hold back."

He ignored Weineck's shock. Standard procedure might have been to hold a number of shells in reserve, just in case there was an urgent call for fire support, but standard procedures would have to be abandoned. As long as there was a hope, however faint, of breaking through the defence lines and punching their way towards the *Reichstag*, the gunners would have to do their utmost.

"The same goes for our remaining air power," he added. "Once the offensive begins, they are to strike at targets within Berlin, doing everything in their power to weaken the defenders."

"*Jawohl, Herr Oberstgruppenfuehrer*," Weineck said. He still looked shocked. "But…but that will cost us badly."

"Yes, it will," Alfred said. "But the *Fuhrer* has ordered us to take Berlin."

He scowled as he turned to the overall map. The traitors were gathering their forces under the protection of their remaining air force - and those damned American missiles. Ideally, he would have preferred to deploy his air power to slow their advance, but that would drain the remainder of his aircraft for very little return. He had to admire the traitors for choosing to leave Berlin uncovered, despite the American missiles; the decision might have cost them quite badly, but it had definitely worked out for them.

"I also want you to redeploy a number of commando teams," he added. "Once it becomes clear that we are storming the city, the traitors will attempt to send their own forces forward to engage us. The commandos are to slow them down as much as possible."

"*Jawohl, Herr Oberstgruppenfuehrer*," Weineck said.

Alfred nodded, curtly. His redeployments were the best hope the *Waffen-SS* had of breaking through the defence line and storming Berlin, but there was no way to avoid the sense that there was nothing he could do to prevent disaster. A retreat now would look bad, yet it would preserve his forces and give him time to bleed the enemy…doing unto them as they'd done unto the SS. And yet, the *Fuhrer* would not listen. He'd gambled everything on taking Berlin.

"And then I have a number of other redeployments that need to be handled," Alfred added, slowly. Maybe they could win the battle…but if they didn't, he'd have to do what he could to avoid losing the overall war. "But we will handle those later."

"*Jawohl, Herr Oberstgruppenfuehrer*," Weineck said. He paused. "Pulling back the Category A units will weaken the ongoing fighting."

"It can't be helped," Alfred said, bluntly. "Let them retake a few metres of territory, if they feel they are not being lured into a trap. We will take the entire city soon enough."

———

Being a barmaid, Katharine Milch had decided shortly after she had started her new job, wasn't something she would have inflicted on anyone, particularly working in a distinctly low-end bar in the poorer parts of Berlin. Her figure, in a uniform that was practically indecent, had been complimented so many times she'd lost count, while she'd had to slap seven men for groping her breasts or pinching her bottom. Indeed, if the bartender hadn't been a brutish lout of a man, she suspected she would have had to fight to save her virtue from the mob.

But it did have its advantages, she had to admit. The men who clustered into the bar at the end of each day were workers, workers in occupations deemed too important to let them go join the army. They were a mass of bitter resentment, caught between the demands of their work and taunts that implied that they were cowards. Katharine poured them endless mugs of cheap beer and listened to their comments, occasionally adding a comment of her own. It was odd, she conceded, but the provisional government might have outsmarted itself when it had legalised unions. There were unions popping up everywhere now.

Idiots, she thought, after hearing one man complaining about having to work overtime in an ammunition factory. It was hard to keep the scorn off her face. *The wolf is at the door and you're whining about not being able to see your wives and children.*

She shook her head at the thought as her shift finally came to an end, then handed her apron over to the next barmaid with an inescapable sense of relief. Her skin *stank* of beer - she'd had a mug thrown over her by a half-drunk lout - yet at least she hadn't had to use any of her training to fight them off. She wanted a shower, even though she'd endured worse during her training, but she knew that wasn't going to happen. Water rationing was growing tighter and tighter by the day, leaving ordinary Berliners increasingly short of drinking water, let alone washing water. She'd just have to wipe herself down when she reached the apartment and hope it was enough.

The streets were dark when she walked home, forcing her to keep a sharp eye out for footpads and rapists. Berlin really had gone to the dogs, she thought, her lips twisting in disgust. Once, the crime rate had been minimal; now, there were thousands of horror stories running through the city, everything from thieves and pickpockets roaming freely in broad daylight to *Untermenschen* rapists running wild. Most of the stories were exaggerated - she'd planted a few herself - but there was a hard core of truth to them. Berlin was dying and the signs of death were all around her. Even if the siege was lifted tomorrow, the once-great city would never be the same again.

She reached the apartment without trouble and strode up the stairs, trying hard to keep from doing anything that might attract attention. There was little so blatantly obvious as someone trying *not* to sneak around, her instructors had taught her. The trick was to remain calm, composed and pretend - if only to one's self - that one had every right to be there. Police questioned the people who seemed out of place, not the ones who looked normal.

At least they won't ask questions if I stay in the flat, she thought. *There are fewer and fewer girls on the streets these days.*

"Message from Odin," Hans said, once the door was closed. "We're to move as planned in four days, unless it gets put back."

Katherine gave him a long look. "Are you sure?"

"The message was repeated four times," Hans said. He'd served with her long enough not to have any great objection to her femininity. She trusted him, just as she trusted the other men on her squad. "Four days...unless it gets put back."

"An all-out offensive on the city," Katherine mused. Their operations had always been planned to take place under cover of an assault; indeed, she was surprised they hadn't been called into action sooner. "And a kidnapping operation."

She scowled. In her experience, trying to be clever - trying to do too many things at once - was asking for trouble. She would have preferred to concentrate on one or the other, not both. But she understood, from innumerable briefings, just how important it was that both parts of the operation were pulled off successfully.

"Check with Loki," she ordered, reluctantly. "See how many men he has in the city."

"Understood," Hans said. "The others have yet to report back."

Katherine scowled. There was nothing so dangerous, she knew from bitter experience, as something that stuck out like a sore thumb…and a handful of military-age men lurking in an apartment definitely stuck out, particularly when they should be on the front lines. She'd had no choice, but to send them out, allowing them to pose as soldiers, policemen or workers…even though it ran the risk of disaster.

"When they do, inform them that we will be making the final preparations for Strike One," she said. Thankfully, the traitors had long since lost control of large parts of Berlin. She had no idea how the *Reich* Council had managed to miss the growing protest mobs, but their successors hadn't learned from their mistakes. "I'll need to speak to Loki about Strike Two."

She closed her eyes in irritation. Loki might have faith in his people, but *she* didn't. Too many of them had slipped up in the months prior to the uprising, before the traitors had taken control of the city. Indeed, she'd been careful to ensure that Loki knew nothing about the other cells…although he would *have* to know, if he was going to assist her with Strike Two.

And if I put it completely in his hands, it might just be screwed up anyway, she thought, darkly. She opened her eyes. *Too many bastards have already messed up - and there's no way to know if they screwed up legitimately…or if they're on the other side.*

"The plan seems too good to be true," Hans pointed out, carefully. "There are just too many ways it could go wrong."

"I know," Katherine said. Anything that looked too good to be true probably was. "And that is why we are not going to be using his plan."

CHAPTER THIRTY-FIVE

Berlin, Germany Prime
23 October 1985

"They're not pulling back," Volker Schulze said. "They're preparing for a new offensive."

"It looks that way," Voss said. He sounded tired. He'd just got back from inspecting one set of defences, Volker knew, and he'd be heading back out in an hour, after he'd given his report. "They're still shooting at us, but the pressure has slacked. Prisoner interrogations suggest that we're facing reservists all along the lines."

Volker frowned. "And there's no hope they're pulling back?"

He shook his head before Voss could answer. It was nothing more than wishful thinking - and he knew it all too well. The *Waffen-SS* wasn't setting up defensive lines to the east, or withdrawing to more defendable territory. They were massing their troops, giving them time to rest and recuperate before they launched another major offensive. And, because their reservists were still keeping up the pressure, the defenders couldn't take advantage of the pause to rest themselves. There was, quite literally, nowhere to run.

"Our forces are still massing here and here," Voss said, tapping points on the map. "They should be ready to advance within five days."

Volker scowled. "Will they be in time?"

"It depends on just what they have in mind," Voss said, honestly. "We're putting together contingency plans to advance earlier, if only to open up a corridor to Berlin, but that would run the risk of allowing them to extract most of their own forces before it was too late."

"Which would prolong the war," Volker mused.

"Or shorten it," Voss countered. "An engagement in open terrain would give them some advantages."

Volker rubbed his eyes. He might have a bedroom in the bunker, where there was no constant shellfire to keep him awake, but he'd barely been able to sleep properly since the siege had begun. The war had to be fought, he knew; the war had to be won...but the Berliners were suffering in a way that would have been unimaginable, a scant few months ago. He'd certainly never dreamed of being their leader, let alone forced to watch helplessly as his city was slowly reduced to rubble. The war could end tomorrow - and that was another piece of wishful thinking - and it would still take years to rebuild.

And the city will be savaged if the Waffen-SS break through the defences, he thought. *It will be the end of days.*

He shuddered, wondering just how many men and women were secreting weapons or poison around their person to ensure that they didn't fall into enemy hands. The reports flowing in from occupied territory were an endless liturgy of horror. Men killed or rounded up and forced to serve the SS; women raped or marched east to be married to SS stormtroopers and raise the next generation of easterners; children taken from their parents and transported to an unknown destination. It was hard to be sure just how many of the reports were actually true - the pre-war intelligence network had been shot to hell - but one thing was clear. The hatred between west and east was growing - and so was the fear.

There's no way we can live together, he thought, grimly. *All we can do is try to slay the monstrous beast in its lair.*

He turned to look at the map, shaking his head slowly. Even if they won the battle, even if they smashed the forces laying siege to Berlin, getting to Germanica would take months. The winter was already starting to take hold in the east, making it harder and harder for the easterners to move troops and supplies westward...his forces would have the same problem, if they wanted to launch an eastern offensive. No, any counterattack would have to wait until the spring...assuming, of course, that they survived the coming offensive. And that would give the easterners ample time to prepare.

"We may have only a handful of days," he said. If there *was* a spy on the council - and young Albrecht had proved it - the SS would know the situation as well as he did. *He* would have cut his losses and withdrawn from Berlin, but the SS clearly disagreed. "Can we withstand their offensive?"

"I hope so," Voss said.

Volker shot him a sharp look. *That* was hardly a ringing endorsement.

Voss sighed. "Our forces have considerable experience in using the terrain to their advantage," he said, heavily. He didn't mention that troops - mainly untrained volunteers - who hadn't learned had died. "But we are short on ammunition as well as everything from rations to hospital beds. A single push forward might be enough to bleed us dry."

"And production isn't keeping up with demand," Volker muttered.

The irony chilled him to the bone. He'd created the very first union, he'd ensured that the workers had the power to resist the government's demands… and now he had to force the workers to produce guns and ammunition in record quantities. And the threatened strikes weren't the worst of it, he knew all too well. The machinery was slowly breaking down, threatening to render the factories useless. His men had no time to fix the damage or even produce more ammunition.

We could ask the Americans for ammunition, he thought, sourly. *But their ammunition wouldn't be suitable for our weapons.*

Voss met his eyes. "We could try to discuss a truce," he offered. "They can have the east and we can have the west."

"They won't go for it," Volker said. "Not after…not after all the bloodshed."

"The alternative is this war lasting much longer," Voss said. "Even if Berlin falls…we do have more troops and panzers at our disposal."

"True," Volker said. He smiled, rather tiredly. "But will the government hold together if we lose Berlin?"

———

"So," her father said. "How are you enjoying married life?"

Gudrun blushed. There had been no hope of a real honeymoon - that would have to wait until the war ended, if it ever did - but they had managed a handful of days away from the maddening crowd. It had been odd, sleeping together without fear of discovery, lying together and talking about their hopes and dreams for the future…the war nothing, but a grim awareness at the back of their minds. But there had been no hope of prolonging the holiday any longer. The fighting was about to get a great deal worse.

"It has its moments," she said, finally.

"Glad to hear it," her father said.

He nodded to Horst, then tapped the table, motioning for them both to sit down. "The good news is that I think we've isolated the spy within the *Reichstag* itself," he said. "By noting the timing of the messages left for Horst" - he nodded to Gudrun's husband - "and comparing them with the servants who actually left the building, we believe that Elfie Fruehauf is the most likely candidate."

Gudrun took a moment to place the name. Elfie Fruehauf was a senior cleaner, if she recalled correctly; a thirty-year-old woman who lived and worked in the *Reichstag*. She'd practically passed unnoticed, even when Gudrun had been trying to get to know the staff. Being unnoticed *had* to be a desirable skill for a spy, she figured. No one had suspected Horst until after he'd confessed to her personally.

Horst leaned forward. "What's her excuse for leaving the building?"

"Apparently, she has a husband who runs a bar," her father said. "They're both from Bavaria, according to the files; they have no friends or family within the city. They certainly don't live together, but they see each other as often as they can."

"Apparently," Gudrun repeated.

"*Reichstag* staff are expected to be on call at all times," Horst reminded her. "I'm surprised they kept her on if she was married."

Gudrun's father shrugged. "Her record is very good," he said. "I imagine - officially - they didn't want to lose her."

He leaned forward. "She has clearance to go everywhere, save for the secure rooms," he added, slowly. "No one would question her if she supervised the maids cleaning the various bedrooms or wonder why she took a room or two to clean herself. She would be completely unnoticed as she placed a note in your room, Horst, and took your reply. And her fingerprints would be everywhere anyway."

"And she takes the notes to her husband," Horst mused. "He must be an SS officer too."

"Probably," her father said. "They were both born in Munich, according to the files, but I doubt we'll find any traces of them."

Gudrun nodded. Munich was the third or fourth largest city in the *Reich*, with well over a million citizens. A handful of records could be inserted into the files by the SS - which practically controlled the registry office - to create a convincing background, at least on paper, for Elfie Fruehauf and her husband. There would be no reason, she suspected, for anyone to remember them. They'd be average schoolchildren, average workers, average soldiers… even a careful check of the records wouldn't turn up any red flags. It would take a thorough investigation to penetrate the cover and that would require more time than they had.

"We are running out of time," Horst said. He looked at Gudrun. "They are demanding more and more details of your schedule."

Gudrun shivered. Horst had made it clear, more than once, that the SS wanted her alive. It was a terrifying thought. She'd been arrested before, but then she'd just been an average citizen caught up in the middle of a riot. Now, they knew just how big a role she'd played in toppling the *Reich* Council. Karl Holliston wouldn't just want her dead, she knew. He'd want her to *suffer*.

"So we grab the bitch after she returns from the next meeting and interrogate her," her father said, curtly. "And we raid the bar at the same time."

Horst shook his head. "There won't be a direct connection between the bar and the commandos," he said, flatly. "Taking out the bar will do nothing more than warn them we're on to them."

"They want to snatch my *daughter*," her father snapped. "I'm not inclined to take chances!"

"If you snatch Elfie Fruehauf," Horst said, "you will reveal that we know she's a spy. And they will *know* that I put you on to her. Our chances of quietly isolating and destroying the commando team will go down sharply."

"As well as make you a target," Gudrun said, quietly.

Horst nodded. "The best we can hope for is having them think I've been arrested too," he said. "But…at that point, they will probably decide they want me dead before I can talk."

Gudrun shook her head. "Then we don't want to blow your cover."

"I feel that way," Horst said, dryly.

"I've had the bar under quiet surveillance," her father injected, sharply. "There are too many people coming and going for us to have any real hope of picking out their contact."

"And if we raid the bar, the commando team will just pull back and get on with their mission," Horst added. He looked at Gudrun. "You really need to stay in the *Reichstag*."

Gudrun scowled. There was nothing she could do for the war effort, but do her best to boost morale. Visiting hospitals and speaking to the wounded, addressing civilians…helping families who had been blasted out of their homes by shellfire find new places to stay…it wasn't much, yet it was the only thing she could do. Giving that up didn't sit well with her, even if she was the only one affected. And if she didn't visit the hospitals, would it suggest to the population that the provisional government no longer cared?

And if we lose the population, she thought, *what happens to us then?*

She felt her scowl deepen as her father and husband argued. The SS had been putting up posters everywhere, insisting that the provisional government was responsible for everything from the siege and shellfire to the atrocities the SS had committed as they swept west. And as conditions worsened within the city, people were starting to listen. Gudrun couldn't help wondering just what would happen if the SS pledged to spare everyone, but the provisional government and its collaborators. She doubted the SS would keep its word - Berlin had been infected by the desire for freedom - yet she suspected it wouldn't matter. Drowning men would clutch at straws to save their lives.

And what would I do, she asked herself, *if my family was starving?*

The thought tormented her for a long moment. There were few families in the *Reich* that didn't have at least one person - a husband, a son, a brother - in the military. Gudrun's brother, father and grandfather had all fought for the *Reich*. But now, almost every military-age male in Berlin who could be spared from their work was in the military, doing everything from fighting on the front lines to transporting weapons and equipment around the city. And everyone else was watching helplessly as their children slowly starved, if they weren't killed by shellfire or mugged by one of the criminals who had started to prowl the streets, preying on innocent civilians. Their lives had gone downhill sharply…

…And for what?

"We need to draw this team out of hiding," she said, interrupting their argument. "Don't we?"

"They won't show themselves on our terms," Horst said, shortly. "Gudrun, I know how these people *think*."

Gudrun smiled. "So we give them a target they can't resist," she said. "We give them me."

Horst stared at her. "Out of the question!"

Her father echoed him a moment later. "Are you mad?"

Gudrun held up a hand. "We need to lure them into a trap," she said. "And to do that, we need something that will draw them out of hiding. And we know they want me, correct?"

Horst took a long breath. "Do you have any idea just how many things could go wrong?"

"You could die," her father said. "Gudrun…"

"I owe it to my conscience to take some risks," Gudrun said. "I…"

"So you have said," Horst snapped. "And they'll engrave it on your tombstone!"

"We tell them where I will be at a specific time," Gudrun said, ignoring him. "And we have a team of our own in place. When they turn up, we snatch them."

"Kill them," Horst corrected. "They won't surrender and they'll be damn hard to capture."

"There's a major push coming," Gudrun said. She'd read the briefing notes with growing alarm. American high-attitude recon aircraft had noted the steady build-up of forces around Berlin, the *Waffen-SS* mustering its power for a final lunge into the city. "We cannot afford to have a commando team running around in the city. Going after me is relatively harmless…"

"No, it isn't," Horst said.

"…But going after a power plant or the defence lines is far more dangerous," Gudrun added, trying hard to keep her voice calm. "We need to deal with them before it's too late."

"By using you as bait," her father said. His voice was very even, very calm. "Gudrun, I forbid it."

"I'm a married woman," Gudrun snapped. It wasn't a tone she would have dared to use earlier, but she was no longer under his authority. "Horst…"

Horst sighed. "It could work," he conceded, reluctantly. "But Gudrun... the risks alone are terrifying. You could die or be snatched."

"Or they might realise it was a trap and fall back, abandoning any plans to snatch you," her father added, angrily. "Gudrun, this is madness."

"We can make it work," Gudrun insisted. She looked at Horst. "Can't we?"

"Maybe," Horst said, He closed his eyes for a long moment. "Too many people would have to be involved. A single leak would be enough to doom the entire operation. And there are far too many moving parts."

"But it could work," Gudrun said.

"Yeah, it could work," Horst said. He ignored her father's glare. "But you'd have to do *precisely* what you're told to do."

Her father snorted, rudely. "*That* will be the day."

Gudrun looked at him. "Father, I'm already a target," she said, gently. "This is a chance to turn that into an advantage."

"Or a chance to get a bullet through the head," her father snapped. "You're in quite enough danger without walking straight into a gunfight!"

"They have orders to take her alive," Horst said. He didn't sound as though he believed himself. "I don't think they'll kill her deliberately."

"Accidents happen," her father said. He sighed, heavily. "I should never have let you go to that damned university."

Gudrun heard the pain - and fear - under his words and bit down, hard, to keep from mustering a sharp response. Her father might be stern, her father might expect her to be more of a traditional girl than she wanted to be, but she'd never doubted her father loved her. Boys were expected to go into danger, to put their bodies between the *Reich* and all harm; girls were expected to remain at home, safe and warm. And yet, she had started the ball rolling that had eventually brought down the *Reich*. She was very far from a traditional girl.

"I will be fine," she said, softly. "Horst is looking after me."

"Too much can go wrong," Horst said, sharply. "There is no way we can guarantee your safety."

Gudrun swallowed, but refused to back down. "Start drawing up the plans," she said. She'd challenged the *Reich* at the height of its power. She was damned if she was backing down now. "And then we will make them work."

CHAPTER THIRTY-SIX

Berlin, Germany Prime
25 October 1985

"All is in readiness, *Herr Hauptsturmfuehrer*," *Strumscharfuehrer* Brandt said, as the sun started to peep over the horizon. "We are just waiting on the order to move."

"Yeah, we must wait for the order to attack before attacking," *Hauptsturmfuehrer* Hennecke Schwerk mused. "To launch without support would be disastrous."

He smiled as he inspected the men. Four days of rest and recuperation - and intercourse and intoxication - had done wonders for morale. The men had been able to sleep in comfortable beds for two nights, often sharing them with girls eager to show the *Waffen-SS* stormtroopers that black uniforms were still the very height of fashion for young men. Hennecke himself had spent two days in bed with a blonde girl who might have been a boring conversationalist, but knew precisely what to do with her mouth and breasts to give a man a very good time indeed. By the time he'd headed back to the lines - and sent the girl to the next stormtrooper who required servicing - he felt so much better that he was tempted to lead the charge into Berlin himself.

And that girl wants to regain her racial certificate, he thought, nastily. *And the only way to do that is to carry an Aryan child to term.*

"I assume the reservists kept prodding the defenders," he said. "Did they actually learn anything useful?"

"Very little," Brandt said. "They confirm that the enemy has dug in over there" - he smiled as he jabbed a finger towards Berlin - "but very little else."

Hennecke shrugged. The stormtroopers might have been pulled out of the line, but the shooting had never actually stopped. Intelligence kept insisting that the enemy was on the verge of running out of bullets and, for once, Hennecke was inclined to believe they were right. He'd heard enough rumours about ammunition shortages confronting the *Waffen-SS* to make it easy to believe that the enemy would have the same problem. And Berlin was completely sealed off from the rest of the *Reich*. They didn't have a hope of shipping more ammunition into the city.

They could try to fly it in, he thought. *But we have enough air defences surrounding the city to make it very difficult.*

He glanced at Brandt. "Did you hear anything about the timing?"

"No, *Herr Hauptsturmfuehrer*," Brandt said. "There's no set time for the offensive."

"Odd," Hennecke mused. Taking advantage of a fluid battleground was one thing, but preparing an offensive without setting a start time was odd. If nothing else, some units could practically be relied upon not to get the word and sit on their asses while everyone else engaged the enemy. "But I'm sure they have their reasons."

He sighed, then turned to look towards Berlin. The battleground was a wasteland, countless buildings knocked down by gunfire or blown up by emplaced IEDs. Hennecke knew just how lucky he had been to escape being wounded or killed in any one of a dozen traps he'd stumbled across during the endless battle. And yet, one final push might just be enough to destroy the enemy defences and carry the stormtroopers into Berlin itself.

And then we can put an end to the war, he thought.

———

Horst hated to admit it, but he was terrified.

Not terrified for himself, he knew. He'd long since grown used to the idea of putting his fragile body at risk. Growing up in Germany East - where one might have to fight at any time - had shaped his mindset, reassuring him that it was better to die in battle than watch helplessly as his family were ravished or murdered by *Untermenschen*. But putting Gudrun in danger was something else. The thought of losing her was terrifying.

He was her husband. He had a right - he knew he had a right - to tell her what to do. And yet he also knew that trying to enforce that right would destroy their relationship. No one could object - legally - if he laid down the law to her and enforced it with his fists, but *Gudrun* would never tolerate it. He'd never be able to sleep next to her again, not without having her slit his throat while he was sleeping. And yet, it was almost worth it just to know she would survive.

But she's right, the coolly pragmatic part of his mind observed. *There's no other way to lure the cell into the open.*

He cursed under his breath as he led the way down to the car. He'd done everything he could to guarantee success, placing trustworthy soldiers in position to intercept the commandos when they finally showed themselves. And if everything went according to plan, *Gudrun* would never be in any real danger. A volunteer, wearing a blonde wig, would play her role long enough to lure the commandos into the open. Gudrun should be safe and sound in the bunker when all hell was let loose.

And yet he knew, all too well, that too many things could go badly wrong.

Gudrun looked nervous, he noted, as they stopped by the car. The driver didn't look much better. He'd been trained in evasive driving - Horst had read his record very carefully before authorising him to work as Gudrun's driver - but deliberately leading someone into a trap was new. And using the person he was supposed to protect as bait…Horst was surprised the man hadn't objected more forcefully. No close-protection team worthy of the name would want *anything* to do with the plan.

"This is your last chance to change your mind," he muttered. The driver opened the door, then turned and headed back to the front seat. "You can back out now and no one will think any less of you."

"Because I'm a woman," Gudrun said, crossly. They'd argued for hours as the plan came together, Horst trying to talk her out of it while Gudrun insisting they went ahead. He still found it hard to believe that she'd come up with the plan, then forced it though despite opposition from both her father and husband. "No one expects much from me either."

"Seems a better deal than we get," Horst said. He'd seen how pride could keep a man fighting when a tactical withdrawal to a superior position would probably have worked better, in the long run. "A man who backed out now would be branded a coward."

Gudrun gave him a sharp look, then settled into the car. She'd insisted on wearing trousers, rather than a dress. Horst was torn between admiring her insistence on practicality and worrying about soldiers admiring his wife's shapely legs. But at least they would let her move quickly if there was an emergency. She'd even spent the last few nights in the shooting range, mastering the small pistol he'd given her. Maybe allowing her to burn through so much ammunition was wasteful, but at least it meant she could defend herself, if necessary.

Unless she loses the pistol, Horst thought. Gudrun was fit - the BDM had made sure of that, if nothing else - but she was no match for a grown man, particularly one who had had intensive combat training. Stormtroopers who had their asses kicked by women only existed in bad American propaganda. *If she loses the pistol, she's in deep shit.*

He settled in after her, feeling an uncomfortable churning in his stomach. The driver started the engine as Horst leaned backwards, trying hard to calm himself. He hadn't felt so bad since the day he'd reported for basic training, when he'd discovered that all the practical work he'd done trying to get ready for the *Waffen-SS* had been largely futile. His instructors hadn't hesitated to tell him precisely what they thought of him too. He'd honestly believed the bastards would arrange a training accident if they thought he couldn't or wouldn't come up to scratch.

"Let's go," he said.

The car slowly rolled out of the garage, passing through two checkpoints without stopping and turning onto the empty road. Their outriders, sirens howling, joined them seconds later, the riders watching carefully for signs of trouble. Horst forced himself to relax, one hand fingering the pistol at his belt as he waited. They had nearly four hours before all hell was due to kick off. He could wait until then...

The waiting is always the worst, he reminded himself, grimly. *I'll feel better when the shooting actually starts.*

———

Katharine Milch waited behind, keeping her weapons well out of sight, as two of her team - dressed in police uniforms - rousted the homeless out of the ambush site. It wasn't ideal, but there were very few truly *ideal* places in Berlin. No matter what she did, she was sure an alert would go out at once and armed troops would rush to the rescue. The timing might just be in their favour - reading between the lines, she rather suspected that the main phase of the final offensive was due to kick off soon - yet it would be no consolation to her team if they were caught in the open.

Limited room to manoeuvre, she told herself. If all went according to plan, the target and her escorts would be trapped, completely at her mercy. *And if we get out before they respond, we should get away clean.*

"That's the place cleared," Hans called. "We can move in now."

"Do it," Katherine ordered.

She glanced at her watch, grimly, as they took up positions. Timing was everything - and yet the timing could not be precise. They were dependent on matters outside their control, matters she knew couldn't be controlled without giving the game away far too soon. If the bodyguard acted fast - and he wouldn't be expecting her move - the entire operation could fail completely. But then, if it *did* fail, she'd have ample time to break contact and vanish before it was too late.

And then we can join the other cells, she thought, tartly. *At least our time won't be completely wasted.*

———

Gudrun could tell that Horst was worried, even though he was doing a very good job of pretending to be unconcerned. He was slumped back in his chair, his eyes half-closed, instead of holding her in his arms or talking quietly. She knew he wouldn't be concerned about the driver - they *were* married, after all - but about the plan. Using his wife as live bait couldn't sit well with him.

At least he let me do it, she thought. She had no desire for a real fight, no desire to find out if he would keep his word to let her have an independent life. It spoke well of him, she supposed, that he *was* letting her be bait. And yet, was it really a good sign? Horst might have been a better husband if he'd refused. *But if he lets me do this, he can hardly object to me being on the council…*

The car shook violently, twisting and turning as it slammed into one of the outriders and roared into a side road. Horst started, one hand drawing his pistol, as gunfire broke out; Gudrun looked up, just in time to see two of the remaining outriders blown off their motorbikes before it was too late. The driver slammed the partition between the driving seat and the passenger compartment, the doors unlocking seconds later as the vehicle lurched to a halt. Horst swore out loud as the gunfire grew louder, a handful of bullets pinging off the car as the attackers - whoever they were - took care of the final set of outriders.

"Stay down," Horst snapped, pulling her to the ground. "Keep your head down!"

Gudrun nodded as she reached for her pistol. Something had gone badly wrong…no, they'd been driven right into an ambush. The driver had betrayed them! She looked up in alarm as the door opened, then realised that Horst was slipping out of the vehicle. Two more gunshots echoed out before he managed to slam the door. Gudrun barely had a moment to pray before the door nearest to her was yanked open and a strong arm caught hold of her. The driver leered down at her as he tugged her into the street.

"Bastard," Gudrun swore, bringing up the pistol. The driver's eyes went wide as she pulled the trigger four times, feeling the weapon jerking in her hand. She wasn't a good shot, not compared to Horst or the instructors on the shooting range, but she could hardly miss at point-blank range. "You…"

The driver tottered backwards and collapsed to the ground, blood leaking from four bullet wounds. Gudrun barely had a moment to savour her victory - or recoil in horror from ending a person's life - before a strong hand caught hold of her wrist and twisted it sharply. She screamed in pain, letting go of the pistol as her new captor pulled her all the way out of the car and slammed her head to the pavement. There was a flash of pain, then the darkness reached out and swallowed her.

———

Katherine smiled as the driver died - he had never been intended to survive, despite being a long-term sleeper agent - and then peered down at the blonde girl beneath her feet. Gudrun Wieland didn't look like much, Katherine decided, as she hauled the girl up and threw her over her shoulder. She'd certainly not realised the driver wasn't alone. Katherine had darted backwards, ready to take cover if Gudrun opened fire on her, but it hadn't been necessary.

She unhooked a grenade from her belt and hurled it into the car, then turned and started to run. Gudrun was lighter than she'd expected, puny and weak compared to an eastern woman, but she had to be sneaked out of the city. And that wouldn't be easy.

Mission accomplished, she thought, as the car exploded behind her. *And all we have to do is lie low.*

She reached into her pocket and pulled out a detonator, clicking off the safety and then pushing the button firmly, transmitting a radio signal across the city. It would set off alarms, she knew, but it was already too late. A series of explosions echoed over the city, ensuring that it would be harder for the defenders to react...and signal the forces waiting on the other side of the defence lines. It was time for the battle to begin.

"The bastard is still alive," Hans grunted, as he caught up with her. "I don't think he's mortally wounded."

Katherine shrugged. Horst Albrecht hadn't been trustworthy, no matter what his handler had said. Either he was an incompetent buffoon, which was unlikely, or he was an outright traitor. He'd had the perfect opportunity to stop the traitors before they became more than a gaggle of students and missed it completely. No, he was a traitor himself. If he hadn't been one when he'd started, he was definitely one now.

She scowled at the thought. Men could never be trusted completely when sex was involved, she knew from painful experience, and Horst Albrecht *had* been fucking the girl she was carrying. And he'd even married her. Katherine was no stranger to doing unpleasant things for the *Reich*, but marriage? No, Horst Albrecht could not be trusted. And if he survived the next few days, he would either be executed by the SS or his fellow traitors. They'd assume he was responsible for Gudrun's capture and take it out on him.

"They'll blame him for this," she said. "And no matter what he says, they'll never believe him."

Horst staggered to his feet, feeling oddly unsure of just what had happened. He'd been attacked by a pair of commandos...they'd been commandos. He was sure of that, if nothing else. Their basic training and fighting style was identical to his, although they'd been far more practiced them himself. He'd shot one, he thought - there was definitely a body in front of him - but the other had started to pound on him before Horst had finally managed to bury a knife in his heart. Or was that nothing more than a hazy memory of something else? His head felt as if he'd been drinking heavily the night before...

Gudrun!

The thought snapped him out of his daze. Turning, he looked towards where the car had been and recoiled in shock as he realised it was nothing more than a burning wreck. The flames were so intense that he knew, beyond a shadow of a doubt, that if Gudrun was still in the car she was dead. And yet, they'd wanted her alive...he stumbled forward and noted, to his relief, that the rear door was open. Gudrun had had a chance to get out...

He cursed as he nearly tripped over the body and stumbled, then glared down at the remains of the driver. Someone had shot him in the chest, three or four times; the damage was far less extensive than Horst had anticipated. *Gudrun* had to have killed him, he realised. The pistol he'd given her was far lighter than the one he carried himself. But three bullets to the heart would be enough to stop anyone.

Should have worn body armour, he thought, as he kicked the driver's body. He'd never suspected the driver, not even once. And yet...in hindsight, he should have been a prime suspect. No one paid attention to drivers. *You swinehund traitor...*

He gathered himself, somehow. There had been a quick-response team on alert, but it had failed to show. The outriders were dead. Explosions were echoing over the city...

...And Gudrun was gone.

CHAPTER THIRTY-SEVEN

Berlin, Germany Prime
25 October 1985

Hauptmann Kurt Wieland wasn't sure if he was being rewarded for good service or being punished for some unspecified offense. His unit had been recalled, shortly after Gudrun's wedding, and deployed to defend the *Reichstag*, relieving a mixed unit of policemen, security troops and military forces belonging to the various political factions. He had strict orders, from Volker Schulze himself, to make sure that *no one* entered the complex without both clearance and a thorough search, but just about everyone who wanted to get in seemed to believe they could browbeat his troopers. He'd come far too close to ordering a complete strip and cavity search on one bureaucrat before the man had hastily backed down and stopped issuing threats to have the entire unit reassigned to Siberia.

Although how he expected to get us to Siberia is an open question, Kurt thought. *I…*

He jerked up as he heard the sound of an explosion, followed by several more in quick succession. Those hadn't been shellfire! And they'd been well within the safe zone surrounding the *Reichstag*. He dreaded to think how many people had hurried into the safe zone, believing that the SS would leave it untouched, only to be caught now by bomb attacks on a scale unseen since the Arab Rebellions. Hundreds, perhaps thousands, of people were dead or wounded…

"Incoming fire," Loeb snapped.

Kurt ducked behind shelter as the first antitank missile slammed into the defences, followed by a hail of RPGs. The first explosion shattered the guardhouse, but the *Reichstag* itself was largely unharmed. Kurt allowed himself a moment of relief - the designers had planned on the assumption that there would be a nuclear war - then started to bark orders as commandos opened fire, pouring gunfire into the *Reichstag*.

"Lock down the building," he bawled. One of the explosions, unless he missed his guess, had been far too close to the barracks. The soldiers on duty would have problems getting to the *Reichstag*, even though they were bare minutes away if they sprinted. And if the bomb had been *in* the barracks, hundreds of good men would be dead now. "Send a warning up the chain. Tell them we need help…"

He swore again as he heard the sound of shellfire, shells crashing down all over the city. The SS had mounted a coordinated attack, hitting the *Reichstag* at the same time as they thrust forward and into the defence lines. Command and control networks were probably disrupted badly, if they weren't down altogether. The defenders knew to hold the line - he'd had similar orders before his men had been pulled out - but it was going to be harder to send reinforcements to plug the holes before the SS rammed an infantry division through them.

"Aircraft," Loeb barked. "Watch the skies."

Kurt nodded, grimly. The SS air attacks had dropped down to almost nothing over the last few days, but now they were back with a vengeance. A missile rose up to blow one of the planes out of the sky, yet the others kept coming, targeting defence lines, garrisons and power plants right across the city. Berlin might survive the offensive, but life in the city would never be the same again.

He shook his head, dismissing the thought, as the shooting outside grew louder. It didn't matter, not now. All that mattered was holding the line…

…And praying, desperately, that help arrived in time.

———

"The main offensive has begun, *Herr Oberstgruppenfuehrer*," Weineck said. "Resistance is still strong."

Alfred nodded impatiently. Taking out the enemy command and control network was a core facet of modern war, but it hardly mattered in Berlin. The defenders had nowhere to run and no reason to expect to be treated well if they surrendered. His forces had taken a handful of prisoners, but almost all of them had been badly wounded before they'd finally stopped fighting and two of them had died shortly after being captured. The basic interrogation - the POWs had been shipped east, on the *Fuhrer's* direct orders - had made it clear that no one dared surrender, simply out of fear of being shot as soon as they were captured.

Damned bastards, he thought.

The thought gnawed at his mind. He was no stranger to the horrors of war - he'd seen more horrors than any pampered westerner - but allowing so many atrocities to be committed had been stupid. They hadn't even had the sense to win the war outright before starting the reign of terror. And he'd wanted to stop it. It would have been so easy to hang a few of the worst offenders, just to encourage the others, but the *Fuhrer* had refused to allow it. Terror might weaken the defenders, he'd argued, yet it had also made them reluctant to surrender. And that gave them the determination to fight on when all seemed lost.

He looked up. "And the enemy reinforcements?"

"No movements as yet, *Herr Oberstgruppenfuehrer*," Weineck said.

"They'll move soon," Alfred predicted.

He kept the rest of the thought to himself. The *Fuhrer* had shot a number of men for 'defeatism' and he had no intention of joining them. And yet, the military logic was beyond doubt. His force, burnt out after weeks of savage fighting, simply didn't have the time to stand off even a single armoured thrust. And the enemy, if the latest reports were accurate, had enough panzers massing in place to launch *two* thrusts. His forces would wind up trapped between two advancing jaws.

We have to break through to Berlin, he thought, coldly. *Whatever happens, we have to get through now. Or we lose.*

———

The enemy were keeping their heads down, *Hauptsturmfuehrer* Hennecke Schwerk noted, as he led his men towards the first enemy position. It had been worked into a suburb of Berlin, a blur of housing, shops and a single large school, but twenty minutes of shellfire had left most of the once-proud suburb in ruins. The school was nothing more than a pile of rubble - he couldn't help thinking that the children would be pleased - while most of the homes had been badly damaged. Only the shops remained intact, although their windows were smashed and several nearby vehicles were burning brightly. Hennecke's commanders hoped to loot the shops to feed their men.

He dropped to the ground as he heard a burst of machine gun fire, then motioned four of his men into a flanking formation while the others opened fire, trying to keep the gunners from noticing that the attackers were trying to outflank them. They'd used the tactic before, time and time again, but this time it failed. Several other machine guns opened fire, picking off the flankers before they had a chance to get into position. Hennecke felt his lips curl in sharp irritation, remembering the pre-battle briefing. They'd been ordered, in no uncertain terms, to break through the enemy defences, stopping for nothing.

Tapping his radio, he called in an airstrike. There was a long pause, long enough for him to wonder if something had gone wrong, then three HE-477s roared over the battlefield, their cannons pouring explosive shells into the enemy position. The machine gun fire stopped abruptly, but the aircraft weren't finished. Hennecke stayed low as one aircraft dropped a handful of tiny bombs on the enemy, then turned and flew eastwards. A missile rose up from the ground, behind them, only to drop to the ground and explode somewhere to the east. The pilots had escaped in time.

"Forward," he yelled, as he rose and ran towards the smouldering remains. "For the *Reich*!"

There was almost no incoming fire, although he kept his head low just in case. The enemy seemed to have been wiped out, save for a couple of young men who were both badly wounded. There was little hope for them, he knew, even if they got to a field hospital in time. He shot them both - it was a mercy kill - and then swore as mortar shells started to land around them. The enemy had had plenty of time to plot out their firing positions…

…And a number of enemy soldiers were slipping forward, trying to launch a counterattack.

"Not this time," he muttered, as he motioned for his men to get into position. "You're not going to stop us now."

———

"What happened?"

"A whole string of attacks, *Mein Herr*," the operator said. He didn't seem to know *how* to respond to a policeman - particularly one with powerful relatives - but at least he was trying to do his job. "One of them was on Councillor Wieland's car…"

Herman blanched. He knew the plan - he knew what was *intended* to happen - and it wasn't an attack on Gudrun's car. Horst had told his handlers that Gudrun would be vulnerable in the afternoon, not midday…something had gone badly wrong. Had Horst betrayed Gudrun, his wife of a week? He doubted it - he was fairly good at reading people - but if he hadn't, someone else had to have betrayed *Horst*. His handlers might have suspected his loyalty all along. And if *that* was the case…

He looked down at the map as report after report came in; bombings and shootings from inside the city, airstrikes and shellfire from outside the city. The quick-response team that had been on alert had already been deployed, racing to a commando assault on one of Berlin's power distribution stations. Most military and government bases had their own generators, he knew, but losing power all over the rest of the city would cause panic…

"See if you can find any patrolmen free," he ordered, finally. He doubted it would be possible. The thousands of men who made up the *Ordnungspolizei* - the men who had continued to serve after the uprising - would be scattered over the city, facing their own nightmares. "If you can, divert them towards the scene of the ambush."

He groaned, inwardly, as the operators went to work. The whole plan might have been Gudrun's idea, but he should never have agreed to it. He should have beaten sense into Gudrun and Horst when they actually tried to make the plan work, rather than risk his daughter's life. And now he was trapped in the *Reichstag*, the building already under attack, unable to do anything to help either his daughter or his new son-in-law. All he could do was wait, watch and pray.

———

Horst slumped down next to the driver's body, feeling oddly unable to move as he battled complete despair. He'd lost everything in less than a second, a feeling so profound that he was barely able to move. And yet, somehow, he managed to force himself to gather his thoughts. The commandos had escaped, taking Gudrun with them - he had to *believe* they'd taken Gudrun with them. They'd risked far too much to kill her when they could have ordered him to end her life.

Unless they doubted my loyalty even then, he thought, as he forced himself to stand. *They might have feared to alert me too soon.*

He picked up Gudrun's pistol and stuck it into his belt, then hastily searched the driver's body for anything useful. The man had been carrying a pistol himself, which Horst took, and an ID card, but very little else. Horst pocketed everything anyway and then stared into the remains of the car. There was no hint that anyone had died, as far as he could tell. He didn't *think* the heat was hot enough to reduce a body to nothing but ash, but the SS *had* a habit of using incendiary grenades to burn down insurgent hovels in Germany East.

They will want her alive, he told himself, again and again. *They will want her alive.*

He shuddered at the implications. Gudrun had been a symbol of hope - the hope of a life without fear - from the moment she'd gone public and told the regime that she, a mere university student, had no fear of them. Merely killing her would never be enough, not if her body was never recovered. Karl Holliston would want to crush her beneath his heel, he would want to make it very clear that he had captured and smashed the symbol of hope, he would want to use her death to boost his cause. And yet, the cause had grown far beyond her...

Her death won't change anything beyond giving us a martyr, he thought. *And that means he needs to turn her against us.*

The sound of shooting and shellfire grew louder as he reached the end of the side street and peered down the main road. One of the outriders was lying dead on the ground, his motorcycle long since gone. People were stealing everything that wasn't nailed down, these days; Horst had no doubt that the bike would be sold shortly, if the thief hadn't already managed a sale. Strip the police signs from the bike and it might as well be a civilian model, as long as no one looked too closely.

He checked the body - the outrider had broken bones as well as a cracked skull - and found his radio, but it was broken. Horst fiddled with it for a long moment, then gave it up as a bad job. There was no hope of repairing the radio without tools, spare parts and time, none of which he had. Instead, he hurried down the street, thinking hard. The quick-response team had failed to show, which meant that there was no hope of help. If the shooting really *was* coming from the *Reichstag*, and it certainly sounded that way, anyone who might have come to help had too many problems of their own.

They must have planned the timing perfectly, he thought. *Hit Gudrun and snatch her, then attack the Reichstag and everywhere else, forcing us to react to them. And then send in the troops to finish us off while we're distracted.*

There was nothing he could do about that now, he knew, but he *could* head to the bar Gudrun's father had identified for him. It was unlikely that the commandos would have taken Gudrun there, but the bartender was almost certainly an SS contact, if he wasn't an outright operative. He might - he might - know where Gudrun had been taken. And if he refused to talk, Horst would *make* him talk. He knew *precisely* how to hurt someone to cause maximum pain, but little real injury. The man would talk, Horst promised himself, no matter what he had to do...

It wasn't much, he knew all too well, but it was the only hope he had.

They'll try to get her out of the city, particularly if the battle is lost, he told himself. He knew his own people all too well. *And if that happens, I have lost everything.*

———

The bunker was oddly aseptic, Volker had often thought. There was a battle raging above his head and another being fought on the edge of the city, but the bunker was calm and utterly composed. He sat in the heart of the war room, safe and secure, even though men were dying as the fighting raged on. And yet, there was nothing he could do about it.

"Power stations are out in Sections Five through Seven," an operator said. "Emergency power is off-line; I say again, emergency power is off-line."

"Seven aircraft have been shot down over the front lines," another added. "No pilots have been reported alive."

"Sniper active near the walk," a third warned. "Police units have been dispatched."

Volker shook his head, then looked at Voss. "Are we holding?"

"For the moment, barely," Voss said. "They're coming at us hard, hammering our lines with staggering force. A number of our guns have already run out of ammunition."

"Then pass the word to the relief forces," Volker ordered. Time had almost run out. "Tell them to come in, guns blazing."

Voss nodded, shortly. "*Jawohl, Herr Chancellor*," he said. "It shall be done."

He strode away to issue orders, leaving Volker alone with his thoughts. Karl Holliston had to be out of his mind. A smart man would have backed off, realising that the *Reich* could be sundered in two - and see who came out ahead, in the months and years to come - but Holliston had sent uncounted thousands of his men to their deaths. And he'd committed atrocities that practically guaranteed that the SS would never be accepted in the west, not now. Too much hatred had been unleashed.

But you were in the SS, his thoughts reminded him. *You knew how fanatical they could be.*

It was a bitter thought. He'd been taught to fight, to take advantage of every fleeting opportunity, but he'd never really been taught to *think*. His masters wanted the ultimate soldier, one who would fight to the bitter end, yet never question orders. He'd fought in more battles than he cared to remember, before he'd finally resigned. And yet he'd never questioned orders.

He shuddered. And he hadn't questioned his son's silence either, had he? He'd never really understood what he'd served until Gudrun had rubbed his face in it. She would have made a fine daughter-in-law...

...And yet, marrying Konrad would have ruined her.

He sat back in his chair, knowing there was nothing else he could do. There was no point in issuing further orders, not now. His people on the ground knew what to do, even if they lost contact with the *Reichstag*. Berlin might fall, but the relief forces would trap and destroy the *Waffen*-SS. The die was cast...

...and what happened now would determine if the *Reich* lived or died.

CHAPTER THIRTY-EIGHT

Berlin, Germany Prime
25 October 1985

"Message from Berlin, *Herr Generalmajor*," *Hauptmann* Franz Winckler reported. "We are to commence Operation *Mausefalle* at once."

Generalmajor Gunter Gath nodded, curtly. He'd hoped for longer, but the orbital imagery he'd been sent had made it clear that time wasn't on his side. His men had worked like demons, moving five panzer divisions and their supporting elements eastwards…it would just have to be enough. If it wasn't…

One last roll of the dice, he thought. *And pray the SS isn't ready for us.*

"Send the signal," he ordered. "The aerial and commando attacks are to begin at once."

"*Jawohl, Herr Generalmajor*," Winckler said.

"And the main body of the advance is to begin in twenty minutes, regardless of the reports from the ground," Gunter added. "We cannot stop for anything."

"*Jawohl, Herr Generalmajor*," Winckler said, again.

Gunter nodded, then turned his attention to the map. All had *not* been quiet on the western front. His panzers might have been held back, but his commandos and more experienced infantrymen had been skirmishing with the *Waffen-SS* for days. The bastards had been working to set up roadblocks, emplacing antitank weapons to delay his forces as they raced towards Berlin. They were doing precisely the same thing *he'd* done, back when the *Waffen-SS* rolled into Germany Prime. The irony was not lost on him.

We probably showed them how to do it better, he thought. *A march that shouldn't have lasted longer than a day was stretched out for nearly two weeks.*

He scowled, remembering the reports from the scouts. Berlin was at the centre of the greatest *autobahn* network in the world, but the roads would have been mined or otherwise rigged to make using them difficult. And merely driving a few hundred panzers down the road would be enough to put them out of commission. His forces risked being drawn into urban combat, whether they liked it or not. But it couldn't be helped. The chance to trap the *Waffen-SS* in a *kessel* - and save Berlin - could not be ignored. It would shorten the war.

And even if they retreat, we will have given them their first true battlefield defeat, he thought, darkly. *That will teach them that they're not invincible after all.*

"The commandos have begun their assault, *Herr Generalmajor*," Winckler reported. "And our aircraft are on the way."

Gunter nodded. He'd held back every aircraft he could, conserving his strength as much as possible while the SS controlled the skies over Berlin. Now, his men would clear the SS out of the skies - winning air supremacy - or die trying. And even if they failed, the SS would no longer be able to call on its flying artillery. Their pilots would have to fight to defend themselves, rather than support the stormtroopers on the ground.

"Inform me when the main offensive encounters opposition," he ordered. "And keep a close eye on our logistics. We don't want to run out of ammunition midway through the battle."

"*Jawohl, Herr Generalmajor,*" Winckler said.

———

Hauptmann Felix Malguth braced himself as the HE-477 roared eastwards, skimming the ground as he hunted for targets. Anything military outside Berlin, he'd been told, was fair game, even though the *Heer* was on the move for the first time in decades. The prospect of accidently strafing or bombing his own men nagged at him, even though he was fairly sure he'd outraced the panzers long ago. As long as he was careful not to cross the lines into Berlin, he could be reasonably sure he was attacking the right side.

And if I fly over Berlin, I might well be shot down, he thought, remembering the warning the pilots had been given, over and over again. Berlin's air defences were good, but they had no way to tell the difference between friendly and unfriendly aircraft. *I'll be shot down by my own side.*

He gritted his teeth as the city came into view, obscured by a growing haze of smoke. The battle was still underway, the SS fighting desperately to break into the city even though they had to know that relief forces were on the way. Felix had no idea why they thought they could still win the battle, but none of the SS stormtroopers he'd encountered had been the sort of people who just gave up. And yet, getting hundreds of thousands of soldiers - and civilians - killed for nothing was pointless. Surely they would be wiser to set up defence lines to the east?

Don't go feeling sorry for the bastards, he told himself, sharply. *You know what they've done to the Reich.*

Cold hatred blazed through him as he caught sight of a convoy, a handful of armoured vehicles and trucks moving westwards. There was no way to know just what they had in mind - blocking the counterattack or escaping before the jaws slammed closed - but it hardly mattered. He twisted towards them, spraying cannon fire over the vehicles as he passed overhead. Five of the trucks exploded in quick succession, followed by two of the armoured cars. The remainder scattered hastily, a handful of soldiers drawing their sidearms and firing after him. It was futile, but he found it hard to care. The more bullets expended uselessly, the fewer there would be to shoot at the men on the ground.

He cursed under his breath as he stumbled across an air defence position, then yanked the HE-477 to the side, avoiding a missile that passed far too close to his aircraft. The SS gunners had to have been equally surprised, he noted; they'd have set the missile for proximity detonation if they'd had longer to prepare before opening fire. But they'd be on the alert now…if they hadn't been on the alert already. The fast-jets had raced ahead of him, trying to sweep the SS fighters from the air. He would have been surprised if the SS stormtroopers on the ground *didn't* know that they were under attack, even before he'd arrived.

You should be running now, he thought, as he caught sight of a line of soldiers scrambling for cover. *You're as naked as the day you were born.*

He resisted the urge to spray cannon fire over their position - it was poor tactics - as he headed east. A helicopter - clearly marked as SS - flashed in front of him, settling down somewhere below. He blew the craft apart with a burst of fire, then caught sight of a line of panzers moving west. They *had* to be trying to take up position before it was too late, hoping to block the oncoming storm. He expended his handful of air-to-ground missiles on them, following up with a hail of cannon fire. The panzers exploded into fireballs, one by one.

Armour is useless when it doesn't have air cover, he thought, as his cannon ran dry. *And there's nowhere to run.*

Turning, he headed west, feeling a grim sense of satisfaction as he retreated from the battlefield. The makeshift airfield was just behind the lines, the ground crews already preparing ammunition and fuel for the planes as they returned home. He would land and take a quick piss while the crew hastily reloaded his aircraft. And then he would go back east and do it all over again.

Better make sure I know where the lines are, he reminded himself, as he overflew a pair of panzers heading east. There was no way to tell which side they were on. *Or there will be accidents all along the lines.*

———

"*Herr Oberstgruppenfuehrer*," *Sturmbannfuehrer* Friedemann Weineck said. "The enemy is attacking to the west!"

"I have eyes," Alfred snarled. He could see the map as it was hastily updated by the staff, red arrows slotted into place to represent the enemy advances. And even if he couldn't he would have known what was going on. The sudden arrival of hundreds of enemy aircraft was more than enough warning that a major offensive was underway. "They're trying to entrap us."

"They're hitting the blocking forces hard," Weineck reported. "Commando and airstrikes have already weakened them badly."

Alfred nodded, grimly. The traitors had had ample time to turn every last town and village to the east into a strongpoint, but his men had had only a few days before the storm broke over their positions. They would fight, he knew, and they would bleed the traitors, but it wouldn't be enough to stop them. Despite everything, the traitors had succeeded in transferring a sizable force from west to east.

And while my men are tired, theirs are fresh, he thought. He had no idea who was in command of the enemy counteroffensive, but he had to admire his nerve. Instead of feeding the reinforcements into the battle piecemeal, he'd held them back - along with his aircraft - until committing them at the best possible moment. *And while my men are running short of ammunition, theirs have access to the largest stockpiles in the Reich.*

"Order the blocking forces to engage as best as they can," he ordered, thinking hard. "Is there any update from Berlin?"

"They're gaining ground," Weineck said. "We can still win!"

Alfred swallowed the sarcastic response that came to mind. The plan had failed. Indeed, perhaps it had been doomed to fail from the start. Even if they did take Berlin - and it was clear that the defenders were fighting like mad bastards, bleeding his men heavily and counterattacking whenever they had a chance - it would be pointless. The jaws of the trap were rapidly closing around him…his men would, at best, wind up fighting to defend Berlin themselves. And at worst, they'd be trapped between three fires and doomed to destruction.

"Order the blocking forces to hold as long as they can," he said. "I have to call the *Fuhrer*."

"*Jawohl*," Weineck said.

It was quiet in the secure room, Alfred noted, even though he could still hear the distant rumble from the battlefield. He sat down heavily, then braced himself as he picked up the red phone. It would connect, automatically, to the *Fuhrer's* office in Germanica. And he knew, beyond a shadow of a doubt, that Karl Holliston would be sitting behind his desk, waiting for the news that his forces had won the battle. Alfred swallowed, hard, as he heard the *Fuhrer* pick up the phone. There was no way Holliston was going to take the truth lightly.

"*Mein Fuhrer*," he said. "The enemy have launched their counterattack."

Holliston snorted. "Block it."

Alfred felt a flicker of anger. Holliston had worked his way up through the intelligence and counter-intelligence side of the SS, not the *Waffen-SS*. The *Fuhrer* was far from stupid, but he had no real idea of the military realities. Block a major panzer thrust? It was easier said than done.

"We can't block the attacking forces while storming Berlin," he said, carefully. "*Mein Fuhrer*, I request permission to abandon the siege and pull back to our defence lines."

"Abandon the siege?" Holliston demanded. "That's a cowardly…"

"We do not have the mobile firepower to continue the offensive while guarding our flanks," Alfred snapped. "*Mein Fuhrer*, we must pull back now or they will pocket four divisions within the *kessel*. And that will be the end!"

He cursed under his breath, then went on. "There's no shame in pulling back and allowing the enemy to expend themselves uselessly," he added. "It's a tactical withdrawal, not a surrender…"

"We can't let them win," Holliston insisted. "Everyone who's currently sitting on the damned fence will join them! They cannot be allowed a victory!"

"They will have their victory, *Mein Fuhrer*," Alfred said, throwing caution to the winds. "I cannot stop them. The only thing I can do is give them a pointless petty victory - driving us away from Berlin - instead of crushing four divisions! If we lose those men…"

He ground his teeth in range. The hell of it was that Holliston had a point. If the traitors and their provisional government scored a victory, everyone who had chosen to sit on the fence rather than join one side or the other would be forced to re-evaluate their position. The spy in the provisional government might change sides - again - while military officers and bureaucrats who had resigned might beg to be allowed back, while they still had something to bargain with. No, the traitors could not be allowed a victory…

…But they were going to get one anyway.

He took a long breath. "I can get the men out of the trap, *Mein Fuhrer*," he said. He knew he was pleading, but he no longer cared. "And then we can launch a counterattack, once the enemy has exhausted itself…"

"Berlin is to be taken," Holliston snapped. "Do *not* give the enemy a victory."

There was a *click* as the *Fuhrer* put down the phone. Alfred stared at his handset for a long moment, then slowly put it down on the table. The *Fuhrer* was mad. He *had* to be mad - or too ignorant to be aware of his own ignorance. There was no way Alfred could take Berlin and, simultaneously, save his men from being pocketed and destroyed. After the atrocities, he had no reason to expect the traitors to show mercy. Why should they?

Do not give the enemy a victory, he thought, as he rose. *And that is one order I can try to carry out.*

He strode back into the main room and glanced at the map. The situation was growing worse by the minute, the enemy smashing their way through the blocking forces with almost contemptuous ease. They were paying for their haste, but it wouldn't be enough to slow them down. And if he didn't react now, he and his men were doomed.

Weineck looked at him. "Orders, *Herr Oberstgruppenfuehrer?*"

I could be shot for this, Alfred thought. Disobeying orders in the face of the enemy was a court martial offence, if anyone actually bothered with the court martial. The legendary Erwin Rommel had once summarily shot an SS officer who was trying to interfere with his command, during the final drive across the Suez and into Palestine. *And my family could be killed too.*

He kept his face impassive with an effort. His family's lives were at stake, but so were those of tens of thousands of stormtroopers. Losing those men would make defending Germany East impossible, ensuring the end of the war. And he *liked* Germany East. The westerners were too soft to do what needed to be done to preserve the *Reich.* Life was far too easy...

And I have to save my men, he told himself. *Everything else is secondary.*

His family might be killed by the *Fuhrer,* he told himself, but they'd also be killed if the traitors won the war. Everyone with any connection to the SS would be purged. There would be no mercy...

"Orders from Germanica," he lied smoothly. "We are to begin a withdrawal back to the Warsaw Line."

He turned to look at the map. "Pull the assault forces back from Berlin, then order the gunners to slow up the inevitable counterattacks as much as possible," he added. "Deploy the Category B units to slow down the enemy counterattack, then move the Category A units to the rear."

Weineck frowned, doubtfully. Alfred didn't blame him. The Category B units were unlikely to be able to do more than slow the enemy, but the Category A units had to be saved to fight again. Without them, integrating the steady flow of reservists into the ranks would be impossible. There was no choice.

"Do it," he snarled. "And then prepare for departure. This place is to be purged as soon as we leave."

"*Jawohl, Herr Oberstgruppenfuehrer,*" Weineck said.

Alfred nodded and turned his attention back to the map, covertly glancing around the room and wondering which one of them was the spy. If someone thought to check with Germanica…all hell would break loose. He'd twisted Karl Holliston's final order into a tangled mess - and he knew, beyond a shadow of a doubt, that the *Fuhrer* would not find it amusing. But there was no choice. A retreat under fire was one of the most dangerous manoeuvres a military force could attempt, but it was better than being caught in a trap and destroyed.

And if I can get the men out, he thought, *I will die happy.*

———

"We're to do what?"

"Fall back," the messenger said. "Orders from HQ."

Hauptsturmfuehrer Hennecke Schwerk stared in disbelief. They were winning! The enemy line was crumbling in front of them! He could feel it. The enemy's counterattacks were weakening and they'd practically stopped dropping mortar shells on the advancing stormtroopers. It was clear, to him at least, that the enemy was running short on everything from men to ammunition. One final push and they'd be in Berlin!

But he knew better than to disobey orders.

"Sound the retreat," he ordered, as a new wave of shellfire crashed down on the enemy positions. Hopefully, the enemy would keep their heads down long enough to keep them from realising that their opponents were falling back. "Deploy two sections to act as a rearguard; we'll leapfrog back to our lines."

He took one last bitter glance towards Berlin, wondering just why they were pulling back *now*. They'd come so close! The thousands of dead stormtroopers would not have died in vain, if Berlin had been stormed, but instead their rotting bodies were being left for the enemy. Victory had been in their grasp, only to be snatched away by…by what? An order to retreat? What was going on?

His thoughts mocked him. *Was it all pointless? Did all those men die for nothing?*

Turning, keeping his expression under tight control, he led his men away from Berlin.

CHAPTER THIRTY-NINE

Berlin, Germany Prime
25 October 1985

"It's confirmed," Voss said, quietly. "The enemy is falling back all along the line."

Volker nodded in relief. The SS didn't know it - he *assumed* they didn't know it - but they had come terrifyingly close to victory. Berlin's defenders had been on the verge of running out of rifle and pistol ammunition, let alone mortar rounds, antiaircraft weapons and everything else they needed to hold the line. Mounting a push from the city, in hopes of overrunning the retreating storm-troopers before they could set up new defence lines of their own, was impossible. It would take weeks, at best, before the defenders could be rearmed…

"Gath is altering his deployments slightly in hopes of enveloping the enemy before they make it out of the bag," Voss added. "But they really reacted too quickly for us to catch most of them."

"True," Volker said. "Someone on the other side must have decided to cut his losses."

"It is the smart choice," Voss agreed. He paused. "We still have a security situation in Berlin itself, though."

"Deploy troops to hunt down the remaining commandos once we are sure we can hold the line," Volker ordered. The attack on the *Reichstag* itself had been beaten off, thankfully, but the commandos had hit a number of other targets and gunfire was still being reported across the city. "And keep warning the population to stay indoors."

He rubbed his eyes, tiredly. Berlin would never be the same, that was sure. The city had been devastated, large parts shelled into rubble…he had no idea if they could even *afford* to rebuild, once the fighting came to an end. And the destroyed factories, power plants and even a hospital would cost millions of *Reichmarks* to replace. The *Reich* might survive the war, only to collapse under its own weight shortly afterwards.

And untold thousands of men, women and children were dead.

"We won," Voss said, quietly.

"I know," Volker said. "But why does it feel like a defeat?"

———

"She doesn't look like much," Hans said.

Katherine snorted as she finished binding Gudrun's hands and legs together. Gudrun was in good health, she'd noted during the brief examination, but hardly stronger than the average schoolgirl. She might be the very picture of Germanic perfection - blonde hair, blue eyes, pale skin - yet she was no soldier. But then, a girl so pretty would have no trouble finding men to fight for her. If she'd seduced a trained SS observer - and Katherine was sure that she had - she could seduce anyone.

Cow, she thought, nastily.

"We'll keep her drugged for the moment," she said. She didn't bother to respond to Hans's remark. The *Fuhrer* and his interrogators could take Gudrun apart at leisure, digging everything she knew out of her mind before hanging whatever was left for treason on an utterly unprecedented scale. "We don't want her waking up too soon."

"If she wakes up at all," Hans warned. "That bump on the head was nasty."

Katherine shrugged. The original plan had been to hole up in the apartment and wait for the fighting to come to an end, but it was clear - now - that the stormtroopers had failed to break into the city. She had no doubt that the traitors would search the city thoroughly, once they were sure they'd won the war. They didn't dare stay in Berlin. *Someone* would have seen something suspicious, she was sure, something that would lead the police straight to them.

"We'll just have to hope," she said, tartly. Hans was right - the sedatives sometimes had unfortunate effects - but the last thing they needed was Gudrun waking up before they were safely out of the city. "Get into your uniform."

She smiled to herself, grimly, as she donned her own uniform, then smirked rudely at the sleeping prisoner. Gudrun would never know the *freedom* of wearing male clothes, would never know how easy it could be to pass for a man. But then, her breasts were too large to be easily concealed by a uniform, while Katherine's were thankfully small. She could pass for a uniformed man with ease.

And everyone in the Reich is conditioned not to question men in uniform, she thought, as she checked her appearance in the mirror. *And no one will question us either.*

She looked faintly effeminate, she decided, but most soldiers who looked at her would dismiss her as a staff officer. They were *expected* to be effeminate, she'd been told. *Real* soldiers *knew* that staff officers were the ones who couldn't hack it, using their connections to be assigned to the rear. They wouldn't see anything other than a young man who confirmed their preconceptions. And by the time they realised the truth, it would be far too late.

"Get the box," she ordered, as Hans returned. "Hurry."

"We'll have to head to the west," Hans said. They carefully lowered Gudrun into the box, then locked it securely. "Too many people moving to the east, I think."

Katherine nodded, crossly. A dozen cells had been expended in the battle for Berlin, but it seemed that their sacrifice had been wasted. She'd sent her remaining team members off to cause havoc across the city, yet in hindsight that might have been a mistake. No, it *had* been a mistake. They could do a great deal of damage before they were hunted down - they *would* do a great deal of damage before they were hunted down - but they would die for nothing.

"Let's go," she said. "Do you have the papers?"

"Here," Hans said. "And if they're not enough...?"

"We fight," Katherine said.

She scowled. The attack had failed, which could only mean that the traitors had launched their own counterattack. And *that* meant that the roads around Berlin were likely to be consumed by savage fighting. Getting out of the city was one thing, but sneaking eastwards was going to be harder. About the only advantage they had was that there would be so much confusion that it would be hard for the traitors to throw out a search cordon...

"Come on," she said. A new hail of gunfire echoed over the city as she opened the door for the final time. "Let's move."

———

Horst wasn't too surprised to discover, as the bar came into view, that it managed to live down to expectations. There were strict public health rules across the *Reich*, but the bartender had clearly decided to ignore them. Even when closed, he could smell alcohol and too many unwashed men in close proximity as he walked towards the building. He was surprised that the bar *was* closed, even though the provisional government's emergency broadcasts had ordered all businesses to close. The bartender must have had other things to do with his time than serve alcohol.

He hesitated, torn between desperation and training. His training had always encouraged him to scout the ground *thoroughly* before charging into battle, but desperation pushed him onwards. He hadn't seen a single policeman or soldier on his run to the bar, nor had he been able to make contact with anyone else. The public telephones had all been deactivated, he'd discovered. He hoped, desperately, that they'd been shut down deliberately, instead of being sabotaged. If the telephone network had been wrecked, coordinating operations across Berlin was going to become a great deal harder.

Bracing himself, he walked up to the door and threw himself at the wood. It splintered under the impact, crashing into the darkened building. Horst moved forward, drawing his pistol and holding it at the ready. He darted into the shadows, keeping himself hidden, but there was no sound that suggested someone - anyone - was within the building. Even the sound of distant gunfire was growing quieter. He crept forward and rounded the counter, then swore inwardly as he saw a body lying on the ground. It was clearly a young girl... cold ice trickled down the back of his spine before he realised it definitely wasn't Gudrun. The dead girl's hair was brown, her exposed legs scarred badly. Horst puzzled over the wounds for a long moment, then checked the body carefully. Her neck had been casually broken.

A barmaid, he thought, as he pulled back. The girl's uniform was easy to place: a blouse and a skirt just barely on the right side of the decency laws. *Just someone who was in the wrong place at the wrong time.*

He tensed as he heard something - a rustling noise - from the rear of the bar. Lifting his pistol, he slipped forward, listening carefully as he peered through the door into the backroom. Another body was sitting on a chair in the rear of the room, head resting on the table as if he were crying into his drink. Horst slipped forward...

...And then jumped forward as he sensed someone hiding behind the door, spinning around to see Schwarzkopf hurling a punch at him. Horst twisted, but it was too late to avoid a glancing blow that sent his pistol flying off into the darkness. Schwarzkopf cursed savagely, then hurled himself forward, slamming them both to the ground. Horst barely managed to land well, trying to push the older man away. He knew how to *kill* Schwarzkopf, but he needed to get answers first; he slammed a punch into Schwarzkopf's chest, then hurled him over, slamming him to the floor. Schwarzkopf grunted in pain, his eyes darting from side to side, then stilled as Horst drew his dagger and held it to his eye. Threatening to blind him would probably be as effective as anything else.

"Traitor," Schwarzkopf managed.

"You're the ones who covered up the deaths of my comrades," Horst sneered. "We could have handled it."

Cold bitter hatred flowed through his heart. He still remembered the betrayal he'd felt, back when he'd discovered that Gudrun was telling the truth. Konrad had been wounded, crippled beyond any hope of recovery, yet no one had bothered to tell his parents. The SS was supposed to look after its people, wasn't it? And yet, Schwarzkopf had clearly killed the bartender just to cover his tracks. The bartender's wife was probably dead too, if she hadn't been arrested when she tried to leave the *Reichstag*.

He gathered himself, meeting Schwarzkopf's eyes. "Where is she?"

Schwarzkopf smirked. "And which *her* are we talking about?"

"You *know* who I'm talking about," Horst said. Schwarzkopf tensed as Horst placed the tip of the knife against his eyeball. "Tell me where she is or I'll blind you."

"She's gone," Schwarzkopf said. He snorted, rudely. "Did you think I would *know* where to find her?"

Horst stared down at him for a long moment. "You took her out of the city?"

"That was the plan," Schwarzkopf said, casually. "Of course, they could have been killed as they crossed the lines. Or shot up by the stormtroopers as they retreat…nice-looking girl like yours, traitor. What do you think they're going to do to her?"

"Damn you," Horst said. "How were they planning to get out of the city?"

Schwarzkopf laughed at him. "What were you doing during training? Fondling yourself? I wasn't told any of the details and if you bothered to actually think, you'd *know* I wasn't told any of the details."

Horst had to pull the blade back just to keep himself from ramming the dagger through the eye and straight into the brain. Schwarzkopf was right. No covert operative was ever told more than they needed to know, just in case they were captured by the enemy and forced to talk. Horst had endured weeks of training in resisting interrogation, but his instructors had made it clear that *anyone* could be broken. It was far safer not to know anything he didn't specifically *need* to know.

And there was no trace of a lie in Schwarzkopf's voice. He wouldn't have been trusted completely, not by the commandos. If they'd suspected Horst - and it was *clear* they'd suspected Horst - they would have suspected his handler too. Horst had dropped the ball - or so they'd claimed to believe - and that meant that his handler had screwed up too, either by believing Horst or not keeping a close eye on him. No, Schwarzkopf wouldn't know anything useful and…

A wave of despair threatened to overcome him. The commandos definitely wouldn't stay in the city, not if they had orders to take Gudrun alive and deliver her to Germanica. And *that*, at least, had to be true. They could have tested Horst's loyalty if they'd merely wanted her dead. But…if they tried to cross the lines surrounding the city, they might just be killed in the crossfire… and, if *that* happened, Gudrun would likely die too.

"You love her," Schwarzkopf mocked. "And if you had kept a closer eye on her, she might not have died."

Horst stabbed him. Schwarzkopf let out a gurgle as the dagger slipped into his brain, his body convulsing one final time before falling still. Horst stared down at him bitterly, wondering why he'd ever liked the older man. But back then he'd been secure in his role, he'd been sure he was doing the right thing. The students could be allowed a great deal of latitude, but they couldn't be trusted. It had been his job to keep an eye on them…

…And he'd done it, too, until Gudrun had opened his eyes.

"Damn you," he breathed. He wasn't sure if he were talking to Schwarzkopf's body…or himself. "Damn you to hell."

Horst searched the body quickly, but found nothing apart from a pistol and two spare clips of ammunition. Schwarzkopf would have dumped everything that might have led a team of investigators back to his lair, taking that particular secret with him to the grave. And he'd mocked Horst…

He wanted to die, Horst thought. He opened Schwarzkopf's mouth and frowned as he saw the suicide tooth, still in place. *And he didn't want to kill himself.*

Gritting his teeth, Horst rose, kicked the body savagely and then searched the bar from top to bottom. There was no sign of anything that might lead him to the commandos; indeed, it looked as though the bar had been stripped of anything useful. The barrels of beer he would have expected to find were missing. Rationing had bitten hard, he knew, but it was still puzzling…unless someone had handed out the beer in hopes of causing a riot. Who knew?

A riot would make a good cover for trouble, he thought, grimly, *and…*

He sat down, hard, after he finished his search. He'd found nothing. He'd found nothing and Gudrun was gone. He didn't even know where to *begin* looking for her. He wouldn't even know if she was alive or dead, unless her dead body was found somewhere in the next few days. And it might not even be recognised before it was dumped in a mass grave…

I might never know what happened to her, he realised. *And yet, if she falls into enemy hands…*

There was nothing he could do to find her, he told himself, as he headed to the door. He didn't have any way to *know* what had happened. And all he could really do was return to the *Reichstag*, report in and hope he didn't get blamed for her capture. If, of course, she *had* been captured…

If she has, he vowed silently to himself, *I will get her back, even if I have to tear Germany East apart.*

———

"The Category A units have made it out of the *kessel, Herr Oberstgruppenfuehrer*," Weineck said.

Alfred scowled, ignoring Weineck's tone. The Category B units had *not* made it out of the trap. One by one, they were being overrun and either crushed or forced to surrender. Some of them had died in place, fighting savagely, but others had simply surrendered once they realised they'd been sacrificed like pawns on a chessboard. Alfred knew he should be angry at them, yet there was no real point. He'd thrown them away, knowing they would be defeated, just to buy a little more time.

"Redeploy our airpower to keep us covered," he ordered. No one seemed to have checked with Germanica - yet - but it was only a matter of time. "And then order the remaining units to move away from the city."

He shook his head, slowly. A German army hadn't been in headlong retreat since...since 1918, when the British had broken their lines and advanced into Germany itself. Even the desperate fighting around Moscow, back in 1941-42, hadn't seen such a retreat, although a number of units had made tactical withdrawals. The *Waffen-SS's* reputation for invincibility had been shattered in a single catastrophic day. Rebuilding what they'd lost in men and material alone would take time, but rebuilding their reputation could take years...

If we have the time, he thought, numbly. He was too tired, too worn, to care. *The traitors will mount a counterattack as soon as possible.*

Weineck cleared his throat. "It's time to evacuate, *Herr Oberstgruppenfuehrer*," he said, bluntly. "The demo teams have to rig the farm to explode."

Alfred nodded. He was tempted to stay behind, to join the men he'd expended during the futile attempt to slow the enemy, but *someone* had to explain the retreat to the *Fuhrer*. If he took all the responsibility upon himself, perhaps - just perhaps - the remainder of his command staff would not be purged. The *Reich* was going to need them, in the weeks and months to come. There was no one else in Germany East capable of preparing for the coming onslaught.

"Understood," he said, taking one last look at the map. "Let's go."

CHAPTER FORTY

Berlin, Germany Prime
25 October 1985

"You utter…"

Horst barely had a chance to duck before Kurt Wieland threw a punch right into his face, sending him staggering backwards. It was all he could do, torn between tiredness and the bitter sense of failure, not to hit his brother-in-law back as hard as he could. Kurt had every reason to be mad at him, but there were limits.

"That will do, Kurt," his father-in-law said. He looked ashen, but grimly composed. "Horst. What happened?"

"He let her get captured," Kurt snapped. "Father…"

"I said, that will do," his father repeated. "Horst…?"

Horst took a breath. "The driver was a spy," he said, numbly. Even in hindsight, there had been no clues to miss. He'd never suspected the driver for a moment. And yet, it was the SS who taught close-protection officers their skills. The bastard must have been seduced back during his training. "He drove us right into a trap."

"And Gudrun was captured," Kurt snarled. "Or killed!"

"There was no body in the car," Horst said, quietly. A police team had gone over the wreckage as things quietened down, but they'd found nothing. "They either managed to get her out of the city…"

"Or she was killed somewhere along the way," Kurt said. His voice hardened. "How do we know you didn't betray her? You *worked* for the goddamned blackshirts!"

"He could have betrayed her long ago," his father said, quietly.

"Unless it was all a plan to put the SS firmly in control of the *Reich*," Kurt snapped.

Horst sighed, feeling too tired to go on. "Only a complete lunatic would come up with such a plan and expect it to work," he said. He wanted to shout, but he didn't have the energy. "We were fooled - we were all fooled - because we thought we were fooling them. Now shoot me or let me decide what to do now."

Kurt looked as if he was ready to go for his pistol, but his father stepped forward before he could make up his mind. "What do you plan to do?"

"Go after her," Horst said, flatly.

"It's suicide," Kurt said.

Horst glared at him. "Would you rather I left my wife and your sister in their hands?"

Kurt started forward. "And what sort of husband would let his wife walk straight into a trap?"

Horst balled his fists, ready to fight. Kurt was right. He should have insisted on using a double from the start and forbidding Gudrun from accompanying them, rather than planning to make the switch in the early afternoon. Gudrun would have made a fuss, but he could have handcuffed her to the bed or simply locked her up to keep her from leaving. She would have killed him, probably - he'd taught her the basics of using a knife as well as a pistol - yet at least she would have been *alive*.

"I don't think he was offered a choice," his father-in-law said. "Kurt, sit down. We need to think."

He met Horst's eyes. "Do you think you can succeed?"

"I think so," Horst said. In truth, he had no idea…but he was damned if he was just abandoning her. Gudrun deserved so much better. "They won't kill her at once, not if they do have her."

"They'll have her in the deepest darkest dungeon they have," Kurt said. "Getting her out is going to be a nightmare."

"There's no such thing as an impregnable fortress," Horst said. It had been Hitler himself who'd pointed out the critical flaw in the Belgium fortresses, back in 1940. Gudrun would be buried beneath the remains of the Kremlin, where the SS had an extensive prison facility…once they got her there, of course. "I'll find a way to get in."

"You might just find a way to get killed," Kurt pointed out.

Horst shrugged. There was no other hope. The provisional government would have to launch a counterattack, invading Germany East before Holliston managed to unlock his supply of nuclear weapons, but it would take weeks, at best, before the invasion force was ready to go. And then it would be moving right into the teeth of a Russian winter. Horst would have been surprised if the military agreed to consider moving before the snows had melted and the roads were traversable again.

They could have her on a plane to Germanica by now, he thought. *And then they'll start breaking her, piece by piece.*

But Kurt was right. It wasn't going to be easy. Slipping across the border - either on foot or in the air - was one thing, but moving from state to state within Germany East would be nearly impossible without the right papers. And it was unlikely he could get his hands on the right papers, after the RHSA burned to the ground. Forging them would be very risky…

"I see no alternative," he said. Getting to Germanica without being caught would be tricky, but he *was* a native of Germany East. He did know how to get around. "Do you have any options yourself?"

Kurt scowled, but shook his head bitterly.

He loves his sister, Horst thought. It wasn't entirely a surprise, but it *was* uncommon - at least in Germany East. Brothers stayed with the family, sisters went off to join other families. And yet, that might not even happen in Germany Prime. People didn't move away from the settlement when they married. *He cares about her.*

"Come with me," he said.

He regretted the words as soon as he said them. Tolerating Kurt for Gudrun's sake would have been easy - Kurt had played his own role in starting the uprising - but asking Kurt to accompany him was different. It was stupid. Kurt was a *Heer* infantryman, not an SS operative or a commando. And yet, he knew he couldn't withdraw the offer. It was too late.

"You're going to be needed on the front," his father-in-law said. "Kurt…"

"I will," Kurt said, addressing Horst. "There's no shortage of qualified officers who can take my place."

"We'll see what your superiors say," his father grunted. "Horst, when do you plan to leave?"

Horst frowned. "I'm not sure," he said. Leaving now would give him a better chance to slip through the enemy lines - the *Waffen-SS* were still retreating in confusion - but waiting a week would let him see just what was developing on the ground. Maybe, just maybe, some kindly soul would assassinate Karl Holliston and negotiate a truce. "At least a day or two from now."

Kurt sneered. "You don't want to leave at once?"

"I do," Horst said, tiredly. His patience snapped. "I'm exhausted, hungry and not in the best of states. I need a good night's sleep and some food before I can even consider departing."

He forced himself to control his voice. "And if you don't want to get yourself killed if you come with me," he added, "I suggest you do the same yourself!"

Turning on his heel, no longer caring if Kurt put a bullet in it, he strode through the door and down the corridor towards the quarters he'd shared with Gudrun. It felt like it had been years since he'd last stepped into them; he closed the door behind him and then sagged against the wall. There were signs of her presence everywhere, from the nightgown her mother had given her for the wedding night to the notebook she'd been writing in…he slumped to the ground, cursing himself under his breath. She'd wanted him to treat her as an equal, but it had led right to her capture…

They won't kill her at once, he told himself, firmly. *There's still time.*

Sure, his own thoughts answered. *And what they'll do to her before they kill her will break her, once and for all.*

He rose, somehow, and stumbled towards the bed. Sleep wouldn't come easy, even though he needed it desperately. Tomorrow…he would have to plan the most dangerous mission of his career, knowing that failure would mean certain death for both of them…

…And, perhaps, the end of the war itself.

———

"The reports are quite clear," Voss said. "They're retreating."

"Good," Volker said. "Can we chase them all the way back to Germanica?"

"No," Voss said. "We're going to have to lay the groundwork for taking the war into Germany East. As it is, the last set of orbital images suggests that the

SS bastards are digging into their former defence lines near Warsaw. Digging them out is going to be difficult."

"Giving them plenty of time to muster their resources for the final battle," Volker said.

"Yes," Voss agreed. "But there are limits to how many reservists they can pull off the settlements."

Volker nodded in agreement. Security in Germany East had to be maintained - or the Russian insurgents would attack the settlements and destroy them. He had no way to know for sure, but he would have bet good money that sending so many reservists westwards had weakened the defences badly enough to allow an upswing in attacks. And sending CAS aircraft westwards hadn't helped either, he was sure. The SS's air power had often made the difference between losing a settlement or slaughtering the attackers.

He sighed. And if there *were* a series of insurgent attacks, he asked himself, what should they do?

"A problem for another day," he mused.

Voss frowned. "*Herr* Chancellor?"

"Nothing," Volker said.

He looked though the window, down at the streets. An impromptu party was already underway, even though large parts of the city were in ruins and thousands of lives - military and civilian - had been lost. He wondered, bitterly, just what would happen afterwards, when the population realised that winter was coming and food - and everything else - was going to run short. Maybe they could bring in help from the west, but would it be enough?

"If we could get him to agree to a truce," he said, "we could end the war for good."

"Holliston won't agree to a truce," Voss predicted. "He cares nothing for anything, apart from his supremacy."

And that, Volker suspected, was all too true.

———

Gudrun fought her way to wakefulness through a haze of pain. Her head was throbbing, her arms and legs felt bruised and weak…as if she'd been beaten savagely, part of her mind noted. Had she been beaten? Her memories were odd, flashes and impressions rather than anything solid; the last thing she recalled was kissing Horst before they went down to the car...

She swallowed, hard, as the memories flashed through her mind. They'd been ambushed, she'd been hit...and now she was a prisoner.

"I know you're awake," a voice said. It was so atonal that Gudrun wasn't sure if it was male or female. "You may as well open your eyes."

Gudrun hesitated, then did as she was told. She was lying on a makeshift bed - really, nothing more than a handful of blankets - in a small metal room. The room was shaking, a faint thrumming noise echoing through the walls. In her dazed state, it took her a moment to realise that she was actually in the back of a van. She wasn't just a prisoner, she was being taken somewhere...

She sat upright, despite the pain, and looked down at herself. Someone had removed her shirt and trousers, leaving her in her underwear; there were unpleasant-looking red marks on her wrists, reminding her of the time she'd been handcuffed and arrested during the first real protest. And yet, she wasn't cuffed now...she swung her legs over the side of the bed, only to fall backwards when her head started to spin. Her legs felt far too wobbly to be *real*.

"I really *would* stay lying down," the voice said. "You were drugged and it hasn't quite worked its way out of your system."

Gudrun twisted her head, looking for the speaker. A man - no, she realised dully, a *woman* - was sitting next to her, wearing a rumpled uniform. There was something odd about her, something that nagged at the back of her mind. And yet, no matter how she tried, she couldn't place it.

Her throat felt dry, but she managed to speak. "Who are you?"

The woman shrugged. "For the moment, I am your captor," she said. "You're heading east."

Gudrun hesitated, then threw a desperate punch at the woman. The woman caught Gudrun's hand effortlessly and yanked her forward, sending her sprawling to the deck. Before she could move, she was rolled over and a booted foot placed against her throat, ready to crush her neck. She froze, wondering helplessly if she was about to die. She'd never been thrown around so easily, even when Kurt had roughhoused with her as a child...

"Let me explain a few things to you," the woman said. "You are a prisoner. You are no match for me or any of your other guards. Even if you did manage to get out, where would you go?"

Her eyes hardened. "You can sit here in reasonable comfort," she added, "or I can chain you to the wall. Which one is it to be?"

Gudrun tried to meet her eyes, but she couldn't. There was something about her captor, she saw now, that scared her to the bone. This was a woman who had all of the human weaknesses burned out of her…the commando her father had suspected, perhaps. And she'd thrown Gudrun around with ease.

And if I'm not chained up, she thought, *there might be a chance to escape.*

"I'll sit here," he said.

The woman nodded, unsurprised. "Enjoy the ride," she said, as she helped Gudrun to her feet. "What comes after is going to be terrible."

Gudrun shivered. She knew the woman was right.

EPILOGUE

Germanica, Germany East
28 October 1985

Karl Holliston sat in his office, reading the latest reports. The enemy trap had slammed closed, catching a number of units he could ill afford to spare, but the most powerful and capable of his divisions had managed to escape. He honestly didn't know if he should give *Oberstgruppenfuehrer* Alfred Ruengeler a promotion - in hindsight, it was clear that he'd made a mistake - or execute him for disobeying orders. Discipline had to be maintained, true, but he'd placed Ruengeler in an impossible position.

He put the report down and leaned back in his chair, thinking hard. Berlin remained in enemy hands, while the enemy had enough firepower in place to deter another stab westwards. That much was beyond dispute, even if the Americans continued to remain out of the fighting. They'd intervened covertly already - and that had been costly - but open interference would be outright disastrous. He could hope that the *Reich's* population would recoil in horror at *any* dealings with the Americans, yet he had to admit it wasn't certain. He had few qualms about slaughtering any number of traitors - and anyone who refused to join him was a traitor by definition - but it hadn't played well on the international stage.

And if the traitors think they're going to be slaughtered, he thought, *they won't surrender.*

It wasn't a pleasant thought. He'd hoped to win the war quickly, before the first snowfall began, but he'd failed. The traitors were still firmly in control of Germany Prime, while his own forces had been badly weakened in the fighting. Replacing the men he'd lost would take years, years he didn't have. Even the news from the commando team - that Gudrun Wieland had been captured and was on her way to Germanica - wasn't enough to make him feel better.

I can make her suffer, he thought. *And I will. But it won't be enough to stop them from launching a counterattack.*

He snorted at the thought. Generations of experience with insurgencies had taught the *Reich* that allowing the insurgents to try to use Germans as human shields would only encourage such behaviour. He had no doubt that threatening Gudrun's life wouldn't be enough to stop the traitors from launching their invasion, when the time came. Her family might take it badly, but they weren't calling the shots. His spy in Berlin had made it clear that the provisional government intended to continue the war. In spring, when the winter had finally departed, the panzers would head east.

The odds weren't on his side, he admitted, although it was something he would never admit in public. His forces had taken a beating, losing far too many panzers and support aircraft for his peace of mind, while the traitors had vast numbers of untouched weapons under their command. They'd probably have control of the skies too, thanks to their American allies; they'd certainly be able to deny the skies to *his* aircraft. And they had absolute control of the seas. It didn't look good.

And yet - and yet - the war was far from over.

He smiled darkly as he opened the secure drawer in his desk and pulled out a simple black folder. The wording of the report was blunt and very clear, even to someone who felt as though he spent half of his life writing or reading reports. There had been no success - yet - in preparing the ballistic missiles for launch, but a handful of tactical nukes were ready for detonation. They could be deployed at his command.

They'll come into Germany East, seeking to destroy us, he promised himself. *But they will find nothing, but fire and death.*

Karl Holliston returned the folder to the drawer, then poured himself a glass of brandy.

The war was *very* far from over.

End of Book Two

Twilight Of The Gods **Will Conclude In:**
Ragnarok
Coming Soon!

APPENDIX: GERMAN WORDS AND PHRASES

Abwehr - German Military Intelligence

Bund Deutscher Mädel (BDM) - League of German Girls/Band of German Maidens, female wing of the Hitler Youth.

Einsatzgruppen - SS extermination squads

Gastarbeiter - Guest Worker

Generalmajor - Major General

Germanica - Moscow, renamed after the war

Hauptsturmfuehrer - SS rank, roughly equal to Captain.

Heer - The German Army

Herrenvolk - Master Race

Junker, German nobleman

Kessel - 'caldron,' German military term for trapping an enemy formation.

Kinder, Küche, Kirche - Nazi slogan, roughly "children, kitchen, church."

Kriegsmarine - The German Navy

Lebensborn - literally 'font of life.' SS-run program for increasing the German population, including measures to encourage breeding and the kidnapping of 'Aryan' children from non-German families.

Luftwaffe - The German Air Force

Mausefalle - 'Mouse Trap'

Mutterkreuz - Mother's Cross

Oberfeldwebel - *Heer* rank, roughly equal to Master Sergeant

Oberkommando der Wehrmacht (OKW, 'Supreme Command of the Armed Forces') - The German General Staff.

Obergruppenfuehrer - SS rank, roughly equal to Lieutenant General.

Obersturmfuehrer - SS rank, roughly equal to First Lieutenant.

Ordnungspolizei - Order Police (regular police force)

Reichsführer-SS - Commander of the SS

Reichssicherheitshauptamt (RSHA) - Reich Main Security Office

Sigrunen - SS insignia (lightning bolts)

Standartenfuehrer - SS rank, roughly equal to Colonel.

Sturmbannfuehrer - SS rank, roughly equal to Major.

Sturmann - SS rank, roughly equal to Private.

Strumscharfuehrer - SS rank, roughly equal to Master Sergeant.

Swinehund - German insult, literally 'pig dog.'

Untermensch - Subhuman.

Untermenschen - Subhumans, plural of *Untermensch*.

Unterscharfuehrer - SS rank, roughly equal to Second Lieutenant.

Vaterland - Fatherland.

Volk - The German People.

Wehrmacht - The German Military (often taken to represent just the army (*Heer*)).

EXCERPT FROM BOOK 2 OF THE CODEX REGIUS:
BEYOND THE SHROUD OF THE UNIVERSE

Chris Kennedy
Available now from Chris Kennedy Publishing
eBook, Audio Book and Paperback

President's Conference Room, Terran Government Headquarters, Lake Pedam, Nigeria, September 27, 2021

"That concludes my report," Lieutenant Commander Shawn 'Calvin' Hobbs said from the podium. "Are there any questions?" He looked around the room and involuntarily cringed. While he had known there would be *some* questions; he hadn't expected that *everyone's* hand would go up.

The president's conference room was unlike any other Calvin had ever been in. At its center was a table which could easily seat 20 people to a side. The floor of the room sloped upward on all sides, with 10 rows of stadium seating.

The leaders of the Terran Government sat at one end of the table, with the president seated at the head of the table in her customary chair. The vice president, the secretary of state and the speakers from both houses of parliament filled the chairs closest to her. The rest of the seats at the table held members of the Terran Republic's Security Council; their staffs and other interested representatives filled the audience seats, as well as most of the aisles. The place was packed.

The people at the table had brain implants which translated any Terran language; every seat in the room also had jacks that allowed users to plug in and get a running translation of the conversation provided by a small artificial intelligence (AI) which had been replicated for that purpose. The AI also kept notes and logs of all the conversations within the room, unless specifically told not to.

Seeing the forest of hands, Calvin sighed. This was going to take forever. With a mental shrug, he pointed to the closest representative.

"We have only just finished the war with the Drakuls," the senator from Japan said, throwing her hands up in the air, "and now this…this…soldier has gone and involved us in another one. Who is he to think he has ambassadorial powers or the right to speak for us?" She looked around the enormous room for support and smiled when she saw most of the heads in the audience nodding.

"I certainly didn't intend to get us into a war, ma'am," Calvin said. "We were helping the Aesir, as we were ordered, when the Efreeti vessel appeared and fired on us unprovoked. We didn't even know it was *there* before then, much less do anything to cause them to attack us. And actually, ma'am, I'm a naval aviator, not a soldier." Although Calvin currently led a space fighter squadron and a platoon of Terran Space Marines, he still considered himself a naval aviator at heart. It had only been a couple of years since the aliens had shown up on Earth and drafted him to be a janissary in their wars; until recently, a Navy F/A-18 pilot was all he ever wanted to be.

"Not only has he involved us in a war with the Efreet, but also a war with these Jotunn frost giants?" the senator from Romania asked. "Both of these are creatures out of myth and legend. And new universes? What's next, vampires? How are we supposed to fight things that don't exist in places our best scientists say are impossible?"

"The Jinn Universe does exist, sir," Calvin replied. "My men and I have been there several times, and in a number of different systems. Their universe is just as real as ours. I lost a lot of good people there."

One of the senators from Domus raised her hand, and he pointed to her. The planet had been discovered on one of Calvin's first missions to space, and their society had joined the Terran Republic the year before. The world was home to two races; one of these was humanoid in appearance, while the other, the Kuji, looked like 6-foot-tall Tyrannosaurus Rexes. Having been recognized, the Kuji princess stood.

"Unlike the rest of this august body, we are less focused on what is already done and can't be undone," said the princess, nodding to the other Domus senator, the humanoid princess. "We are more worried about what will happen next. Lieutenant Commander Hobbs has already shown these races inhabit a number of stars and planets in their universe, most of which are also inhabited in *our* universe. How do we know they won't all of a sudden pop up on our planet or jump into our system and start dropping bombs on our cities?"

"I'm sorry," Calvin said, "but the bottom line is that we *can't* know whether they are there until we go into their universe and see. Even then, there is no way to protect against them; we can't stop them from jumping into our universe. The only thing we have going for us, we think, is that there aren't any stargates in the other universe. The Jinn have to transfer into our universe to use our stargates if they want to move around quickly. They don't have faster-than-light space travel in their universe, so it would take many years to go from one system to another."

"So the only ones we really have to worry about would be the ones already there, or those that come through the stargate into our system?"

"Yes, ma'am," Calvin said. "At least, that's the way we understand it now. There may very well be creatures that inhabit your planet in the other universe; in fact, I would bet there are. It seems like most of the planets that support life in our universe are also inhabited in the Jinn Universe."

"A follow-up, if I may?" the princess asked. Gaining permission, she continued, "It is necessary for our continued security to determine if they exist on our planet. How do we find out if they are there?"

"There are a couple of ways to find out, ma'am. If we want to do it stealthily, we can use one of the transportation rods we brought back to send a few people to their universe and look around. Unfortunately, we only have a few of them, so it will probably be a little while before we can do so. We are working on making more rods, but there is a substance we need that is only found in the other universe. In order to make all the rods we need, we are going to have to find a supplier in the other universe."

"What about the friendly race you met? The Sila?" Terran President Katrina Nehru asked, happy to be headed back in a positive direction.

"Yes, ma'am," Calvin replied. "We have had contact with the Sila on a couple of occasions. They all left a common planet when its star went nova, and they now inhabit several planets we know of, but they don't have contact with each other. Most of their planets have been conquered by the Efreet and ruled by them ever since. We helped one planet throw off the Efreeti yoke; I'm sure they would help us against the Efreet."

"How big is the Sila Navy, exactly?" the Russian representative asked.

"Almost nonexistent," Calvin admitted. "The Sila only have a single destroyer; however, they have been artificially held back in their technological development by the Efreet. If we give them a boost, I think they'd make great allies."

"Oh, so now you are qualified to give us treaty advice?" the French representative asked. "After involving us in a war with two previously unknown star nations, you are going to tell us who we should have as our allies too?" He spread his arms as he looked across the entire auditorium. "Honestly, I don't see the need for this body to exist since we already have you to determine who our allies and enemies should be."

With that, many of the representatives began shouting their own comments and criticisms. As the moderator struggled to regain control of the meeting, Calvin opened up his in-head calendar display and began cancelling his other appointments for the day. This wasn't going to end any time soon.

The Situation Room, Fleet Command HQ, Lake Pedam, Nigeria, September 29, 2021

"That concludes my report," Calvin said for the second time in three days. "Are there any questions?"

Unlike the chaos that followed this question in the governmental headquarters building, the mood in Fleet Command was somber. Everyone in the room could see the magnitude of what the fleet had been tasked with. How could you defend an entire planet, much less its individual cities, when aliens could emerge anywhere, at any time, and attack? What did they have that could stop an Efreeti ship from appearing and conducting an orbital bombardment of Earth before any of the Terran forces could stop it?

Nothing.

It could happen in the next five minutes, and the military would be completely unable to prevent it. Everyone knew it, and no one had a solution. All the eyes in the room turned to Fleet Admiral James Wright, the head of the Terran Navy, who sat at the head of the table.

For his part, the admiral looked out the window at the Terran Governmental Headquarters, visible across the lake, deep in thought. Finally, nodding to himself, he returned his gaze to the podium. "So Calvin," he said, "you've had the longest to think about it, what are your recommendations?"

Although the question might have seemed out of place to some of the non-American members of the staff, Admiral Wright had a long, personal relationship with Calvin, going back to the Sino-American War of 2018. Although their working relationship had been strained at first, the admiral had come to count on Calvin's decision making. That trust was rewarded with a string of Terran victories across a number of systems in two universes. And, more to the point, Calvin had more off-world fighting experience than any other Terran officer.

"I don't think we have a lot of choices," Calvin said. "We have to take care of Terra first. Don't get me wrong; I'd love to help the Aesir, and they need all the help they can get. Even with the information we gave them, they are going to be overwhelmed by the combined forces of the Efreet and Jotunn if they don't get any help. Still, we have to take care of Earth first."

"I'm sorry," Admiral Ackermann said. "Who were the Jotunn again?"

"The Jotunn are frost giants allied with the Efreet," Calvin said. "They stand about 16 feet high and weigh over a ton. Not only does their size make them difficult to stop on an individual basis, their ships are similarly oversized. For example, their battle cruisers are about the size of a Mrowry dreadnought."

"That is about 1.5 of your miles in length," Captain Andowwn, the Mrowry attache to the Terran military, replied. A felinoid race, the Mrowry were the Terrans' closest allies on the galactic stage, with the elven Aesir close behind.

"That is…quite large," the German admiral said. "We will need more ships if we are to meet them in combat."

"That's the problem," Calvin said. "Well half of it, anyway. As much as I'd like to help the Aesir, I don't think we can. Unless something changed while we were gone, we barely have enough ships to defend our own planets in the face of this new threat; if we send some to aid the Aesir, we are leaving ourselves perilously open to attack."

Admiral Wright's eyes found the only civilian in the room. Not surprisingly, he was tapping on a data pad. "Mr. Brown, could we get a status on ship production?"

Andrew Brown jumped as his name was called. Brown ran the Fleet Material Management Network, or 'Replicator Command,' whose sole purpose was to ensure the Republic of Terra's replicators ran as efficiently as possible. Products of advanced alien technology, the replicators could take raw materials and turn them into any finished product for which they had a blueprint. The biggest replicators could even produce super dreadnoughts, the largest class of ships.

Calvin had first met Andrew Brown when he was the plant manager for Boeing's Airplane Programs Manufacturing Site in Renton, Washington, during the war with China. Brown's experience managing aircraft production facilities had been instrumental in his success with Replicator Command... although it looked to Calvin like Brown's hairline was rapidly receding, probably due to the stress involved.

"Ah, yes," Mr. Brown replied. He tapped the pad two more times. "Our fleet remains at three ships, the cruiser *Vella Gulf* and the battleships *Terra* and *Domus*. We also have the former Efreeti cargo ship *Spark* that Lieutenant Commander Hobbs brought back, if you count it. Although we do not have many active ships, our ship building facilities are just beginning to hit their stride."

He looked at his pad. "The republic is up to five replicators—"

"Excuse me," Calvin interrupted. "Did you say *five*? You've been busy."

"Yes, we have," Brown replied with a smile. He looked around the room and saw questions on several of the faces. "For those of you outside of Replicator Command, replicators range in size from Class 1, which can only make minor items, up to Class 8, which is capable of producing a super dreadnought. Class 1 replicators are found on some of the medium-size and larger ship classes where they are used to replace equipment that breaks. Class 8s are enormous in size, and are relatively static."

Brown's focus returned to Calvin. "In addition to the Class 2 replicator on the moon and the Class 6 we got from the Mrowry, we also towed the Class 8 you captured back to our asteroid belt. I knew that wouldn't be enough, so we made a Class 5 replicator with the Class 6, and another Class 6 with the Class

8. We sent the Class 5 to Domus so they could begin shipbuilding, and we stationed the new Class 6 in the asteroid belt with the Class 8. It took some time to do all of this, as well as to create the infrastructure required to operate them effectively."

He smiled. "I'll tell you what, though," Brown said, pausing for effect; "once you get a Class 8 set up, it can generate infrastructure *fast*. The amount of material it consumes in a day is nothing short of staggering…but you wanted to know about our ship status. All five replicators are now in operation making ships, and you will see a number of new ships very soon."

He motioned, and the lights dimmed. "If you look at the screen, I can show you what I mean." He tapped on his pad, and a picture of a tube in space appeared on the screen. "This is the Class 8 replicator four months ago. For scale, do you see these little points of light?" He indicated a group of about 50 small dots. "Those are *Reliable*-class shuttles, and each is over 200 feet long. The replicator is over two *miles* long."

There was a collective intake of breath. Even though the officers knew the replicator was big, few realized just *how* enormous it really was.

"For the record," Brown continued, "the dots represent one *day's* worth of production." The crowd gasped again. "Of course, that was one day's worth before we had all of them to help tow asteroids to the replicator. We actually ran out of raw materials at 8:00 in the morning. If we hadn't, we could have built several hundred more that day." Another gasp.

"Here's the Class 8 today." The picture changed, and the crowd had its biggest gasp yet. Emerging from the replicator was a ship that dwarfed it. "The super dreadnought *Thermopylae* should be ready next week. It is fully three miles long and masses over 10 million tons."

"Oh, man," Calvin said. "I am soooo ready to have that on my side."

"In addition to the *Thermopylae*," Brown continued, bringing up the next picture, "we also have the battleship *Hood* within a week of completion at one of the Class 6s and the battleship *Yamato* finished at the other." The picture changed to a battleship alongside one of the replicators. "Now that we have everything in place for mass production, we will have the makings of a fleet soon, but even with a Class 8 replicator and two Class 6s, it still takes time."

"Time we don't have," Calvin said. "And, even when we get them, they won't be able to make the jump to the Jinn Universe until we get the metal required to make their jump modules…and the time required to refit the modules into the ships. Also, we're still working on developing effective weapons and tactics for fighting the Efreet, but we haven't figured *them* out yet, either. And even with implants, training the crew isn't going to happen overnight. The bottom line is we simply aren't ready for a fight with the Efreet."

"Speaking of which," Admiral Wright said, looking at Brown, "Do we have a source for getting the unobtanium, or whatever the hell you need to make the jump modules?"

"The caliph in the anti-Keppler-22 system has said he would be happy to let us mine it there."

"Anti-Keppler-22?" one of the wet navy admirals asked.

"Anti-Keppler-22 is the system in the Jinn Universe that corresponds to Keppler-22 in our universe," Brown explained. "The problem with getting the needed material from there is the system isn't close to here, and the material decays in this universe if it's untreated. Somewhat explosively. If a ship left anti-Kepler-22 with 100 pounds, there would only be 10 pounds remaining by the time the ship arrived here, if the ship wasn't destroyed in the attempt. It has to be kept very closely confined and processed immediately, or it is quite dangerous."

"How much do we need for a jump module?" Admiral Wright asked.

"We need a little more than a pound of the metal for each module," Brown replied, "and the larger a ship is, the more modules it needs to be able to jump; for example, battleships need eight." He sighed. "I hate to suggest it, but I think the best thing we could do would be to send the Class 2 replicator from the moon to Keppler-22 'b,' or, even better, to jump it into the Jinn Universe and have it make the jump modules there. It could also fashion more of the transportation rods needed to jump people between the universes while it's there."

"What about the indigenous people on Keppler-22 'b'?" Admiral Babineaux asked from down the table. "Will they mind if we set up on their planet?"

"I doubt it," Calvin said. "The people there are the equivalent of the Mayan Indians of a millennia ago. They still think of us as gods or demi-gods when we go there. They shouldn't be an issue. I don't think there'd be a problem with running the replicator in the Jinn Universe, either. I'm sure the caliph would love to have us there to help defend the system while his nation learns to defend itself."

"As I understand it, we can't stay in the other universe long-term, though, can we?" Admiral Wright asked. "Isn't there some sort of disease or something you get?"

"Yes sir," Calvin replied. "The two universes aren't completely compatible. Just like some of the metal we need from their universe breaks down here, silver and gold from here break down in their universe. Something also happens to people who stay too long in the opposite universe. Eventually, they sicken and die. We can operate the replicator in the other universe, but any Terrans manning it will have to come back to our universe periodically, or they will die. One of our pilots, Lieutenant Dan Knaus, was trapped in the other universe for a couple of months, but he crossed back and forth several times and doesn't appear to have any long-term health issues."

"Got it," Admiral Wright said. "Although the situation won't be remedied within the next couple of months, we're making progress on our lack of ships and jump modules. But I think you said that was only half the problem?"

"Yes sir," Calvin replied. "In addition to not having enough ships capable of taking the fight to the enemy, the other part of the problem is that we don't know the nature of our enemy; we don't know what we're trying to defend *against*. We don't know for sure what's on anti-Earth and anti-Domus although we have anecdotal evidence that the Efreet are across the shroud of the universe from Earth."

Admiral Wright raised an eyebrow. "Shroud of the universe?" he asked.

"Yes sir," Calvin said. "That's what the Sila call the boundary between our two universes. They think of it as a veil that can be pierced, and, to answer your earlier question on what we ought to do, I think we need to pierce it here on Earth and find out what the hell's on the other side."

"Wouldn't it be better not to antagonize them?" Admiral Babineaux asked. "Perhaps they don't know we exist. Shouldn't we build up our strength first and then cross over in force?"

"No sir, I don't think so," Calvin replied. "Captain Nightsong, one of the Aesir, was here several hundred years ago, and he said there unequivocally *are* Efreet on anti-Earth. Even worse, they already know we exist too, because some of them have crossed over in the past. If anti-Earth is really the Efreeti capital, as we've been told, then it's better if we find out first, before they find out about us. I'd rather negotiate with our ships holding their orbitals than vice versa."

"They may know we exist," Admiral Babineaux said, "but it is unlikely they know we are the same people who destroyed their ship. They probably don't even know about the attack. How could they? Wouldn't the Efreet have to use our stargate to get to their capital to tell them?"

"We have been *told* the Efreet don't have faster-than-light drives, but we don't *know* that for sure," Calvin replied. "Are you willing to bet the future of the Earth on that, sir? I'm not." He turned to Admiral Wright. "Honestly sir, I think we need to mount a small operation across the boundary to find out what we're dealing with, not only here, but on Domus, too. That is the *only* way we're going to be able to prepare for them."

"I take it you are volunteering to lead this mission?" Admiral Wright asked.

"Yes sir," Calvin said. "My platoon has the most experience with cross-boundary operations. The first few times you go beyond the shroud, you are violently sick when you get there. I wouldn't want to take a bunch of people who had never been to the Jinn Universe before and have them throwing up while we're taking enemy fire. My troops have been there, and we are acclimated to the jump. We can do this, sir. And then, once we determine the nature of the threat, we need to do the same on Domus." He paused, then added, "It's the only way to be sure."

Praise for Chris Kennedy's Best Selling Codex Regius Series:

"Chris Kennedy's Search for Gram, takes humanity, the most recent newcomers to interstellar space—and the reader—on a roller coaster exploration of alien cultures with ancient animosities and startling technologies. There's action and skullduggery in plen-ty, and along the way Kennedy gives the reader a look inside questions of morality, ethics, and the true meaning of personal responsibility, not simply to others, but to one's self."

—David Webber, author of the
Honor Harrington series

"Chris Kennedy's "Beyond the Shroud of the Universe" is, above and beyond anything else, an unabashed, no-holds-barred roller coaster of space opera action. If you like your Star-Wars-meets-John-Ringo thrills direct, undiluted, and not overly convo-luted or complicated, this is the book for you. Seatbelts required."

—Charles E. Gannon, Nebula Award-nominated
author of Raising Caine

46259182R00203

Made in the USA
San Bernardino, CA
01 March 2017